ALL OVER AGAIN

Quick Decision - Book Two

by Samantha Keathley

Copyright © 2016 Samantha Keathley

All rights reserved. No part of this book may be reproduced in any form or by any means, electronic or mechanical, without the written permission from the author. All characters in this book are fictitious. Any resemblance to actual persons, living or dead, businesses, companies, events, or locales is entirely coincidental.

This book was written for entertainment purposes, not to provide medical, emotional, or physical advice.

First Edition

Cover design by Terry Keathley

The Lord is near.

Philippians 4:5b

To my family

Thank you for giving me this opportunity to tell some of our story.

Chapter 1

The empty seat to my left has drawn my attention every few minutes for the past two hours, along with the handsome man who failed to persuade me to give it to him. The crowd jumps to its feet, erupting in applause as my favorite band finishes their last note. I join in, but quickly grab my dress coat and start to rush to the exit. I gently move around the two women who are blocking me from the aisle. They don't even notice; the stage still holds their eyes. A quick glance around confirms that no one notices me. Good! I focus my attention on the exit sign. My car is in the parking lot across the street from the Times Union Center. I pick up my pace, hoping the encore holds the audience in place. My purse slides down my arm and I replace it back on my shoulder as my hand brushes the embroidered name, April, on the shoulder strap. It was a Christmas gift from Ryan last year. I push the door open and the wind whips my hair into my face. Pulling my coat around my shoulders, I make it across the street and start the big incline up the hill to the parking area when I hear someone's footsteps behind me.

"I see your guest never showed up." The handsome man from the concert states as his stride begins to match my hurried steps.

"He has a reason." An excuse I've already heard before, I'm sure!

"My name's Paul." He extends his hand, but I ignore it. His smile doesn't quite meet his eyes as he drops his hand. Making it up the hill, I glance around the parking area, hoping to spot my car, and then I look back at Paul. He smiles again and his dimples hold my attention for a fraction of a second. I step away and continue to walk.

"April." I say as I try to decide how to end this conversation without being rude. He continues to walk next to me.

"Did you enjoy the concert?" He asks.

"Yes, the music was very dynamic and I loved the way they sang in harmony!" I say as I continue my search. Why didn't I memorize where I parked my car? Probably because I thought Ryan would help me find it.

Paul puts his hand under my elbow. "Since you're alone, I'll walk you to your car. It's not safe for a beautiful woman to be walking alone here at night."

"Thanks, but that's unnecessary, Paul. I'm fine walking by myself." I turn to leave, but he continues to hold tight to my elbow.

"You never know what type of crazy people are around. I think it's best I walk you." He insists.

My hands start to sweat a little even though the temperature has dropped since the sun went down. I try to jerk my elbow away from him, but his grip holds firm.

"Let go!" I say as I grit my teeth.

"Why, April? I'm just trying to make sure you make it to your car safely."

I shake my arm up and down, but it doesn't work. His fingers start to dig into my skin. The last time I was approached by a stranger my self- defense skills were poorly used. I vowed to never let that happen again.

I stop struggling and yell, "Help!" Then I take my free hand and thrust my palm, upward into his nose. A sickening crack meets my ears and blood spurts out of Paul's nose, if that's really his name. He releases my elbow and takes ahold of his nose. His eyes turn dark. I scream a few more times, but Paul and I are the only people in the parking lot. No one comes running to help, I freeze, shocked by what I did.

"Wow, you are one messed up woman, April. I was just trying to help." He growls, "I bet you broke my nose." He takes a step back, shaking his head.

I start to run away. My eyes grow blurry. My car sits two lanes over from where I am. I cut across, attempting to distance myself. Scanning the next row, I don't see him anywhere in the muted moonlight. My grip tightens on my keys. The alarm on my car starts to blare. I fumble with the key ring until I find the right button. It quiets. I scan the cars hoping my alarm doesn't draw him back to me. I race to unlock my door. I only press the button once, hoping that I only unlock my door, but didn't hear it unlock so I push again. And that's when I hear all the doors unlock. I jump into my seat and close my door. A cackle greets my ears and I scan the parking lot. Where is he? I lock the doors promptly, and then look around again. A couple walks in front of my car. My car starts on the first try, and my shoulders loosen. Wiping my sweaty palms on my newly purchased flirty red sundress, I plug my dead cell phone into the charger. I turn on my headlights, and start to put my purse on the passenger seat. Pausing, I notice the 30th birthday card my daughter, Lysa, gave me before I left for the concert. Birthdays are overrated anyway. Spending them alone is fine, right? Maybe my expectations are too high. I plop the purse on top of the card, my only one, and begin my hour and a half drive home to Windham Mountain New York, alone, again.

Chapter 2

EARLIER IN THE DAY

    The steady drizzle begins to seep into my shirt. I stop walking and lean up against the wall of the bank hoping the small overhang from the building will block some of the rain. I take out my phone and pretend to be interested in what's on it. I have a perfect view of the bank's front entrance and the parking lot, which is where the blue Honda parked moments ago.

    "Ryan, he's heading your way." Nick's voice invades my earpiece. I hear him approach before I see his black, about size 11 dress shoes come into my vision as I look passed my phone at the ground. I casually push off the wall as I see our man walk by. Dark hair, medium build, business casual attire. I step in line behind him and start to follow as I pretend to talk on my phone.

    "Sure you don't need me to pick anything else up for you, Mom?" Nick chuckles at my question, but doesn't reply. I watch our man head into the bank.

    "Sure, mom I'll stop there too. Right after the bank." Now that Nick knows where I'm heading, he can go get the car in case we need to leave right after this stop.

I hang up and follow him in. My hat is pulled low but I don't think he notices me anyway. He puts his hand into his pocket and pulls out a withdrawal slip. I snap a silent picture as he hands it over to the teller but I'm not sure how clear the image will be. The next available teller waves me over. I hand her a $100 bill and ask for change. She quickly counts out the twenties and hands them over.

"Is that all, sir?" She asks.

"Yes, thank you." I pocket the money and see our suspect walk out the door. Nick pulls up to the curb and I slide into the passenger side. Perfect timing! The car pulls out of the parking lot and turns left, driving right by us. We follow him but keep several cars in between.

"Where do you think he's going now?" Nick asks.

"I think he probably went to one of his usual places; grocery store, girlfriend's, or home would be my guess." I yawn out the last word.

"Yeah, I agree. The bank today was new for him." He steps on his break as the car in front of him makes a right-hand turn.

"I need to talk to April. She knows something is off. We have had too many clients pulling me away from home. I was hoping to tell her about the business after it closed but I don't think this job is ever going to end."

"I know, Ryan! We closed all of our cases as fast as we could but this one is taking forever, so after this gets resolved, you can let your PI business die and we can both go back to working for your dad's construction business." The Honda passes through the red light right when the light changes from yellow, but Nick stops and we both watch as he continues down the road.

"I don't think I made the best choice in not telling April about this months ago. I know I couldn't tell her in the beginning of our relationship but there never seemed to be a good time." I run my hand through my hair.

"Ryan, I'm not sure how wise it would be to tell her now! We both signed that stupid contract for this case and if she flips about this business we still have to finish it," Nick stresses. "And that would be a major problem because you signed that you would see this through to the end where the clients were completely satisfied." The light turns green and Nick continues forward. We don't see the car but chances are our guy Tim is heading home.

"Nick, I remember what I signed, but every time I look into her eyes, I feel guilt. Why is that, Nick? I'll tell you why, because I'm guilty. She's my wife! And she should know about this." My jaw tightens.

Nick isn't going to understand; he isn't married and he doesn't have to make excuses for his tardiness. I shouldn't have brought it up, but the longer I keep this secret, the more distance I create with April. My stomach churns each time I look into her eyes, so I've started avoiding them. I don't want anything to cause disharmony in my marriage, but I think this already has.

"Why didn't you tell her when you got married?" Nick says.

"Do you remember how we *got* married?"

"Yeah, Nancy had something to do with that." Nancy is April's older sister and Nick would like Nancy to be his girlfriend.

"Nick, seriously! She didn't want anything to do with me when we first married. She said 'I do' to protect her loved ones. Do you think she would have been receptive to my telling her about my second job?"

"Well, you could have said something then, but not now. It's too late." Nick states.

"I made a mess of things and I'm not sure how to make it right. That's what I'm trying to figure out now!" I throw my hands in the air.

"Alright, Ryan, I get it, calm down. You stress me out!" Nick says as he reaches for his Mountain Dew. "I'm one street away from his house. What do you want to do if Tim isn't there?"

"I'll answer that after you get there." I pinch the bridge of my nose. I grab my Sprite and take a sip. It's flat! But I finish it anyway. In the driveway sits the car we're looking for.

Nick circles the block and pulls into a great spot for us to watch the house, car, garage, and driveway. We sit for hours and nothing happens. Absolutely nothing!

I glance at the car clock as a van with a plumber's ad on the side pulls up. Our replacement. "Our shift is over now so let's head home."

"I hope something happens soon so we can end this gig." Nick massages the back of his neck.

"I wish! Each time I meet with the clients, they tell me we're missing something. They have no problem paying us more and the wife insisted on this 24/7 surveillance. I hope it helps, I'm glad we were able to hire two more people. If this keeps up, maybe we can hire a couple of more people so that we can stay home more." I stretch my legs as far as the car will let me. "Do you want me to drive, Nick?"

"No, I'm fine. You should nap, you've been a bit cranky today." Nick comments. I grunt but know he's right. I recline my seat and try to find a comfortable position.

We have about an hour before we reach Windham Mountain so I try to nap. My name is Ryan Nolsen and Nick, at times, can be a difficult person to deal with and even more difficult when he's right. He is also my best friend. We went to high school together and he heard of my love for April throughout those years. About how no other girl had such beautiful strawberry blond hair and how her light blue eyes looked my way once while I walked down the hallway to class. I insisted we made eye contact and Nick said she was just looking where she was going. I talked less of her after high school because I knew he was tired of hearing about it. Nick kept encouraging me to move on because April refused to talk to me. He told me that a woman that angry with a man, for no reason, was only trouble. I didn't listen and I completely disagreed.

    The years went by with no words passing between April and me, but my heart still ached for a relationship with her. Some might call me stubborn, and maybe I am, but I knew she was the one. We only talked for a few minutes before we exchanged our vows but I knew it was the right thing to do. Several months ago, her sister, Nancy came up with the idea. It was the best decision I ever made; after all, it's what I've wanted for so many years. I only had a short time to pray about it, but I sought after God throughout that whole night. After we were married we went to Helen for counseling, which we desperately needed. It took some time but we learned to communicate. We built a friendship over the first weeks of marriage and she fell in love with me as time went on. Why we did this is a story for another time.

    She could tell when I wasn't happy before I would say anything. And I was able to figure out when she was sad, even if she said she was okay. She knows me. She already senses that I'm hiding something from her. She has also pulled back a bit from me. Now she doesn't readily share about her day when I get home. She is still having nightmares from the events that happened months ago but she doesn't talk about them either. She knows I'm not being truthful with her; she knows I'm hiding where I go and that my business trips aren't related to the family carpentry company. How do I explain this to her? Should I continue to keep my mouth shut until this is over? Is Nick, right?

I pull my phone out of my pocket and realize I had it off all day. After it turns on, twelve text messages pop up and three missed calls. Yikes! What's going on?

"Nick, what day is it?" My heart beat starts to double its normal rhythm as I continue to read April's messages.

"May 1st. Oh, today's April's birthday, isn't it? Or should I say tonight, it's almost

9 pm. Man, you really are striking out!" Nick snorts.

"Tell me about it! I bought April tickets to a concert months ago for her birthday. I totally forgot about that. Concert's tonight." I call April and her phone goes straight to voicemail. I leave a quick, 'I'm sorry' message and hang up. Not sure what to do.

Glancing up beyond the road, I can see the mountains in the distance. The Ford shifts gears, indicating our start up the steep climb. The curves remind Nick to slow down, as does the single rail that blocks one from falling off its steep ledge. This single road connects one way of life to another; many people would be stranded if something happened to it. Now to figure out how to connect with my wife, the truth would be a good start. Maybe.

* * *

My name is April Nolsen. I have an 8-year-old daughter named Alyssa, who insists on being called Lysa since she turned 8, and I married a man I couldn't stand being around because someone was after my daughter and it was the best protection and cover I could find. Fortunately, now I love my husband, Ryan. I know it's not ideal to fall in love with a man after you marry him, but it makes for a good story and I did it for the safety of my family. Oh, and he loves me too. He has loved me since high school, but I wouldn't even talk to him back then because of something I thought he said once. It was childish of me! It turned out he was defending me against a bunch of guys.

Our relationship has been wonderful for a few months. We did almost everything together, even grocery shopping, but within the past two months Ryan started working all the time. And I mean all the time! I guess I still need to adjust some. Maybe it's normal.

He has stopped making eye contact with me and he has been avoiding my questions about where he's been going. He has had three overnight, out of town, maybe, business meetings this month alone. I don't need to ask Helen what the classic signs are - I wasn't born yesterday. Was it the catch he was after and not me? Was I just a challenge all those years and now he realizes he made a mistake? How does a wife approach her husband with these thoughts? Maybe I don't want to know the truth. Or maybe I do.

"Mommy?" Lysa skips into the living room and throws herself down next to me on the couch.

"Yes, sweetie, what is it?" I put the shirt I just folded on top of the other folded clothes and push the basket away from my feet.

"Can you say yes?" She tilts her head a little to the side, smiling.

"About what?" I pull her into my arms. She likes to get confirmation first, when she thinks I'm going to say no.

"I want to spend the night with Aunt Nancy in the guest house." My sister, Nancy, lives in the guesthouse, which is attached to our house.

"I picked you up from Aunt Nancy's just a few minutes ago. It's a little late but if she's free I don't see why not." A great idea for her and Nancy, *and* I won't have a distraction when Ryan gets home!

"Mommy?" Lysa leans back so she can look at my face.

"Yes, Lysa."

"I love being here with you and daddy."

"Me too, sweetie, me too." She wraps her arms around me and we both enjoy the cuddle time.

She is doing very well in her counseling sessions with Helen. Helen suggested that we all meet with her as a family, so we can figure out what our normal family looks like. We said it was a good idea but neither Ryan nor I made the call to schedule it. Lysa is happier than I've ever seen her. I wonder if it is necessary to bring up more of the past; which would happen with Ryan and me there. Helen is my sister Nancy's best friend and a gifted counselor. She would say it is necessary to talk about our fears. I'm still having nightmares but Lysa isn't and I don't want her to remember details that she has already forgotten.

I wasn't able to protect her when she needed me most. That's my job as her mother, but I failed. It haunts me still, when I sleep. I'm glad Lysa knows how to let God be in control. I still have one hand gripping what I think I control. I could learn from my daughter.

"I think I'll go pack now. I can't wait to surprise Aunt Nancy! She looks so sad lately. Do you know why, Mommy?" Lysa asks as she jumps up from the couch.

"Umm, no, I haven't asked her." Where is this conversation going?

"I know why. She didn't tell me, but I know."

"Really? Please share." I pat the couch cushion next to me and Lysa sits back down.

"She's sad because Nick isn't around. She misses him. And I miss Daddy. They have been going away a lot and I really miss him, so I'm sad like Aunt Nancy, and you too mommy. You're sad too. I know you miss Daddy."

"That's true, I do miss Daddy, but how did you know Nick has been going with daddy?" How did I miss this huge piece of information?

"Because Daddy said he was there."

Should I believe like my child?

"And it makes sense because that is why Aunt Nancy is sad too. I've asked her and she says she isn't sad, but I can tell she doesn't want to be just friends with Nick; she wants to marry him. And do you know what?"

"Yes, Lysa?" I shift uncomfortably on the couch.

"I want Nick to be my uncle, so maybe I should tell him to marry Aunt Nancy."

"Uh, Lysa, slow down. That isn't something you should do." Oh, boy! She's a little young to be playing match-maker.

"Why, Mommy? They need help. They don't see that everyone would be happy if they just get married. Maybe I'll write them a letter telling them they need to get married."

"Lysa, honey, that's not a good idea."

"Why, Mommy? I'll tell them to do it for me." She puts her hands together and gives me a pleading look. How do I explain this to her?

"Mommy, I know it will work. Please let me write it, please!"

"Lysa, I'm sorry, but no, you can't. The idea has to come from them."

"But if it would make everyone happy, don't you think we should tell them?" She looks at me with pleading eyes.

"No, honey. Some things need to be figured out on their own. If this is why you want to go to Aunt Nancy's, then it's best you stay home with me."

"Mommy, please let me go. I promise not to say a word about it; I promise!"

"Okay, okay, you can go."

"Thanks." She hugs me again and gives me an extra squeeze as she gets up from the couch and runs to her room to pack. Oh, how fun that would be, Lysa writing letters! I laugh to no one in particular.

"What's so funny?" Ryan's voice startles me. When did he get home? I didn't hear the garage door.

"Hi. How was your trip?" Do I really want to know?

"It was okay. Nick and I didn't finish the job, but we're getting close. So, what's funny?" He asks again, sitting down next to me.

"Oh, Lysa. She asked to spend the night with Nancy and she also wants to write a letter to her and Nick explaining that they should get married."

Smiling, Ryan leans closer to me, "Now that could be interesting. What did you tell her?"

"I said no."

"Oh, I would have said yes." He laughs, and I toss a pillow at him.

"Ha! Well *you* can tell her yes, but I'm staying out of it." Maybe!

"I'll think about it, but the idea does have a ring to it." He clears his throat and says, "April, I'm so sorry I forgot about the concert and your birthday! I turned my phone off and forgot to turn it back on. Please forgive me."

"It's really hard to forgive you right now, but yes I forgive you. I'm still hurt though."

He reaches into his bag and pulls out a present. I take it and open it. A gasp escapes my mouth. It's a beautiful gold necklace with a large heart surrounded with diamonds.

"Happy Birthday!" He says.

"Thank you, Ryan! Please put it on." I turn around and lift up my hair. He secures the clasp and it falls gently onto my skin.

"It's absolutely beautiful!"

"I'm glad you like it." He pulls me into a hug. I nestle my head into his neck and he kisses the top of my head.

"I really am sorry. I miss being home and I wish I could change my work schedule. I have this one contract left from before we were married and as soon as it's finished, I won't take anymore weekend work for a long time. Okay?"

"Okay. Do you know how much longer it will last?"

"About a few more weeks. I shouldn't have to be gone every weekend, but what I can do is work less during the week. I'm sorry. I know I've been working 7 days a week. Maybe my dad can take a couple of my days until this project is over. Would that be better?"

"Yes, I suppose."

I examine my nail polish, seeing a chip on one of my fingers.

"Is there something else you think I can do?" He asks.

"I would like you to explain what you're doing there and where 'there' is that you are going. I don't even know and is Nick with you?" He shifts his weight and briefly looks at me.

"But I did tell you where it was the first time I made a trip down there."

"You were vague."

"Are you sure?"

"Yes, you said something about a small town…"

"Yes, we have been traveling about an hour south from here to Kingston. We're doing the normal business stuff. Nothing exciting, just work that is progressing far too slowly for my liking. Maybe Nick can go a time or two without me so I can stay here with you. I'll ask him." He pulls me into another hug.

Maybe he is only working. After all, Nick is with him. I rest in his arms, planning to schedule that family appointment with Helen. She's right; we do have a lot to learn.

"Daddy, Daddy, Daddy! You're home!" Lysa runs and jumps at Ryan right as I slide out of his arms. I've learned to avoid getting hurt; I need to move fast when Lysa is excited.

"I didn't hear you come in; when did you get here, and why didn't you call me?"

"And why are you not in bed, little lady?" He counters.

Ryan starts tickling Lysa, ignoring her questions, and off they run throughout the house.

Chapter 3

Lysa spent last night at Nancy's but she arrived back home almost before the sun came up. I turned on the kitchen light and heard Lysa descend down the stairs from Nancy's. She was probably watching for the light to turn on. I fed her a chocolate muffin April made yesterday. My phone starts to move on the counter. I have the ringer off because I didn't want to wake April.

"Lysa, sorry sweetie, I have to take this call." Lysa shrugs and walks to the couch as I put my phone to my ear.

"Hey, Nick. What is it?" I walk to the kitchen and fill a glass with water. Leaning my elbows on the counter, I look out the window and notice the grass hasn't been mowed. When did I last take out the mower? I thought it was a couple of days ago. There are several pieces of a swing set I was assembling, scattered on the ground where I left them when I was called back to work. They take up most of the back deck. This job is not more important than my home life, and my marriage. But the truth is, I'm treating it that way.

"...so Ryan we have to go back."

I must have missed something. "What?! When and why?" My voice gets louder with each word.

"John says we have to go back. He says our guy has been meeting with a few different people. He has taken pictures but is concerned he's going to miss something."

I'm the boss. John isn't in charge so why is he acting that way? I set it up where he would call Nick if there were any trouble because I can't always talk freely, but that doesn't mean I'm to be bossed around.

Nick continues, "He said that we need to get there right now. I'll pick you up in twenty minutes, make it thirty, I'll knock on Nancy's door first, and then I'll get you."

"Why would it take you twenty minutes to get here? You live down the street." I ask. The house projects forgotten.

Nick hesitates. "Yeah, well, I was in the middle of washing my laundry."

"Really, Nick?" He can't trick me.

"Okay, I recorded yesterday's game and it's the end of the fourth quarter."

"Laundry, nice. Truth is, you have been starting to stink a bit. I'll call John after you pick me up, see you when you get here." I put my phone back in my pocket and dump my glass of water into the sink. I have to pack, again, and how am I supposed to tell April I need to work again so soon? This is not typical in the construction business. She will know I've been deceiving her and this is really going to hurt her. I hear movement on the stairs.

"April?"

"Yeah?" She steps off the last step and sits down on the couch. Ryan scans the room but can't find Lysa.

"Nick just called. There's some type of emergency at our out-of-town site. I'm so sorry, but I need to go back and so does Nick. He is picking me up in a half hour."

Sighing, she looks down, and starts to pick at her nail.

"But this might be the last time I have to go." I hope!

"Huh? How is that? Ryan, that makes no sense." April stands, and throws her hands into the air. "If the project isn't supposed to be finished for a few more weeks, an emergency shouldn't make it end quicker."

"Uh, you're right about that but I'm going to find someone else to take my place. This isn't fair to you and Lysa or me either. I want to be here every day with you. I don't like spending the night somewhere else, listening to Nick snore. Please know that April, I really want to be home." I slowly pull her toward me and lift her head gently until I'm looking into her eyes. "You know that right, April?"

"I think so." She looks at me and adds with more confidence, "Yes, I do, I know you want to be here." But she sighs and pulls back.

"I have to pack again. Nick should be here soon."

I look at her one last time before I walk to our bedroom. She's genuinely sad but I can't think of anything helpful to say. I know that recently April planned a couple of candlelight dinners and had Nancy take Lysa out, and both times I'd called to let her know I was running late and wouldn't make it home for dinner. When I arrived home a place setting for one awaited me.

* * *

I thought marriage would be different. I don't have to worry about money anymore; which is a relief. I have a beautiful place to live and my sister lives in the apartment above us. I know God has really taken care of me.

If I think of what I struggle with the most, I would have to say complaining. I can do an amazing job not finding God's blessings in my life, and others' too. I'm trying to change that so when I start thinking 'poor me', I try to name the many blessings God has given me today. Today's blessing is that I have a husband who does an amazing job providing for my family and me. I truly am thankful about that.

"April, I'm packed. I have something for you and Lysa too. Here, open it." He hands me a long, rectangular box. I open it to find, not flowers which was my guess, but a box filled with truffles. All different kinds!

"Thank you, Ryan. I love truffles!"

"Yeah, I know." He wraps me in a hug. "Please forgive me for leaving again. I feel so bad, I'm really sorry. Can we do a retake on your birthday day?"

"Yes, we can and I forgive you, Ryan. Please find a replacement when you're down there. We have so much catching up to do. I have a long list of stories I want to share with you." I didn't even tell him about Paul yet. I rub my elbow, which still hurts a bit.

"When I get back, things will be different. Okay?" I hope he can keep that promise.

"Okay." I shrug.

"Good, where's Lysa?" He asks.

"Not sure. Let me call her. Lysa!" I shout.

"Yes, Mommy." She shouts back but walks in a second later.

"I have to go back to work again." Before she has time to pout, Ryan holds out his gift to her.

"What is it?" She looks at the box and smiles.

"You're going to have to open it to see."

Lysa takes the present and opens it; she finds a baby doll that can crawl on its own. "Wow, super cool, Daddy! Thank you! I love it!" She hugs Ryan quickly, and races back to the toy. She tries to rip it from its triple knotted, multi-taped, and wire wrapped contraption. Before too much frustration, Ryan asks for the toy and works to free the baby with much frustration of his own.

"Mommy, I think I'll name her Sally."

"That's a great name." I say as I watch Ryan pull at the wire and tape at the same time. He mumble's something. The doorbell rings. Ryan frees the baby and turns on the switch. The baby starts to coo when I open the front door. Cute!

"Hi Nick. I'd be lying if I said I'm glad to see you, but please come in anyway."

"Thanks for the warm greeting, April. A moment ago, Nancy had a similar response." Maybe Lysa is right; they might be in need of some help.

"You're so welcome." I try to keep my tone in check.

Nick steps in and closes the door. "Ryan, are you ready?"

"Yes." He grabs his bag and hugs Lysa and Sally. Lysa moves to the floor to play. He smiles at me, and pulls me into him and I hug him tightly. I'm going to try to trust him and I will miss him.

"April, I'll call you tonight, okay?"

"Sure." I whisper. Nick waves before they step outside. I close the front door after they get in the car. I grab my box of chocolates and try to decide which one to eat first.

"Mommy, let's go to Aunt Nancy's."

"Alright, Lysa, let's go and see if she is up for company." I put the box down but I know there will be a lot of empty wrappers soon.

Chapter 4

Nick gets behind the wheel. I pull out my phone and check the picture I took from the bank. It has the account numbers on it and a withdrawal for $5,000.00. Not sure what it means, it might mean nothing. Young people usually don't have that much cash on hand so I'm curious now. Up until this point I thought Tim was just the boyfriend of a wealthy daughter.

We made it back to Kingston in record speed. John led us through Tim's movements over the past couple of hours. He visited his girlfriend and they went to her parents for a very brief visit. He went to church. None of these events required a call to us, and none of these activities warranted us to return. John is close to getting fired and Nick too. And I would fire them if I weren't married. Now we are sitting in front of Tim's house.

"How did we get into this mess, Nick?"

"You started it, remember?" Nick questions my question as he peers through his binoculars.

"My dad started it. Well, not really. Before you started working for him at the family business, we had one client named Brad. He was very friendly and made huge promises about when he was going to pay us. My dad felt the need for us to do some research into his background to see if the money our client said was there, really was. He was asking us to build him a strip mall down the mountain. It was going to be huge. We were all excited about the project and couldn't wait to get started. But my dad said we had to wait. The man also thought had all the necessary permits on hand to start and the land was leveled. It seemed that he already hired someone and something went wrong. My dad didn't want to hire a private investigator so he found online classes for a PI license and asked me to take them. We discovered that we needed one more permit before we could start the building project and it would take a few weeks for it so we had a little time for me to get started with my classes.

"My dad took me off all the other jobs I was doing and I spent all my time studying and researching how to become a Private Investigator that specializes in financial crimes. We were sure there was more to this nice guy. When I finished the courses, and got my license, my next step should have been to work for an actual company. I had no experience and, well, no experience. We didn't have any time for that and we already put some time into this project because the permit came through, as I was finishing up my classes. This man wanted it done yesterday so my dad figured we could start with digging because that was just our time; we already owned the necessary equipment. My dad didn't hire anyone else to speed up this process and the man started to complain that my brother and dad were not enough men to get this job done in a few months like he had envisioned. My dad reassured

Brad that shortly we would have enough men on the job; we had to finish up another project first. My dad also reminded him that the first payment was past due and the man reached into his pocket and gave him the check. He said he forgot to put it into the mail and that was why he came down to the site today; to hand deliver it.

"I had a new job that I didn't know how to do. My dad informed me that I have great intuition and that this was the right side-job for me. I went to work trying to dig up information on our new client. It didn't take long for me to find out that he did hire another construction company before us. I called them and found out that Brad's first check bounced when they tried to deposit it. He assured them that he wrote the check from the wrong account and he gave them another one. A different man just ripped off the owner of that construction company, and he said he wasn't about to do that again on such a big project with an even bigger risk. He cancelled the contract, which he could do because there was a clause in his contract. One bounced check was under the termination agreement.

"I told my dad all of this and he still wanted more evidence. I, at this point, wished I spoke up to my dad, letting him know that I didn't enjoy digging into peoples' private junk but I knew this was for the company. So far there was no crime committed on our clients' end, only suspicion.

"My dad was leaning toward terminating the contract too, but he again asked me to keep looking. I decided to follow him a bit. Surveillance sounded like fun work to me so I tailed him as he left the construction site. My dad went to the bank to deposit the check and my brother stayed to continue digging out the foundation; a full basement below each store was desired.

"After following Brad to a bank, one restaurant, and then to his home I called it a night. I took notes and decided to do it again tomorrow. After four days of keeping track of this guy, I saw that he was shady. He visited a different bank each day. At this point I still didn't meet Brad so I followed him into a couple of the banks and heard that he was setting up loans. This would be fine but on my latest bank visit, I found out that he was close to filing for bankruptcy.

"After my dad heard this, we terminated the contract and refunded his check. A couple of years later a strip mall was built there but Brad must have sold the land before it was built. It would have been exciting to build it, but my dad made the right decision. Shortly after that incident a few side jobs came up for PI work. I let everyone that wanted to hire me know that I didn't have experience, but no one cared. They just assumed I would do my best and that was it. I never advertised and I asked everyone I worked for to not mention my name. I had a confidentiality contract. I didn't want people knowing I did this. That's where you came in Nick, but you know that already. Thanks for being the face for this business. After this case, I'm leaving it to you."

"What? No, you're not!" Nick fumbles with the binoculars.

"Okay, we'll just close shop then." I shrug.

"You thought I wasn't paying attention to your very long story, huh? Throwing that last part in there like that." He grunts and puts the binoculars back up to his eyes.

Smiling, "Yeah, you caught me. See you're good at this. And you have your license now too."

"Nice try, Ryan. Taking over your business is not going to work for me and your story was long, almost put me to sleep. Do we have any Mountain Dew left?" He places the binoculars onto the dashboard.

I reach behind the driver's side seat and pull open the cooler. The ice melted long ago and the few remaining sodas are floating at the top. I grab two.

"Here you go, the ice is all melted." I wipe my soda off on my shirt.

"I'm not surprised about that. I didn't have time to refill it or add more sodas during our quick trip home."

"You could have skipped the end of the game." I smile.

Nick's hand stops short and he glares at me.

"Ok, no biggie, drink your warm soda. It doesn't matter to me." I pop the top to my Sprite. "I thought John said our guy was on the move? I haven't seen any movement since he went inside his home. If he were leaving in a hurry it would have happened by now. I don't think he's going to mess up by getting a little spooked. He isn't acting like a guilty person, which tells me, he has been doing this for a long time or he's innocent."

"If he is innocent then everyone involved wins. It gets trickier if he isn't." Nick states.

"Ryan, we have been doing this together for a couple of years now, are you sure you want to close shop? I know there is still one guy out there you want to get. What about him?"

"That's personal, to you also. I'm still searching for him, I won't let that one go, but I'm not planning on taking any new clients. Where do they come from anyway? I've never advertised." I guzzle half of my soda and put it in the cup holder.

"Ryan, you are forgetting something." Nick says in between sips.

"What's that?" I ask.

"You're *really* good at this!"

I grunt in response and begin to fiddle with the defroster. Without having to say anything to Nick, he turns on the car so we can get rid of the fog on the windows.

"Well, Ryan, your best is the best. Your success rate speaks volumes and people recommend you. That's why you keep getting phone calls. Remember last year, you worked for the construction company for only, what was it, 70 work days or something crazy like that?"

"Yeah, that's about right. You didn't work much more than that, either. I needed your help on most of these cases. The big problem is that we need to travel to them."

"That is a problem now but before you got married, it wasn't an issue. And I've been trying to see Nancy more but I have no free time. I agree; it's a good time to close shop. Plus, the two new guys your dad hired aren't very good at building. We need to get back there before that business starts to get complaints. Your dad would be mad then."

"I'd be mad too! We've worked so hard building up a reliable name. We can't have someone come in and ruin it." I rub my eyes a bit. The moon is bright tonight. I glance at the clock, one a.m. "Ok, Nick let's recap what we have. We were hired to find out about our client's daughter's boyfriend, Tim. They both want what is best for her and that they think Tim is after her fortune. After we did a thorough background check and looked into his financials we found no evidence indicating that he was doing anything illegal or deceitful. After we brought them this information, the wife insisted we needed 24/7 surveillance to make sure we weren't missing anything."

"We started that 5 weeks ago and still nothing that would suggest he isn't a good guy." Nick yawns.

"Yes, and after we presented that to our clients the dad was in agreement that we should call it quits, but the mom insisted there was more to find. She said it was her woman's intuition. Yesterday, we followed him into the bank and I took a picture of his withdrawal slip. It states that he took out $5,000.00."

"That's a lot of money for a kid." Nick sighs.

"I think so too, which puts us back to something we're missing." I pull out the last sour cream and onion potato chip from the bag. It doesn't have much crunch as I bite down on it. Yuck! I need to go to the gym.

"Then John calls in a panic because he was having a tough time tailing him. He lost him in between dropping his girlfriend off at home and his own house. John went straight to Tim's house and called us. It took Tim ten minutes longer to get home. He must have done something during that time. That was probably the only thing significant that happened all night. Maybe you should fire John. He royally messed up."

"I was thinking that too. So, looks like we still don't have much." I slouch back into my seat.

"I think Tim is in for the night. All the lights are off and they have been off for almost an hour." Nick looks at me.

"Yeah, I agree, let's head home. Our replacement is here anyway. I'll make a decision about John tomorrow. I can call a couple of contacts and double up on the evening. We don't need to spend more time here tonight. Let's take some time off soon."

Chapter 5

Ryan came home around three this morning. I called Nancy around nine because Lysa wanted to stay with her this morning. That left me alone and with a start of a headache. Shopping might help.

Kohl's is having a great sale on jackets and I want one in red. I have never had a red jacket before and I'm not sure if they still have any, but I saw a cute one in their catalog a few weeks ago. Walking toward the woman's section, I spot Karen Kingsbury's latest book. Maybe I should get lost in a book tonight. I pick it up.

There are a surprising number of people here, but no red jackets. Maybe I can order it online? Their toy department on my left shows amazing sales on Lysa's favorite collectable, Zoobles. They are originally $10.99, marked down to $4, and the sign says to take 50% off the sale price. I grab three. I love a good sale! Looking around a bit more, I realize there is nothing else I want to see so I try to locate the front of the store.

The checkout line moves fast. When it's my turn the Zoobles ring up as $10.99 so the sales clerk calls the manager. Waiting with a stranger can be weird, especially when I don't feel like talking.

Prompted, I ask her how she was doing. "I'm doing horrible!" She says.

"Why?" I ask struck by the oddity of someone answering so honestly.

"Yesterday was my birthday and I didn't get anything. Not one thing. Not even someone acknowledging my birthday."

"Oh, that's horrible!" My birthday was better than that.

I think saying Happy Birthday to her now would be insensitive so we both stand, in silence, as we wait for the manager to come. The overhead blinking light alerts those around that someone is holding up the line. The last two people on my line leave for a different checkout and the woman behind me gives me the look. The cashier shrugs her shoulders and tosses her stringy blond hair, from a bottle, over her shoulder. The manager takes care of everything and I leave with my purchases. Feeling hungry, I drive thru Burger King. I'm not a huge fan of fast food, but I don't really know how to cook so I can't be too picky. Maybe tomorrow I'll experiment? As I eat a couple of fries my thoughts go back to the cashier with a rose tattoo on her neck. To not get anything for your birthday isn't fun. It seems like she was all alone.

I start to open up my wrapper but I can't eat; I need to go back to the store. I put my sandwich back in the bag and put my car in drive. She needs a present and I just bought her one. Easing off the brake, I contemplate how crazy I'll sound, but that isn't what's important. Looking like a fool to those around me isn't a big deal. Doing God's will is much more worthwhile. Parking again, I search my unorganized and over-stuffed purse for a pen. A black pen will do. I write, 'Please, remember, Jesus loves you' on the inside cover and start toward the store.

I know Lysa has a birthday party to go to next month, so I'll pick up a couple more Zoobles. I grab them and move faster to checkout. I've already nicknamed the woman, Rose. Her eyebrows are furrowed and her mouth is in an upside down U. She is doing all the proper motions for her job, but she has no happiness. Glancing at her left hand, I don't see a ring. Her aging hands place items in a bag. The couple with a tired baby in front of me finishes up.

Rose looks at me and says, "You're back." No smile, just recognition.

"Yes, I am." I smile.

A woman gets in line behind me. Rose remembers how to override my Zooble purchases, so we don't have to wait for the manager, making my time with her very short. She puts them in a bag and blows at a few stray hairs that have escaped from her hair tie, reminding me of a weeping willow tree in the winter, thin and wispy and in need of care.

I reach into my purse; my heart beats faster as I pull out the Karen Kingsbury book I purchased earlier.

"I know you didn't get anything for your birthday yesterday, so I want you to have this. Happy Birthday!"

Rose looks at me as if I'm crazy; then she slowly smiles and says, "This is for me?"

"Yes, it is. Happy Birthday, and remember Jesus loves you."

Smiling broadly, she adds, "Thank you!"

"You're welcome."

"I have some time off from college so I'll have time to read it now. Thank you!"

College? I thought she was in her forties.

"Happy birthday!" I say again.

She hands me my receipt and I wave goodbye as I grab my bag. A good friend of mine has often encouraged me to reach out to someone when I'm down. She's right, when you give, you also receive far more than you expect. Now I can eat!

Chapter 6

She isn't sure how this is going to work. She should have figured it out before today because as soon as she finishes walking to the podium she has no choice but to open her mouth and speak. Her left hand moves down her skirt, ironing out imaginary wrinkles, as her right holds shaking papers. Being a Christian counselor, in a small room, with one to two clients at a time was the only profession she thought she would have. In seconds, that will change. She's not sure if this will be her first of many speeches or her one and only. She's thankful she doesn't know the answer to that, for now she can focus on this daunting task ahead.

Reaching the podium, she puts her papers down and looks out at the crowd. There must be at least 200 women sitting out there staring back at her. There are even women standing in the back without chairs. Quickly, she looks down at the podium. Arlene said this was supposed to be a small gathering, maybe twenty or so. Arlene is the woman in charge of the advertising for tonight. She sent out an email to all the church women, and opened it with, "If you're a woman, you might be missing this key? Come find out what you might not know you're missing, but definitely need! Our very own Helen Frances; a well-known Christian counselor, will be teaching." She takes a sip of water, puts the cap back on, and places it on the floor next to her feet, realizing that there is nothing more she can do to stall. She opens her mouth, closes it, and then opens it again.

"Ladies, thank you all for coming tonight. My name is Helen Frances and I work for Christian Associates. I have been a counselor there for eight years helping women, couples, and families experience growth and healing. Today's topic is going to be a tough one for many of us, but tough for me in a different way. I was happily married for 10 years when my husband passed away very suddenly. One of his dreams for me was to talk to groups of women, but I'm not sure he envisioned this many of you because I know I didn't. I do wish he was here to see this. So, without delaying let's get right into today's topic. What I want you all to do is think about your body. Are you happy with it?"

Giving the ladies a moment to think, she reaches down for her water.

"If anyone here feels they have the perfect body, please stand up." No one stands, she waits, and still in a room full of hundreds of women, no one stands.

"Look around." She gives them a few seconds to do that. "Those of you who thought, 'so and so next to me is beautiful, I wish I could look like her' isn't standing! Here is where our huge problem is. It's not a physical problem, but it's our mindset. We have been taught by society what beautiful is and that no matter what we look like we won't ever measure up. This is wrong thinking.

"Have any of you felt that if you could just lose 10-15 pounds, then you'd be more comfortable with yourself? I've been there and let me tell you that if this is what you are waiting for, it will not happen. You will continually feel uncomfortable and/or unhappy. I want you all to know that God loves your body! He created us in his own image, all as individuals, all different, and all out of love. Let me say it a different way: He loves your body the way you look right now! For those of you who don't believe me, let's say it out loud. Please repeat, 'God loves my body the way it is right now.'" Lips move as mumbles and some sniffles come forth. "I want you to know that by not believing God, you have let yourself believe the lies of the enemy. Do you want the devil to continue whispering in your ear? Now say it like you mean it." This time a bolder confirmation rings out. "Women, I want you to know that you have the power to overcome this lack of confidence and self-image issues. You might be holding on to what someone else has said about you or your body or about what you have seen Hollywood portray as the body to have.

"When you get home, I want you to try something. Lock yourself in a room with mirrors and look at yourself. This is going to be hard for most of you, but remember that God loves your body.

As you stand there, find something that you like about yourself. Also, ask God if there is anything He would like you to change. Being healthy is important and you are worth taking the time for. But say as you stand there, 'God finds me beautiful.' Say it however many times it takes for you to start believing it."

She talks for another twenty minutes, giving women tips and sharing her heart. When she closes, one woman asks when the next meeting will be, and others nod and ask also. She informs them that she will schedule it with the church and Arlene. At the mention of her name, Arlene stands and explains that she will send out an email as soon as we get it scheduled. She also informs the crowd that there is an email list on the table in the lobby that anyone in the group can sign if they weren't on the original list. With all of that done, Helen makes her way to the back where she is greeted with a long line of women waiting to talk. Woman after woman confide in her about how unhappy they have been with their body, their insecurity setbacks, and how they are now starting to believe for the first time that they are beautiful.

As the next woman approaches she glances up and sees Nancy and me. We give her a thumbs-up signal as we head out the side door. She called us last minute to invite us tonight. I'm so glad my mom was free to watch Lysa, this talk was worth listening to. We had no idea what the talk was about. I'm shocked that not a single woman in the room was content with their own body.

* * *

Nancy and I walk to her car. We are parked at the far end of the lot. "April, what did you think of Helen's talk?" She asks as she unzips her purse and starts looking for her keys.

"Well, I didn't stand up, if that's what you mean. It was interesting. I was expecting her to tell everyone to do his or her homework like she normally does in her counseling sessions." I walk around to the passenger side.

We both open our doors and slide in. "I was thinking of setting up an appointment with her for the family, but now I bet she'll be booked for months. She does have a way of making a person feel uncomfortable but at ease at the same time. There are many things I don't mind about my body, but there are also areas I wish I could change. There are areas I could tone up, but there are things that can't be changed." I rub my hand over my chin.

"I think she wanted us to get to a place where we can be content with the things we can't change and to see that we can also do something about the things we want to change. What do you want to change but can't, April?" Nancy looks my way but quickly sends her eyes back to the road.

"Nancy, I would change my chin if I could. It's a little bit too pointy."

"What? Are you serious?" Nancy's usual quiet voice raises, "There is absolutely nothing wrong with your chin."

"I guess this is why Helen brought up the topic. I never voiced that before, it's just something I've noticed over the years when I look in the mirror. I can see now how I need to accept it as me. It's how God made me. I'm going to take Helen's challenge when I get home." Saying that to Nancy will help keep me accountable.

"Me too. I've been unhappy about a few sagging body parts, but I've made no movement toward fixing them, and I know I can. I don't exercise regularly, but I do eat well for the most part. I can see how not being happy with my body has really had an impact on me. I've ignored it, but now that Helen talked about it, I really want to make my way toward being content with the things I can't change and change the things I can." Nancy nods.

"I'm the opposite, Nancy. I eat horribly when Ryan isn't cooking, but I do run regularly." I lean my head back against the seat.

"I've noticed that since I turned thirty I've been gaining weight. A friend was telling me the other day that when she turned thirty-three she looked back over the past three years and realized that she has gained an extra five pounds each year. She didn't change anything; her diet has been the same for the past ten years. She still has the same exercise routine, walking up and down the stairs to do laundry and walking to and from her car. She insisted that she didn't and doesn't do much more than that. Fifteen pounds is a lot. I don't want to think about what that could mean for her by the time she turns forty." Nancy turns down our street.

"I agree. That could be us soon." I cringe. "Now the question is, do we do nothing and just let it happen or are we going to be proactive and come up with a plan?"

"I like the way you think, April. Let's come up with a plan. I think we actually need two plans." Nancy smiles at me.

"And why would that be Nancy?" I wonder.

"First we need an exercise/diet routine and second we need to figure out how to be content with the things about our body we are not happy with. You know, the things we can't change." She parks and we get out of the car, giving me a moment to think.

"The first one sounds easier. I'll take that one."

"Nice, April, steal the easier one." She playfully shoves my arm.

"Well, I am the younger sister." I state, and put my hands on my hips.

"I'm not sure why that makes sense, we aren't kids anymore, but I'll take the challenge. I do think the answer might be different for each of us, but I'll explore it." She adjusts her purse strap on her shoulder.

"Great, because I already have visions of what we need to do." I start walking toward the door with my keys in my hand.

"You might have to try harder than that. I've had visions of me exercising for years." Nancy says.

"Oh, Nancy, don't you worry. I will motivate you to exercise like you have never been motivated before. Do you remember our gym teacher from middle school? She had a problem with walking." I put the key in the doorknob and turn it.

"Yes, I remember Ms. Baraski. She said walking was too easy. The moment we entered the gymnasium we had to be running. If one of us decided to walk, then we would have to do laps after gym class. I was so relieved when the principal caught on to why so many kids were consistently late for their next class. That was torture." She grunts and shakes her head.

"I agree, and I like to run. She was something else. After she was forced to change her teaching style, she did prove to be a great asset to the school. She knew how to teach and get everyone into shape. What if we give her a call?" I suggest.

"Absolutely not, April. There is no way I'm going to subject myself to her again. Do you know what she did when I sprained my ankle?" Nancy asks as she takes off her shoes and puts her purse down on the end table.

"No, I don't. What did she do?" I sit on the couch and kick my shoes off.

"She filled a bucket with ice and a bit of water. Then she made me place my leg in it up to the middle of my calf. As the kids were running around playing some sport, she would walk by every minute and kick the bucket. She only let me take my foot out every 10 minutes and I had two rounds of it. Do you know what that means April?"

"That she liked to torture you, Nancy!" I shrug.

"Yes, but it also means that she kicked the bucket twenty times. She was crazy and it hurt so much. There is no way you are going to call her, so please think of another plan. Or we could switch plans." Nancy says hopefully.

"Oh no. That's okay. I'll figure out something else. No need to worry!" I state.

"Oh, that is exactly what I'm going to do, worry. You are already looking at Ms. Baraski for motivation. This might turn out very badly."

"Now, Nancy, I will only have your best interests in mind. You can trust me." I ease back into the couch and let my body relax.

"Actually, I think we need to both, do both. The point was to be content right where we are."

"Yes, but to see how we can be healthy too and change what we want to change." I point out. Nancy isn't going to get off that easy.

"We need to find the balance." She states.

"Nancy, does Helen have this balanced?" I ask as I sit up straight.

After thinking a minute, "Actually, she does. She doesn't gloat about it, but she is content and she likes her body. She is healthy also. Yes, she has it balanced." Nancy looks at her watch.

"Well, then we have inside help." I point out.

Laughing, Nancy gets up. "I better go home, it's late. Do you want me to send mom down with Lysa or do you just want me to send Lysa?"

"Please send mom too. It would be nice to visit with her a bit. Thanks for letting them stay in your apartment. Lysa loves being there." I hug Nancy.

"I love having her there." She slips her shoes on, grabs her purse, and heads out the door.

Chapter 7

This morning my phone woke me up too early for my liking. Ryan didn't stir. It was Janice asking if I was free to come over. And a thought came to my mind. I said yes and called Nancy. I filled her in on my thoughts and an hour later, Lysa was settled on the school bus and we went to Janice's house.

"April, did you and Nancy come over here to talk to me about eating healthy and dieting? Is this some kind of intervention?" Janice glares at me and gets up from the kitchen table and starts washing the dishes in the sink.

"Oh, Janice, absolutely not." I stand and start to walk toward her, but she turns abruptly.

"Good, because I was about to kick you out." She states as she dries her hands, and makes her way back to the kitchen table where Nancy sits, smiling. I join them.

"Janice, there's no need to get upset." Janice is my best friend. She would never kick me out but she has threatened to do just that repeatedly over the years. "We came over here for your help. We went to Helen's talk last night and it stirred our thoughts about changing a few things and we wanted your help." I state.

"What April is leaving out, Janice, is that you seem to have figured out a way to eat healthy and exercise without anyone's help, and we were hoping you could let us know how you did it."

Janice asks for more information so we take turns filling her in on what Helen's talk was about.

"And so we want to be healthy. April's in charge of the exercise part and I'm going to attempt to figure out how we can all be happy with those parts of us we have been so unhappy with." Nancy finishes.

"Nancy, April swindled you. Have fun with that one." Janice smirks.

"Thanks, yeah I know she did. She pulled the 'I'm the younger sister card.'" Nancy says as she shakes her head.

"She usually does. Once she tried the 'I'm the younger friend.' But that didn't get her anywhere!" Janice confides in Nancy like I'm not sitting at the same table.

"Uh, I'm right here, you two. I can hear you." I go to the teapot, fill it, and turn on the stove.

"We know." Janice laughs. "It's fun picking on you. Anyway, both of you know that I have struggled with my weight most of my entire life. I have always had the metabolism of an 80-year-old woman. But also, when I was a child, I ate whatever I wanted. My parents gave me all the candy and chocolate I could eat. Anytime, and I mean anytime, I asked for ring dings or chocolate bars, three boxes of each would appear in the pantry. There were no food limitations, and I never learned how to stop eating something I wanted more of. If I wanted the whole bag of chips, I would eat the whole bag or if there were ice cream in the freezer, I would skip putting it in a bowl and just grab the whole container. I got to be huge before I understood the effects of my actions. The consequences were already established when I started kindergarten, habits ingrained in my mind.

"I also learned that eating made me feel better when someone poked fun at me. I wasn't involved in sports of any kind and gym class was always my worst grade. The gym teachers didn't know how to handle me, either. They would make hurtful comments, thinking that I was unaware of my size. Stuff like, 'You know, Janice, if you just walked more, you could be so pretty,' or 'You have style Janice, now let's run some laps and get you the body.' I gave up at an early age. There seemed to be no one who understood me. I had no self-control and no self-worth. I hated everything about my body and I knew everyone else around me did too.

"I did discover hope though. I had friends, like you two, but I didn't talk to you about these feelings because, well, honestly you wouldn't have understood. But you did help. You saw me for who I was, not my size and you never tried to change that. You didn't try to get me to go to this class or that lecture on dieting and I appreciated that more than you know."

"Wow, Janice, I had no idea. I'm so glad you feel comfortable to share this with us now. If you don't want us to talk about this anymore, we don't have to." I say as I give her hand a squeeze.

"Oh, it's okay. To answer your question, I have been eating healthy for a long time. You both know I love to cook, so for years now I have been making dietary changes. I'm very slow to change so I would only make one change a month and perfect that throughout the month before moving on. I wasn't a fan of salad so I experimented with many different low calorie dressings to make it something I enjoy. I have tweaked so many recipes that I have enough for a cookbook. I have learned how to enjoy healthy food, and I don't keep tempting ingredients in the house."

"Do you make everything you eat?" Nancy asks. She shifts forward in her seat.

"I try to make most things. I have learned that if I want potato chips, I need to peel the potatoes and slice them really thin, then cover them with oil and salt, and you get the picture. I would have to make it, instead of having to just walk to the pantry to grab a bag to eat. This saves me from indulging a lot of the time. I have removed a bunch of the temptation, and I also don't keep potatoes in the house." The teakettle whistles and Janice gets up to turn it off.

"I like that Janice but I don't know how to make much of anything. How about exercise?" I ask as I help her get out the mugs and the tea selections.

"I go to a gym. I have learned that I don't do well soloing it. I need someone to keep me accountable. When I did try on my own, it would last for a month or two then I would fall back into my old ways and do nothing at all. Now I have a personal trainer whom I meet with three times a week. She also asks me how my other two workouts went that week so even though she wasn't there; her asking keeps me in check. She and I set monthly goals, and I try hard to meet them. In the past eight months, I've lost 83 pounds. I still have a long way to go, but I hope that when I reach my ideal weight that I'll have made a life change. I don't want to go back. I know I would have given up a long time ago if I didn't have God helping me every step of the way and my trainer cheering me on also.

We each pick out a tea bag and make our drinks. "A big help came from the radio. I remembered a DJ talking about New Year's resolutions over a year ago and how most people set some goals and most of the people fail to reach them. He was explaining how a pastor decided to encourage people to pick one word that they want to use to describe what they want to change about themselves that year. I thought, 'what would be a good word for me?' I came up with the word 'positive' at first, but I thought I would benefit more from the word 'healthy'.

"Then I tried to figure out what I thought that looked like? I've spent time exploring that word, 'healthy'. I knew it meant that spending time eating chocolate was out. Then, I tried to plan a schedule but rethought that idea and figured that the Pastor didn't mean planning beyond the word but focusing on it in that moment. Each time I was presented with an opportunity to be healthy or not, I would just let that word sink in. And make my choice for that moment. I didn't focus on my planned schedule for the next day, but on whether or not I should take a brownie from the tray that was being passed at the brunch I was attending. Everyday stuff like that. It's usually easier to decline when the word 'healthy' comes to mind."

"This's amazing, Janice. You're amazing." I lean over and give her a hug.

"Wow, Janice, 83 pounds in eight months! Is that too fast?" Nancy wants to know.

"My trainer has kept a close eye on my diet and assures me I am eating well balanced. I also took a nutrition class at Columbia Greene. It was fun to be in a class with teenagers!" She sends us one of her 'yeah right' looks.

"You have been thorough then." I lean forward on the table. "Would you be interested in teaching us?" I ask.

"There you go again with one of your crazy ideas, April. I haven't even reached my goal yet." Janice pulls her lime green t-shirt down a bit. Her bangle bracelets jingle as she puts her hand back around her teacup.

"It seems to me that you figured out how to and I know you can be an inspiration to others. You can start with us." Nancy states.

"If I didn't know you better, I would think you were mocking me. You both already have the perfect bodies!" Janice wags her finger at us.

"Actually, we don't think so." I say.

"Then you need to talk to someone else because I think you're crazy! Helen can help you with that!" Janice's eyes grow big. "Or you should go to the eye doctor cause your eyes aren't working well!"

"Well, that's helpful." I throw my hands into the air. "Uh, how about this, Janice, can you teach us how to cook some healthy meals?"

"Now, that's something I've wanted to teach you for years, April. You do need to learn." At least I got her to commit to something.

Janice adjusts her hot pink eyeglasses as she settles into her chair, formulating her plan. I know I need to jump in here before she has me over here every night learning a new dish.

"Great, let's get started tomorrow. I'll bring Lysa or you can come to my house." Looking at the clock on the microwave, I hug her and we walk to the door.

"Thank you for opening up to us, Janice. You really are an inspiration. We all have something in our lives that is challenging, even though the world can't see some of those challenges, God always knows. I'm glad we came over. You should come to the next one." Nancy adds as she sits down to put on her shoes.

"But I'm not married."

"Neither am I. We went to support Helen; we had no idea what she was going to talk about. Nor did we expect to take so much away from it either. See you soon." Nancy hugs Janice also. We wave and walk to the car.

* * *

Nick slides open the passenger side door and hands me a soda, then gets into the car. "Ryan, has anything changed?"

"Nope, not a single thing. Well, my eyes keep going out of focus every few seconds. I've been blinking a lot, so that's new."

"Not sure what to say about that. You probably need sleep or you need to stop staring at Tim's place." Nick reaches into the paper bag. "I have dinner. I hope you like, oh, I know you aren't going to like it, but it's all I could find within walking distance."

"I can't place the smell." He hands me a small wrapper.

"Well, it's a cheeseburger; I'm just not sure what the guy put on it." Nick pulls his burger out and we both unwrap them.

"Okay, sounds edible." I take a bite and I can't figure out what the sauce is on top.

"I taste the onions and it seems like mushrooms in a BBQ sauce. Is that what you ordered?" I ask.

"I really don't know, I asked for the special. Do you like the fries?" Nick asks.

"You never gave me any fries."

Nick looks in the bag. "They must have forgotten your fries. You can share mine." He holds up his fry box, but I shake my head.

"I think I'm going to call John again and have him repeat what he saw."

I reach for my phone while I balance my food in my other hand. He answers on the first ring.

"Yes, Ryan, did you catch him?" John wants to know.

"Catch him doing what?" I ask.

"That's your job, not mine." What did I see in this guy when I hired him? "He was moving around a lot. It seemed suspicious so I thought he would do something today."

"Where did he go?"

"I already told you." He states.

"And I want to hear it all again." I say as Nick chuckles.

John sighs loudly into the phone. "He went to the gym this morning and then home. He had on different clothes and his hair was wet when he came out. Then he went to a restaurant, he walked in by himself and out again by himself. He went to a bank and came out after three minutes. Then he went home for an hour and then he headed south on route 92 for 30 minutes. He went to a flower store, went inside for five minutes and came out with some flowers. Then he drove for another 37 minutes in the opposite direction and knocked on the address of 9 Blossom Ave. He handed the flowers to the woman that answered the door and went inside for a half hour. When he came out I followed him home and that's where you found him when you arrived."

"Okay, thanks John. You have the morning shift tomorrow." The sauce starts oozing out of the top of my burger and onto my fingers. I lighten my hold.

"Yeah, I know. He was moving around a lot and interacting a lot today. Isn't that odd, Ryan?"

"No, not this kind of stuff. He went to the gym, ate lunch, bought flowers and spent some time with a woman. The only thing suspicious was the visit to the bank, but he could have just taken out money to pay for the flowers. John, from now on you will tail him and take notes. You are to only call Nick and let him know, in detail, what happened and he will make the decision based on what he thinks is the best course of action."

"Man, I thought this was it. What about the suitcase?"

"What suitcase?" Did John almost forget to tell me a piece of important information, something that could be significant?

"He left his house this morning with a suitcase in his hand."

"What did it look like?"

"Umm, let me think." I really shouldn't have given John this second chance.

"It was black and fairly big. Looked full."

"Where did he put it?" I demand.

"In the back seat of his car and I didn't see him take it out either."

"Okay, John when you are back on duty, watch him and communicate better with Nick. Also, Nick and I are going back. I'm going to put Howie on the case tonight and you are on days still. Do you understand?" I ask.

"Yes, Ryan, I do, and sorry. I'll do better next time." He better!

I slid my phone back into my pocket. I take a few deep breaths. I need to hire experienced people next time. Wait, this is my last job so I don't need to waste time interviewing anyone. I slowly let out my breath.

"Nick, can you call Howie and see how fast he can get here? I want to get home!" I start to rub my neck. "While your scheduling that with Howie I have something to check out." I say as I start to open my door.

"Sure."

I toss what's left of my burger onto my seat and close my door. I walk down the street to Tim's car. I look up at his apartment and see some lights on. I take out my flashlight and shine it into the backseat of his car. On the seat sits a black bag. I check the backdoor handle to see if it's locked. It doesn't budge. I was hoping to do this the easy way. I pause; breaking into a car is illegal. So far I've done nothing wrong, so far! I try the driver side handle. It's locked.

"Hey!" Two guys start walking toward me. The taller of the two starts to reach into his pocket and I know now is the time to leave. A dog starts to bark, then another one. Two-porch lights flicker on. I turn as fast as I can and sprint to the car. I hear one of the men curse. I don't waste the time to look back to see if they are gaining on me. I make it to the car and swing open my door.

"Go!" I shout to Nick but he already has his foot on the gas before I even close my door. The men are in front of our car but Nick doesn't slow down. I brace myself for the bullets to hit our car any moment but Nick goes faster and they jump out of the way.

Now I want to know what's in that bag!

Chapter 8

I finish chopping the cucumber and place it in the bowl. Lysa mixes it in and we both wait for Janice to give us more instructions.

Her bracelets jingle against the side of the bowl as she moves it toward her to take a look. "Do you want red onions in the salad, April?"

"No, Lysa, do you?" I glance at my daughter. She has grown a couple of inches in a couple of months.

"No, thanks." She wrinkles her nose.

"Okay, so that salad is done. April, how does the chicken look?" She asks but I'm convinced she already knows.

I pick up the lid to the mini grill and look at two pieces of meat that have dark lines on top and because Janice said to turn them over when they looked like that a few minutes ago on their other side, I'm going to guess that they're done. "It looks ready to come off the mini grill." I give her a look that hopefully shows I'm more confident than I am.

Janice leans over me and pats me on the back. Lysa hands me a plate and I use the tongs to take off the chicken.

"Lysa, how is your pasta coming along?"

"I don't know." She shrugs.

"April, is the pasta done?" I know how to make pasta so I take out a noodle and confirm its doneness. I drain the water out and put the pot down.

"Lysa, you did a great job setting the table."

"Thanks, Aunt Janice!" We finish bringing the food to the table and pray for our meal.

"Janice, this salad dressing is amazing!" I drizzle more onto my salad.

"It's my favorite one and now you know how to make it." She adds more salad to her plate.

"Thanks for coming over on such fast notice."

"No problem. I wasn't doing much but laundry and that can do itself for a while.

"What's that smell?" Lysa asks.

"Not sure," I say. Janice and I look at each other and we both jump up at the same time and race to the kitchen. On the stove, above the pasta pot is billowing steam or smoke. Janice beats me to the pot and removes it from the stove.

"Looks like I forgot to turn off the stove." I cringe.

"I'd say! That's what it looks like." Janice tips the pot to put water in it. All I see at the bottom is black chunks.

"I'm a lost cause." I mumble.

"Nah. Lysa, how did the pasta taste?"

"Good." She says.

"And everything else?" Janice inquires.

"It was all tasty."

"See, April, you did well. You forgot about the stove but I bet you will remember from now on." Janice leaves the burned creation to soak in the sink.

"Okay, that's true. I'll try again." I eye the sink and hope that the soapy water works a miracle. We all walk back to the table and enjoy the remainder of the meal.

"Lysa, it's time for you to finish your homework."

"Sure, I have to read for twenty minutes so can you call me when my time is up?"

"You bet." She gives me a quick hug and skips off down the hall to her bedroom.

"What's wrong?" Janice puts her hands on her hips.

"Why does something have to be wrong? Can't I just invite a friend over to hang out and teach me how to cook?"

"You could, but I know when something is wrong. We've been friends too long for me not to know." Janice starts tapping her florescent orange toenails.

"Okay, you're right." There's no fooling her, we are as close as sisters. "I'm lonely. Ryan has been working all the time and this past month or so he has started these weird business trips where he is away for two or three days at a time."

"Are they planning to build where he is traveling to? Where's he going?"

"That's the thing, Janice. I don't know exactly, somewhere in Kingston. At first I didn't ask because I was hoping he would tell me. Then as time went on, I just felt dumb for not knowing. Maybe he mentioned what the project was and I wasn't paying attention. He's vague." I plop down on the sofa and Janice joins me.

"Does he go alone?" Janice asks.

"No, Nick goes with him every time, I think. That's what Lysa says."

"Interesting." She picks up her phone.

"Yeah, I guess." I say as she starts pushing numbers. "Who are you calling?"

When Janice is on a mission she doesn't let anyone get in the way. She holds up one finger to me to let me know to wait a minute.

"Hi Nancy, it's Janice. How are you doing?... That's great...I have a quick question for you. Where's Nick?" There are a bunch of pauses and Janice adds a few uh-huhs and hangs up.

"So what did she say?" I lean backward and grab a blanket from the back and wrap it around me.

"She doesn't know where Nick is and she said frankly she doesn't care. Then she asked me if there was something I knew that I should be telling her. When I confirmed there wasn't, she calmed down, but only a little. Maybe it was a bad idea to call her. I was hoping to find out something that could help you, but Nick isn't talking either. Have you called your in-laws?" She asks.

"No, I haven't." But it has crossed my mind.

"Why not?" She demands.

"Because I want Ryan to tell me what he's up to. Shouldn't I find out from my own husband, not his parents?" I counter.

"You do have a good point, April. Okay, I'll let it go, for now." She relents.

"Thanks, Janice, I think." A sigh escapes my mouth.

"Nothing to think about, you're welcome."

I know Janice is planning to talk to Ryan's parents at some point and it really isn't worth trying to stop her. I trust Ryan so there isn't anything to worry about. I'm just lonely, right? Maybe I trust him.

"Good. Now we should go get some dessert."

"Uh, do we really have to go back in the kitchen?" I whine. "I think I've reached my limit."

"Don't worry April, I brought a fruit salad."

"Wonderful! No heat involved so I can't start a fire this time."

"All part of my plan." She says.

I lightly punch her in the arm. She scrunches her nose as the left side of her lip curls up, making me laugh.

"How are things going with you, Janice?" Janice tends to focus on other people instead of herself. It's hard to get her to share personal information but over the years she has relaxed a bit with me.

"I'm alright, but I had a really bizarre thing happen." She leans back into the couch and closes her eyes.

"Does this involve Douglas, the cop?" I ask, mimicking her position.

"Yes, it's about *him*." I sit up straight. "He and I have been dating for a while now and I was thinking that maybe he was the one. The first few months went really well, but the last two dates have been awkward. He seemed distant and throughout the date he would give only one -word answers to my questions. I tried really hard to get him to open up and he wouldn't. I don't know what I did wrong. I really like him, a lot. Maybe I'm in love with him." Janice's voice trails off.

"Uh, that's weird. How much did he talk normally?" Wow! I had no idea she was serious about him. I thought they went on a couple of dates. That was it.

"A lot! About as much as me."

I clear my throat.

"Okay, he didn't talk as much as I did but, uh, you know what I mean. It was never a one-sided conversation. That's why I don't get it." She sniffles.

"Maybe I should call him and ask." I reach for my phone.

"Nice try, April. I'm not giving you his number."

"Just trying to help." I shrug. "At least I asked. I didn't just call and hold up my finger after I dialed and had you wait to find out what was going on."

"This is different." Janice states.

"Not sure I see how." I shrug.

"Okay, I get your point, April. I'll fill you in next time." She looks down at her toenails, she changed them hot pink earlier.

"Fill me in or ask?" I stand up and fold the blanket.

"Alright; I'll ask first."

"Good. Are you sure you don't want me to call him?" I say as I toss the blanket back on the couch and make my way to the kitchen.

I take out three bowls. Janice lifts the lid off the salad as I place them on the table and turn back to get some spoons.

"Yes, I'm sure. I'll wait and see if he calls me."

Janice scoops some fruit into each bowl. Sitting, I enjoy my first mouthful.

"I agree. Maybe when he does call, you two can talk on the phone. He'll have to talk then, right?" I ask.

"I guess he would. I do talk a lot sometimes so I should try to calm that down a bit, but who's to say he is going to call again. Over the past month I've been the one initiating all our dates and I mean, all of our dates."

"Maybe he wants to be doing that, it's possible. Please let me know if he calls."

"Yeah, I will." She says, her shoulders hunch over a bit.

"How are you feeling?" I ask as I lean a bit closer.

"I feel hurt by his lack of interest, but I'll get over it. He seemed like a really kind guy too. He met many of my requirements. Maybe that's my problem, I have too many requirements. It's time for me to re-evaluate my list and decide what I'm not going to budge on and what I should cross out. Oh, I don't know April." She throws her hands up and her spoon falls to the table. "I like the guy, why does something have to be wrong? Dating is so complicated. You are so lucky to have skipped this part. I wish I knew who the right guy for me was, then I wouldn't have to go through the feelings of my heart being broken."

I wait a second to see if she has more to say. "I wish I knew the answer for you, too, Janice." I say between bites.

"Well, enough about me, April, for your second cooking lesson, I want you to duplicate this salad sometime this week."

"Oh, I do appreciate your going easy on me. Okay, challenge accepted. I better call Lysa before she realizes I lost track of her reading time."

Chapter 9

Howie pulled up a minute before Nick and I made our fast get away. He said the guys got up from the ground and took the black bag out of the car. They had a key, and then they walked away. He said Tim didn't come to the window or the door as far as he could see so Nick and I decided to go home.

"Ryan, wake up. You're here." Nick's hand shoves my shoulder hard.

"Oh, thanks for driving Nick and I wasn't sleeping. Are you going to see Nancy tonight?"

He grunts.

"What does that mean?" Nick is a clam when it comes to his relationships.

"I don't want to talk about it."

"That's obvious. We've spent hours together and you never mentioned a word." I unbuckle my seatbelt.

"Yeah, well let's keep it that way." He presses the unlock button even though the doors were already unlocked.

"Alright, man, but if you change your mind, please let me know. I might be able to help." I say.

Nick's jaw is clenched tight. "Would you be mad at me if I quit before we finish this contract?"

"Umm, maybe, that wasn't what I was thinking you would say."

"Yeah, that's what I thought. I won't leave you in this mess so never mind about me quitting. Bye Ryan."

"Wait…" I open my mouth to ask him what he meant, but he put up his hand.

"Ryan, don't worry about it. I don't want to talk about it."

"Okay, I didn't want to talk about April and my first fight either."

He grunts again and waves me out of the car. I grab my bag and close the car door. Not looking back, I jog to my door as I hear Nick peel out of my drive. All the lights seem to be out. Maybe I missed April and she's already in bed. I hurry to unlock the door. Putting my bag and shoes in the hall closet, I turn and drop my keys in the bowl April put on the end table in the living room. I can see her figure move slightly with the drop of my keys. The television is still on.

I quietly move to her side and start to gently pick her up.

* * *

My legs burn, I knock a branch away, but I need to keep moving. Faster, I need to move faster, which way should I go? There is no time for guessing. I turn, I don't know where I am, but that doesn't matter. My foot pushes off a rock and I keep moving. My chest hurts; my heart races, and I see my breath in front of me. The chill in the air doesn't settle through me; I don't have time for that.

My body gave out a while ago; I'm only running because my brain says I don't have a choice. A slow drizzle starts and my pace slows slightly. I turn my head to listen. He's out there and he's still coming. I need to move and I don't know where to go. Is it safe somewhere around here? Can my legs keep going? I've been running for a long time now. When I heard him, I took off into the woods. I wish I ran the other way; maybe by now I would have found someone to help me if I did. In front of me, I only see trees and dead leaves and rocks and more trees. I don't know where to go. I slow some more. What should I do? If I stop, he will find me. I know he saw me.

I listen again and I still can't tell if someone is back there. My heart races and my chest squeezes. Fear holds me still. My head twists, I hear a sound, and my heart jumps as my ears try to find it. I don't want him to get me. The sun is setting which helps me figure out which way is north. I stop. I live north from here, I think. I rested long enough. I need to run more. I take off without pacing myself. I know I'm going to run out of energy again but I have no choice. He'll catch me if I stop again. I try not to think of what will happen. I focus on running. I can get out of here. I used to run in the woods when I was in high school. I can find a way out. North, I have to stay north. The sun hasn't fully left me yet; I still have a couple of more minutes to use its help. I duck under a tree branch and race over some boulders. The rain has lightened and the suns' rays are almost gone. My arm hits a branch and I jump thinking for a second that he caught me. My shirt pulls backward as I continue forward. I'm not going to stop. I hear the tear and my arm starts to sting. Touching my sleeve, my skin feels wet. I quickly glance at my finger and see blood. I push harder. I know I have more in me. I can outrun him.

The sun decides to call it a night as I take my last hint of direction from it. My breathing is getting too labored and my feet are slowing against my will. I must push myself. My brain says to keep on, but my body won't let it. I hear a sound. I turn to look, but I can't see in the dark. Why did I stop running? I'm trapped. I hear his footsteps behind me, or is he in front of me? I put my back up to a tree and I try to silence my breaths. My hands tremble and I can't keep still. I'm making too much noise. I need help, but there is no one safe here. I feel him; he grabs my back. No, not again.

I scream!

"April, wake up. It's me, Ryan." I try to wake her, but she fights me. I was picking her up to put her in our bed but she starts kicking her legs and screaming. I don't want to drop her so I hold her tighter. She fights harder. She swings her arm and it hits me in the eye. I'm not going to make it to the bedroom; I turn to put her back on the couch.

"April, wake up. It's me, Ryan." I say in her ear. "You're having another nightmare."

I get her back on the couch and let go. She is still swinging at me. Her leg kicks high and makes contact with my throat. Stunned and short of breath, I step back. Her eyes are still closed. I work on regaining my breath and balance. Unsure of how to wake her, I brush her hair out of her eyes but I leave my other hand up to protect my face and throat.

"April, please wake up. You're safe. It's just a bad dream." I don't touch her this time.

Her eyes slowly open and she looks at me. I smile, hoping that she can start to feel safe now. As she moves her matted hair over her shoulder, I notice her racing pulse. She reaches out and wraps her arms around my neck. I cradle her in my arms and sit back on the couch.

"Ryan, I, I, I'm so glad you're here. It was a really bad one this time but the same thing. I was running and he was after me. It wa...was so bad." I tuck her into my arms, hoping to lessen her trembling.

"I... have noticed...that when...you go away overnight my nightmares get worse." April takes a slow breath.

"I am going to try my best not to go away again at night for a long while. I miss you too much." I thought the nightmares had stopped. Another way I have failed my wife.

"That would be good. I've missed you too. I've been so lonely here. I love the house and all, but on nights like this, I become fearful. I don't want to be alone." Her shaking has stopped.

"I'm here now, April. I'll try to be here more, I really will."

Chapter 10

Morning seems brighter! It took a while to get rid of the headache that formed after I woke up from my nightmare last night. I don't know if it was fear that kept me up for hours last night or the throbbing at the front of my head.

Pushing the covers aside, I stretch, longing for the hazelnut coffee that lingers in the air. Ryan typically gets up before me. Lately he has been leaving while I'm still in bed. I hope I didn't miss him. My feet find one slipper where I left it the night before. My toes lose in locating the other, but it's not a concern, I pick up my pace and move toward the kitchen. I don't see him; my shoulders lower as I make my way to the coffeemaker. Did I dream he came home last night? If I did then who made the coffee? I take a sip, enjoying its flavor.

"How did you sleep, April?" Ryan said.

"Huh, where did you come from?" I say as I jump up from my stool, spilling a little of the hot liquid onto my hand. I grab a napkin off the table and wipe up the mess.

"I was in the office looking at some paperwork." His hair is tousled.

He meets me halfway for a hug. I quickly return the hug and try to pull away but he holds me tight.

"Uh, I'd like to enjoy this hug, but I have my coffee mug in my hand." I state trying to take a step back.

"Would you like me to put it down for you?" He asks.

"No, that's okay, I'll just drink it."

He chuckles to himself.

"What?" I throw him a look.

"You don't function well until you've had your coffee."

"I'd argue with you but I know that's completely true. I'll hug you when I finish." I move toward the couch.

"Okay," smiling, he asks, "What are your plans for today?"

"I don't have anything specific just a long 'to do' list." The cup warms my hands. "Lysa will go to school and then come home and I guess at that point I'll see what she wants to do." I say as I look up.

I scream! "What happened to your eye? Where you in a fight? Does it hurt?"

"Slow down, April. I'm okay, and no I wasn't in a fight." He reassures me.

"Then what happened?" I demand.

"Nothing really, it was just an accident." Ryan says.

"And what type of accident are you talking about?"

He sighs. "When I came home last night you were having a really vivid nightmare. I picked you up and was trying to carry you to bed. You started swinging your arms a lot and let's just say you have a mean right hook."

"Oh, no. I did that?" I put my cup down and move closer.

"It's no big deal." Ryan shrugs.

"No big deal! It's a huge deal. I'm so sorry. Does it hurt?" His eye is swollen and has many shades of purple all around it. I can't believe I did that!

"Not really. I think it looks kind of cool."

"Sure, yeah, right," I throw my hands into the air. "If word gets out that I gave you a shiner, yikes, we can't tell anyone." I put my hand over my mouth.

"I was thinking that too." He puts his arm around my shoulder and pulls me into him.

"Should I put make-up on you?" I have to make this go away.

"You aren't getting close to me with your make-up. I was thinking that we stay home this weekend instead. We have a little you and me time. I already talked it over with Nancy. She is completely fine watching Lysa; the only thing left is for you to agree."

"Now that sounds wonderful. Too bad you had to get hurt for it to happen." I sigh.

"Actually I was planning on surprising you with this weekend at home before I got home. The black eye just confirmed it. All I have to do is some paper work but I won't look at that for a while."

"Great. Let's cuddle a bit on the couch." I pull him toward the couch. He hesitates.

"Sure, I just want to grab a cup of coffee, and I'll be right in. Oh, and when I get to the couch, I'd love to hear why you're only wearing one slipper." He says over his shoulder as he makes his way toward the heavenly hazelnut.

* * *

"April, sweetie, Janice is on the phone. I was going to let you sleep, but she sounds upset."

"Huh? Isn't it morning? Why did I go back to sleep?" Ryan doesn't say anything, just holds out the phone. "Oh, Janice, right." As I sit up, I try to focus. My hands each rub one eye; but the blurriness still lingers. I blink. I must have been, oh wait, blinking makes my eyes a bit better. Ryan hands me my phone.

"Hello."

"Hi, April. He called!"

"Who called?"

"Did I wake you up? Because if I didn't, you should know the answer to that."

"Okay, Janice, let's start over. Hi Janice, I just woke up, and I'm not thinking clearly or seeing clearly for that matter because you woke me up. Well, Ryan woke me up, but he only did that because you called."

"He called!" She practically screams into my ear.

"Who called?" I better wake up soon or maybe I should hang up and go back to sleep. This isn't making any sense to me. Janice sounds so angry. Is she mad that I don't know who called or is she upset at the caller?

"Why aren't you saying anything, April?" Janice demands.

"What did he say?" I decide to play along and hope that it starts to make sense soon.

"He said that it's over!" Her voice wobbles.

"Oh, no!" She's talking about Douglas. My back straightens as my feet hit the floor. "Why?"

"I don't know why, really." She sniffles. Ryan taps me on the shoulder.

"I'm so sorry, Janice. Oh, can you hold on one minute?"

"Yeah." She whispers.

I look up at Ryan, a little annoyed.

"April," Ryan whispers, "Why don't you go over to her house and I'll do my paperwork now, and then when you come back we'll spend time together."

"Are you sure?" I ask.

"Yeah, she needs you right now."

"Okay." I whisper back to Ryan.

"Janice, I'll be right over, okay?" I say into the phone.

"Okay, thank you and Ryan too. He whispers loudly, I heard what he said." She chuckles, then sobs.

"I can hear you too, Janice!" Ryan shouts.

"I'll be right over." I add before I hang up.

I give Ryan a hug and ask him to forgive me for being annoyed with him. I hope we work this well together throughout our marriage.

"I'll see you soon. How long do you need to finish your paperwork?"

"Two or three hours should be about right. Stay as long as you need, I have a couple of house repairs I've been wanting to get to so if you're not back when I finish going through the papers, I'll start that."

"Okay, do you ever relax?" He hasn't taken a day off in a while but it seems like he isn't really taking one off today either.

"Ha, ha. I do. And I will this weekend, but I like to get things done sooner than later."

"Not me. I like to procrastinate as long as I possibly can. Do you think that will cause conflict for us in the future?" We are opposites in many ways.

"Probably," he says as he pulls me back to him and into another hug, "but if we learn how to balance each other we could work very well together."

I squeeze his hand and grab my keys from the bowl. My shoes are on the mat by the door. Slipping them on, I wave as I walk out the door.

My car is fairly clean and it smells like bananas, rotten bananas. When was the last time I had a banana in my car? When the road straightens, without any cars coming my way, I glance around trying to find the culprit. With no luck, after several tries, I park in front of Janice's house. Janice needs me so I'll have to look for the banana another time. Her curtains are drawn and I notice no sign of movement as I ring the bell. I have a key so I decide not to wait for her.

"Janice, I'm here! Where are you?" I shout as I close the door behind me.

I keep calling her name, but only my lonely echo comes back to my ears. The kitchen, living room, bedroom, and dining room are all on the first floor and they're all empty. The bathroom door is open and from here, I can see she isn't there either. In the garage hangs an old bicycle above her car. She drives a bright yellow Honda civic. Lysa calls it a banana every time she sees it. She says it's a game she learned in school. Anyway, there is no sign of Janice in the garage. She knew I was coming over, so, where is she?

I step back into the house and peek in her backyard. She hates her backyard so I didn't think she would be out there, but I know I only have the basement left to search, which makes the outside more appealing. There are several steps that lead down to a concrete patio. She isn't out here either. As I enter the kitchen I hear a loud scraping sound coming from the basement. I guess she's in the dreaded area. Her stairs are bare wood with thin boards for my feet. They appear rickety, but I have no choice but to trust each one to do its job. It's dark and dank down there. The only light is on around the corner; as I walk to it, I can see Janice's shadow as she moves a large container.

"Here, kitty, kitty. Where are you?" She says impatiently.

"Janice, what are you doing?" Is she losing her mind?

"April, come on!" She throws her hands into the air, "didn't 'here kitty, kitty' give you a clue?" She snaps out.

I didn't want to tell her that maybe Douglas broke up with her because she was too blunt in speaking her mind.

"Yeah, I heard that, but you don't own a cat." I point out.

"I do now!" She moves around a big container.

"Oh. Is it a stray?" I ask. I was here a couple of days ago and she didn't have a cat nor did she mention wanting one.

"No, I went to the pound yesterday. I thought maybe I needed to learn how to take care of something living. I wasn't sure if I knew how to be motherly so I thought a cat was a good start." She puffs the words out as she continues to move boxes around.

"Oh, that sounds like a good idea, but you have always been great with Lysa."

"I know, but she always goes back home. I have never raised anything, and I wasn't sure I knew how." Janice gives me a defeated look and sits down on a box.

"Okay. What did you name the cat?"

"I named him Dougie." As she says the name her shoulders start to shake. I put my arm around her and let her cry for a minute. Then I steer her toward the steps.

"I can't leave Dougie." She starts to turn around.

"Janice, the cat is afraid right now; he will come out when he's ready. Let's put his food bowl at the top of the stairs, and when he comes up to eat, we'll close the basement door."

"Okay, you're right." She relents.

She lets me walk her up to the kitchen. I make some coffee, and try not to stare at Janice's clothes. She has on a bright orange top that hurts my eyes when I look at it, with matching eyeglass frames. She owns frames that have several different colors that she swaps out when she gets tired of one look. She enjoys buying clothes that match them. She also has a headband to match with a yellow flower on the orange band. I try to resist seeing what color her socks are. Her hair is very stylish. I have never tried to emulate

Janice's style, but it works well for her most days. I don't think now is the time to tell her orange makes her look a bit washed out.

Her coffee spills a little as I walk the couple of steps to the table. I wipe up the floor, and wait for her to say something. She normally has no problem filling in gaps of silence. This must be bad.

"So, Janice, why did you get a cat?" I hope this eases her into sharing.

"I wanted to."

"Okay."

"Well, I've been waiting for Douglas to call. I was determined not to call him because I was thinking that I was being too pushy, so I refused to call him. I was sitting around waiting for the phone to ring and it wasn't doing its job. While waiting, I remembered Douglas asking me if I was ever able to take care of a pet. I told him that I've never owned a pet before and he just said, 'Oh'. I didn't think much of it at the time, but then I thought maybe he was wondering if I would be able to raise children. His wording was odd so I figured maybe he thought that I couldn't, and that was why he was so quiet lately. Last night I went out and picked up this cat. And I learned a lot already. He was right." She stands up quickly from her chair where we're sitting in the kitchen; her knee knocks the table.

She goes on, "I can't raise any children. I can't even get a cat to come out of my basement, how would I keep kids alive? No wonder he wasn't calling me. I'm a failure. I have nothing to offer, nothing to give and now I see why I've been alone all this time. No one wants me!" She sits back down and put her head in between her arms on the table.

"Janice, you need to slow down. You know you can't compare one night with a cat, to raising children. You will make a great mom. You know how to cook amazing food and you are very loving and caring toward Lysa. She has always loved spending time with you, and so do many other people in this world. You cannot let one man and his foolishness take that away from you. You are an amazing woman." I hope she sees that I am speaking the truth to her.

"I was happy, but it doesn't matter now anyway. He shattered my happiness."

"Why?"

"He called!" Oh, yes. I do remember this part.

"Why don't you tell me what he said?" I give her arm a light squeeze.

I stand and put my arm around her, leading her back to her chair.

"He said a lot of nothing, is what he said!" When Janice is upset, she doesn't give the information you ask for, but instead moves her hands around a lot and continues to rant.

"And that would be?" I hope to bring her back to our conversation.

"He started saying that he noticed I have lost a good amount of weight since we met. He said I look great and that's where I lost him. He didn't really make sense after that. He started mumbling about how he really likes me and then he went on about how we don't fit together."

"Did you ask him what he meant by that?"

"Did I ask him what he meant?" Her hands go up into the air as her legs bump the table, again. No coffee spills, surprisingly. "Of course I did. He just said the same thing again. And then I said, 'how do we not fit?'"

"And?"

"And nothing. He made no sense. Why hasn't Ryan befriended him yet?" Janice throws a curve ball.

"Uh...," I'm not sure where she is taking this, "he's been busy."

"Yeah, I know, but he could have solved this one for me. He could have called him for me." She says as if this should make sense.

"I'm not sure if he would be comfortable with that." I say.

"Maybe I'll ask him anyway. He seems to be good at this kind of stuff."

"I'll warn him." I mumble.

"That's fine, but I'll still ask. April, I thought he was the one." She groans.

"He still could be. Did he say he doesn't want to see you anymore?"

"Actually, he said he was going to miss me. I said if that was him breaking up with me, he would have to come over and do it face to face. He said he couldn't, and yes that he was indeed breaking up with me."

She pounds her fist into the table. Coffee sloshes up the sides and all around the outside of the mug. I'd clean it up but this might be a lost cause.

"Oh, that does sound final."

"Yes, it does! I wish I knew why though. I'm so frustrated! What did I do wrong? He didn't seem to mind my take-charge personality. Actually, he never let me push him into anything. He was equally opinionated and I loved him for it, most of the time. He even loved the way I dress; he said my wardrobe showed my personality well."

"Did he switch back to his church?" Douglas started going to our church about two months ago.

"I don't know. We just broke up, but I didn't see him Sunday and I looked. And why would he break up with me, if he were going to miss me? That doesn't make sense to me. Do you think I should go to his house?" She seriously considers this idea.

"Umm, I need to think about that a bit." If I tell her a flat out no, she will have her car keys in her hands in ten seconds flat.

"Yeah, you're right, I should go over there." She gets up, and starts to walk over to her shoes.

"Janice, that isn't what I said."

"Well, you didn't say it, but that is what you meant." Nope, she's not even close.

"Actually, I really meant what I said; that I need to think about it."

"April, help me out here, I should go over there, right?" Janice's voice rings higher with her last word.

"Janice, I know you would like me to say, 'Let's get in the car now and find out what this is all about' but I'm just not sure that is the best approach." I make sure she is looking at me as I talk to her. "Sometimes waiting is the best approach. Maybe he needs time to miss you. To realize what he is actually giving up."

"Maybe I should wait a bit then. I'll wait until tomorrow night when he's on duty, and I'll call in a disturbance."

"Janice, I hope you're joking, because that isn't funny and I think it might be illegal." I shake my head. My head starts to ache. Maybe I should call Nancy or Helen to come over and help.

"I'm joking, April, lighten up. But I do want to know what is really going on. I still think he is the one I'm supposed to marry so shouldn't I be over there pursuing this?"

"Janice, listen, your emotions are all over the place. You need to take some time right now to think. He needs time right now to think also. And so do I, so please just stop wanting to do anything, but think right now." My voice is surprisingly even, I'm thankful it didn't mimic my frustration.

"April, okay, I see your point. He needs time to realize that he misses me and wants me back. You're right. I'll give him some time."

That wasn't quite what I said, but at least we aren't driving down the road heading toward Douglas's house.

"So Janice, do you have any food?" I need to change the subject for a little while.

"You know I do. Alright let's go have a cooking lesson."

"Umm, I was wondering if you have anything ready."

"Nope, I don't so if you want to eat, you have to cook." She states.

"Okay, what do we make?" I'm not sure what is worse, having to cook or talk Janice into leaving Douglas alone.

She opens the fridge door. I don't know if I'm really helping her by distracting her, but I need something to eat. I haven't eaten yet and I also need time to think. There's a lot to think about!

Janice drops a piece of food on the floor and the cat races over to eat it making Janice smile. And me too! At least one problem is solved.

Chapter 11

I have all the notes from every man that has contributed to the surveillance job, which isn't many in either category. I'm about halfway through reading and I can't find anything wrong with this man. He seems clean, a bit too clean maybe, but maybe not. He doesn't work either. It seems that all he does is meet people for lunch or dinner, go to the bank, school, church, girlfriend's, and other miscellaneous errands. He gives the appearance of being a good guy. A little over the top, fake maybe, or maybe a bit too friendly with people he just meets. He wants to be liked. His frequency to the bank needs to be investigated more, and if that can be explained, then I'll have to close the case. There's no proof that he isn't who he says he is. Finalizing this will bring me home and give me time to focus on my family. That's what I want but I need to be sure. I can't let what I want sway me to miss something critical.

I have his credit history, but that is all I can get legally. I have a friend who could help me get more information, but I don't feel right about crossing into those gray areas. I need to find out another way; reaching for my phone, I take the opportunity to freely talk to Nick. Stretching my legs onto the black leather ottoman in front of me, I remember April saying that it's too big for the office room. I agree, but it is so comfortable. He answers after three rings.

"Nick, where are you?"

"I'm at my place." He seems distracted.

"Oh, is Nancy there?" Maybe that's why.

"No, she doesn't want anything to do with me!" Oh, that's not good.

"Why is that?"

"Ryan, it's *this* job! She feels I've been abandoning her like her dad did. She says I walked out without explaining where I was going. I told her I had a job to do, but that wasn't enough information for her. I thought I left on good terms. She went on and on about me not being honest with her, and if I can't communicate better then we shouldn't spend so much time together. Then she told me that I never said how long I was going to be gone and that when I was gone I never answered her calls. I told her my phone died, which is true, but she wouldn't hear anything I had to say. I didn't ask her if it was her time of the month or anything, even though I was hoping that was the reason for this outburst. I don't understand women. Here I thought we were really getting to know each another. Now, I'm not so sure."

"Wow; that really stinks!" Should I say anything else?

"Yeah, I'm starting to see why you were all upset about not being able to tell April. I get it. Did you find a way to tell her now?"

"Unfortunately, no, Nick, but we aren't taking any more clients for a long time or ever. Hopefully, Nancy will be able to see you more after this project is finished, and then realize that you aren't going to walk out on her like her dad did. That's a good point though, I should be more sensitive with April about their dad."

"Oh, I'm so frustrated!" He growls.

"Yeah."

"I should have hugged her instead of getting all defensive. Man, I'm messing this one up."

"We'll get through this with God. I'm going to see if the other guys can handle the surveillance for this weekend. I want you to call Howie and see how everything is going. I also want you to tell Howie and John that they are to follow our guy into the bank the next time he goes there. I want as much information as we can get. I want to know what he is doing in there. Okay?" I push the ottoman away from me so I have more room to stand up.

"Yup. I'll call him now. Oh, Ryan…"

"Yes?" I hesitate a moment before I pull out the coke from the mini fridge.

"How are things going with April?"

"Okay. We're planning a stay-cation this weekend which means I might be limited to text messages. If anything serious develops, give me a call."

"A stay-cation, that's a good idea. Was it yours?" Nick is quite the talker today.

"Actually it was. I really miss her and I want to spend as much time as I can with her."

"Sounds good. Have fun. Oh, and if you see Nancy can you put in a good word for me?" Now he's using his brain.

"Of course, Nick. And I know you aren't asking but my advice is for you to continue to pursue her and woo her." I pop the top and start to sip the soda.

"Yeah, that could be hard if she doesn't want to see me."

"Nah, you're a smart guy. I bet you will think of something. Oh, and when I see her, I'll let her know your horrible working hours are my fault. I'll work on being a better boss."

"Now that might help. I like the sound of that…your fault. Yeah, please let her know. Thanks, Ryan." I can hear him smile.

"No prob. Bye, Nick."

I toss my phone onto the end table, and pick up the papers I wasn't finished looking at.

A helicopter sounds. I look out the window and see it go by. A loud thud from the roof startles me. It sounded like a heavy object being dropped from a high distance or at least higher than my roof. Strange. There are plenty of trees on my property but none near my house. I wonder what it could be. My stomach growls so I put my papers down and head to the kitchen. April made brownies yesterday; I pop one into my mouth then start to search the refrigerator. There's some chicken salad left over. After adding a little cayenne pepper and lettuce, I bite into my sandwich.

Exploring the roof wasn't on my 'to do' list today, but I can't think of what could have made that noise. I need to make sure there's no damage. Finishing my sandwich, I put my boots on and go into the garage. My ladder is hanging on the far left. My truck might be too close to the wall for me to get it out, but maybe not. Putting my feet sideways, I'm able to lift the ladder up and sidestep out. I open the garage door.

The back of the house is easier to get on the roof. Once I'm around the back, I start extending the ladder. After finding a secure spot, I start to ascend. Three, then two, now one step left. As I approach the top, I see that the shingles all look in order in the back of the house. I pull myself up onto the roof and I walk around toward the front and see more of the same, but the chimney has a huge bag sticking out of it. I grab it with my right hand and give a tug. It doesn't budge. Huh. Where did this come from? Putting both hands around the plastic, I lean back, and pull as hard as I can. It breaks loose and I stumble several feet toward the edge of the roof by the front of the house. My left foot slides to a stop as my heel lands in the gutter and my toes see the sky. The bag slides passed me, falling to the ground with another thud, leaving me sideways but still on the roof. I wipe the sweat from my forehead, and slowly sit up in hopes to relieve my dizziness and calm my heart. Man, that was close.

After several minutes my curiosity wins over my dizziness, and I start to descend. Three rungs down, I hear a crack coming from below my right foot. My foot slips and my hands slide; I try to stop, but gravity pulls.

* * *

"Ryan, try to stay calm. "A strange voice says. "You've had a bad fall and I'm putting an IV into your...Ryan you need to relax." She places a hand on my shoulder and pushes me down. I have no strength to fight.

"What happened? Ouch, I'm in ...so... much pain." My eyes won't open. I'm not sure where I am but I don't care, I only want the pain to stop.

"You fell off the ladder. I'm Stephanie, one of the EMT's here to help you. I want to get an IV started so we can get you some morphine for the pain you're in."

That's all she needed to say, I'll be still just as long as she takes this sharpness away.

"What happened?"

"Do you remember climbing the ladder?" She turns to her partner and says something about no short-term memory or something like that.

"Uh, no." What ladder?

"Ryan, please tell me the last thing you remember doing?" She puts the IV in.

"Um, I remember talking on the phone to Nick." I try to move my arm and shooting pain fills my whole body.

"Okay, do you know Nick's phone number?" Look in my phone! What's with the twenty questions?

"Yes, it's…oh, my head feels funny. It feels warm." I open my eyes and see the sky.

"Good, that's the morphine. We're going to wait a few minutes for the morphine to take effect. While we wait, Charlie is going to get a history from you."

Stephanie points to my left, and I see a man with a black hat pulled down past his eyebrows. He is holding a clipboard that goes up passed his nose. All I can see are his eyes, but he's a bit far away or maybe my eyes are blurry.

He asks questions like, what my phone number is, address, if I was on any medications and medical history.

"Ryan, what happened?" April panics, rushing to my side.

"Um, who are you?"

"Oh no! Ryan! You don't know who I am?" She kneels down next to me. April runs her hands through her hair and lets out a groan.

"What happened?" She turns fast and grabs Stephanie's arm. Before Stephanie could respond I realize the morphine is making things funnier than they really are.

"April, look at me." I say.

She turns back, "Wait, you know who I am now?"

"April, I'm sorry I'm on some stuff that Stephanie gave me. I was joking, but obviously, you didn't find that funny." I try to shrug my shoulders.

"So you know who I am?" Her eyebrows rise; her hand squeezes mine.

"Yes, I know who you are."

"Do you know we're married?"

"Yes, I know we're married."

"Oh, good. That was probably the worst joke you have ever told!" She lightens her grip on my hand. "What happened, Ryan?"

"Honestly, I don't remember. I remember us spending time together earlier today and I remember Janice calling. You went over to her house and I worked a bit and talked to Nick on the phone. After that, it's a blank. I don't even know who found me here on the ground."

"I don't know either. Are you in a lot of pain?" She looks into my eyes.

"Not as much right now, but I was before the IV."

Stephanie walks back over to Ryan. "From what we can figure, it looks like you were in a fight and you took a bad fall off the ladder. It's a puzzle to us though because there wasn't another person here and you fell off the ladder. Did you get into a fist fight first or were you fighting on the roof? Do either of you have any insight?"

April and I groan at the same time. We both forgot about the black eye. The EMT stares at us.

"Okay, Ryan, we would like some answers, but that can wait. It's time to go. We are going to lift you. Your wife needs to stand back." She motions for the help to come over.

Stephanie is the one in charge. There are two other men with her that she introduced as Charlie and um, I don't remember, but she said they were fire fighters. Stephanie and some other woman, I don't remember her name either, are the EMT's that have come to help me.

My neck is in a brace and I have tingling up and down my legs. As they turn me onto my side, sharp pain shots throughout my back. I can't move my neck much because of the brace. Stephanie was asking me about climbing a ladder? Why would I be climbing a ladder today? I need Nick here.

"April?" I reach out my hand hoping to find her.

"Yes, Ryan." She tries to get closer but has difficulty with all the people surrounding me.

"Can you have Nick come over here and look around? Please let him know what happened, and let him know I was climbing a ladder, but I have no idea why." I hope my voice was clearer than my thoughts.

"Sure, I'll call him while I'm following you in the ambulance." Her voice is shaking.

They put a board under me and then all four lift me onto their stretcher. With each, unavoidable bump, sharp pain shoots through my back. There is a thick blanket under me with straps hanging. Stephanie and, I remember her name now, Beth start buckling the straps around me.

"Ryan, we are going to wheel you into the ambulance. Please keep your hands on your lap. If you want, you can hold this strap."

They start to move me.

"Will this thing tip over?" Right now, all I want to do is avoid pain.

"No, we have you." Stephanie reassures.

"Did you ask me to keep my hands in so that I don't tip it?" I'm still not a believer in the safety of this stretcher.

"No, we asked you to do that so your hands don't get bumped on the way into the vehicle."

"Has anyone ever fallen off before?"

"Ryan, don't worry, you're in good hands. We are going to lift you now."

The fire fighters step back. Why are they stepping back? Stephanie is at my feet and Beth is by my head. They wheel me backward while the legs of the gurney go out by my head. I grab the strap tightly. Stephanie's face shows no concern. I can't see what Beth is doing. These women don't look strong enough to lift me. There is another bump and more sharp pain runs throughout my back. Stephanie says something to Beth about being careful, but I don't catch her phrasing. April is standing next to me, Lysa is sniffling, her head buried into April's side. Nancy is standing behind them with her hand on Aprils' shoulder. Of all the days for Lysa to only have a half day of school.

"Lysa, please come here." She turns her head and looks at me, but doesn't move forward.

"I'm okay Lysa, okay?" I try not to scare her.

"Okay." She says timidly, while wiping an eye.

"I'll see you soon. I love you." I reach out for her hand.

"I love you too, Daddy." She says.

I give her hand a quick squeeze, and Stephanie pushes the gurney. The wheels fold up by my feet and I look at this petite woman holding me up. Stephanie sits beside me in the ambulance. I never saw Beth leave but from my limited view, she isn't in here. We start to move.

"Ryan, have you had any previous injuries to your back?" Stephanie has a clipboard in her hand.

"No."

With each dip in the road comes a twinge. The hospital is about an hour away.

"Ryan, I'm going to give you more morphine, but before I do, can you tell me if you now remember why you were on the ladder?"

"Um, Nick and I were talking and uh, at some point...there was a loud noise on the roof. I'm not sure if I was still talking to Nick or if...uh, anyway, there was a noise and I wanted to make sure everything was fine so I took out the ladder. I went on to the roof and I found, I found...well I don't know what I found, but I need to talk to Nick. Do you have a phone I can use?" I ask.

"Ryan, you need to slow down. What happened when you started to go down the ladder?"

"I slipped. I don't know why. I climb ladders for a living, why would I slip?"

"I don't know." She has her head down, and continues to write. "Was the ladder wet?"

"No, I don't think so. I started to go down the ladder and one of my feet went to the next rung and it didn't hold." I tried to get up but the straps held me in place.

"How old was your ladder?"

"Stephanie, I only have the best equipment. I wouldn't let it get old. I need to call Nick."

"Sorry, I don't have your phone. Your wife probably has it; soon you will be able to make your call."

"Okay, I'll wait."

This makes no sense. I need to be at my house looking around. I couldn't have just slipped, could I? My brain's fuzzy. I wiggle my toes and think about what needs to be done next. Forced procrastination stinks!

* * *

"Nick, I'm so glad you're here!" Nancy rushes toward Nick. "That was fast."

"I was already on the road when April called. Nancy, please tell me what happened!" Nick pulls her into a quick hug.

"Sure. Lysa came home early from school today because it was a half-day. April called me and asked me to meet the bus. We were playing a board game, when we heard a loud thud on the roof. I didn't think much of it, but I was going to mention it to Ryan when he came home. I didn't know he was home already. Anyway, we went back to our game, and a couple of minutes later we heard Ryan on the roof. He must have heard the noise, and went to check it out. Then we hear Ryan yell, and we also heard the ladder fall. I don't know how it happened. I raced outside and saw him lying on the ground. I yelled for Lysa to bring me my phone. I went to Ryan but he didn't stir. I checked for a pulse and he had one, but he was unconscious. The ambulance came within ten minutes, but during that time Lysa was panicking, and I was trying to keep her calm. When the ambulance arrived, we backed up, and Ryan started to come to. Oh, I was about to call April, but she pulled into the driveway right then so I didn't need to."

Nick motions for Nancy and Lysa to sit on the grass.

"The EMTs knew exactly what to do. They lifted him onto a stretcher after putting on a neck brace. He was able to move his arms and hands just fine. I didn't notice his legs." Nancy finishes.

Lysa starts to cry. Nick reaches out, and pulls her into a side hug. Sniffling, Lysa starts to calm. Nancy looks into his eyes. Her heart skips a beat. He is handsome. The thought sends chills throughout her body. The realization confuses her. She's known Nick for a very long time, but he was always a family friend. He and Nancy have had many conversations about life and God over the years. He's Ryan's best friend. Is it right for her to have feelings for him? Her husband Phil has been gone for almost three years now. Some days it feels like yesterday.

"What's wrong, Nancy?" Nick closes his fingers around Nancy's.

"Oh, I'm concerned about Ryan."

He knows there's more but he doesn't push with Lysa right next to them. One day she'll share her heart with him. He knows that his recent travels have put a strain on their friendship.

Lysa calms.

"Okay. Let's look around. Why don't we start at the ladder?" Nick gets up and offers Nancy a hand up.

They walk around the house. The ladder is on its side lying on the ground. Nick walks the length of the ladder then goes back to one end and gets down on the ground for a closer look. He takes out his phone and snaps several pictures.

"Nancy, come here. Look at this." She looks at what he's talking about.

"These three rungs have all been cut. They weren't cut all the way through but look at this one. It's the second cut one, but it didn't break yet. Someone wanted him to fall." He lets out a loud breath, and calls the police.

She doesn't know what to think about the ladder. Why would anyone do that? When did, this happen? And when were they here to do it? Who would want to hurt Ryan? It was meant for him, because neither April nor Nancy would even carry a ladder this big and no way would they use it. Nick is off the phone, and starts to pace.

"Nancy, let's look in the garage." He starts to walk.

"Alright." Nancy and Lysa follow.

They make their way around the other side of the house and see a big, black garbage bag. Nancy stops.

"Nancy, you okay?" Nick looks her way.

"That wasn't there yesterday." She states and grabs Lysa's hand. She takes a step back, bringing Lysa with her.

"Are you sure?"

"Yes. It wasn't even there this morning."

"Maybe Ryan put it there."

"That's possible." But she doesn't sound convinced.

"How many thuds did you hear, Nancy?" Nick takes out his phone and starts taking more pictures.

"I heard one on the roof, and then two more. I thought they were Ryan and the ladder falling but that doesn't make sense. I heard the ladder fall last. Maybe it was the bag I heard fall, and then the ladder. Also, there was a helicopter flying over the house. It sounded really close, but that has happened before, I think. I thought it was just those Eric Brothers again. You know they have their own chopper that they fly all around up here." She waves her hand at the sky.

"I'll ask them about that later. Let's move away from the bag, and I'll call the police back." He leads them quickly to the front of the yard, and up to the road. Maybe Lysa should have gone with April. Nancy decides to call Janice to come and get her. Her mom left yesterday to go to Florida with April and Nancy's youngest sister Ella to look at colleges.

"Nick," Nancy asks after he hangs up the phone again, "do you think we should be concerned?"

"No, but I don't want to take chances, either." He runs his hand through his brown hair.

"Okay, Nick, we have known each other for a long time now. And I was wondering…" Before she could finish, two police cars come to a stop in front of the house. They block off the road on both sides. When they finish, a big van pulls up, and a man steps out wearing a full bomb squad uniform or at least that's what Nancy thinks it is. She has never seen one before. She can't see what he looks like, not even his hair color. Another man exits from the drivers' side, half sporting the same attire. He reaches into the back seat, and pulls out the top half of his suit.

"This is so cool, Aunt Nancy! Look at them!" Lysa points in one direction then another. Her eyes grow bigger with each new thing she sees.

Nancy decides not to let her know why they are dressed like this. She hopes Janice arrives soon.

"Are you okay, Nancy?" Nick asks as he puts his hand on her shoulder.

"This is a bit overwhelming." She whispers.

"Yeah, a bit, but it's better to be safe. I don't think there is anything to worry about. I need to talk to the person in charge. Are you going to be alright with Lysa?" Nick has already started walking in the opposite direction but maintains eye contact until Nancy replies.

"Nick, I'll be fine. I'm not going to move unless someone tells me to. Janice should be here soon to pick up Lysa."

Neighbors start coming out of their houses. She doesn't know many of them because she only moved into Ryan's guest apartment a few months ago. She regrets not taking the time to get to know some. Maybe she should now. Oh, wait, she told Nick she wouldn't move. Why would she tell him that? She decides to sit on the grass by the road, far away from the black bag. Lysa sits too.

She misses Phil every day. She knows he wouldn't want her to be alone for the rest of her life. She knows he wanted her to have a baby to love as much as he wanted one also. She's thirty-two years old; too young to be alone for the rest of her days here on earth. She never planned on falling for Nick; it just happened. She was going to tell him before the police arrived, but now isn't the best time. She wants to be honest with him right away. He has never admitted his feelings for her so it could all be one-sided. He comes over often, and they have gone on a number of dates, but all he has ever done was say he had a great time or gave her a brief friend-like hug, until today, but that hug wasn't romantic either. It was one of concern. She knows he cares for her; she's just not sure if it will become anything beyond friends.

She has been afraid. She loved Phil with all her heart. And then she lost him. She's afraid to have feelings for Nick. She has been mad at him these past couple of weeks because he has canceled plans with her repeatedly because of business travels. She knows his business very well and there is no reason for him to be traveling this much. She knows he is going with Ryan so she's more curious then lacking trust. What are they doing?

Maybe she's misunderstanding why he wanted to spend time with her. Maybe he feels bad for her because she lost Phil. That could be it. Ryan came over a lot after Phil passed away, but she knew his intentions were to help with fixing things and to spend some time with Lysa. He wanted to be her dad and April's husband and she saw it as a very good thing. She also selfishly wanted him to marry April. He has always been a great role model for Lysa, and now that the adoption is final, he is officially her dad.

"Aunt Nancy, Aunt Janice is here but she can't get through." Lysa points down the road.

"Okay, let's walk you over to her then." Once they get to the car, Nancy fills Janice in on what has happened and they decide that

Nancy will stay with Nick while the two of them will go to the hospital to wait with April. Nancy walks back to the grassy area where she was waiting before and sits down again.

"Nancy!" Nick is waving his hands. Getting up, she dusts off her pants, and walks over to him.

"What did they find?" She hopes it's something like garbage.

"It was a bag full of bricks with a note stuck to one of them." He explains more as the bomb squad drives away. There are still a couple of policemen, but almost everyone else has left about as fast as they arrived. The roadblock was moved also. She missed all of it.

"And?" She rubs her head.

"There was no bomb, but the police did say a crime was committed. The ladder was definitely cut and we're all thinking that the bricks were meant to fall on the roof so that Ryan would climb up the ladder and fall." Nick says with distaste.

"Who would do this, Nick?" Nancy clasps her fingers together.

"I have no idea." He shakes his head.

"I have known Ryan for a very long time, and there has never been anyone that has disliked him except April, but you know that story."

"What did the note say?"

"All it said was 'leave me alone'."

"Huh, Ryan must know who it is then." Maybe.

"Nancy, is there anything you need to get or do before we go to the hospital?" He gently takes her elbow and starts to walk toward the driveway.

"Yes, I need to grab my purse." He drops his hand and they walk side by side, but not too close to touch. It is things like this that convince her that he is only around as a friend.

"Nick, I'm sorry I wasn't very nice to you the last time we talked. Can you forgive me?" Her words start tripping over each other, because she can't hold back the need to ask forgiveness.

"Yes, I can. I'm also sorry I keep traveling and that I didn't answer my phone when you called. It was dead and I left my charger at home but I will try to plan better so I don't have to cancel on you anymore." He says.

"It's okay. It's not like we're dating or anything. I was being too possessive of your time." She says over her shoulder as she pushes open the door and walks into the house.

"Yeah, uh, well I'll wait here for you." He says, as the door slams shut in his face.

What just happened? Now he won't even come inside! Maybe I need to talk to Helen. She makes it to the top of the stairs and grabs her purse. Nancy doesn't get it. When everything happened last year with April, he was right beside Nancy the whole time. He didn't say he cared or anything to that effect, but his actions showed it. Jogging down the stairs, she realizes that she's mad. Nick is standing outside the doorway, and he steps aside while opening the door for her when she gets to the landing. She decides it's better not to say anything at all before she has had time to think.

Chapter 12

"April, how's Ryan doing?" Nancy asks, rushing over to hug me.

"I don't know yet. He's getting an MRI now. They did some X-rays first. I only saw him a little bit before they took him back. The hospital is full. His room number is H2a. Do you know what H stands for?" I spit out.

"No, I have no idea. What?" Nancy takes my hand in hers.

"It stands for Hallway. They have him in the hallway, but hopefully he should only be there a short time. Nick and Nancy, do you mind staying here with Lysa? Janice went to get some coffee and I want to call Ryan's parents." I give Lysa a quick hug.

"Sure, we'll stay with Lysa."

I stand and Nancy takes my seat next to Lysa, Nick begins to pace. I can see that things aren't going well between them, but now isn't the time to ask. They'll figure it out.

My cell phone doesn't work in the hospital. I walk to the elevators, and out one of the many side doors.

"Hi, April. How are you doing?" Ryan's mom loves to beat people to the greeting.

"Hi. Ryan fell off a ladder, and he is at St. Peters now. He hurt his back. They're running tests now." I barely choke out the end of my sentence as my emotions finally surface.

"Oh, no! Hold on." 'Ryan's been hurt, we need to get to the hospital,' I hear her shout to her husband. "April, which hospital did you say he's in?"

"He's at St. Peters. I'm going to go back to him now. I'll see you when you get here. We are still in the emergency room. If that changes, I'll call your cell if I get a chance."

She hangs up before I get my last word out. I turn, use a Kleenex, and quickly make my way back to Ryan's side or at least the place where I can wait to hear from him. In the waiting room, Lysa sits, leaning on Nancy's shoulder. When I rush in she jumps up, and hugs me.

"Mommy, did you hear anything about daddy?" She pulls on my sleeve.

"No sweetie," I say as I hug her back. "Did you?"

"No." I walk her over to Nancy. "I'm going to go to his hallway spot in the emergency room and see if he's there. I'll come back soon. Okay?"

"Okay, mommy, but can I go with you?"

"Lysa, I'm not sure. How about this; I'll go in alone now, and find out if you can go in with me next time. Alright honey?" I prefer for her to be out here but I'll keep my word.

"Okay, mommy. I'll stay with Aunt Nancy." She sits back down and sticks out her lower lip.

"Thanks Lysa. If you want, Aunt Nancy can turn on the television, and see if there is anything for you to watch." Nancy and I share a look.

"I'll take care of her, April. You go and see how Ryan is." Nancy's back is toward Nick. Interesting.

I turn, and push through the double doors. Walking around, I turn a couple of times, looking for Ryan's hallway spot. Now lost, I know asking is my only hope in finding him.

"Can you please tell me where Ryan Nolsen is?"

"Umm, one moment." She types several keys on her keyboard.

"He's in his room, H2a." I hold my tongue about already knowing that because I'm on the verge of being rude.

"Where is that?"

"Oh, make a right at the end of the counter, and then a left at the end of the next hallway. He should be right around that bend." She gives the directions without taking her eyes from the computer screen.

"Thanks." I follow her directions while trying to avoid the hallway confusion and chaos. I am not the only one who is undergoing stress. At the last turn, I see Ryan propped up with two pillows under him. He has his eyes closed. I stand by him, and gently put my hand into his.

"I'm a happily married man, so do you mind letting my hand go!" He mumbles.

"I'm happily married also." I whisper back, giving his hand a squeeze.

"April, you smell good." He says, his eyes still closed.

"Thanks, Ryan. You don't look too good. How do you feel?"

"I felt better earlier today before falling, but the muscle relaxers and pain meds are helping." He has a slight slur to his words.

"Did the doctor say anything yet?" I ask, as I sit gently on the edge of his bed. I quickly jump up, realizing that I still have no idea the extent of his injuries. Sitting on his bed could cause a problem.

"April, relax. Maybe a nurse can get you a chair."

I look around and see one right against the wall by his bed. Pulling it over to his side, I sit and reach for his hand again.

"I know you asked me a question, but I can't remember what it was." He turns his head and winces.

"I was wondering if a doctor told you anything yet." I repeat.

"Umm, no, maybe, I don't know. It's all a blur. Did I mention that the pain meds are helping?" He asks.

"Yes, Ryan you did. Okay, I'll go look for a doctor to find out what's going on." I run my hand gently over the side of his face, careful to avoid the swelling he still has around his eye. "I'll be back soon."

"Okay, I think I might try to take a nap. Naps are good, don't you think April?"

"Yes, Ryan." I pat his shoulder lightly, as a chuckle escapes.

I'm glad he isn't in unbearable pain right now. He is definitely loopy. Hearing Ryan joke warms my heart.

* * *

The constant movement around me makes it hard to rest. I have identified most of the workers on shift. There is the blond nurse who checks people in. The janitor who moves his cart down the hallway, and about eight or nine minutes later, he is back again waiting in the intersection. I never see anyone talk to him. He waits a few minutes, and then takes off down the left wing. A tall, slightly overweight man, with a comb over, walks passed me. He has a tag on him, but he isn't wearing scrubs or a white coat. He appears to be on a mission. There are several female nurses talking at the station along with an average height male. I don't know what his role is. He flirts with one nurse for a little while, then moves across the little hallway to another station, and chats with another nurse closely. The janitor comes back and waits near me again. The check in nurse is busy, and doesn't waste time chatting with her coworkers. My nurse rarely makes an appearance. I have seen her two times and I've been here for, umm, a long time.

I think April said she would be back soon. I saw her walk through the doors straight ahead of me, but she hasn't walked back yet. The janitor exits on the right with his cart following. The big double doors several yards in front of me open. I was hoping to see April, but it's a nurse with curly brown hair. She is pushing a gurney. It steers to the right, and she bumps into the wall. She cringes, and tries to straighten it out. Backing up, she hits the double door with her back. She shakes her head, and moves forward again. The bed starts to move to the right again. She pulls her arms back to her body, and the gurney stops moving toward the wall. Now it has stopped moving, but has not progressed forward since she entered the doors. She lifts her right foot, and pushes down. I can't see from this angle if anything changed, but she seems frustrated. She tries again. It must not have worked because the next thing she does is jump with both feet landing on a lever. The bed shimmies as she continues to jump up and down with both feet. After five or six times, she gets off, pushes her hair back over her shoulder, and stands tall, peeking around to see if anyone noticed what just happened. I don't know when I went from smiling to chuckling, but the movement hurts my back.

She slowly starts to move her wheels forward. She lets out a sigh as the bed goes straight. Ten steps and she will be right in front of my bed. My hand holds my bed rail. Eight more steps and I still don't know which direction she is planning to take. One more step and she starts to turn toward her right. She needed to turn two steps earlier, but I wasn't in a place to instruct; I just don't want to be jostled. Her shoes squeak as her arms move to her left. Her bed misses mine, but hits the wall in front of me. She pulls it backward a couple of steps, and proceeds forward. A nurse quickly side steps, and the male nurse that likes to flirt, moves too slowly as the gurney taps him out of the way. Disappointment lingers as she moves out of my sight. It was fun to watch but I wouldn't trust her driving a car.

I think I'm invisible. I've been here for over an hour, and no one has informed me about what is happening; I think. I don't know if that is a good sign or not. I can move my arms fine. I think my neck is fine also, but they still have a neck brace on it so I can't be completely confident. I think I saw a doctor, but I can't remember now. The janitor is back and so is the man with the comb over; neither talks to anyone. My eyes grow heavy as the janitor's cart passes by.

Chapter 13

"Mommy, what color is daddy's hair?" Lysa asks.

"It's dirty blond." I reply.

"No, mommy!" She jumps up from her seat, and puts her hands in the air. "Daddy has clean hair mommy, not dirty. And if it is dirty you need to go back in there, and clean it for him because he needs help right now. Mommy you need to help him. Please go and clean daddy's hair." Lysa starts to cry.

"Honey, calm down." I pull her onto my lap, and hug her tight as I whisper into her ear, "The name of the hair color is called dirty blond. His hair isn't dirty, okay?"

"Are you sure?" She pulls back and looks at my face.

"Yes, I am." I nod.

"Okay, because mommy I think you should go, and check to make sure it isn't really dirty. That's something we can do to help him." She gets off my lap and grabs my hand.

"I will. I came in here to check on you. I saw daddy, and he was asleep, but I'll go back, and sit by his side for a while. And I'll check his hair too." I run my hand down her head.

Lysa calms. I don't want to let her go, but I also don't want to leave Ryan alone. I spent a while searching for someone to give me information on how he is doing. In the process, I turned myself around, and was lost for around 20 minutes. I still haven't located anyone who can help.

"Lysa, do you want to go home or stay here a little longer with everyone that is here?" She looks tired.

"I'll stay here. I want to know how daddy is doing." She moves over to Nancy and sits in the empty seat.

"Okay, when I find out what's happening, I'll come back, and let you know, then you can go home to rest." I've lost track of time. I know we have been here for hours and we still don't have answers.

"Please tell daddy I love him." She rests her head-on Nancy's shoulder.

"I will." I turn to the crowd. "I'll be back as soon as I know something."

With each trip, I become more acquainted with my surroundings. As I approach Ryan's bed I can see that he's still asleep. I go to the nurse's station, and wait for the nurse to turn around. My foot taps, and I check my phone. Shifting from on foot to the other, I finally speak up, "Excuse me."

"Yes?" She answers with a clipped tone.

"I was wondering if the doctor has been around to see my husband, Ryan Nolsen." I watch her type something quickly.

"He has." She says with the same annoyance.

"And?"

"And, please give me a minute to look it up."

I wait.

"Umm, ok, here it is. Ryan needs surgery. We are admitting him, and he will be brought up to the fourth floor shortly." I cringe.

"Okay, I have a lot of questions. Is there any way I can talk to the doctor?" Not surgery! I put my hand on the counter.

"It's probably best you talk to the surgeon, and he will be in to talk to you and Ryan when he is brought upstairs."

On my way back to Ryan's hallway spot, I see a nurse steering a bed. I step aside because she was heading straight toward me, and as she passes me, I notice its Ryan.

"Ryan, how are you?"

He reaches out his hand. "I've been better."

The nurse doesn't slow, which leaves me to briskly walk behind. I hope she doesn't bump the gurney into anything or anyone. Looking at the little blessings, I thank God that He constantly confirms that He is here with me. I'm glad I found Ryan before he left to go upstairs. The nurse doesn't try to make small talk on the way up to the fourth floor. She seems lost in her own world, which is fine with me because I don't want to attempt small talk right now either.

The woman pushing the bed hits the wall as she turns into the room, which causes Ryan to let out a groan. An actual room!

"Sorry." She says as she snorts out a laugh.

"Ryan, how are you feeling?" I rush to his side.

"I'm hurting. I think the pain meds are wearing off."

"I can get someone." I say.

"Sure that would be..." Ryan starts.

"Hello, Ryan. I'm Dr. Collins. I'm going to be performing your surgery. You will be here in the hospital for about a week. The nurse will bring you a day-by-day chart so you will have an idea as to what you will be able to do each day. You will be seeing a physical therapist while you're here, and two or three times a week for several weeks after you go home."

"Will he be able to do everything he was able to do before?" I'm so confused. There must have been a conversation without me.

"Most likely. The surgery isn't very invasive. It should take about one hour."

"Okay, can you please tell me what is wrong with his back? I don't even know that. I don't even think Ryan knows that."

"Of, course, your husband has two herniated discs in his back, L1 and L2."

"Oh." No!

"Your husband is in good hands. My team and I have been doing these surgeries for many years." I hope he is being truthful and he is really good at what he does and not just cocky.

Nodding, I grab a tissue from my purse. Now isn't a very good time to tell Ryan and the family my news. I wanted to tell Ryan a couple of months ago when I found out. He has been so busy with work that I haven't felt we had the right moment. Before his surgery isn't a good time either. I'll tell him, then the family this week. I've waited too long already. Because of the beating I endured almost a year ago my doctor wasn't sure I would, first, be able to conceive and second carry the baby this long. She says I'm still high risk but the baby looks healthy and so does my uterus. That was three days ago that she said that. I was planning to tell Ryan then. I didn't want him to get disappointed if I miscarried. He has waited so long to be a dad. Now I think I should have told him two months ago when I found out. I think I messed up this one.

"...and that is about it." The doctor concludes.

"See, April, I'm going to be fine." Shoot! What did the doctor say?

"I think you will too." I'll worry until I see him after the surgery though.

"I'll be fine." Ryan whispers.

"Alright, Ryan the nurse is here to get you all ready. April, there is a waiting room around the corner from here. If you and your family go there, when the surgery is over, I will let you know how everything went. We are scheduled to start in 20 minutes and the surgery will take about one hour."

"Thank you, Dr. Collins." I look down at my watch and calculate ahead to the end of surgery. "I'll see you at 7:40 pm."

"About." He says with a smile and nods at me on his way out.

"Ryan, I love you so much." I say as I hold his hand in mine.

"I love you too. There is no need to worry, April. I'm going to be fine." He squeezes my hand. His face is tight with pain.

"That is the third time you've said that to me. I think your pain meds are working just fine." I say as a smile creeps across my lips. Squeezing his hand back, I let go and stand. I turn my back to him so he can't see my lip tremble.

"Okay, Ryan, I'm here to get you ready." A cute nurse with Elmo's head scattered all across her shirt says with too much enthusiasm for me.

I take a deep breath, lean over, and kiss Ryan. "See you soon."

"Yes, you will. I'll be…"

"Oh, no, you don't. You are not allowed to say 'fine' again, but I pray you will be."

He smiles at me. At the door, I hesitate. Am I making another mistake? Should I tell him now? The nurse walks over to me, and smiles while she closes the door, and I realize that my choice was taken away. I lost my chance. What if he doesn't make it? What if he never knows about our baby? I'm thinking too extreme. I take another deep breath. I dab my eyes, and walk quickly to the waiting room downstairs where everyone else is.

"April what's wrong?"

"Um, Ryan has two herniated discs in his back. He is going into surgery any minute now. We can wait upstairs in a room there. The doctor said he will let us know how everything went right after he completes the surgery."

"Let's go." Nick says as he tries to grab Nancy's hand, but Nancy already has a hold of Lysa. I enjoy the distraction. They really need to sit down and have a good talk. Ryan's parents and Janice follows.

"Mommy, is daddy going to be okay?" Lysa makes her way to my side.

"Yes, he is. After the surgery, we will go in, and see him for a tiny bit, maybe. That's up to the doctor. Then we will go home, and get a good night's sleep. Daddy will come home after a few days, but we can come here and see him every day." A tear falls onto my shirt.

We find the waiting room with little problem.

"Does anyone want some coffee?" Nick asks.

"Yes, I'd love a decaf with lots of cream and sugar." A yawn tries to bring oxygen to my brain.

Nancy gives me a sideways glance. I quickly look away. I'm surprised she hasn't figured it out yet. This might clue her in.

Hopefully she doesn't ask me anything tonight. I think I might cry if she does. I have to tell Ryan first.

"Okay, anyone else?" Everyone shakes his or her heads, except Nancy.

"Yes, I'd love a coffee. You know how I like it, right?" Nancy asks or maybe it's a test. They must have had a huge fight.

"Regular, three creams and three sugars." He says and looks intently at her. "And Lysa what would you like to drink?"

"Can I have French fries and a chocolate milk?" She has her head settled into my lap.

"I will try my best." He says as he pats her head.

I'm going to have to let Nick know that she doesn't care to be patted on the head. She finds it too babyish.

I don't feel like talking. I look out the window down at the parking lot.

* * *

Did I miss my chance to tell April the truth about me being a Private Investigator? I know it's a slim chance that I could die, but if I do and she finds out from someone else, she is going to think I betrayed her. I can't let that happen. Maybe I should write her a letter. No, that won't do. The nurse said I was all ready for surgery and that she needed to step out for a couple of minutes. Having this extra time isn't good for me. It makes me think about who could have cut my ladder. I have a couple of ideas. Unfortunately, I can't confront them at this time. I wish I were able to move around, and do what I do best; solve this problem. Having to be bed ridden for a bit, and then have days or weeks where I'm not fully back to my normal self is going to hold back my investigation. I need to find who is responsible!

Nick is going to have to help figure this out with me or maybe even for me. He has been working with me for a long time now. I trust him. I know he can figure this out. I also know that I don't need to tell him to get started on it either. I bet he is forming a plan right now. I can rest in that. But, now, what do I do about April? I saw how she paused at the door. She knows there's something I'm not telling her. Why did I wait? Why?

"Ryan, it's time to go." The cheery nurse says as she opens my door.

"My head is fuzzy, and why are you so happy?"

"Ryan, serving makes me happy. When I get stuck thinking about myself, and my own problems, I ask God whom I can help. Helping someone else gets me off of my poor thoughts, and serving you and others makes me happy." She pats my shoulder.

"I like that. Thanks for sharing, and serving."

"Ryan, you're welcome." She starts to move my bed.

"What's your name? I forgot." I rub my eyes.

"I'm Sandra."

"Sandra, when I'm stuck in bed healing, instead of focusing on what I can't do at the moment, I'm going to remember this conversation, and spend time praying for you and others. That is how I'll be able to serve. Thank you for a new perspective!"

Chapter 14

The chopper lands and two men get out. One is carrying a gun at his side and the other is straightening his tie. They walk to an old farmhouse and the door opens for them. Inside, dominating most of the space is a table and a few chairs. Behind the table sits a lone chair, a laptop open and the person occupying the chair types with heavy fingers.

"Did you get the job done?" No eye contact is made.

"Yeah, we did." The guy with the tie says.

"How bad is he?"

"Bad."

"Alive?"

"Yeah, but he won't be getting in your way for a long time." He pulls out a chair and looks around for something to drink. The guy with the gun stands in the back.

"Well, I didn't want him bad. I said slowed down."

"I did just what you asked; he's a lot slower than before." He chuckles.

"What did you do?" The laptop lid closes.

"Don't worry about what I did."

"I only wanted you to scare him, not cripple him."

"Well, you should've been more specific. Your fault, not mine, now pay up." The man stands.

An envelope is pushed across the table. The two men leave and get back into the chopper.

Chapter 15

Not even dating! What was that comment about? He's been dating her for over a year. What did she think they've been doing all this time? He's been dating her slowly, because he didn't want to pressure her after she lost her husband. Man! Nick needs to hit the gym. He'll wait until after Ryan is out of surgery.

Ryan's mom likes to talk. She is practically trying to persuade April to agree to her moving in for a while. She wants to help, she says. And I know she does. April is thanking her for her help. Nancy sits and listens. She doesn't add a single word to their conversation. Lysa is leaning on April's shoulder. She looks tired. Nick tries to make eye contact with Nancy, but she avoids him. The silent treatment! She even has her shoulders turned away from him. She's intentionally sitting sideways in her chair. Her back might regret that later.

Nick didn't grow up around women. He doesn't have any sisters and his mom left when he was little. He's not used to this. His dad and him are close. When they had a problem, they took the direct root and would say what the problem was. Sometimes it got loud but the situation was resolved faster than this.

He went away to college and after his first semester his dad asked him to come home for a visit. Nick did and that was when he introduced to his dad's girlfriend, Ellen, who became his stepmother shortly after. It was awkward but Nick saw that his younger brothers were happy and his dad too. He was happy for them but he was starting his own life and didn't quite know how to accept this change. He and his dad are still close. Ellen and Nancy haven't met yet but she did meet my dad and brothers on different occasions when they have come up to visit. Dad usually comes when Ellen has other plans. Nick thinks they understand how he's still uncomfortable. He doesn't understand women at all. Maybe he should remain single. Maybe that's the best thing for Nancy. Maybe Nancy tried to fall in love with Nick but realized she could only love Phil. Nick decides to take a step back and re-evaluate, it's probably best they go their separate ways.

Nick focuses on what happened to Ryan and the job. Who did this to Ryan? He doesn't see why the guy from their present case would do this. They thought he was innocent. As far as Nick knows, Ryan's other clients have been happy with the job he has done for them. He pulls up his memo pad on his phone and starts working. He jots down question after question for Ryan.

Ryan's dad is sitting with his arms crossed in the seat next to his wife. He hasn't added anything to the conversation. He looks deep in thought then he looks Nick's way, and raises an eyebrow that follows a nod. Nick nods back, understanding that they will talk later. He knows this wasn't an accident. Nick is sure he is going to offer his help. This could get complicated. Nick focuses on car colors as he looks out at the parking lot. Ryan has all his notes at his house. Nick needs to see them. What have they missed? Nick was hoping this job was ending soon so that he could seriously date Nancy, but now that isn't happening he has time to help figure this out.

"Hello, Ryan's family." The doctor comes into the center of the waiting room. "I'm Dr. Collins, I know you all want to know how things went, so I won't keep you guessing, I'll just tell you; Ryan is doing well. The surgery went as planned, and I'm very pleased with the results. Ryan will need to stay in bed most of this week. He has a therapy schedule, and we will be monitoring him while he stays here. Are there any questions?"

"Can we see him?" Lysa asks.

She was almost asleep when the doctor came in, but when he asked if there were any questions, she was on her feet jumping, while raising her hand. She didn't wait for him to call on her, just blurted her question out. Now she is hopping like she has to go to the bathroom.

"Yes, you can go in and see him, but he is very groggy, and isn't making much sense." He looks at Lysa and says, "This is very normal but you can only stay a minute. He needs his rest."

"Okay. I'll be very good. Mommy let's go. We can go see daddy." She pulls on April's hand. April hesitates. Lysa pulls again, and April follows.

"Where is he?" April asks.

"I'll take you all to him."

He walks out, and everyone follows. It doesn't take long to be standing next to Ryan's bed. Lysa is the first one there. Ryan gives her a half smile.

"How are you doing, kiddo?" He tries to grab her hand but misses by several inches.

"Daddy, I'm fine. How are you?" Lysa moves her head about two inches from Ryan.

"I'm okay. Tired." He says.

"You should get some sleep daddy." Lysa yawns. "Me too, I'm tired."

Everyone in the room wants to talk to him but Nick stays in the back. Nancy is also in the back. Lysa, April, Janice, and the Nolsens talk to Ryan until the doctor clears his throat and asks everyone to leave. Nick opens the door so they can all walk through.

"Nick."

After everyone has exited except the doctor, he lets go of the door.

"Doc is it okay if I have a minute with Ryan?" Nick asks.

"One minute." The doctor steps out.

"Nick, I'll be quick, you have to find out... find out who did this." Ryan tries to sit up but quickly changes his mind.

"There was a message in the bag you took off the roof." Nick rests his hand on Ryan's shoulder, hoping to persuade him to stay still.

"What did it say?"

"It said, 'Leave me alone' and there were a bunch of bricks in the bag."

Ryan's features grow tight. "Okay, umm, that could be from a couple of different people."

"Really? Do you think it could be from this case we have been working on? You know, the one we can't seem to solve." Nick runs his hand through his hair. He wasn't expecting Ryan to say there could be multiple sources.

"It could be, but there are a couple of other people I haven't been leaving alone either. And Nick, I still have my memory, I didn't forget about the case we are working on." He tries to smile at Nick.

"Guys, your minute is up." A nurse sticks her head into the room.

Nick's fist clenches. They didn't get anywhere.

"Nick, it's okay. If I get a chance I'll text, or email you. I'm so tired right now anyway." He closes his eyes.

Nick walks out.

He's alone.

Ryan has always been the one to come up with the plan and tell Nick what to do. Now he has to do that by himself. He's a construction guy, not a PI.

Chapter 16

I turn the knob, and walk in quietly. I don't want to disturb anyone. I carefully click the front door shut, and hope I didn't wake her up. The lights are out on most of this floor. I can see the televisions' commercial lights dancing from the family room. I put down my bag, and walk toward that room. Going by the steps, I continue to remain silent. The family room is before me, and I can see her sitting on the couch with the remote in her hand, and a glass in the other one.

"Hey, Janice. I'm back. They let me see Ryan for a little bit when I went to drop off his bag. I'm glad I decided to buy him new stuff so I didn't have to make the long drive back and forth." I sit down next to her and grab a pillow to hold.

"That's good. I know you were hoping to see him. How does he look?" She mutes the television and turns toward me.

"He looks okay. He's still tired so I didn't stay long. We really didn't say much to each other. Hopefully tomorrow we can talk." I sigh.

"I'm fine staying here for the week. I can help with Lysa and the cooking." She grins.

"Thanks. I know the first time she will want to go to the hospital. Maybe you can come too, and then after her visit, you can sit with her in the waiting room or just bring her home." I look at my watch. 10 pm. I want to go to bed.

"Sure, no problem."

Janice took a week off before Ryan got hurt. She was going to use it to get over Douglas. Maybe her being here instead of at home alone will be beneficial to both of us. Not sure where that leaves the cat.

"Janice, you are such a good friend. I feel that over the years you have given more to me than I have to you." She'll deny it.

"That's not true. We have equally annoyed one another over the years."

I throw the pillow at her. I'm too tired to argue. She blocks the pillow. "Okay, has Lysa stayed asleep since I left?"

"Yes." Her eyes glance back at the screen. The commercials are over.

"Good. This might trigger nightmares for her."

"Yeah, it might." Janice and I share a knowing look. Last year was tough on all of us.

"What are you watching?" I ask.

"Oh, I was just flipping through the channels when you walked in. I couldn't find anything good." She turns off the screen.

"I'm tired; I think I'll go to bed." As I start to walk down the hall the doorbell rings. "I wonder who that could be."

"Maybe it's Nancy." Janice stands and folds the blanket she was using.

"No, she would let herself in. She has a key." I start to walk to the door but Janice is closer and beats me there.

Janice peeks through the peephole. "Oh, no," she whispers, "It's Doug."

"Why would Doug be here?" I say as I gently shove Janice out of the way so I could open the door.

"Hi, Doug, anything wrong?" My mind races to Ryan. Why would a police officer need to come to my house after 10 pm?

"Nope, April. I was just stopping by to see how you're doing. I heard about what happened to Ryan earlier and I wanted to make sure you and Lysa are fine."

"We're doing fine. Lysa is asleep, and I'm about ready to turn in as well."

"Good. I'm glad to hear that. I'll be sure to stop in again tomorrow, and I'll stop over to see Ryan too." He takes a step back, and then hesitates.

"Okay, thanks, Doug." I know he saw Janice's car out front. "Did you want to say hi to Janice?" I lean to grab her arm, and pull her next to me in front of the open door.

"Oh, hi, Janice. You look, uh, great. How are you?" He doesn't step closer.

Maybe this wasn't a good idea. He looks like he is ready to bolt. I think I just prematurely tore the band aid off Janice's wound.

"Hi, Doug. You look good too. Have you been exercising?" He looks down and pats his stomach.

"Yes, I actually have been." A corner of his mouth turns up, and he takes a step back.

Janice stands there with her arms crossed.

"It was great seeing you Janice. I have to go." He nods at her, and walks back to his car. He parked right next to Janice.

"He knew I was here." She says while closing the door.

"Yes, he did."

"I'm not sure what that means. Did he really come to check on you or to see me? And if he came to see me, he didn't say much nor did he make future plans."

"He does know your number."

"That's true, but he hasn't used it lately." Her shoulders drop. "He confuses me."

"Me too, Janice, me too." I put my hand on her shoulder.

"I think I'll go to bed also."

"Okay. Sleep well."

"I'll try." Janice says with a sad laugh.

"Yeah, I'll try too."

* * *

I peek in and see Lysa sleeping soundly. I'm glad she's able to sleep. I cross the hallway and start to get ready for bed. I don't understand how Ryan fell off the ladder. It doesn't make sense. Maybe after some sleep I'll be able to make more sense out of it.

I can hear Janice settling into her bed. I know she's hurting.

God how can I help her? She has been with me throughout all of my pains and struggles. She has constantly reached out to me, guiding me toward Your truth and love. I want to do the same for her. I would like to get up, and go into her room, pick up her cell, and call Doug and give him a piece of my mind. I know that isn't the best idea, so I'll stay here. I don't want to hurt her more. It was stupid of me to drag her out from behind the door, and make her face Doug. I don't know what I expected to happen. Maybe that he would apologize, and ask her out. Or wrap her in a big hug. I want her to have what I have now with Ryan, but I understand how it has to be the right time. God, I pray for Doug, I pray you please help him to see what Your will is regarding Janice. Please give him wisdom. I don't understand why he really came over tonight. I don't think it was to check on me. I think he saw Janice's car, and that's why he stopped. He acted so weird though. He didn't seem like he wanted to talk to her. So why stop by? I'm so glad You are in control of these things God.

Thank You, God, that Ryan's surgery went well. Please heal him fast. I don't think he is going to be a good patient. Please touch his heart as he waits in bed healing, and use that time for him to grow closer to You. Please keep this little one inside me safe. Please let me know the right time to tell Ryan about the baby. I think I should have already, and so I pray that you please soften his heart toward me when he finds out I held this information from him. Thank you, God, for Your miracles, and Your blessings in my life.

My eyes sting, but my heart has peace.

Chapter 17

Thinking back to her last conversation with Nick, she realizes she didn't communicate her feelings well. She was leaving the hospital with everyone after Ryan's surgery when Nick pulled her aside.

"Nancy, do you have a minute?" He looks sad.

"Sure, Nick, what's up?" She shrugs.

"I want to know what happened between us earlier."

"Umm, I'm not sure I understand either. We were talking, and then you wouldn't step into my house." Nancy starts to get defensive.

"Before that," his eyes shift past Nancy to the building behind them, "I mean when you defined our relationship as 'not dating'."

"I was just speaking the truth; we aren't dating but..."

Nick cuts her off. "Okay, I think I'm starting to understand." He takes a step back.

"You do?" Her eyebrows rise.

"Yeah, I do." His hands turn to fists. "Yeah, I'll see you around, my friend."

"Uh, that's not what I thought..." Nancy looks at him with confusion. She thought they were going to finally define their relationship as dating.

"But it's what you said." He touches her arm, looks into her eyes, and nods. He opened his mouth, but closes it, turns and walks off to his car without a backward glance.

Nancy shivers. She stands there for about 10 minutes trying to figure out what went wrong. How did the conversation turn them into being only friends? Why didn't she open her mouth, and share her feelings with him? Now he believes all she wants is a friendship with him. She was trying to hint to him that she wanted to move from friendship to dating, but she didn't say that. She only hinted. Now she has more proof that hinting doesn't work; it never worked with Phil. Why would she think it would work with Nick? She should have spoken her mind instead of hoping he would share his with her. She's not sure what he's feeling though. Maybe it's only friendship for him. Friendship; she wants more, but she'll take what she can get. Being his friend is better than not having him in her life. She has felt for the past year that they had formed a great friendship. He was someone she looked forward to sharing the details of her day with. He seemed that he wanted to hear them too. And he was open with her too, until these road trips started.

* * *

Flight five! I only have two more to go. It was a long drive, but this should be worth it. Her breath starts to come out in short puffs. She can do this. The elevator would have been easier but it wouldn't have helped her toward her goal. One more to go! She was trying to be quiet. Speed isn't an issue; no one knows where she is and who she is going to see.

She opens the door to the floor she wants to be on. She peeks through and sees no one. That's good! Most people have left for home by now. She moves with quick silence hoping to not bring any attention to herself as she makes her way to the office she wants. The door is cracked open and she hears voices coming from within. She leans against the wall to keep from being seen, uncertain what to do.

"You know, it doesn't matter what you think Helen." A male voice says.

He is not lined up with the crack in the door, but Helen is. Her left hand is in a fist at her side behind the oak desk, but her face remains poised, not revealing any emotion.

"Why set up an appointment if my thoughts don't matter to you, Stan?" She looks at him. Silence. Nancy's stomach starts to growl and she takes a step away from the door, hoping no one heard.

"I wanted to be able to tell someone and now I have. You can't tell anyone what I did because we have a patient/doctor confidential relationship." Nancy can hear the smile in his words.

"I can choose not to have you as a patient anymore." Helen says.

"You can but you won't. You know if you shut me out, you won't know what I'm doing and that will bother you too much."

"Stan, this has been going on too long." Nancy takes a step back toward the door.

"I haven't done anything in a while." A chair scrapes the floor.

"Or so you say." Helen's mouth twitches.

"I'll see you next month Helen. Thanks for the visit. It was great seeing…" Nancy races down the hall to the bathroom.

Her heart races as she lets the door quietly close behind her. What was that about? Helen has never mentioned a hostile client but then she doesn't talk about her patients. She waits until her heart rate returns to normal and opens the door and walks to Helen's office.

The door is wide open and Helen is standing behind her desk, organizing files. She looks a little pale but when she spots Nancy she smiles broadly.

"Hi Nancy, it's great to see you!"

"Great to see you too!" Nancy gives her a hug.

"What brings you down the mountain?" She goes back to sorting her files.

"I wanted to talk to you but I should have called first. If this is a bad time, I can go." Her voice trails off.

"Oh, this is a perfect time! I just finished with my last patient of the day and I was going to head home." She didn't give any hint that it went poorly. She seems like the usual Helen. "What did you want to talk about?"

Maybe she should go? But she really needed help. "Helen, I haven't been open with you about my relationship with Nick."

"Okay. Are you telling me this because now you want to be?"

"Yes. Last year Nick started writing me emails and I would write him back. It was neat to get to know him that way. He also would come over to help out with things around the house. Stuff like, fix the leaky faucet or unclog the sink. He would come over just to ask if I had anything for him to do and if I said I had nothing for him to do, we would talk and drink coffee. I was growing to enjoy his company. I was looking forward to his next visit.

"Recently, he started traveling with Ryan on some odd business trips. He didn't explain anything about his trips, and when I asked he didn't offer any new information. I started to get frustrated. He has been gone almost every weekend in the past two months and he works for the business during the weekdays. I realized I was missing him and have grown to like him, maybe even love him now. Now we are barely on speaking terms."

"You must have left something out." She looks at me with a smile.

"Helen, first let me say this is hard for me to share with you. I didn't plan on finding anyone new. I also don't want to be alone for the rest of my life. Please forgive me for keeping this from you." Nancy shoulders slump.

"It's okay, Nancy. Really! I actually knew something was going on and I was only waiting for you to be ready to tell me about it. Now why aren't you two on speaking terms?"

"Well, I mentioned that we were only friends. I was hinting that I wanted to be more than that, but he took it as me saying, 'I only want to be friends.' He looked sadly into my eyes, said 'see you later, friend' and then walked away." Nancy puts her head in her hands.

"And what are you going to do about that?" Helen walks to her safe, under her desk and unlocks it, puts the files in and locks it back up.

"I'm not sure yet."

"Okay, well you'll figure it out."

Nancy whips her head up and stares at Helen. "That's all you are going to say?"

"Yes, that's it. This isn't a counseling session. I'm your friend and I know you are smart and that you will figure it out." She crosses over to Nancy.

"What if I want this to be a counseling session?"

She yawns. "I had a lot of clients and honestly I have nothing but a listening ear right now. I'm all out of good advice." She chuckles.

"Okay. How about I'll pray and think and we'll talk about this again later?" Nancy hopes Helen agrees.

"Sounds good. Oh, did you have any dinner yet?"

Nancy shakes her head.

"We ordered in for lunch but I didn't have time to eat. Let's go to the kitchen and see what's left."

They make their way to the kitchen and Helen pulls out boxes of leftovers from the fridge. The containers are full of salads, lasagna, and chicken parmesan. We put them out and help ourselves.

"I'm sorry, Helen." Nancy says in between bites.

"For what?" Helen wipes her mouth with her napkin.

"For falling in like."

"That's a ridiculous thing to be sorry about." Helen flicks her fork in Nancy's direction but that's all she says.

When they finish, Helen and Nancy put the dishes in the office dishwasher.

"Nancy, when will your mom and Ella come back from their college shopping?"

"In a day or two. They haven't decided yet. Ella isn't sure if this is the right college for her, and so she is pulling mom around to all the different malls and eateries to see if that will help her make up her mind."

"Oh, boy. That doesn't sound like…"

Nancy raises her hand. "I know and I tried to tell my mom but Ella is, well, she's Ella."

"Probably best not to get involved."

"That's what I was thinking too. Ella has had three mothers for a long time. I can see how we have overprotected her. Now it's time for her to make her own decisions."

With the kitchen put back in order, they grab their belongings and head to the door.

"Your mom is doing a good job."

"Yes, she is. She sounded really tired on the phone last night though. I worry about her living alone when Ella goes to college. I should have thought ahead before I sold my house and moved in above April."

"You were brave to move out. I'd miss my house. You have been encouraging me to see that maybe it's time for me to put up that dreaded for sale sign." Helen sighs.

"Is that what you want, Helen?"

"I'm not sure. I have an endless list of house repairs. My house looks like it's condemned, all except for the lack of wood covering the windows."

"It doesn't look that bad." They start walking to the elevator.

"Each time I look around, I find another repair. I can't afford to fix it up and I'm not going to ask the church to do any more than they already have. They've been a huge help these past few years, but the whole house is falling apart. I think it's time to call a realtor. Who did you use?" Helen sighs.

"A guy named Greg Palmer. He goes to our church. I looked through the booklet the church distributes to help promote businesses that we represent. He did a great job. I was pleased."

They step into the elevator. Nancy pulls out her phone and starts scrolling through her phone book.

"Here it is. Greg Palmer, Realtor 555-1211."

"Wait a second." Helen starts unzipping her purse. "I don't have any paper."

"Helen, put it into your cell phone."

"Oh, that would be easier." Nancy waits for Helen to give her the signal that she is ready. "Okay, 555-1211. I feel better already. My house is a huge stress for me. I'll miss it because it reminds me of my husband, but it's time for me to move on. I'll take pictures."

"I'll help you pack." Nancy puts an arm around Helen's shoulder and gives her a light squeeze.

"Thanks, I'll need help. I'll call him tomorrow. Now that I've made up my mind, I want to get things started."

"I don't have to work tomorrow so if you want to start cleaning and packing I can help you. Janice is staying with April this week while Ryan is in the hospital helping with Lysa so I'm free." They make their way to the front entrance. A steady rain plinks the windows.

"Sounds like a plan. We can also discuss your little dilemma, and if you want advice still, I'll give you some."

"I always value your advice, so yes, I would like to hear it, but I'll wait until tomorrow. It's been a long day." Nancy rubs the back of her neck.

"How's Ryan doing?" Helen asks.

"His surgery went well. He needs to spend the next several weeks healing, but the doctor thinks he will be back to his normal self by then."

"That's good. I'm glad he'll make a full recovery."

"Yes, but I think that means that Nick will be traveling even more now." Nancy sighs.

"Ah, Nick. We shall talk about him tomorrow." Helen pulls out her umbrella from her big tote bag. "I'll walk you to your car."

They step out into the rain. Nancy's thoughts focus on who would want to hurt Ryan.

Chapter 18

Her breathing started coming out in quiet wheezes about thirty seconds ago. The heat was taking its toll. She needed to sit down before she falls down.

"Mom we looked at most of the campus and the local malls here in Florida. I really like it, but I don't want to live so far away." Ella whines.

"Ella, the choice is yours. If you would like to go to college close to home, you can do that. Even if you want to live at home, I'd love that, but please make the decision based on what you and God want." She steadies herself against the nearest wall. Unfortunately, it's outside the hotel, not inside.

"I will, Mom. I'm ready to go home tomorrow. I've seen enough to make up my mind. How about we go back to our room and change into our swimsuits and go to the beach?" She folds her hands together, under her chin.

"You keep me young Ella, thanks." Agnes says.

"Anytime Mom! Oh, and you're still young."

Ella puts her arm around her mom's shoulders as they walk through the hotel's front door. The air conditioning helps her breathing immediately. Their room is down a long corridor off to the right of the front desk. Getting there isn't much of a problem. Agnes has been exercising over the past four months and she's moving around a lot better than she did several months ago. The classes she started attending, which are only filled with older people, have done a great job to help increase her energy. Six months ago, she wouldn't have considered this trip with Ella. It's been decades since her last vacation. These past few days have been great. Mother and daughter were able to open up to each other, crossing from a child/parent relationship to friends, a bit. She still might need parenting, but now they respect each other more.

Ella uses the card and lets them in the room. Ella's bathing suit is hanging in the bathroom.

Parenting her three daughters has had its hard times, but she's thankful for this new phase. She will continue to mourn the loss of her marriage. He was and still is so special to her. For a long time, she doubted his love. Why would he just leave? She questioned what she thought they had together, but she knew in her heart that it was real. She still holds hope that he will return one day. Sixteen years he's been gone; sixteen long years; sixteen lonely years. Friends tried to convince her to remarry but she hasn't considered it, but maybe when 20 years have passed, she might entertain the thought. For now, she'll focus on what's happening today.

Ella is graduating from high school soon, and then she is going to college. She doesn't know where that will be. It could be far away. When she starts to think about that her heart tends to beat a little faster. It was at college that April had been... oh, she would not focus on that. Ella is in God's hands and that is a wonderful thing. Agnes does hope she goes to school close to home. She had a boyfriend over this past year that really wasn't a good influence. It took her a bit of time to listen to the family and understand that he was only after one thing. He broke her heart when she refused to give in, and he dumped her for that. Agnes is very proud of her. She did what was right and even though he said he would come back and be her boyfriend if she would share herself with him, she stuck with her morals and said no. She didn't believe his lies. He stormed off saying how he wasted this past year being involved with her. Saying that opened Ella's eyes to what type of man he was. She then realized she was in love with the idea of being in love and really didn't have feelings for him. She has matured these past couple of months. Going to college is a big step and Agnes thinks she's ready.

"Mom?" Ella says as she opens the bathroom door.

"Yes, Ella."

"I still have no idea what I want to be." She crosses her arms and plops on the bed.

"That's okay. You don't need to know yet."

"Are you sure?"

"I know so. Most freshmen don't know what they want to be. The neat thing is that God will help you figure that out. My best advice to you is to get involved in a Christian group on campus. There are a number of different ones depending on where you decide to go. Search and check out the ones your college has and become involved." Agnes reaches for her bathing suit.

"I remember going to one meeting that time I stayed with April for a week." She sat up straight in bed, her eyes widening. "I was a kid and I went to all of her classes and to her Campus Crusade for Christ meeting. It was so much fun. I stayed up so late, but it was worth it. I will definitely do that mom. April really had a lot of friends before, well, you know. I felt like everywhere we went, she was saying hi to someone she knew."

"She did have a lot of friends. I don't know if she keeps in touch with them or not. I know you'll make lots of friends too."

"I hope so; I'm a bit nervous about going."

"You'll do fine." Agnes says as she touches her arm.

"Mom, are you going to get changed now? The beach should be fun. Now I feel like our vacation can start." She reaches for the remote.

Wiping away a tear, Agnes squares her shoulders as if that might help prepare her for the empty nest that will be home in September. Two of her girls live near, but it's not the same. They both have their own lives. Her heart is warmed that April married Ryan and she thinks Nick is in love with her Nancy. They have both been through rough times, but now life seems better for them. She hopes Ella doesn't have to have as many hard times as her two older daughters have had. Ella doesn't remember her father. She didn't ask about him ever. She was 2 years old when he left. Agnes's shoulders sag. Maybe she should have tried to remarry when he didn't come back. Maybe all her girls would have had that void filled. The problem was she still loved him and even now she still loves him. And she has forgiven him for leaving. Does he think about them? Maybe he isn't even alive.

"Mom, what's taking so long?"

"Oh, uh, sorry honey; I was daydreaming. Give me a minute, I'll be right out."

"Okay. I'll grab some towels and sunscreen."

Minutes later they have sand between their toes. The sun is shining and the wind has picked up a bit from this morning. They place their towels on the sand and apply the sunscreen. Ella is starting to attract some attention. She dresses modestly, which Agnes is pleased with. Months ago, she wouldn't go to the beach with her because she would have pushed to wear something skimpy. She has grown so much in such a short time.

"I don't know if I've ever sunbathed before. What an odd thing to start doing in my fifties. I don't think I'll make a habit out of it. As I start to perspire, all I want to do is go for a swim in fresh water!" She chuckles. And picks up her book.

Ella seems to be enjoying herself.

"Ella, do you think you should turn over?"

"Oh, umm, I must have fallen asleep. How long have we been here?"

"About a half hour."

"Thanks mom." She says while flipping over onto her back.

Agnes doesn't know if she can do this much longer. If this is what vacations are, she hasn't been missing much.

"Mom, I think I'm going to not date anyone for a while."

"I like that idea." Agnes tries to hide her excitement over that statement.

"Yeah, I thought you would. Mom I want to spend time figuring out what I would like to do with my life. I don't want to be distracted by guys. I'm taking my future seriously and to throw my chance to do well in school by being in a relationship isn't worth it. I want to pursue my interests. Maybe I'll volunteer at the hospital or with children. I don't know if I want to be a teacher or a nurse or a cook. I like to cook, but I don't think I love it that much. I like to help people, but I'm not sure if being a nurse is the way I want to help. I love kids. I've enjoyed being Lysa's aunt. I know I haven't been much of an aunt this year because of that relationship I was in. I let him take up all my time. Never again am I going to do that. I want to be the best aunt possible. I really have enjoyed watching Lysa grow all these years; playing with her was the highlight of many of my days."

When Ella starts to talk, she usually keeps going for a while and Agnes loves that about her. It takes a bit of time for her to open up, but when she does she shares her heart and her thoughts.

"Also, mom, I want to be a better daughter to you. You have given so much of your time to provide for me. I've watched you work two jobs, sometimes three, to care for all of us. I still don't understand how you have made time for me also. And you do. Whenever I want to talk, you put down what you're doing and you listen to me. I know you didn't have that with Nancy and April for a while, but I'm glad you figured out how to balance it all. You really are a wonderful mom, the best mom ever!" She leans over and hugs Agnes.

"Thanks, Ella. I wasn't always available; you just don't remember is all. You are an amazing daughter Ella, and I will be praying for you as you start your career search."

"Thanks mom." Ella pulls two waters out of the bag and hands one over to her mom.

"Ella, my face feels very hot. Does it look red to you?"

"Umm, yes it does. Did you flip over onto your stomach?" Agnes shakes her head. "Then let's pack up and go get lunch. All this lounging has worked up an appetite in me."

"I like your plan, Ella. Food sounds great. Food and air conditioning!"

Chapter 19

My gym teacher in middle school taught me that women don't sweat; we perspire. I have lived with this being truth until I woke up this morning. Sweat beaded across my hairline. When sleeping, I saw him chasing me again as I ran down the jogging trail. I pumped my arms as my legs sprinted forward. I could hear the pounding of feet behind me keeping pace with mine. I turned slightly as I passed the big oak tree, and that is where he tackled me to the ground and that is when I woke up. Each time I have this dream I get a little bit further away. The last time the oak tree was about 20 feet in front of me. I wish the nightmares would stop. My legs shake as if I actually participated in a 5k. I'm not sure they can hold me long enough for a shower, but I need to be clean right now.

After my shower, I'll go visit Ryan. I know Lysa will want to go, but I won't wake her up yet. She hasn't been getting enough sleep, and when that happens she can be moody. Letting her sleep will be best for everyone. The water is warm enough. As I step in, I think about everything that I need to get done. I mentally start writing a list. I'll ask Nick to take care of the lawn so Ryan won't have to think about that this summer. I towel off quickly and find a piece of paper and a pen. As I begin writing my head starts to hurt.

For the most part, I've stopped drinking caffeine since I knew I was pregnant so I'm well passed a caffeine headache. Still need to tell Ryan. My head pounds as I try to focus on my list. I write, 'tell Ryan' but my handwriting isn't legible. Is it my eyes or my hand? The sun shining through my window is too bright. Maybe I need to sleep a bit more. I get under the covers, and pull my comforter over my head. The dream starts to replay in my mind as sharp stabbing pain shoots throughout. My stomach starts to churn, and I race to the bathroom. My head feels like it's going to split open. Exhausted, I collapse on the bathroom floor.

"April, are you okay?" A voice asks.

I can feel a hand on my shoulder, but my head hurts too much to open my eyes to see who it is.

"April, are you okay?"

"No, please stop yelling, Janice. My head…"

"I wasn't yelling, but why are you on the floor?"

"I, I don't know." It's too bright in here.

"Are you hurt?" Janice enquires.

"Yes." I say as quietly as possible. Even my own voice hurts my head.

"Okay." Janice sits next to me. "Where are you hurt?"

"My head."

"April, I'm going to take you to the hospital. Lysa is finishing breakfast now, so I'm going to get you into the car first."

"Call Nancy first to get Lysa." I choke out. "I don't want her to see me like this. She can't know anything is wrong."

"Okay, let me help you to bed."

"No." I make a pathetic attempt to push her hand away. "I need to be by the toilet."

"Okay." She says as she gets up and walks to the door.

* * *

"Nancy," Janice whispers, not wanting Lysa to hear, "I need you to come and pick up Lysa. I have to take April to the hospital."

"Did anything change with Ryan?" Nancy asks.

"No, as far as I know Ryan is fine, it's April. She collapsed on the floor and says her head hurts a lot. She's been vomiting, but this doesn't look like the stomach bug. Her head is where she says the pain is."

"Okay. I'll be over as soon as I get dressed. Tell Lysa I have a surprise for her and want her to spend the day with me. It's best we don't tell her anything."

"April said the same thing. Okay, I'll get her ready." Janice quickly closes her phone and rushes to the kitchen to motivate Lysa into getting ready faster.

"Lysa, I just got off the phone with Aunt Nancy, and she says she has a surprise for you. Can you go get dressed and brush your teeth quickly? She will be here in a couple of minutes." Janice says as she places a forced smile onto her face.

"Sure, I love surprises." She jumps off her chair and races to her room. That went well. Janice tip toes up the stairs and peeks in on April. She is curled up in a fetal position on the bathroom floor. She isn't moving and her skin is pale. She touches her cheek. Maybe she should have called an ambulance. She thought taking her would be faster, but maybe not. April hasn't stirred. Janice races back downstairs to open the front door and wait for Nancy, forgetting that Nancy has a key.

How can so many bad things happen to one person? April lived most of her life in fear. Janice listened to her over the years tell her she wasn't going to do something and Janice knew it was because April was afraid. It controlled her reactions throughout most of her days. As a child, she feared failing her dad. He was a good dad, but he had his own life obstacles that left him sometimes vacant. April tried so hard to please him and when he would respond to her with low enthusiasm she would try harder the next time to do better. When he left, she felt that she failed. She thought maybe she didn't try to do her best in school or maybe she didn't help him fast enough when he asked for her to do something. She saw her mom lose herself in her jobs and again she felt guilty over not being good enough. She feared getting married and losing her husband as well. When college came around and that monster came into April's life, Janice thought she would never recover. She lived in fear every time she went somewhere in public. She didn't want to have to fight, but she did for Lysa. Janice thinks she would still be living in fear if Lysa weren't born. They are all so blessed to have her in our lives.

"Aunt Janice, I'm ready."

"Oh, good Lysa. Aunt Nancy should be walking down the stairs any second." Janice pulls her into a side hug.

"Actually, she's walking toward us right now, Aunt Janice."

"Oh, you're right, Lysa. I must have been day dreaming."

"Come Lysa, let's go for a drive." Nancy says as she steps off the last step.

"Bye, Aunt Janice. I'll see you and mom later. Oh, I want to say good-bye myself."

"Umm, Lysa, I'll let her know, she's in the bathroom. You'll be back later and then you can tell her all about your day."

Lysa runs up to Nancy and hesitates. Janice doesn't like making her wait but seeing April the way she is now is a very bad idea.

"Hi, Janice. Please give me a call in a bit." Nancy says with urgency.

"Sure, I will." Janice closes the door and race up the stairs. April hasn't moved. Janice checks her pulse, slow. She gently shakes her arm.

"April, it's time to go to the hospital."

"Good." Her voice barely reaches Janice.

"Can you walk?"

April gives a slight nod and Janice helps her to her feet. It takes some effort, but they make it to the car. She turns off the radio and April keeps her arm over her eyes. The drive is long and April's moans are painful to hear. Janice tries not to go over any of the speed bumps as she pulls up by the emergency entrance at Albany Med. They walk into the waiting room and find a seat for April. It doesn't appear to be crowded. She hopes for April that it isn't a long wait. Looking over, she notices April has her head in between her knees. Janice answers the nurses' questions, hands over the insurance card, and asks for a bucket. She hands a garbage can to her, and Janice places it on the floor in front of April. Not even a minute later, Janice is holding April's hair back, and when she is done, Janice gets her a couple of paper towels. Janice cleans everything up then they wait for April's name to be called. We follow the nurse to a room in the back. A different nurse asks a couple of questions and takes her temperature, pulse, and blood pressure.

"Your blood pressure is low." The nurse says as she writes the number down.

She informs us that the doctor will be coming in shortly. April looks to have fallen asleep. Janice wonders if she has eaten anything today. Maybe she is really worried about Ryan. She unzips her purse and starts pulling out old papers as she continues to wait.

"Hi April, I'm Dr. Stevens." A tall middle-aged man; about six two enters the room. "What seems to be the problem?"

"My head, it feels like I'm bleeding."

He looks around her head. "Well, I don't see any blood."

"Is the baby okay?"

"Ah, now I understand." He says. "When was the last time you felt the baby kick?"

"This morning, I think. I only just started to feel her kick this week so it's still faint." April says without moving, or opening her eyes.

"Okay, let me send someone in to do an ultrasound." He walks out the door.

Janice stares at April, but doesn't say anything.

"I haven't even told Ryan yet, so you need to be quiet about this." She whispers.

"I will, but why haven't you told him?" Janice leans forward so she can hear April's response.

"At first, I wanted to wait to make sure the baby was healthy. You know what the doctors said about thinking I couldn't have any children after what happened, so I wanted to make sure the baby was healthy and my body was doing what it needed to do. Then when I found out things were looking good I tried to tell him, but he started working a lot and going on those long business trips. There just hasn't been a good time yet. And now he's in the hospital, and I'm not sure if things are fine anymore so it's better he doesn't know yet."

"April, you need to tell him either way." Janice reaches out and gives April's hand a light squeeze.

"I know that now and I will." She grabs her head, and slowly rocks back and forth.

A nurse walks in with the ultrasound machine. She pulls up April's shirt, and squeezes the warm liquid onto her stomach. She slowly moves the wand around, pushes some buttons, quickly picks it back up and starts to clean it off without saying a single word.

"Is everything okay?" Janice asks.

"The doctor will be back in with all the information."

"Really? You aren't going to tell me anything?"

"Sorry, I can't." Can't or won't?

She walks out and April tries to clean off her stomach. Janice takes over for her.

"Hi, it's me again, Dr. Stevens." He walks in and sits on the stool. "Everything looks great with the baby. It is common sometimes for women to have bad headaches or a step below a migraine when they are pregnant. You can take some Tylenol, and drink plenty of water and go to bed."

"This doesn't feel like a bad headache. It feels like I'm dying." April chokes out.

"Sometimes that's how they feel." He says to April, then turns to Janice, "Please take her home and put her to bed."

"Okay. Are you sure that's all you can do for her?"

"Yes, I'm sure. This is just a pregnancy thing." He states.

With that, he leaves. Janice helps April off the bed, and they make their way slowly back to the car which is still parked in the emergency entrance. Oops! Thankfully it wasn't towed away.

"I'm already staying with you for a few days April, and don't worry, I won't tell anyone you're pregnant. I'll cook and take care of Lysa; all you have to do is rest and get better."

"Thanks, Janice. You know you would make a good nurse. A much nicer one than the one I had today."

"Maybe I'll go back to school for nursing when you are all better." April doesn't respond.

Janice drives back to April and Ryan's house. She gets April back in bed and calls Nancy and then Ryan. It was hard not to say anything about the pregnancy, but she knew that it isn't her news to tell. She thinks Nancy knows already. Thinking back over the last four months Janice should have figured it out also. She remembers what the doctor told April years ago about her not getting her hopes up for carrying a baby full term. Interesting how God can bless. Janice is still in shock, but very happy for her. She deserves some happiness. She wonders if it's a boy or a girl. It will be fun to be an aunt all over again. She hopes it doesn't confuse the little one when he or she discovers that Janice isn't really their mom's sister, but a close friend. When Lysa asked why she calls her Aunt Janice, April told her that she was an Aunt by privilege. Lysa was so cute when she said 'it doesn't matter how Janice became her Aunt she was just thankful that she was.'

April continues to groan in her sleep. Janice hopes this resolves fast.

* * *

The ceiling has some blood on it, two very noticeable streaks, going in opposite directions. If this was not a hospital, I would start asking questions but flowing blood happens here often. My whole body works but the pain keeps me lying here all day, staring at the ceiling wondering what happened. A curt knock and then the door opens without waiting for me to reply. I hope it's April.

"Hey, Nick. It's great to see you."

"Ryan, you look good. How are you feeling?"

"I'm feeling okay. I had a light therapy session this morning, and I have another one in an hour or two. I can't remember what time it's scheduled for, but I figure I'm not going anywhere so it really doesn't matter. Janice called and said she took April to the hospital. She said not to worry, the doctor said it was a step below a migraine and it was normal for what she is going through right now. I'd be pulling my hair out if Janice wasn't there helping her. She really has been such a wonderful friend to April over the years, almost too wonderful. I think Janice feels responsible for April. I think she has taken the role of protector and provider for April since college. I'm thankful for her, and that she is willing to stay with April right now. Not many friends would do that."

"I agree; there aren't many people out there like that." Nick sits in the only chair in the room.

"Anyway, we need to solve this case. I was so close to telling our employer that there was nothing unusual about this man, but now I'm here in the hospital. This causes doubt for me. How about you, Nick?" I try to sit up, but pain shoots through my back.

"I have doubts as well."

"I'm not sure where my doubts lie though. The pain meds I'm taking have really left me in a fog, and each time I think I'm on to something, I fall asleep. Nick, you need to be sharp. I'm too slow to figure this out." The truth hurts.

"'I think we can do this together. How about we start from the beginning when you were hired?"

"Sure, that sounds good. I was approached by Mr. and Mrs. Edward Willis ten months ago. They were concerned because their daughter was showing an interest in a man they felt was 'shady'. They said they couldn't put their finger on what the problem was, but they thought he was after her inheritance somehow. They wanted us to find something wrong with their daughter's boyfriend, Tim. They wanted to have concrete evidence to show her why he wasn't the right person for her. We spent all our time digging through his history and watching him closely. Mrs. Willis insisted five months ago that he needed to be watched 24/7 so we arranged for that. Do you have all the notes, Nick?"

"Yes, I picked them up from your house. I didn't have time to look anything over yet. Here it is." Nick picks up my brief case, and puts it on the bed.

I shift slightly, groaning as I reach for the handle. After a few twists, the latch pops open. Nick rolls up his sleeves. I would have done the same, but the hospital gowns don't have long sleeves.

"Okay, I have three sets of notes. Up until the last two months we mostly had the guys switch on and off until Ed and his wife had insisted that we were the ones that needed to do the surveillance. I don't know why he felt that was necessary, but we did as he asked."

"That did make our lives harder." Nick grunts.

"It did. Anyway, let's each grab a stack. Let's make notes of where he went, dates, times, and with whom he was with, along with anything we feel might be important. Here's a notepad Nick, and a pen." I pull them out of my briefcase.

Nick takes both. We work for a while, rarely using our vocal cords, and barely using our pens. The physical therapist arrives.

"Are you ready for therapy, Ryan?" Jill asks in her usual cheery voice.

"Umm, you caught us in the middle of some research, but I think we could continue this for hours, so yes, I'm ready." A sigh escapes my mouth. I'm really not looking forward to this.

Nick took another stack and adjusted the lunch tray by the seat in the corner. He lowers his head, continuing his work.

"Ryan, our goal for this session, is to get you out of bed and walking some. Do you remember this morning how you did log rolls?" She asks with a chipper voice.

"Let's see. I'm supposed to keep my spine straight, in a neutral position, holding my stomach in, and slowly roll from one side to the next. Am I right?" I made sure to memorize the instructions. I don't want to slow my progress any.

"Yes, that's it. Let's start with that." Jill lowers the bed into a horizontal position. I rock slowly from one side to the next. This isn't that bad. I can't wait to get out of bed and walk.

"Okay, now I'm going to have you sit up. Remember to keep a straight back. I'm going to help you with that, but I want you to try not to rely on me. The more you can do on your own, the quicker your recovery will be." She smiles.

Jill supports me as I lift myself to a sitting position; along my hairline moisture forms. I that this!

"Whoa. I think I need to move a little bit slower." I grab my head. "My head is woozy."

"Unfortunately Ryan, it's normal to feel lightheaded after surgery. This is your first time sitting without the support of your bed. Now let's get you to your feet."

She's joking, right? "Uh, what happened to light therapy?"

"That was this morning, now you have work to do."

"I'll try." The fuzzy feeling has only subsided a little.

"Good. Slowly, move your feet to the floor. I'm right here supporting you." She has her hand on my back and the other under my arm.

"Are you sure you can hold me up if my legs don't?"

Nick coughs but doesn't take his eyes off his work.

"Ryan, where's your faith?" Jill chuckles. "I know what I'm doing and yes I'm confident that I can hold your weight if your legs don't."

Excuses aren't working to get out of this. I've broken out in a full sweat and I haven't even stood up yet.

"Okay, I'll try."

"Slowly move your feet toward the floor."

Jill adjusts me to help get them there.

"Keep going." Each inch takes effort. "Look, Ryan, you did it. Now slowly start to straighten your legs."

"Am I supposed to be out of breath?"

"Yes, that's normal too. You have been through a lot and therapy is hard but I can guarantee you will be happy you are putting the effort in now."

As she talks, she supports me, as I stand tall. Spots start to overtake my vision.

"I suppose you are going to ask me to take a step."

"Yes."

"I was afraid of that."

I'm not sure what I said that was funny, but Jill's infectious laugh puts a smile on my face and boosts my confidence. I could see April becoming fast friends with her. I wish April were here. She would be on my other side encouraging me to take this first step. I hope she's feeling better soon. I haven't even talked to her on the phone today.

"Ryan, Ryan?"

"Oh, yes. Sorry, I was deep in thought."

"I thought you were just procrastinating."

"Yeah, that too and the spots in my vision aren't helping."

"Take your time, and please let me know when you are ready, okay?"

"Okay, I'm ready. Let's get this over with."

Putting all of my weight on one foot creates a wobbly effect in that leg. How did I get so weak? With the next step, I do a little shuffle movement giving me an ancient look.

"You're doing great. Keep going, you're almost to the door."

Man, I didn't want to go that far. Concentrating, I make several more shuffles. Unfortunately, they were all in the opposite direction of my bed.

"Is there any way you could wheel my bed to me?"

"Nice try. You can do it. Each time you do this, you will get better at it and it will be easier for you."

"That's good because right now I'm feeling very dizzy." Somehow I turn and start walking back. I try to go a little faster so I can sit down, and make this feeling stop.

"Ryan, please slow down. I don't want you to fall." Jill insists.

"I'm almost there." I grunt.

"Yes, you only have a couple of steps left, but I don't want you to fall." I ignore her. "You're one stubborn man Ryan."

"Yes, I...."

Sitting back down on the bed, I grab the bedpan and lose my lunch.

"That's also normal. Anesthesia can have that effect. Let me get you a wash cloth."

She goes into the bathroom and comes out with a wet hand towel.

"Thanks."

After it's all cleaned up, Jill helps me lie flat.

"You did great for your first session."

"You mean second session." I state.

"Nah. This morning doesn't count. This session you worked hard. I'll see you tomorrow."

"Thanks, I think."

With a wave, she walks out the door. I can hear her laughing down the hallway. That was brutal. I hope tomorrow is better.

Chapter 20

I think I'm bleeding! I can't figure out where, but I'm convinced I am. I feel the baby moving, so my body is functioning enough to support him or her. I can hear myself groan occasionally. The noise shoots pain throughout my head so I try to keep quiet. Unfortunately, the groans slip through my lips before I can control them. The central air hasn't done its job lately; my sticky hand tries to move the sheets down off my back. Slow movements are easier to handle.

My stomach has emptied four times since I've been home from the hospital. Walking is too overwhelming for me so Janice has placed a garbage can next to my bed. Sleep is hard to find. When I was a child I would watch television when I was sick. Sometimes I would fall asleep watching it. The lights flickering from the square box wouldn't sooth so I'm not going to try and turn it on. The noise from it would be too agonizing. Hoping sleep will come is about all I can do. Maybe the doctor is right and I'll feel better in the morning.

I know I'm stressed about Ryan being in the hospital. Also about my decision not to tell him about being pregnant is weighing heavy on my heart. Why did I make such a quick decision and stick with it? At first it was to protect him from the hurt of losing a baby;

which is what I thought would happen. Each week that passed I had an opportunity to speak up. I think I was mad at him because of the amount of time he was spending away on business. I know I was mad at him. I should start being honest. If I can convince myself that the lie is true somehow, that makes me think that I'm right. If my brain weren't hurting, I'd explore that more. Lying in a darkened room with noiseless sound has caused my thoughts to rick-a shay. Sleep would be a pleasant dream.

"Umm, April. I heard you groan so I knew you weren't asleep. Do you want to talk?" Janice asks.

"Nnnot really. Nnoiiise hurts my head, head worse."

"Is it hard to talk?"

"No. It, it, it just hurts to tttalk."

"Okay. I'll leave soon."

"Please, don't leave."

"I meant I'll leave your room soon so you could sleep."

"Oh, ok."

"Have you fallen asleep yet?" Janice comes over to the bed and adjusts the sheets.

"No, I've been thinking too muuuch."

"Okay, I'll go and let you sleep. I'm putting your cell phone on your nightstand. When you wake up, can you send me a quick text?"

"Yes, I, I can."

"Good. Oh, and I need to make sure you are drinking enough water. You have a few reasons to stay hydrated." Janice bends the straw and puts it right up to my lips. Slowly water flows down my throat. There isn't relief with anything I do. I keep drinking, knowing that I'm going to lose it later. It's worth trying for the baby. A while ago Helen was encouraging me to find the blessings from God every day in every situation. It's easy to do when things are going the way you want them to, but usually during those times I forget to thank God for them. Today, I am blessed because I have so many people around me who care about me and are willing to help me through this tough time. Also, that Lysa isn't here watching me go through this. *Thank You, God!*

* * *

April drifts off to sleep right after Janice takes the straw out of her mouth. If she keeps stuttering after she wakes up, Janice is going to take her back to the hospital. Gently closing the door behind her, she starts to make a list of the things she needs to do around the house. Cook the chicken; wash Lysa's clothes...answer the door. Who could that be?

"You better not have woken up April." She mumbles as she hurries to the door.

"Hi, Janice. I wasn't expecting you to answer the door."

"Well, sorry to disappoint you, Doug, but I'm the only one you are going to talk to, so what do you want?" Her hands defensively land on her hips.

"Oh, I'm not disappointed. I'd love to talk to you."

"You have a funny way of showing it. I don't live here and you weren't expecting me to answer the door, so I really doubt you love talking to me because you haven't called me in, oh I don't even know how long it's been." Her face begins to turn pink.

"Umm, okay, you have a point."

"That's all you're going to say? You have no explanation?" She counters.

"You're beautiful, Janice."

"That's it! You avoid my question with a comment about beauty. Men!" She reaches back to slam the door but he knows what she's about to do; he already has his foot in the way before she can get a grip on the door.

"Doug, why are you here?"

"I wanted to know how Ryan was doing."

"He's improving."

"That's great."

"Yeah, it is. If you want to know how he is tomorrow, go visit him. I'm going to be here for a few days and I'd prefer not to talk to you." She reaches for the door again but he stays in the way.

"Oh, that's good to know. I'll be seeing you soon then, Janice. Bye."

"Bye, hey, wait. Why will you be seeing me soon?"

"Oh, I don't know." He smiles.

"Why won't you be honest with me?" Yelling isn't her usual choice for communicating, but this man makes her so mad!

"I didn't lie." He states in a straightforward manner.

"But you avoid the truth. Do you think you are going to hurt me? Well for your information you already have, so it would be better for me if you just told me the truth as to why you broke up with me."

She watches his mouth open and close and she decides she can't look at him another second. She closes the door.

She hears his car door close and his engine start. She likes honesty. He said he hasn't lied. He said she was beautiful so maybe he likes the look of her face but not her personality. Ha! She knows she can be a bit overbearing, but so can he. That's one reason why she thought they were a good fit. She needs someone that will stand up to her. She has strong opinions and she likes to share them, she likes a good debate. If she were to ever get married she'd have to work on that, maybe. Forget about him. He has broken her heart once, why is she giving him the opportunity to do it again? She doesn't know.

What was she doing before the doorbell rang? Oh, right, she was making a list. Maybe she'll start cooking and then figure out what to do next. She cooks when she's angry.

It took her twenty-five minutes to let her shoulders relax. The kitchen smells amazing with a delicious and very calorie conscious meal for herself. She doesn't think April will be up to eating but she's going to make chicken soup once she takes all the chicken off the bone. Maybe that would help. She should have her try some crackers and Sprite first maybe.

* * *

Lysa races across the warped hardwood floors. Her sock snags on a nail that slightly sits above the floor. It pulls and she loses her balance. Her hand reaches out and she grabs the nearest thing to her, Helen.

"Ms. Helen, when are you going to call Mr. Palmer?"

Helen chuckles. "I was thinking about calling him after lunch, Lysa."

"Oh, that's good." She leans down and rubs her foot. "I'd like to see him again. I met him one time when Aunt Nancy was selling her house. He was a really nice man so I was hoping he would come over today and maybe have lunch with us."

"Really? I'm sure Mr. Palmer is a busy man with the way the house market is right now. Houses are selling like hot cakes."

"I guess, but how will we know unless we ask him?"

"That's a good point Lysa." Not sure what else to say, Helen starts moving her blankets from the hall closet and into the plastic containers.

"Lysa, can you please bring those empty boxes upstairs into Ms. Helen's room?" Nancy calls out from the kitchen.

"Sure, Aunt Nancy."

Lysa skips to the boxes and grabs four. As she stands, the boxes start to wobble.

"Lysa," Helen starts to say.

"I think I'll only take two at a time." Lysa decides.

"Good idea."

As she makes her way out of listening range, Nancy approaches Helen. "You know she does have a good point."

"You too, huh? My goodness, it runs in the family." Helen rolls up her sweatshirt sleeves.

"What does?" Nancy questions.

"Oh, perseverance maybe or something along those lines."

"Nice! I like the way you phrased that, so uplifting and positive."

"Ha, you know I was being facetious." Helen snorts and moves a couple of boxes out of the way.

"So…"

"You aren't going to quit, are you?" Helen sighs.

Nancy shakes her head and Helen gives her a half smile and walks to her phone. She pushes a few buttons and walks out of the room. Nancy starts to follow her, but realizes she's heading to the bathroom. She won this round!

Looking around, she decides to busy herself by making lemonade. Homemade lemonade is so good. Then she starts making lunch.

"Yes, Nancy is here at my house right now…. oh yes, sure you can come over and see her…I bet it has been a long time…lunch today…well it just so happens that Nancy is in the kitchen making lunch right now…you'll be here in fifteen minutes…oh, that sounds great…we have been packing so there are boxes and stuff all over the place…you'd like to stay and help…sure I'd never turn away help…see you soon….okay, bye."

"Uh, what did you do, Helen? Was that some type of revenge?" Nancy glares at her.

"Oh, no. That was a very odd conversation. I don't think Greg knows about Nick." She places the phone on the counter.

"Why would I tell my realtor that I'm in a relationship?"

"Only because he has a crush on you and it would be a good idea to let him know that you aren't interested. Or are you?" Helen teases.

"Ha! Helen, he is a nice guy, but I didn't even give him a second look because I like Nick even though I didn't know that when I sold my house."

"Ah. Okay, well you can let Greg know that when he comes over for lunch but maybe after he agrees to be my realtor." Nancy's eyebrows rise. "I'm only joking, Nancy. You should let him know you aren't interested as soon as possible."

"Yes, I will. Oh, boy. Are you sure he wasn't just being nice?"

"I'm sure."

"Yikes. Okay, I'll let him know. I never encouraged him, Helen. Never." Nancy drops into the nearest chair and sighs. Boy was this getting messy.

"I didn't think you did. Sometimes being single is all the encouragement one needs."

"True."

"You should watch out then because once he knows about Nick he might come after you. He is a really nice guy so that wouldn't be bad or anything."

"There is one thing you are forgetting, Nancy."

"What's that?"

"You still are single."

"Oh, right, I am." She pulls the brown and white pillow onto her lap and gives it a hug.

"Yeah, you are."

"It's either Nick or singleness. I'll make that clear to Greg."

"What will you make clear to Greg, Aunt Nancy? Oh, is Mr. Palmer coming over?" Lysa says as she comes back down the stairs.

"Yes, he is, for lunch." That one was easy to answer. Nancy's glad Lysa didn't wait for an answer to her first question.

"Yay." Lysa sits next to Nancy and leans against Nancy's side. "When's lunch? I'm hungry."

"We will be eating as soon as Mr. Palmer gets here."

"Okay." Lysa sits up. "Ms. Helen, I found three dolls upstairs and some clothes that I think fit them. Can I play with them?"

"Yes, sure you can."

"Thank you so much!" She tosses her hair over her shoulder as she rushes back up the stairs.

"That's something we both missed out on."

"Huh, what do you mean, Helen?"

"Having children. She is so excited about little things and she talks all the time. I wish we each had a chance to have children, but I'm glad we aren't single moms right now either. Maybe one day we might have a child or two. We're both still in our early thirties, so it's possible." She looks at me with wet eyes.

"Helen, of course it's still possible. I know we miss our husbands terribly but I know neither of them would want us to go through this life so alone."

"I know, but I'm not ready to move on."

"There's no rush, Helen."

"I haven't thought about having a baby in a while. We never tried. We talked about trying in the future, which would have been around now. Maybe that's why I'm thinking about babies."

"Babies can be…oh, do you mind getting the door, Helen? I need to finish throwing together the salad." Nancy tosses the pillow and rushes to her feet.

"Convenient, Nancy. I did notice that you stopped all work on lunch until the doorbell rang. You are trying too hard to play matchmaker."

"Well, for your information, I'm good at it. Look at Ryan and April."

"Your methods aren't, oh, what's the word?" Helen gives her a look.

"Please get the door, Helen, and stop stalling."

"Maybe if I stall long enough, he will just go away." She crosses her arms.

"Maybe, and then who is going to sell your house?"

"I'll get the door but I'm not looking forward to this." She sighs. "You tricked me, Nancy. If I knew this was your intent I would have found someone else."

Helen might be mad at Nancy now, but she'll get over it soon enough. The table is set and the food is all out except for the salad and the dressings. If Nancy stalls in the kitchen any longer than necessary, Helen is going to retaliate. Nancy tosses some cheese on top and with slow steps walks to the dining room table.

"Hi Greg." Nancy smiles. Greg comes over and gives her an awkward hug. Lysa walks in at that moment.

"Hi, Nancy. It's been a little while since I last saw you. How have you been?" Greg takes a step back and removes his suit jacket.

"I'm doing well." Nancy says.

"No, you aren't, Aunt Nancy?" Lysa comments.

"No?" Greg raises his eyebrow.

"Oh, and why would you think that?" Nancy turns to Lysa.

"Because you were crying over Nick not being around. I know you are sad because he has been traveling a lot. Mommy has been sad about Daddy traveling a lot also."

Maybe Nancy was wrong about Lysa helping the conversation, but at least she doesn't have to figure out how to bring up Nick.

"You're right, Lysa. I have been sad about that."

"So are you going to forgive Nick now so that you can marry him?" Lysa inquires and Helen chuckles.

"Lysa, we will speak about this later, okay? Why don't we all sit down? The food is ready."

"Sure, I'm hungry. Are you hungry, Mr. Palmer?" Lysa looks at Nancy and gives her a slight smile as she makes her way around the table so that Helen and Greg have to sit next to each other. Nancy can't believe it; matchmaking runs in the family.

"Yes, I'm very hungry, Lysa. Do you ladies mind if I say grace?" Greg asks.

They all bow their heads and listen to him pray. Nancy resolves from now on she is going to meddle less. She's setting a bad example for her niece and the look on Helen's face confirms it.

"Oh and I hope you forgive Nick too." Greg adds, with a chuckle after he says amen.

"Me three." Helen chimes.

"Okay, everyone I'll forgive Nick. Can we eat now?" Nancy's cheeks turn a slight shade of pink.

"I most certainly think we can." Greg says as he winks at Lysa, while picking up the potato salad.

"Mr. Palmer do you think you can sell Ms. Helen's house?"

"I will try my best to sell it quickly and get her the best price also." He passes the salad to Helen.

"I know there are so many repairs so I'm not expecting much for the house. Before my husband passed away this house was in excellent condition. Now it seems that everywhere I turn, something is falling apart. Do you really think you can sell it?" Helen asks.

"Yes, I do. I don't think there are too many repairs either, but we will take a look after lunch. I'm not concerned. I think this house will be off your hands soon. Where are you planning to move to?" Greg asks in between bites.

"I have decided to rent. I don't want to own a house anymore. I know nothing about house repairs and I don't want to think about them ever again. Along with mowing the lawn and shoveling the snow."

"Sounds like a plan. Have you started looking at places to rent?"

"No I haven't."

"I can take you around this week to a few places and if there isn't anything you like, then we can just keep on looking."

"You help people look for places to rent?" Helen isn't convinced this is a normal thing.

"I have helped many people look for places to rent. Tomorrow I'm free from one to four so we can start looking then, if you're free. Before I leave here today you can let me know what location you want to look in, and if you want to rent in an apartment or a single or double house."

"Okay. Great." Helen looks at her plate, her appetite strong.

Lysa and Nancy focus on eating and listening to Helen and Greg talk. Nancy knew they would like each other. And they already set up a date for tomorrow. That was fast!

"Thank you for lunch, ladies. It was delicious."

"You're welcome." Lysa and Nancy say in unison.

"Helen, can you please show me the house?" Greg looks at his watch, then stands and picks up his plate. Nancy takes the plate from him and stacks the rest of them and brings them into the kitchen.

Helen visibly slouches when Greg says, 'the house.'

"Sure. Lysa, would you like to help give the tour?"

"You bet! Mr. Palmer, please follow me. Here is the dining room but you already saw it when we were eating. Through this doorway is the kitchen." She steps through the doorway and waves her hands around. Greg gets a quick look before she quickly steps out and starts to lead everyone up the stairs.

"Lysa, do you know how many bedrooms there are up here?" Greg asks.

"I think so, but let me go and make sure. I think it's four but..." She dashes back and forth as the adults wait in the hallway. "Yes, I'm right, it's four."

"Great, can you show me the bathrooms that are up here?"

"Right this way. There are two, one is blue and the other is flowery. I hope the new people that live here like flowers. There are a lot of them in that bathroom."

The blue bathroom, as Lysa calls it, is a full bath with blue paint on the wall. The flowery one is off the master bedroom and the shower curtain has some huge flowers on it. The walls are slightly pink and the tub, sink, and toilet are all white.

"Helen, these bathrooms look good and the kitchen looks updated."

"My husband re-did the kitchen six years ago and the bathrooms were redone right before we bought the house."

"How old is the roof?"

"I think 15 years old, but I'd have to check on that."

"Okay, I looked at it while I was waiting outside and it looks like it's still in good condition. Lysa can you show me the rest of the downstairs?" Greg asks.

"This way everyone. First we will go to the brown sitting room."

"Which room is that?" Nancy whispers to Helen.

"I'm not sure." She shrugs.

Lysa walks to the living room. Ah, there is a brown rug with lots of chairs.

"Next we will go to the delicate room." She leads them to the family room where Helen has her glassware and china spread across a big coffee table, waiting to be packed away.

"I think that is it for this floor. Oh, wait; there is another bathroom down that way. It's small so I'll let you go by yourself."

"Thanks, Lysa."

They watch him walk toward the half bath that Helen tastefully decorated.

"Aunt Nancy, I'm tired of giving the tour, can you finish so I can go back to playing with those dolls?"

"Sure, Lysa, I think there is only the basement left anyway."

"I know." She says with a smile.

"She can have those dolls when she goes home with you today." Helen says after Lysa ascends the stairs.

"Are you sure?"

"Yes, they were a gift from some distant relative. I don't remember who gave them to me, unfortunately, but I have no attachment to them. I was a teenager when they arrived in the mail."

"Okay, Helen the bathroom looks good. Oh, where did our little tour guide go?" Greg looks around.

"She's upstairs playing with dolls. She doesn't want to go into the basement." Helen answers.

"I don't either so I'll start cleaning up the lunch dishes." Nancy adds.

"Okay, lead the way Helen. I think you are going to be surprised by how much you get for this house. You do have some repairs but they are all minor ones. I have someone who can fix them up for you and he doesn't charge much. Do you have a lot more of your mortgage to pay off?"

"We have, I mean," She stutters. "I have $134,000 left."

"That's great. After I see the basement I'll tell you the listing price."

And that's all Nancy heard as they left the main floor. She needs to talk to Nick; it's unsettling having tension between them.

Chapter 21

The bucket fumbles in my shaky hand, but I manage to bring it to my face in time. Janice hurries into the room and places a cool washcloth on my forehead. She takes the bucket before it slips from my grip and I fall back onto my pillow. She cleans up my mess. The baby wakes with faint quick kicks; probably wondering when food will make its way to him or her. I'm wondering as well.

"Distract me, Janice, please. Whisper me a story."

"Sure, what shall I whisper? I know, I'll tell you about my journey to health." She tries to whisper.

"Please."

"Okay, I made a commitment to exercise and eat right some months ago. Before I started exercising, I did something a little odd and I'm not saying this is a good strategy, but it worked for me. The two days before I started workouts, during my meal times I ate my high calorie meals that I loved to eat and really thought about how they tasted. I did this with chocolate and other sweets too. I was surprised at how I didn't care for the tastes of many of the sweets and with most of the high calorie meals, I took notice of the feeling I had afterward. The overstuffed stomach and the kind of sick feeling some of the greasy food left me with after eating them. I started to take the power out of the food. In my mind, I was putting these foods high up on a 'must have' pedestal. They were my 'go to' foods when I was feeling a little down or lonely. One by one I took count of my favorites and I eliminated the power each one had in my mind. I started to rethink and started to renew my mind by changing my thoughts about them. I told myself the truth about them. They didn't make me feel better during or after having them, but worse. Some were also my habit foods; things I thought I liked but realized I don't even like the taste of. I might have liked it years ago but not anymore. I spent years being in the habit of eating them that I never questioned my buying them. These foods didn't have control over me anymore.

"I had one other problem. For a very long time I didn't want to give up any foods. I liked being able to eat what I wanted to eat. I felt I deserved this right. After realizing these truths, then I wanted to change. The truth was that I was so out of shape I couldn't play a game of tag with my niece and I was too big for all the pants I own. The truth was that the control I felt I had, hadn't been the controlled outcome I wanted. I only controlled the moment and my choices made me out of control of my size. I set goals but they weren't for the world's version of a perfect body, but rather one of health and energy.

"Deciding to take time for me and knowing that my health was worth fighting for was what I focused on. I have spent my life giving to others. Serving others is so important to me. I saw how with each passing year I had gained more weight; a few pounds each year. I was never really thin and I honestly don't want that to be my goal. I want to be healthy; I want to be able to do things with friends. I don't want my weight being the reason I can't do things anymore. I see that since I have taken the time for me to get healthy, I'm helping and serving others more. I can do so much more with the energy I now have.

"I'm not as tired as I used to be, and I love that. I don't wake up wanting to go back to bed because I feel I didn't get enough sleep. I love having energy.

"I set small goals. I look at the next pound I want to lose. When I was 180, I said to myself as I worked out and as I made meal choices, '179, I'm looking to weigh 179.' I have long-term goals as well, but I don't concentrate on them too much. I don't want to get discouraged, so I focus on the next pound to be lost and I exercise hard to lose it. April?"

"Yeess." I choke out.

"You don't look well."

"I sstill," I pause, "feel like I'm dying."

"Okay, we're going back to the hospital." Janice moves around the room. My eyes are closed or maybe the room is dim, either way I can't tell what she's doing. Honestly, I don't care; all I want is this pain to stop. The door closes. I don't think she believes I can get to the car on my own. I'll wait; that's all I can do anyway. I want to talk to Ryan. What if he finds out about the baby from someone else? Janice pops back in the room. She lifts my arm and wraps it around her shoulders while her other arm goes around my waist. She pulls me up and a groan escapes my lips. Janice lifts me and my shaky Jell-O legs wobble with each step down the hallway and to the car.

When she starts the car the radio automatically blares. She quickly silences it. "I'm trying to go slow over the bumps." Janice informs softly as we start down the road.

"It doesn't matter. The pain can't get any worse."

Maybe they can put me to sleep until the baby's due. Or make the pain stop somehow. Finally arriving, Janice circles into the emergency entrance, puts the car in park, and races to my side. Before she opens the door, she turns and grabs a wheelchair that's sitting outside the lobby. Pushing it over to my door, she fumbles to open it and hold the chair at the same time. I start to ease off the seat and Janice catches me before I fall. I slide into the chair and place my head on my right hand. Bright lights greet my not wanting eyes.

Janice takes charge and speaks to the nurse. Waiting among hurting people doesn't ease my pain. About an hour goes by and my name is called. Janice maneuvers to the left and then a sharp right. She has a bag in her right hand and her purse over her left shoulder. The weight doesn't slow her down. We enter our assigned room. A nurse asks questions and Janice answers them. I'm asked to walk to the bed. My blood pressure, pulse, and temperature are taken. The nurse informs me that my blood pressure is low, very low. I mumble that it normally is. She leaves, and Janice and I wait. Without me asking, Janice dims the light and puts a blanket over my legs. The baby moves as if sensing comfort.

"Hello, again." In walks Dr. Stevens.

"Oh, you, again." Janice clenches her jaw.

"I've already told you what her problem is. She needs to drink plenty of liquids and get plenty of rest. This is just a bad headache."

"Just a bad headache? Have you opened your eyes and looked at her? She can't function. This is not just a bad headache. Where did you go to school?"

"Jjjanice...." I start but can't finish.

"April, you need to go home and rest. We have done all we can do while you are pregnant. This should pass by morning."

"Dr. Stevens!"

"Yes?" Hi jaw tightens as he turns toward Janice. "Janice, is it?"

"Yes, it is. April doesn't have a ride home so you will have to figure out what is wrong with her before she can go home. She will have to be able to make arrangements herself and in the amount of pain she is in right now, she cannot do that." Janice says as she stands to her full height.

"You're right here so you can bring her home now." He gives her a smirk.

Janice reaches out and squeezes my hand. "Actually, I can't drive her home. I have to go. Someone will get her when you do your job and fix her!" Janice storms out of the room.

I don't think she's going to come back either. Dr. Stevens huffs and storms out also, leaving my door open.

"Stephanie, there is a patient in there without a ride home. See if you can call someone to pick her up." He orders the nurse.

"Sure, Dr. Stevens."

A moment later in walks another nurse.

"Hi. My name is Stephanie. Is there anyone that I can call to pick you up?" She asks in a soothing alto voice.

"I can't think of anyone."

"What about your husband?"

"He's at St. Peter's recovering from back surgery."

"I bet that's stressful."

"Yes."

"What's your name?"

"Aaapril."

"Nice to meet you April."

"Please help me. I'm in so much pain. It can't be good for the baby."

"April, how about I try to make you more comfortable and while I'm doing that, you can think about who we can call to pick you up, okay?" Stephanie places her hand on my arm.

"Thank you."

"You're welcome."

Stephanie fluffs the pillow and hands me a cup of ice water with a straw. She understands that I need things with minimal movement. She then hands me some Tylenol. I take it, trusting that she gives me the right amount. I didn't want to tell her that I'll be vomiting it up soon but I'm trying for my baby. Ryan's baby. I need to talk to him. Why is life so hard sometimes? *God, I need you.*

"Did you think of anyone I can call?" Stephanie asks gently.

"Sorry, I can't. My sister is watching my daughter so she can't come. I can't have Lysa see me like this. My m-m-mom is away with my younger sister so they can't come. My husband is in the other hospital and I have no other friends. Janice is stubborn. She isn't going to come back until the doctor figures out what is wrong with me. I feel like I'm bleeding. Please help me Stephanie." I reach my hand out but only grab air.

"I will. Why don't you sleep some? I'll check on you in a little bit."

"I'll try."

"Good, I'll be back soon." The door closes.

Two right turns and one left and Janice realizes she shouldn't work in a hospital. She's lost! And mad at Dr. Stevens. She should have taken her to a different hospital. Who would think that he would still be on duty? April will thank her later for storming out. That Dr. Stevens better get to work, and examine April. April is a strong woman and a step below a migraine wouldn't keep her in bed. He doesn't know what she has been through. Maybe she should go back and tell him; no, that wouldn't do, then he might force April to leave with her. She hopes they treat her well. It's hard walking around in circles trying to leave this place, knowing April is bent over in debilitating pain. *God please send an angel her way.*

She makes a decision to follow the red tape on the wall down the hallway to the right. In front of her sits the gift shop and a blue tape alongside the red one. She sticks with the red line; it represents her current mood. How long should she wait before she calls to check on April? After several more turns, the red tape vanishes. Oh, brother! Picking the tape color that matches her mood and outfit isn't the best logical method for exiting a building.

Sitting down in the nearest waiting room, she decides to make a couple of calls. The first is to her boss, asking if she can take another week off.

He wasn't thrilled but wasn't really upset either. She knows her value in the company and without her there, his job is harder. He has always said that she can't quit because he could never replace her. She knew he wouldn't give her a tough time taking off because she rarely has and she has months of time saved up from the years she has worked there. The job is enjoyable so there wasn't really a reason to take off. One would think being single she would use her time to vacation anywhere she wanted to. The times she tried she came home more depressed seeing all the honeymooners and lovebirds. It was hard not being content with singleness and right when she started to be last year she met Doug and he had to go and ruin her happiness. Forgiving him has been difficult.

"Ms., do you have an appointment?" The receptionist asks from behind her glass shield.

"Oh, no. Sorry I was just looking for a place to sit. I got lost trying to leave the hospital so I sat here to collect my thoughts." Janice looks at the receptionist and her surroundings as if seeing where she is for the first time.

"Okay, I think it would have been wiser to ask someone for help. You almost made it to the exit. Go out this door and make a left. Follow the walkway which will take you over the street and when you see doors, you are at the parking lot. It's up to you to remember where you parked your car. I wasn't with you when you pulled in." She chuckles.

"Oh, actually, I parked in the emergency entrance."

"You didn't park your car?"

"No." Janice cringes. Hope the car is still there. Can she get lucky twice?

"Well, if it hasn't been towed yet, go..." And on she went telling her which turns to make.

Following the directions for the first three turns worked well but now she's lost again. Should have written it down. Wandering is fine; she doesn't want to leave April. They could refuse to look at her but hopefully that isn't what happens. She picked up the blue line a couple of turns ago. She decides to follow this one too. Maybe some food and coffee will come along the way.

* * *

"April, it's Stephanie. Are you feeling any better?"

"No." Speaking hurts.

"Did you fall asleep?"

"For a little bit, I think." I start to shrug my shoulders but the pain stops me.

"Okay. I'm going to take your temperature and blood pressure." She moves around the room a bit. She hasn't turned on the light, which I'm very thankful about.

"Your temperature is normal but your blood pressure is quite low."

"It usually is low."

"Probably not this low." Stephanie says. "April?"

"Yes, Stephanie."

"I'm going to turn on the light. I want to get a better look at you. I know that the light will hurt your head and I'm sorry for that." She sounds sincere.

"If you are going to try to help me, please turn on the light." I squeeze my eyelids a little closer together.

"Okay, I'll turn on the one over your bed."

She leans her arm over the top of the bed, keeping her head parallel to my head. The light glows as Stephanie looks at me, really looks at me.

"April, I'm going to be right back. Okay?"

"Okay."

She dashes out of the room, forgetting to close the door behind her.

* * *

"Cheryl!" Stephanie rushes up to her. "Where is Dr. Stevens?"

"I'm not sure. Why?"

"Problem with the woman in C36."

"He can't be far. His shift ends in thirty minutes so he wouldn't be on a break now. Do you want me to page him?"

"Yes!"

Cheryl pages the doctor. The nurses continue to talk in quick hushed tones. All Janice can hear is that something is wrong with April. Fortunately, she managed to get herself lost back to where she started. April's room is only steps away. She hears the page for Dr. Stevens. Someone believes April. The nurses continue their conversation with hands moving in all directions. They are not pleased with Dr. Stevens. The nurse named Cheryl says something about being fired. She wishes she knew how to read lips. Dr. Stevens comes into view from the left of the nurses' station.

"Who paged me?" He bellows loudly as he pulls himself up to his full six feet.

"I did."

"Well, what is it Stephanie?"

"Umm," Stephanie says.

"Stop pausing. I'm busy, so make it quick."

She leans in and whispers something to him. His eyes grow big, raising his eyebrows close to his hairline as his nostrils flare; he runs his hand through his hair and walks to April's room. Two more nurses join him along with the one he called Stephanie. Janice starts walking toward the door. She doesn't need to fear them sending April home now, but she thinks she needs to fear what they found. She cautiously steps into the room. There stands Dr. Stevens shining a light in April's eyes, talking in a soothing tone.

Chapter 22

Flip. Flip. Flip. What is that annoying noise? I open my eyes and see the spotted ceiling. I look at my body and the hospital gown is still there. I wish it were all one big nightmare. Flip. Flip. Flip.

"Huh, what happened, Nick?"

"Ah, uh..." Nick puts the book down and stretches his hands over his head, releasing a giant yawn. "When the therapist left and I mean as soon as she walked out the door, you fell asleep. You didn't make walking look easy."

"That's real encouraging, Nick."

"In no time at all you'll be back to doing push-ups and running. The way I look at it is that the worst is over. You walked for the first time, next time it will be a bit easier."

"I hope you're right, Nick." I look for a clock. Can't find one. "So how long was I asleep?"

"I'm not sure. When you fell asleep, I thought, 'that looks like a good idea, I think I'll do the same,' so I did." He rubs his neck. The chair he napped in only reclines a little.

"Did you not sleep well last night?"

"Actually, no. Nancy and I had a fight or something. I'm kind of confused but I'm going to go over there and talk to her soon. I wanted to get this case finished first, but it could take a long time and then Nancy and I are stuck not knowing what we are to each other. I know it's eating me up inside. I don't want her to be going through this either. I want this, whatever this is that Nancy and I are, to be defined and friendship isn't the word I want to define it as even if that's what she's calling it." Nick pushes the footrest back into the chair and gets up and fills two cups with water.

"Maybe you should go over there now?"

"I'll go soon. We need to work first." He hands me a cup of water, but I'm flat on my back. Before I say anything, he hands me the controls so I can slowly raise the bed.

"Are you sure?" I raise it higher than the last time and no dizziness comes, a small victory, but good progress.

"Ryan, let's get this thing done." Nick drinks his water in one gulp and throws the cup away.

"Okay. Where did we leave off?" A yawn escapes.

"We were trying to figure out if there was some pattern in his routine or see if something was suspicious and let me tell you, nothing is." Nick crumbles his cup and tosses it into the trashcan in the corner of the room.

"Alright. Let's look at this from a different angle. Why don't you read the notes from the conversations we've recorded?"

"Sure, that sounds less boring. Let me look for them. Give me a minute." Another yawn escapes. "Ryan, keep your eyes open, we have work to do."

"I will, just hurry up finding it." I close my eyes.

"Here it is. Let's see, I'll start with a conversation you had with Mr. Willis."

"Can you hand me that pen and pad over there? I want to take notes." Nick leans two feet to my left and retrieves the items.

I clench my jaw, and tighten my hand into fist. "I know, I know, you are thinking I could have gotten it myself but, man, am I tired! Thanks." That's my lame excuse!

"No prob." He readjusts his pants, as he sits back in his chair.

Turning my head to the right, I maneuver the pad and my right hand so that I can write with less pain.

Nick starts. "It says, 'December 1st, Willis's residence, 45 Chancy Court. 3:45pm. In attendance, Ryan Nolsen and Mr. Willis.

"How is your day going, Mr. Willis?"

"Fine. Mrs. Willis is out shopping."

"That's good. I wanted to only meet with you anyway."

"Then I guess this works out but it's not good for my bank account."

"Sorry about that. When, did you first meet Tim?"

"I met him when Amy brought him home for dinner 4 or 5 months ago."

"And what did you think of him that night?"

"I didn't think much. He seemed like a nice guy. He pulled out the chair for Amy when we were sitting down for dinner. He was interested in the family business. He asked several questions about my restaurants. Amy even seemed interested in the answers. She has never shown an interest in what I do, ever. That seemed odd, but maybe she was only interested in what Tim was interested in. You know what I mean?"

"You mean she likes Tim so she will pay attention to whatever comes out of his mouth."

"Yes, she was and still is infatuated with him."

"Okay, what else did you talk about?"

"Let's see. I asked him about what he plans to do with his life, stuff like that."

"And he said?"

"He said that he was finishing up grad school in one year with an MBA."

"Did he say what he wanted to do?"

"No, he said he was exploring his options."

"Where did he meet Amy?"

"He met her at the library. They were both studying; he was sitting a few tables from hers. He said he was going to get a drink and wanted to know if she would like one also. When he came back he handed her a soda and asked if she minded if he sat with her at her table. From then on they've been inseparable."

"How do you feel about that?"

"I want her to be happy. She has never shown an interest in any boy before. I mean she has dated somewhat, I suppose, but it has only lasted a couple of months. She has been so happy these past few months. I don't want to take that away from her, but her mother and I feel there is something off. I can't explain what it is that is troubling me, but that's why we hired you. Find out what it is. I hope it isn't anything, honestly. I want Amy to be happy. I just don't want to see her get hurt."

"That makes sense. I will work hard on this case, but I want you to know that my job is to find the truth. I won't alter or slant it and I might find nothing."

"I'm not asking you to alter what you find. I also want the truth and Amy happy too, but I'm not sure both of those are possible."

"Has Amy acted strange at all?"

"Not that I'm aware of."

"Anything different with her behavior?"

"She is cheerier, but that's all I can think of. We don't really see her much."

"Does she still live here at home?"

"Yes, she comes home late at night most nights, but not too late. She is still a responsible girl. Her grades are good, maybe even a little bit higher than before Tim."

"That's good."

"Yes, it is."

"I'm still unclear as to what you have noticed that has made you and your wife suspicious."

"Just a feeling."

"Who's idea was it to call me, you or your wife?"

"Uh, both of ours."

"Who brought up hiring a private investigator first?"

"I told you, already, it was both of us."

"I'm not trying to upset you. Usually one person comes up with an idea and the other person agrees. It's unusual for two people to have the same idea, at the same time, to hire a private investigator."

"Well, we both did."

"Okay. What was your wife's first impression of Tim?"

"She didn't like him."

"Did she say what she didn't like?"

"She thought he was way too interested in the family business and she also thought Amy could find someone cuter."

"What do you think?"

"I don't know; he looks fine to me."

"I meant about his interest in the family business."

"He just asked several questions. Not too unusual, I guess."

"Okay, is there anything else you would like to tell me about Tim or your daughter?"

"I can't think of anything else."

"Thanks for your time. I'll be back to talk with Mrs. Willis soon.'"

Nick puts the notebook down. "Ryan, that's all it says. It would have been easier to listen to this but I know you have the recordings in your safe and I don't know the code."

He knows I'm not going to give him the code. "Did you get anything from that Nick?"

"No, you?"

"Not a thing." I sigh. "I feel like we were hired to be a matchmaking service."

"Yup! Do you want to move on to other conversations, Ryan?"

"I'm quite tired, but we really need to make some progress. If someone didn't injure me I would close this case. Nick, why can't we figure this out?"

"I'm really not sure. Maybe there isn't anything to figure out. Maybe the person that hurt you is from an old case."

"That's possible. This is so frustrating."

Nick flips through several pages. "Ryan, you really need to start using a laptop for your notes."

"Maybe, I know this is old school, but it has worked for me for years and I...."

Nick interrupts. "Yeah, yeah, I know why fix something that isn't broken. Well, I think it's broken. All I would need to do is type in a couple of words and I'd be able to find the exact document we want to look at."

"Maybe. We can discuss it if we ever take another case. We have a couple of women that need to know what we do for a living before we continue."

"Yeah, alright, I found the pages with your first conversation with Mrs. Willis, '"It says, 'December 2nd, Willis's residence, 45 Chancy Court. 1:05pm. In attendance, Ryan Nolsen and Mrs. Willis." Nick clears his throat.

"Hi, Ryan, please come in."

"Hi, Mrs. Willis. How are you doing today?"

"I'm doing well."

"Good. Is there somewhere we can sit and talk?"

"Yes, follow me. I think the living room will be a great place. Would you like anything to drink?"

"No, thank you. Mrs. Willis I'd like to ask you some questions so I have a better understanding of what my job is."

"Sure, ask away."

"Can you please tell me about the first time you met Tim."

"He came over here for dinner one night. For weeks before we met him, Amy has been telling us about him, going on about what a great man he is. How his career choice is really important to him. He has goals, she says and direction. He knows what he wants. She even added that he wants her in his life. I could tell she was thinking about marriage. According to Amy he has never mentioned marriage, even now, but she still thinks that's what he intends. So anyway, he came over for dinner. He was too interested in the family business. My husband owns several restaurants. He has diversified, and has made wise purchases over the last 30 years. He has also stored away golden secrets about the business, many that I don't even know. Tim was trying to find out personal business information when he was here that night."

"What questions did he ask?"

"Oh, I don't know, too many if you ask me."

"Do you remember any of his questions?"

"Umm, let me think…. He wanted to know how many restaurants we own. Also, where they are located, and how much time my Eddie spends in each one. He asked who oversees them, who his right-hand man was. Stuff like that."

"Is there anything else?"

"I can't remember."

"What you did remember is good and if you think of anything else he asked, please let me know."

"Okay."

"What else happened that night?"

"We ate prime rib and mashed potatoes with gravy and an assortment of vegetables. He said he was eating like a king and loved the food. Amy made the dessert, chocolate cream pie with homemade whipped cream on top. It was so good and so bad for us. I must have gained five pounds in one meal. Tim seemed to really enjoy himself. He gushed over Amy's pie and said it was the best he ever had. He hung on all of her words and he was polite to Eddie and me. I should have loved this guy and that's why we called you, because we don't. There is something peculiar about him."

"What did he say about his upbringing?"

"He said his parents traveled a lot so he lived with his grandparents. He saw his parents several times a year throughout his growing up years, but he lost his excitement in anticipating their next visits. He had a great relationship with his grandparents and he viewed them as his parents. He even told everyone that they were his parents. Oh, Tim didn't tell me any of this, Amy did after he left. She said he had a great childhood. His grandparents felt so guilty about their daughter and son-in-law's behavior that they spoiled him rotten. He was given anything he wanted. Mostly he asked for time. There were times he asked for toys, but what he really wanted was to spend time doing things with them and so they did lots of things together. Amy said they took him to Disney Land every year. They bought an RV and travelled around the US stopping wherever there was a big attraction. This fascinated Amy. She even hinted that she would like to do this with Tim one day. She is falling hard for him and I don't want her to get hurt. What type of parents leave their child? If you ask me, they abandoned him and I think he must have some deep scars that will never heal. And that's one reason why he and Amy shouldn't be together. What if he does what he learned from his parents and abandons Amy? Or what if he makes Amy abandon her kids and leaves them with me to raise? Oh, I can't think of that; how horrible."

"Mrs. Willis, can you please tell me more about Amy?"'

Nick looks up from the notebook. "Nice switch, Ryan. I think she would have spiraled much further down that path if you didn't change the subject."

"Yeah, she was starting to move her hands a lot and she, at some point, got up and started pacing. She really is afraid for her daughter and herself. As you were reading I kept thinking that we really need to talk to his grandparents or parents and find out more. I know we couldn't locate them before, but I think we need to pursue that."

"Okay, I'll work on that tonight."

"So will I. Thanks for bringing me my laptop."

"You're welcome." Nick looks down and furrows his brow. "Ah, here is where I left off."

"'Mrs. Willis, can you please tell me more about Amy?'"

"Amy? Oh, yes. Amy is a delight. She is an only child. She was so perfect when she was born that Eddie and I said we could never have another child because no other child could be so perfect. She did everything early, she crawled early, walked early and said her first words at such an early age that it confirmed for Eddie and I that she was the only child we could ever have. She always had excellent grades and perfect teeth and hair. When she took ballet she, well, she was perfect at whatever she did.

"We were surprised she didn't want to go away to a prestigious college but were thrilled that she didn't want to leave home yet. She is kind and likes to help others. She once found a bird with a broken wing and she picked it up and brought it home. We made a home for it and she slept right next to its new nest. When the bird was able to fly again, she took him back to where she found him and let him go. I thought she would have had a tough time with letting him go, but she said he needed to go back to his home where he belongs. She has compassion for anyone hurting. Once there was a baby skunk that looked homeless to her when she was hiking and if her father weren't with her she would have brought that thing home too. It wasn't just animals that she cared for.

"One day she came home from school, I think she was in the sixth grade, and she said that the boy sitting next to her told her that his dad lost his job. She watched him for a whole week and then told us that he doesn't have much food to eat and sometimes he didn't have anything for lunch. Do you know what she did? She started to give him her lunch. I noticed that as soon as she got home from school she was eating nonstop until dinner. This went on for two weeks when she finally told me what she was doing. After that, I made two lunches, and she shared them with him for the rest of that year. His dad did get another job that summer and they moved away. She became pen pals with him then and I think they still write to each other."

"She has a very loving heart."

"Yes, she does. I'm telling you, she is an amazing daughter. It's a good thing we only had one child."

"What is your daughter going to school for?"

"Premed."

"When did she decide to become a doctor?"

"Umm, I'm not sure. We have just always talked about how loving she is and how she would be able to help so many people if she became a doctor. She is so smart. I'm so proud of her."

"Is she excited about being a doctor?"

"Well, why wouldn't she be?"

"It's just a question."

"Yes of course she is! She says it's a lot of work and she studies all the time, but that it's worth it."

"Those are her words?"

"Yes, well, umm, yes."

"How involved are you in the family business?"

"Not very. Eddie handles almost everything. He is such a great provider. I do some of the decorating."

"What is your job, Mrs. Willis?"

"I take care of things around here, of course. I arrange for the maid to come in and clean, and I have several big parties a year that I find the right caterers for and everything that goes into that. It's a lot of work, but it keeps Eddie happy so I'm glad to do it. And of course, I do all the shopping. There are so many things that need to be bought to run a home."

"Okay, do you know how many restaurants Mr. Willis owns?"

"We own 15 or so. I lose track because he buys new ones and sells old ones all the time."

"I can understand that."

"Are we done Mr. Nolsen? I have to get back to work, this house can't run itself!"

"I'm done for now. Is the home number I have for you, the best number for me to reach you at?"

"Yes, it is. Thank you for working so hard to find out who the real Tim is."

"You're welcome, Mrs. Willis. My job is to find the truth no matter what that is."

"Oh, I already know there is something wrong with Tim, so you just need to figure out what it is."

"I'll do my best."

"And that's why we hired you. You have a great reputation."

"Thanks."

"You're welcome. Now I must get back to work, do you mind seeing yourself out?"

"Not at all."' Nick closes the notebook and puts it back in my briefcase.

"Ryan?"

"Uh, yes, Nick."

"Were you sleeping?"

"No, I was only resting my eyes."

"Sure." Nick puts his hand on Ryan's shoulder but quickly draws it back; his normal joking shove could hurt him. "After reading that, I think the problem is with Mrs. Willis. No one is going to be good enough for her daughter. I doubt Amy is ever going to find someone she approves of."

"I agree with you there. What time is it?" I lay completely still, hoping the itch on my calf goes away on its own.

"About 3:30 pm."

"How about we take a little break? I need a nap before dinner and you need to go and talk to Nancy. Can you come back here around 8:30?" The itch is slowly moving around my leg now.

"Sure, I can do that. Rest up, buddy, because we have work to do tonight."

"Yeah, oh, and if you see April please tell I love her."

* * *

Ryan was snoring before the door clicked shut behind Nick. Walking through the parking garage, he tries to remember which level his car was on. Oh, right…it's next to the sign that says '2nd level'. What should he say to Nancy? He doesn't want to settle for this 'friendship only' stuff. After he adjusts his seatbelt, he turns up the radio hoping for some encouragement or wise words.

Swinging into the driveway, he doesn't see Nancy's car. After five or six rings, no one comes to the door. He tries April and Ryan's, and yields the same results. He reaches into his pocket and pulls out his cell to call Nancy. On the third ring, he hears her sweet voice.

"Hello."

"Hi Nancy, I'm at your house now. Are you, by any chance, free to talk? I can meet you wherever you are." He shifts uncomfortably as he waits for her to respond.

"Sure, I'd like that. I'm at Helen's with Lysa. We are helping Helen pack. She's putting her house on the market."

"Okay. I can come over and help." He starts to walk to his car.

"Do you remember how to get here?"

"Yes, I do. Do you want me to pick up any snacks?" He asks.

"No, that's okay. We have plenty here for all of us."

"Oh, good. I'm hungry. I'll be there in a few minutes."

He couldn't get there fast enough. What if she doesn't want them to continue in this relationship or whatever it is they have been in? He needs to clear things up and he'll start with sharing his heart. Man, this is going to be difficult. Pulling into a flower store, hoping that this will help him explain how he feels. There is no way he's going to go to the grocery store and buy flowers from there. He's not going to show his love with cheap flowers that will wilt tonight and be dead by tomorrow.

A wave of different fragrances meet him as he walks around the store, he realizes he doesn't know what type of flowers she likes, but he does know what he wants to say with them! He strides with renewed purpose to the front counter.

"Two dozen red roses, please."

"Sure. Just give me one minute to wrap them up." The petite woman says as she goes to the refrigerator and starts gently pulling out flowers.

He walks around, looking at the variety of loose flowers and arranged ones. Circling back to the counter he can see that his purchase is ready. He pays and makes his way back to his car. Two minutes and he'll see her again. His hands are sweaty and his heart starts to race. He still doesn't have the words to say to her. Hopefully the flowers say a lot. Why is communication so hard? Last time he tried to tell her how he felt, he stumbled over his words. He didn't want to change the status of their friendship to a dating relationship because he thought Nancy needed more time. Now he thinks he let too much time go by. He spots Nancy's car and slowly pulls his car in behind hers. Getting out, he remembers that there are going to be other women around witnessing our conversation. This could get awkward. As he stands up straight, Lysa runs up and hugs him.

"Hi. How is my daddy doing?" She asks.

"He is getting better. He walked to the door and back today."

"Is that good? He used to do that all the time." She looks up at Nick.

"That's good. Tomorrow he will probably do more than that. Each day he will get stronger."

"Oh, that's good. When will he come home?"

"I'm not sure of the exact day, but he should be coming home soon. I can try to find out tonight when I go back." He opens his passenger door and retrieves the flowers.

"Oh, that will be great. Thanks. Can I go with you?"

"Not tonight because I'm going to be there working with your dad, but maybe tomorrow you can visit him. I'm sure he'll love that."

"I'll ask mommy to take me if she is feeling well."

"How is she?" They walk side by side up to the house.

"I don't know. I know that she stayed in bed this morning and Aunt Janice had Aunt Nancy pick me up. They think I don't know, but I'm eight now and I know a lot." She whispers to Nick.

"I'm sure you know a whole lot." Chuckling, he looks around for Nancy.

"I do. Are you here for Aunt Nancy?"

"Yes, do you know where she is?"

"She's right inside. She knows you're here. I wouldn't be allowed out in the front yard on my own. Are those flowers for me?"

"Lysa, you know who they're for."

"I know, Aunt Nancy." Her shoulders lowered slightly.

"Maybe next time I'll bring you flowers." Nick gives her a side hug.

"Would you?"

"Maybe, you'll just have to wait and see."

"Yippee!" She shouts as she skips ahead of him up to the front door. He'd love to be a part of this family; hope it's God's plan. His steps slow as he becomes conscious of the possibility that today could be the end of their relationship. He should have sought her out sooner. Stepping into the house, he sees Nancy standing next to the door, making room for him to enter.

"You look beautiful, Nancy. These are for you." He hands her the flowers but makes no move to hug her.

"Thank you, Nick. They're gorgeous." She smiles broadly at him.

"Not as gorgeous as you though."

"Thanks." She brings the flowers to her nose and takes a big sniff, then sighs. "Would you like to sit down?"

"Sure." Nick does a three-sixty. "Wow, you two have been busy. When did you start packing?"

"We started this morning. Helen decided yesterday to sell the house."

"That's a good idea. This house is quite big for one person."

"And Helen says it's falling apart." Nancy shrugs.

"Where is she?"

"She snuck out the back door and took Lysa down the street to get some ice cream." Nancy sits down on the recliner, leaving Nick no choice but to sit several feet away.

"Ah, good."

"Yeah."

"Nancy…" He starts.

"Yes, Nick." She leans forward but says nothing else.

"I was mad, Nancy, when you said we weren't dating or anything and we were only friends."

"Uh-huh."

"Nancy, I don't know the right way to say this, so I'm just going to say it. I have wanted to give you the time you needed to heal from Phil's passing. I have no idea how long you need and I want to be sensitive to that, but I also want you to know how I feel. I think of you constantly and it hurt so much when you felt we only had a platonic relationship. Nancy, I want to date you. I have such strong feelings for you. You are a special woman and I want to move from friendship to dating if you are okay with that."

"Umm, yes, I'm okay with that." She whispers.

"I don't want to twist your arm or anything." Nick looks into her eyes and wants to kiss her.

"Oh, you aren't twisting my arm. I didn't mean to sound like that. I've liked you for a long-time Nick and I'm thrilled to take what we have into a dating relationship." She smiles.

"Great." Her lips invite him but he holds back.

He pulls her to her feet and into a warm embrace. They stay that way until they hear Lysa skip up the walk chatting nonstop to Helen.

"Thanks for coming over today, Nick. I feel so much better. I've hardly slept since we last talked." They step apart.

Nick leans in for a quick whisper. "Me too. I've missed you too much. Let's never fight again."

"It's a deal." She whispers back.

"Hi, Nick. It's so good to see you." Helen says from the entryway.

"You too, Helen. I'm here to help, so what can I do?"

"Do you mind lifting the boxes and storing them in the garage?" She smiles.

"That works. Better than me packing boxes. If I did, I think you would want to secretly repack them so nothing would break."

Helen chuckles.

"Glad I chose wisely. All the boxes that are closed are ready to go in the garage. I color coordinated them, so if you can make five different piles that would be helpful. Actually, I already labeled the sections in the garage with their corresponding colors hanging in their section."

"Dummy proof, I like that." Lifting the first box, he sees the blue label that says, 'Kitchen' on it. The door leading to the garage groans as he uses his foot to open it all the way. He easily finds the blue sign. As he moves throughout the house he finds red labels for Helen's bedroom boxes, yellow labels for bathroom and linen closets, orange for dining room and living room, and green for guest bedrooms and miscellaneous. As he enters the garage his phone rings. It's tucked deep into his pants pocket. He has two boxes that belong in the yellow section. He delivers them there and pulls his phone out before it stops ringing. He sees it's a call from John. What now?

"What is it John?"

"We lost Tim."

How long ago?"

"About two hours ago. I looked everywhere he normally goes. He's off the grid."

Nick's jaw tightens. This is why the Willises wanted only Ryan and me to do the surveillance. "Go back to his house and wait for him there. When he gets there, call in."

"You're not going to come down?"

"No. Just do what I said." Nick ends the call and pockets the phone. He hears a noise and looks up to see Helen standing in the doorway. He quietly groans. How long has she been there?

"Helen, when did you say you started packing?"

"This morning." She wipes some hair away from her face.

"How did you accomplish so much?"

"Nancy and Lysa have been a huge help."

"Impressive!" Nick's shirt clings to his skin more now than an hour ago when he arrived.

"Thanks, Nick. We have worked hard; maybe we should take a break. Would you like some lemonade?"

"I'd love some."

"Great, I'll get it. Nancy's in the living room, by the way." She says over her shoulder as she makes her way into the kitchen.

"Thanks, I'll see if she needs any help."

The living room is splattered with delicate items and boxes awaiting them. Lysa hasn't joined Nancy so maybe she is still playing with the dolls in Helen's room. She was having a lot of fun making them talk and changing their clothes each time he walked by.

"Hi, Nancy, need help?" She looks up and the glass she is holding slips from her hands, but she makes a quick move and catches it before it hits the floor.

"Why don't we sit down for a bit?" Nick suggests.

"Sure." She moves to the couch. "How is Ryan doing?"

"He was sweating bullets when he had his therapy session earlier today." Nick joins her and wraps his arm around her shoulders.

"What did he have to do?"

"He had to stand up and walk to the door and back."

"Is it normal for him to have that much difficulty?" She leans her head against him, liking the feel of him so close.

"According to his therapist, yes. She said he did very well."

"Good, then. Did she say how long it would take for him to be back to normal?"

"Nope, but I can try to find out when I go back there tonight."

"Okay. When do you think, you'll leave?"

"I was wondering if I could have dinner with you first." He pulls her a little closer and presses his lips to her hair.

"That would be great. I'm still watching Lysa so she would have to come."

"Why don't I go and pick up something and we can all eat here? I know you ladies are on a mission packing, and I don't want to slow any of you down." He removes his arm and starts to stand, instantly missing her closeness.

"Thanks, Nick." Helen steps into the room. "I heard you say you're picking up dinner. I appreciate that. I haven't taken time to figure out what we are going to eat." Helen comments as she hands him a glass of lemonade.

"You mean you don't have everything planned?"

"Haha, Nick, yes, I don't have everything figured out. I've been a little busy." She waves her free hand around the room.

"I'm only joking Helen. I'd love to pick something up. What do you want pizza or subs?" Nick grabs his sneakers and bends to put them on.

"Pizza." Lysa shouts down the stairs.

"Does that sound good to you two?"

"Yes." They say in unison.

"Alright, I'll be back soon."

Chapter 23

He adjusts his blue hooded sweatshirt a bit lower as he approaches the last security camera. Turns his face away and adds a slight limp to his left leg. He doesn't hesitate, but walks casually to his destination. The door opens with a slight sound, but his patient doesn't stir. He wonders how good the hospital staff is. He will find out soon enough. He grabs the IV line with his latex covered hand and the syringe from his pocket. Should he empty it or not? He chuckles. How easy it is to take a life. He finishes and puts the cap back on and pockets the syringe.

He isn't a man that takes unnecessary risks so he gives the person in the bed one more look, places a piece of paper on the food tray, and exits the room, just as quietly as he entered it. A slight smile forms on his face.

Chapter 24

"You look happier then you did an hour ago Nancy."

"Yes, I am. I was expecting a marriage proposal, but he asked if we could start dating. Better than not knowing where we stand but this is a long way off from a ring on my finger." She sighs.

"I'm sorry we didn't have time to talk before he came over, but it looks like you didn't need my advice anyway." She smiles while wrapping a mug in newspaper.

"That's okay. It would have slowed down our production. We really have accomplished a lot today." Nancy takes a second to look around.

"Yeah, we did. You should see the garage. Nick's moving the packed boxes out there really helped me see the progress."

"Helen, do you see me with Nick?"

"Professionally I wouldn't answer that, but as a friend, yes I can see you two being very happy together, just as long as you do your homework."

"I won't forget your homework assignments. I know in the beginning I needed things to go really slow, but now that I know I want to marry him, I don't want to just date. It's funny, isn't it?"

"Yes, it is."

"I guess I don't see the point in dating when I know I want to marry him."

"Maybe he doesn't know yet."

"Oh, yeah, that could be it, maybe he doesn't. I, kind of, thought that when I'm in love with someone the other person would be in love with me as well. Maybe he doesn't love me." Nancy shoulders start to sag.

"I didn't say that. You have waited this long, I think you can wait more. Enjoy your time dating, just keep strong boundaries."

"I remember your talk on dating from a couple of years ago."

"Good. And if you want a refresher, I can print it out. I don't think we packed the printer paper yet." Helen starts to walk to the office.

"Thanks, maybe later. And I packed your printer paper already." Nancy chuckles. "You can email it to me sometime and that would save on clutter in my small apartment."

"Okay, anyway, have you heard from Janice?"

"Not since this morning when she brought April back home after the ER visit. She said April was going to take a nap. I hope that's all she needs. It must be hard for her with Ryan in the hospital. Can you keep a secret?" Nancy puts the set of table clothes in the container and leans over to Helen.

"Of course I can. I do that for a living."

"Right, I think April's pregnant." Nancy whispers.

"She didn't tell you?"

"No, she hasn't told anyone, but I've watched her over the past couple of months and she seems to be. She has been tired lately. I know because she has asked me to watch Lysa. Isn't that great news?" Nancy smiles broadly.

"Yes, but you aren't sure?" Helen adds a couple more table clothes to the pile.

"No, I'm not, but I'm usually not wrong about these things."

"You haven't said anything to anyone else?"

"No, only you. I'm waiting for April to tell me. And she will soon, I just know it."

"That would be great news. So, you think that's what's going on with her?" Helen's eyebrows rise.

"I hope so. Sorry, Helen, I haven't packed a single thing since we started talking."

"That's okay. We've done a lot today. Maybe we should stop and I can work on this tomorrow. Do you think Nick would mind moving the last few boxes into the garage?" She asks.

"Probably not, but you can ask him when he gets back."

My phone buzzes from the table next to me. Picking it up, I see Janice's number. Maybe it's time to bring Lysa home.

"Hi, Janice. How is April doing? Uh-huh…. You took her back to the hospital…. they're running tests…yes, I can keep Lysa for the night.... okay...please call me as soon as you know something...Bye." Nancy sinks into the couch.

"Is everything okay?" Helen wants to know.

"I'm not sure." She pauses, rubs her hand through her hair, and takes a deep breath. "Janice took her back to the hospital after her nap. She said that they're running a bunch of tests. She doesn't want anyone to worry. She also said that no tests results have come back yet, so as of right now there is nothing to worry about. I'm confused; this would have to be more than just a pregnancy."

"Sounds like it to me too." Helen sits next to her.

"She gets her physical every year and she has been healthy every time. I'm not going to worry."

Nick's car pulls up to the front of the house, but Nancy's suddenly not hungry.

* * *

A nurse wheels my gurney down the hallway to get an MRI. There was no more waiting. Right after Dr. Stevens came in and shined a light in my eyes, he told the nurse to take me to get this test. They must have discovered that I'm dying. I feel like I am. I want to see Lysa and Ryan before I do.

"April, we are going to put you in a big donut- like machine. We're going to take some pictures of your head." The technician explains.

"Remember, I'm pregnant." I choke out.

"Yes, I remember."

"Is this okay for the baby?"

"Dr. Stevens ordered it and he knows you are pregnant."

"Okay." That wasn't an answer.

She helps me get situated for the scans. Time goes by as I try not to move or groan from pain. Also, I hope I don't get sick. My toes curl. I try to relax my mind. I wish Ryan were here to hold my hand.

"April, we are going to bring you back to your room now. The tests are done and the doctor wants to do a Lumbar Puncture. He needs to check the fluid in your spinal column. This will help him determine what to do next." She pushes a button on the wall and the doors open.

"What's wrong with me?" I cover my eyes with my arm.

"I don't know, but hopefully the doctor will know soon."

"Yeah."

She drives me back to my room. The doctor and several nurses and maybe other doctors are there as well. No one introduces himself or herself, but Stephanie takes her place right by my head. She starts to explain what's going to happen.

"April, we are going to have you curl into a fetal position on your right side so you are going to face me. I'm going to be right here next to you the whole time. The doctor is going to clean your back and then numb the area. He is going to insert a needle into your spine and remove some of your spinal fluid. The whole procedure should take less than ten minutes, but it will hurt. You can hold my hand and I'll give you a step-by-step explanation as to what the doctor is doing. Okay?" She wipes some hair out of my face and tucks it behind my ear.

"Okay, thank you, Stephanie."

"You're welcome. Your friend Janice is in the waiting room and I'll get her after the procedure is over, after you will have to lie on your back for at least a half hour. I recommend longer though. The doctor is going to start cleaning your back with iodine. It will feel a little cold but painless.

"Now he is going to use a needle to numb your back. This will hurt a bit. You can squeeze my hand if you want April."

I try not to squeeze but fail. I'm glad she told me the truth.

"Now he is going to insert the needle. It will hurt and you will feel pressure."

I feel the needle go in and I squeeze my eyes shut. A tear escapes down my nose and onto the sheets.

"The needle is in and now Dr. Stevens is collecting the fluid. He isn't going to move the needle at all until he has filled the vials."

A nurse behind me let's out a gasp and Dr. Stevens makes an odd noise.

"Stephanie?"

"Yes?"

"What's that noise about?"

"Umm, I'm not sure, but the doctor knows what he is doing. He has performed this procedure hundreds of times."

"Okay, I thought you said this will be over in ten minutes." My jaw hurts from clenching.

"It will be. We are only five or six minutes in, so it's more than half way over. You are doing great." She gently runs her hand over my hair.

"I don't feel great." I cry softly.

"I hope that changes in the next couple of days for you. Here, why don't you blow your nose?" I grab the tissue from her and clear my nasal passage.

"Oh, do that again, April. When you did that, the fluid came out faster. Right now, we are just waiting for enough fluid to fill the vials. It's slow, but we're almost done."

"I think I'll try to nap after this." The pain continues.

"Okay, the doctor is finishing up, only a couple of more drops. There." She pats my hand. "Okay, April, he is going to remove the needle. He's all done. Now Cheryl is going to clean your back and put a Band-Aid on. Then we are going to roll you onto your back. Remember it's best to lie flat for over 30 minutes. Do you want me to get Janice now?"

I nod. She turns and leaves the room. The doctor leaves without saying a word to me. Stephanie returns with Janice.

"How are you feeling?"

"The same. Awful."

She puts her hand gently on my head, and starts to brush my hair back.

"Stephanie, has there been any news as to what is wrong with April?"

"Not yet, the doctor is going to look at her scan now, and we should know more from the lumbar puncture within the hour. Janice, April needs to stay flat on her back for more than a half hour. Please stay with her and make sure she does."

"Okay, thanks, Stephanie."

"Janice?" My voice is barely audible.

"Yes, April?" She leans in close to me.

"There is something wrong."

"The doctor is trying to figure that out now."

"No, I mean, they found something out when they did the spinal tap, but no one would tell me. I couldn't see anything. Can you go and find out?"

"Umm, but I'm supposed to make sure you don't get up."

"I won't get up."

"Okay, I'll see if I can find Stephanie."

"Thanks."

Janice opens the door and is greeted with a bunch of people talking in hushed tones outside the door. Stephanie is right there questioning another nurse.

"What did you see in there, Cheryl?" She puts her hands on her hips.

"There was blood in the spinal fluid."

"Oh, no. She is such a sweet woman and she's pregnant."

"Yeah, I know. Don't get attached Stephanie."

"Too late." Stephanie lets her hands fall to her side.

"I figured that. They are getting a room ready for her up in neurology now. We'll be moving her up there soon." Stephanie looks away.

"Stephanie?"

"Yes?"

"Let's go out after our shift okay?" Cheryl puts her hand on Stephanie's arm.

"Yeah, I'll need that."

"Me too."

Janice comes back into the room and sits down in the only chair. There were a few different conversations going on at once so maybe Janice didn't catch the one I heard with Stephanie. She avoids my eyes, maybe that's for the better. I close mine and try to rest.

Chapter 25

Jill, the physical therapist, sees the man with the hooded sweatshirt leave Ryan's room. He avoids her eyes and rushes down the hall. She stares hard. She was on her way to check on the patient next to Ryan's room, but instead opens Ryan's door. She turns on the light and sees his face is pale. She opens the door and calls out to the nurses' station to hurry and get the doctor. She looks for any signs of blood and doesn't see any. That man did something. What? She looks at his IV and makes a quick decision to pull it out.

A couple of nurses come in.

"Why did you do that? Now I need to put it back in!" The nurse with ducks across her shirt spits out. She picks up the IV, but Jill stops her.

"Look, he hasn't stirred. Something is wrong." The doctor rushes to his side and starts examining Ryan. After a minute, Ryan lets out a groan. His color is improving.

"What happened?" The doctor asked. Jill explained what she saw and what she did.

"It looks like you saved his life, Jill." The doctor bends down and picks up a cap for a syringe. "Whoever you saw put something in his IV. It's a good thing it's on a really slow drip otherwise... We need to run tests and make sure he doesn't have too much of whatever he was injected with still in his system." The doctor pats Jill on the back and starts giving orders. He tells her to wait until the police arrive.

Ryan opens his eyes and groans when he sees Jill.

"No Ryan I'm not here for a therapy session."

"Good, cause my head really hurts." I close my eyes and realize that there is a lot of activity going on around me. "Jill why are there so many people here?"

She explains and I let it sink in that someone wants me dead.

* * *

I call Nick and fill him in on all that has happened. Tests were run and I'm fine, all my organs are in good order and the drug didn't do any damage. Jill saved my life. The police are looking at surveillance footage. Jill gave her best description and Nick told me John lost Tim.

"Hey, Ryan." Nick enters the room, in record driving time.

"Hi, Nick. Have you seen April?" I want to find out about April before we jump into my needing a bodyguard.

"No. She wasn't there when I went to your house. I found Nancy at Helen's house. Lysa was there too. They were helping

Helen pack. She's putting the house on the market." Nick pulls his chair up to the bed and sits.

"That's good. She was concerned about that house. She was thinking it was falling apart, but it seemed to be just a lot of little things were going wrong. Nothing major, really. I hope it sells quickly so she can relax some."

"I don't know if the house will sell quickly, but she packs in super speed. She had everything labeled too. I'm sure that wherever she moves to, she will be unpacked and well organized in a short time."

"How did things go with Nancy?"

"Very well. We are officially dating."

"Umm, okay, I thought you were already dating." I lift up my cup of water and empty it.

"Now I defined it. We never said it aloud, and when Nancy said we weren't even in a dating relationship, I knew I had to do something about it."

"Are you happy with just dating?"

"Maybe we will go out on a couple of dates, and then I'll speed things up. I'm happy that she is ready to be in a relationship with me. I wasn't sure all this time, and now I know. Dating is good." Nick pops open a soda I had sitting on the end table.

"That's great, Nick. Did she mention April at all? I haven't heard from her all day." I push the button that moves my bed to a sitting position.

"No, she didn't. I went out for pizza and when I came back things were a bit bizarre."

"How?"

"Well, Lysa did all the talking."

"That's not bizarre."

"No, I mean, Nancy seemed deep in thought. She didn't say much at all. Actually, neither did Helen but Helen overheard me talking to John so maybe she told Nancy what I said."

"Did you ask them about it?"

"I tried, but Lysa was there. I'm hoping that Nancy isn't having second thoughts. She would tell me, right?"

"I think so. I doubt she is having second thoughts. You're a great guy and she knows that. Maybe she just needs time to adjust or they were trying to figure out who you were talking to."

"I'll call her tonight after we finish up here. So, we can't work too late, okay?"

"Sure, what time is it now?"

"6:30pm."

"Let's get started then. I'm not sure how long I'll last. I didn't get much of a nap."

"So it's official now? Someone is trying to kill you?"

"Seems that way. There will be a police officer at the door tonight so I should be able to sleep." I pull my hand into a fist. If someone else comes in, I can't even defend myself.

"What would you like me to read, Ryan?" Nick picks up the logbook.

"The conversation we overheard between Amy and Tim."

"Let me find it.... Here it is. December 15th. 8:20pm. Coffee Shop, Amy Willis and Tim Stevens sitting together at a table in the far-right corner of the local hang out."

"Ryan, where were you?"

"I was sitting behind them in the corner. I recorded their conversation as I enjoyed a latte."

"Oh, anyway, here goes," Nick settles back in the chair, "'Amy, when is your exam?"

"It's this Friday. I've studied so much; I think I'm ready."

"Ready for you or for your parents?"

"My parents are pushing me to get this degree, but I can see the benefits also."

"If you had a choice, what would you major in?"

"I'm not really sure. I haven't taken the time to figure out what I want."

"Maybe you should. I think it would be sad for you to work in a field you hate."

"That would be sad and frustrating. I'm not sure what I'd like to do, so I might as well keep doing this until I figure it out."

"But will you take the time to figure it out?"

"Maybe, just maybe."

"Are you able to go to the fellowship meeting tomorrow night?"

"I wouldn't miss Campus Crusade for anything!"

"Great. I wasn't sure because of your exam coming up."

"I'm ready. Even if I wasn't, I'd figure out a way to fit it all in. How about you, are you going?"

"Yes, I'll be there."

"Good. So, how are your grandparents doing?"

"They're getting really old. You know I went home over the weekend and they seemed to have aged considerably. My granddad walks with a tiny shuffle now, and my grandma needs her hip to be replaced. It was hard to see them. I think I need to visit more often. It's hard being this far away from them. Oh, and they said they would like to meet you, so maybe on one of my trips home, you could join me."

"That sounds great, how about after finals?"

"Sure. Amy, how are things with your parents?"

"Umm, the same really. They want too much from me. After all, I'm so perfect they refused to have another child because they felt he or she couldn't compare to me. Yikes. I need to forgive them, huh?"

"Yes, you do and probably many more times when different things come up that hurt you. Forgiving can be hard to do."

"Have you forgiven your parents for abandoning you?"

"Yes, but I still have a lot of hurt."

"I'm sure you do. When was the last time you saw them?"

"Umm, let me think? It must have been over a year ago on Christmas. They came into town and stayed with my grandparents. Dad said I'm a man now and mom dabbed at her eyes and said she was sorry."

"I asked her what she was sorry about, and all she did was lower her head into her arms, and shake it. She hugged me too. It was odd. I don't think I've ever seen her cry before, but truthfully I haven't really seen her much to know if that behavior is common or not. In my mind, I call my grandparents mom and dad. When I did that as a child my grandmother corrected me, but she said I was her son. I felt we had a mutual agreement that we both thought it, but didn't say it. I guess it's like I was adopted and I occasionally see my biological parents. I had a happy childhood though. I was well loved and didn't feel like I needed anything. My grandparents taught me to love God, and I know if I weren't raised by them I wouldn't have seen how to do that each day. I'm glad I was raised by my grandparents. Please don't feel sorry for me."

"I don't feel sorry for you. Well, your grandparents' legacy of loving God has blessed my life as well, so I'm glad with you that you were raised by them."'

Nick closes the book and puts it back on the end table. "That's all you have Ryan."

"They got up after that and threw out their drink containers and left the store. I didn't think I needed more. At that point I was convinced the Willis's weird feeling was that Tim is a Christian. I didn't think there was anything more to it. Do you?"

"No, I don't, not until someone tried to kill you twice. We have reviewed everything over the past couple of weeks. I don't think we missed anything. We haven't found Tim's parents. Maybe we can figure this out once we find them."

"Yeah, sounds good. Okay, I'll spend time trying to find them."

"I will too. I have my laptop here; I'll do some research online when I'm awake enough."

"Hey, Ryan?"

"Yeah."

"Has the doctor said anything to you about when you're able to go home?"

"Not yet."

"Lysa misses you."

"I miss her too. I'm not sure it's a good idea for me to go home soon. I don't want to bring danger to them."

"So what else is there to focus on besides finding the parents?"

"I can't think of anything else. We followed Tim around a lot. We attended the Campus Crusade meetings, which were amazing, and we felt he was genuine with his faith and honest about who he is; so no, we can leave him alone now, it's his parents we need to locate."

"Good and yes, it would be nice to be in college again. Free time and an awesome group to hang out with and worship God with too. Can you hand me my pen and notebook?"

"Yeah." Nick hands me the items, along with a sheet of paper.

"I'll see you tomorrow, Ryan." He starts to walk out the door as I open the paper. "Wait!" I say.

Nick comes back, but I don't take my eyes off the note. "What is it?"

"It seems like it's from the person that tried to kill me. It says, 'Now you'll finally listen, Ryan. Nick, you better stay out of this or you will be next.'"

Chapter 26

When Janice came back into the room she left the door ajar. Too many conversations went on at the same time for her to comprehend any of the English spoken. After a couple of minutes one person from the crowd noticed the door and abruptly closed it. April appears to be sleeping, except for the huge furrow in her brow. Does one have pain when they're sleeping? Maybe she's only resting. She's not upset about the door being closed; she wasn't able to formulate any diagnoses from their conversations; closing it hopefully blocks out the noise, so April can sleep.

Blood in the spinal fluid! What does that mean? Is she going to die? Stephanie and Cheryl made it sound like she was. Janice isn't sure what to do. Calling anyone right now would cause a panic and add lots of questions she doesn't have answers to. When April wakes up, maybe Janice will ask her what she wants to do.

A faint knock, and the door opens.

Stephanie walks in, "April is being admitted and I'm going to bring her upstairs to her room. Upon our immediate arrival, she is going to have a procedure called a cerebral angiogram."

"What's that?" April murmurs.

"April, the doctor is going to insert a thin tube into a blood vessel in the groin. The tube is called a catheter, which will be guided to your brain. Once it gets there then an iodine dye is injected into it, this makes the area the doctor is looking at show up clearly on the x-rays."

"Sounds painful." She whispers.

"It is. I won't lie to you April, but I just switched with a nurse upstairs so I can be with you throughout the procedure."

"Thank you, Stephanie. I really appreciate it. Oh." April goes completely still.

"What is it? Are you in pain?"

"The pain hasn't stopped, but the baby just kicked. It's like a little reminder to keep fighting."

"Yeah, I agree. Keep fighting, April, keep fighting." Stephanie says as she adjusts the blanket.

"I will."

"Okay, I'm ready to go."

Stephanie gets behind the bed and starts to push it out the door. Janice grabs her purse and the bag she packed for April. Looking around, she sees she didn't forget anything. Sticking close behind them for fear of getting lost, helps distract her from not knowing the answer to Aprils' problem. Janice knows later she'll regret not paying attention to where they're going, but she's not lost presently so who cares about later.

"Stephanie?"

"Yes, April."

"No Dr. Stevens! If he is going to perform it, I'm going to a different hospital."

"April, don't worry. He isn't performing the exam."

"Good. I don't like him."

"Not many people do." She slams her hand over her mouth and lets out a small groan. "Oops, I shouldn't have said that."

"That's okay. He's arrogant or has experienced some sort of grief he hasn't been able to process."

"His wife died last year and he couldn't save her. It was very tragic. He has become very bitter and quite unpleasant to be around. Before that, everyone loved him."

"He's battling depression."

"Probably."

"Thanks for the distraction, Stephanie. Now I feel sympathy for him, instead of anger. He really needs to go to counseling. Janice, can you pass along Helen's card?"

Looking through her purse, she already knows she doesn't have one, but hopes for it to magically appear anyway.

"Sorry, I don't have one."

"When we get to the room, I'll tell you the number."

"Okay, but I doubt it will do any good. Here we are; your new room."

"Thanks."

As they enter the room, Janice puts their things down on the chair in the corner. April is still lying flat on her back. She hasn't moved since the lumbar puncture.

"April would you like some water?" Stephanie asks.

"Yes and some Chap Stick. It's in my purse. Oh, did I bring my purse?"

"No, but I do have a bag that I threw together for you. Maybe there's Chap Stick in it, but I don't remember packing that."

"I'll get some, I'll be right back." Stephanie says.

"Do you want to try to sit up?"

"No, please find a straw."

Janice slightly adjusts April's head on the pillow and puts the straw into the cup of water. She takes a sip, and relaxes her head back as she closes her eyes. Stephanie returns with the Chap Stick and hands it to April. She has a little trouble getting the cap off and goes a little outside of her lip line but she seems satisfied with the results.

"Sure, and April as soon as they are ready they will take you to the exam room. I'm going to be there too, so you can ask me all of your questions or just hold my hand."

"Okay." April shivers.

"Can I go too?" Janice wants to know.

"No, I'm sorry you can't, Janice, but I'll keep you informed as well. As soon as I can get out to you I will. I'll be back in a minute; it looks like April could use more water." The door clicks, announcing her departure.

"Janice?"

"Yes?"

"I'm afraid. I've never had this done before."

"I'm afraid too." Janice holds April's hand.

"I can always count on you for your honesty. I appreciate that about you Janice. You're such a good friend."

"You're welcome. You're my best friend."

"Mine too." Janice let's a tear fall but doesn't move to wipe her cheek.

"I'm going to help you through this April, whatever this is. I'm not going to leave you."

"Thank you. After this I want you to live your life. For so long you have been helping me live mine, but it's time I let you live yours. I've leaned on you more than I should have. You deserve to be happy."

"I am happy, April. I have enjoyed watching Lysa grow all these years and I wouldn't trade that for anything. I wouldn't trade it, April. Please know that. I have made my own choices and I wouldn't change them either."

"Okay, I've felt guilty and I think you have too because you weren't with me years ago when everything happened. Janice, it wasn't your fault and you didn't do anything wrong. Please know that."

"I've been trying to believe that for years. April if I were there you wouldn't have gotten hurt."

"You don't know that for sure. You couldn't have been with me every second of every day. If it didn't happen that night, it would have happened later. That's the only difference, the time. It was still probably going to happen. Do you believe me?"

"I haven't thought about it that way. Knowing everything we know now, I believe you. I'll need time to process that though."

"Hi, April. I have some water here, with some ice."

"Thanks. Do you know how long I have before the exam?"

"A few minutes, maybe, just relax and we will know more after this exam."

"You think you will have the answer to what is going on with me?"

"I'm pretty sure we will know soon."

"Okay. Thanks, Stephanie."

"You're welcome. I'll be back soon."

"Okay."

"April, do you want me to call anyone now?"

"No, Janice, please wait until after the test. I want to be able to tell them what is wrong with me."

"Okay, I'll wait."

Like a ping-pong match, Stephanie walks back in.

"April, they're ready. Janice, you can wait here or in the waiting room. The cafeteria is still open."

"Thanks."

Stephanie and another nurse wheel April away. April has given Janice a lot to think about. She couldn't have saved her from what she went through all those years ago. All this time Janice has been blaming herself, thinking that if she were with her, none of it would have happened. April is right; she believed those lies. She tried telling her this in the past, but she wouldn't listen. And Janice can't save her from what she is going through today.

God, please heal April. She is going through so much again. I don't know what is wrong, but I know this time that I am not in control and that I cannot save her, but You can. Please help her through this painful exam she is about to have. Please give the doctors wisdom to find out what is wrong and wisdom as to the best way to fix her. Also, please protect the little baby growing inside her. Please keep them both alive.

I'm not sure how to get over my guilt. I've been holding onto it for way too many years. God, please help me believe the truth, Your truth. Thank you.

* * *

People in scrubs walk back and forth preparing the room for the procedure. The seriousness of the situation keeps a businesslike atmosphere. No talking. Clanking of tools greets April's ears. She keeps her eyes closed.

"April, we are going to sedate you. You will be awake, but more relaxed. You probably will not remember much of this."

"Stephanie, should I be afraid?"

"The exam will be painful, but I know you will get through it."

"I mean should I be afraid of the results?"

"Let's wait and see what they find first, if anything at all." She squeezes my hand.

"I overheard them saying there was blood in my spinal fluid."

"Yes, there was."

What does that mean?"

"Well, it could mean that the doctor missed the spot and caused you to bleed."

"Stephanie, do you think that's what happened?" I lift my eyelids open a fraction and see deep sympathy.

"No, Dr. Stevens is one of the best here, and he has never made a mistake with a Lumbar Puncture procedure before."

"So then?"

"Also the blood we found was brown which means you had been bleeding for days."

"In my head, right? I told him when I first came in, I felt like I was bleeding in my head." My eyes close by themselves.

"Right, in your head. Now we are trying to find out what is bleeding."

"Okay and then you can fix it."

"That's what we're hoping for. But I'm not a doctor and I don't know how to read the results so I'm not going to be able to answer more questions about what they find during this exam. You will have a nurse from this unit, neurology. She will be able to answer your questions better than I. But for now, I want you to rest and try to relax. I'll be with you the whole time, and I will not leave until you are back in your room with Janice."

"Thank you, Stephanie."

"You're welcome."

* * *

"Jill, are we almost done with therapy, right?"

"One more lap and then you can sit back in your bed and towel off."

"Can I towel off first?"

"Okay, but next session I want you to push yourself."

"Isn't that what I've been doing?"

Jill chuckles. "Somewhat."

"Really? I feel like I just ran a marathon."

"I know it's hard work, but you will be thankful later."

She hands me a towel and brings me a chair to sit in. This little respite slows my heart to a somewhat normal beat. I push through the last lap and make my way back to bed. Nick and I still have no leads as to where Tim's parents are living. I'm going to need to sleep before I can think about where to look next.

"Jill, before you leave, I have a question."

"Sure, what is it Ryan?"

"Why are we having therapy this late at night?"

"Because it's your lucky day! I work late tonight, and you needed to have therapy again. I have a feeling you will want to be back on your feet soon so I'm here to help you accomplish that."

"Okay, fair enough. Thank you, Jill and thank you for saving my life earlier today!"

"You're welcome. Sleep well. I'll be back in the morning."

"You work too much."

"I know, but I love my job."

She turns off the light as she leaves the room. This is the first day that I haven't talked to April since we have been married. She must be feeling terrible to not call. I tried earlier today, but only got her voicemail and she hasn't responded to any of my texts. I hope I can talk to her tomorrow.

Slowly, I rotate from one side to the other, repeating this every five minutes or so. I can't stop thinking of April. I reach to the nightstand and grab my phone. After five rings and her sweet voice telling me she isn't available, I leave a message. I try Janice and then Nancy.

"Hi, Ryan. How are you doing?"

"I'm okay, Nancy. Have you heard from April?"

"No, I haven't. Janice is with her, but I don't know what's going on?"

"She was at the hospital, but I'm not sure if she is still there." I move my bed into a sitting position.

"I know that part, but she isn't answering her phone."

"Maybe she's sleeping."

"Maybe. I tried Janice also, but she didn't answer either."

"I haven't heard back from Janice yet, either. How about we call each other when one of us hears something?"

"Sure. I'd prefer to talk to April, but I'll take whatever I can right now. It's hard being stuck here in the hospital not being able to move. I'd be driving home right now if I could."

"I know you would. How about you talk to Lysa for a minute before we go back home?"

"Thanks, Nancy."

"Okay, hold on one minute."

"Lysa, daddy is on the phone." I hear Lysa shriek.

"Hi, daddy. How are you feeling?"

"I'm feeling okay. I walked a lot today, so that's good."

"Great, when are you coming home?"

"I don't know yet, but I'll try to get home as soon as I can. I'd like to be there right now with you and mommy."

"Me too. Can you make that work for tomorrow?"

"I don't know yet, but I'll try. I'll keep working hard in my therapy sessions so I can come home sooner." First, I need to find out who is trying to kill me.

"Okay, daddy. You work hard. Do your best."

"I will, Lysa. How are you doing?"

"I miss you and mommy."

"When was the last time you saw mommy?"

"Last night. She was in bed when Aunt Nancy picked me up this morning, but we should be going home soon so I can see her then."

"Good. How about you call me when you see her?"

"Okay, I will. I love you daddy."

"I love you too, Lysa."

I put the phone back on my nightstand, and try to relax. Nancy is going to call me soon. But I know there is something wrong.

Chapter 27

Stephanie did not lie; the angiogram was intensely painful. Stephanie is wheeling me back to my room. There is some type of bag on my groin, I can't remember what Stephanie said it was called or what it is for.

"April, we're back to your room and Janice is here." She pats my shoulder.

"Thanks, Stephanie."

"What now?" Janice asks.

"Now we wait until the doctor comes in. I'm not sure which doctor it will be. Right now, there are two doctors looking at all the results and they will formulate a plan. As soon as they do, they will be in to discuss it with you. Things will move fast so…. oh, hi Dr. Stevens, Dr. Evans. I thought your shift was over, Dr. Stevens." Stephanie steps next to Stevens and tries to whisper that last part.

"No, it's not." He lifts his chin, dismissing her. "April, we have reviewed all of the tests and you have an AVM. Your arteries are as thin as your veins and one burst. Normally, thin arteries are fine; you were born with it and shouldn't have had a problem with it. Have you undergone an enormous amount of stress lately?"

"Yes." I choke out.

"We need to do immediate surgery or you will die."

"What about the baby?" My hands tighten around the sheets.

"First we are going to terminate and then we will work on your brain."

"No!" I yell and immediately grab my head.

"To which part?"

"All of it. I will not have an abortion." Strength fills my voice.

"April, listen, you will die if you don't have the brain surgery."

"I will not have an abortion!" As the words leave my mouth an amazing peace surrounds me. My God is faithful. And I know this is what I need to do.

"April, you will die and your baby will die, if you don't have the abortion."

"I will not have the abortion!"

Dr. Stevens tries several other arguments and each time I repeat myself. I will not have an abortion. As if to confirm, each time I say it, the baby flutters within.

"April, I don't think you are of sound mind right now."

"I will not have an abortion!"

"We'll see about that!" He storms out of the room.

* * *

"She's an idiot! She wants to kill herself. What type of crazy woman would do that?" His hands are moving around at a very fast pace.

"Dr. Stevens you have to calm down." Stephanie says.

"Calm down! She'll be dead in a day or two, or one week, tops. I'm not going to let her make such a stupid mistake."

"It's her mistake to make, Dr. Stevens." Stephanie tries to calm him with a quite tone.

"We'll see about that."

He goes over to the computer and starts typing like a mad man. She isn't sure what he is up to. She thought his shift ended a while ago. When Hannah called in sick a little bit ago, Stephanie took her shift because she didn't want to leave April. Now she isn't sure what it is but she feels she needs to be her nurse for the remainder of her stay here. She knows that isn't physically possible, but she's determined. She will work doubles for as long as she can. She doesn't have anyone at home that will care if she's there or not, and the extra money will help. She grabs a fresh pitcher of ice water for April and walks back to her room.

"April, how are you doing?" She gently puts the pitcher down on the end table and pours some into a cup.

"Not good."

"Here's some water."

"Thanks, Stephanie." Stephanie puts the straw in my mouth. I haven't thrown up in a long time so I drink it all.

"No problem."

"You didn't come back to try to change my mind, did you?" April asks in a reserved voice.

"No, I think you are making a brave choice."

"Stephanie, I know God will protect me and my baby. And if we were meant to die then we will, but I know He is in control and I trust Him."

"You have an amazing faith, April." She places the empty cup on the table and looks around the room.

"God is amazing."

"Yes, He is. You haven't eaten anything since you have been here. I'm going to get you a dinner plate."

"Do you think I'll be able to keep it down?"

"I don't know, but we need to try, you need your strength. It has been a number of hours since the last time you vomited so it's worth trying. Also, you have a saline IV so you should be well hydrated. That will help a lot."

"Okay, I'll try."

"I'll be right back."

Stephanie says as she leaves the room. She's amazed at April's faith. What would she do? She doesn't want to think about that. As she calls the kitchen, she looks around for Dr. Stevens. He no longer occupies the computer. Where did he go?

"Cheryl, where did Dr. Stevens go?" She looks in the office and around the hall.

"I'm not sure, Stephanie. He made a snort, grabbed some papers from the printer and left. Maybe he went home." Cheryl continues to look at the monitor in front of her.

"I hope he went home." But Stephanie had a feeling that wasn't the case.

Each time she goes to check on April, she expects the worst. April seems to be resting now after she ate some of her dinner, which is good. Janice hasn't left her side.

"Stephanie?" Janice's face is etched with fear.

"Yes, Janice."

"I thought April was asleep, but I'm not sure now. Please check to see if something's wrong?"

"April?" Stephanie gently shakes her shoulder. There's no response.

"Let me page the doctor. I'll be right back."

Dr. Stevens arrives before Stephanie takes two steps out of the room.

"What's wrong, Stephanie?" His lips send her a thin smirk.

"I think April is in a coma."

"Let me check."

He enters the room and examines April.

"Yes, she's in a coma." He turns, not saying a word.

"Stephanie, what do we do?"

"Pray, Janice. And call her family." Stephanie says quietly.

"What do I tell them?" Janice gives her a helpless look.

"Explain that April is bleeding in her brain and that she has now slipped into a coma."

"This is really hard. I can't tell her husband that. I can't tell anyone this." Her hand starts to tremble.

"You can do it, Janice." Stephanie grabs her hand and moves her to the chair. "I'll sit right here with you. Maybe you can call a good friend of Ryan's first so that they can go and tell him in person."

"Okay, I'll call Nick and he can go to Ryan."

"That's a good place to start."

Stephanie sits and listens to Janice start to make one gut wrenching phone call after another. She is saving Ryan for last hoping to get support for him first.

* * *

"Which room is Mr. Ryan Nolsen is?"

"He is in room 214b." The nurse says.

"Thanks." He strides to the room. He has a pen and some papers in his hand. He knows what he has to do. He has to save a life today.

"Ryan Nolsen's room?" He says to the officer at the door.

"Uhh, yes. And who are you?" The officer stands taller.

"I'm Dr. Stevens." He holds out his credentials and explains the situation to the officer. The officer steps a side and lets him enter the room.

"Sorry, to wake you, Mr. Nolsen, but it's urgent." He says.

"What is it?" I try to reach the light switch but the man turns it on first.

"Is April Nolsen your wife?" He asks.

"Yes, she is." I push the button for my bed to a sitting position.

"She has been admitted to Albany Med this afternoon. We found blood in her spinal fluid after I performed a Lumbar Puncture."

"Wait." Why is he here? Is he really a doctor? "You're her doctor and you came over here to talk to me?"

"Yes, like I said this is an emergency. Another doctor did an angiogram and we found out that she has an AVM. We discovered that her arteries are as thin as her veins and one burst and now she is bleeding in her brain. We need to perform brain surgery right away, but she is unable to consent because she has slipped into a coma."

"What?" I sit up as straight as I can and start to move off the bed.

"I know this is a lot to take in." He puts his hand on my shoulder to stop me from standing. "But I need you to sign this consent form so that we can save your wife's life."

"Hand it to me!" He says.

Now that is the response Dr. Stevens wanted to get the first time, but it doesn't matter now just as long as he can save her. Ryan signs without reading a word of what it says on the form. He is making this too easy. It doesn't matter, he can save her now, and he will be happy that his wife has survived. He points to the other spots he needs to sign.

"Thank you, Ryan. You have just given us permission to try our best to save her."

"Please keep her alive." A groan escapes my lips. "We haven't even had our first anniversary yet." I sink back into my bed, helpless.

"I'll try my best, Ryan. And I'm the best at what I do."

"Okay."

He suggests I call a friend to come and sit with me.

"I'll have someone call you as soon as she is out of surgery."

"Thank you."

The doctor races out of the room, hoping he isn't too late.

Chapter 28

Janice wipes a cool cloth over April's forehead. Stephanie has come in and out of the room multiple times, she doesn't do much, but she checks on April each time. Both ladies are nervous. The door opens and they both stop what they are doing and stare at the man who fills the doorway. He moves to the end of the bed and starts to push April toward the door.

"Where are you taking her, Dr. Stevens?" Stephanie puts her hands on her hips and squares her shoulders.

"I'm going to save her life." He grunts at her.

"How?"

"She needs to have an abortion, and then go up to surgery."

"But she said no to an abortion."

"Yes, Stephanie she did, but when she went into a coma, I went to her husband and he signed the papers." Dr. Stevens smirks.

"You did what?" Janice yells.

"You heard me just fine! Now if you will both excuse me; I have a life to save!"

"Wait. Let me see those papers." Stephanie demands.

"They've already been filed; you can go look yourself."

Stephanie makes her way out to the nurses' station to find the paper, while Janice makes a phone call. Opening it up she sees that the papers are all there and they are signed. What should she do now?

She needs to go back to the room and follow Dr. Stevens. There must be something she can do. She told April she wouldn't leave her.

"Ryan, did you sign papers that says April can have an abortion?" Janice asks. Her voice shakes.

Stephanie was standing a few feet away, but there was no missing his response, 'what?' rang clear.

Stephanie didn't have time to listen because Dr. Stevens has already made his way down the hallway; and Stephanie needed to catch up.

* * *

"What do you mean April's pregnant?"

What is she telling me? I just signed papers to save my wife, but kill my baby?

"Yes, she's 4 months along and she has been longing to tell you, but she first wanted to make sure things were fine with her body carrying the baby and that the baby was okay. I only just found out myself because I took her to the hospital. She was so distraught because you didn't know."

"Okay, Janice. What did April want?" My back and neck tense and pain shoots throughout my body.

"April didn't want the abortion. She wanted to wait until after the baby was born to have the brain surgery. She said she knew God was going to make everything okay."

"What did I do?" I sink back into the bed.

"Well, Dr. Stevens came in, and is taking her to get the abortion now."

I couldn't say anything; we just kept the phone to our ears without speaking. We both know the other is praying and that is all we can do. I have no control. I'm helpless in this bed. I can't go to my wife. I can't hold her hand and let her know I'm there with her because I'm stuck here.

* * *

Dr. Stevens has gone mad. Stephanie has never seen him do something like this before, and he certainly doesn't know how to steer a gurney. He hit a wall two turns ago, and now he ran into another bed that was stationary in the hallway.

"Where am I going?" My mouth moves, but my eyes are too heavy to open.

"April, is that you talking?"

"Yes, Stephanie, where am I going?"

Dr. Stevens stops pushing. Stephanie glances up at him, but doesn't let him intimidate her.

Stephanie leans down to me. "Dr. Stevens was taking you to have an abortion."

"I said no to that." I say.

"But your husband said yes when he signed the papers." Dr. Stevens spits out.

"Did you inform him that I was pregnant?" I open my eyes and look right at the doctor.

"No, I thought he knew."

"No, Dr. Stevens, I haven't told him yet."

"It doesn't matter, you still aren't of sound mind. You can't make that decision." He starts to push the gurney.

"Yes, I can and I just did. And I bet you didn't tell Ryan you were going to perform an abortion when you handed him the papers to sign." I turn my head toward Stephanie, "Stephanie, please take me back to my room."

"Sure, April. My pleasure!"

Dr. Stevens storms off again. Stephanie just witnessed a miracle. This baby was meant to live. Stephanie can't believe what just happened. Wait, she does believe it! A miracle!

Stephanie takes April back to the room. Janice is sitting with her head down, and phone to her ear but no words are coming out of her mouth.

"Stephanie, you brought April back?" Janice chokes out.

I can hear a voice on the phone.

"I'll put you on speaker, Ryan. Please explain, Stephanie."

"April woke up and said that her husband didn't know she was pregnant, and that she was of sound mind to make the decision herself. A miracle, I just witnessed a miracle." Stephanie says excitedly.

"April?"

"Yes, Ryan?" My brow furrows.

"I love you."

"I love you too and I'm so sorry I didn't tell you." My breathing starts to speed up.

"That's okay. How are you feeling?"

"I'm hurting, but I'm glad that our baby is safe now." I take a deep breath.

"Me too. I can't believe it! I need to see you."

"That would be wonderful." I say.

"I'll see what I can do. Maybe I can get transferred to your room."

"I don't think that will work, but after all that has happened today, it wouldn't be a bad idea to ask." Stephanie says. "Let me see what I can do."

"Thanks, Stephanie."

My baby was on its way to leave this world before he or she even entered it but instead a miracle happened and a heart continues to beat. *Thank You, God!*

Chapter 29

Ryan is still alive. He didn't want him to die but he did want him to suffer and because that woman went into his room right after he left, Ryan didn't suffer. He did hear that Ryan would have died if she didn't go in the room. Next time he should research how much of the drug to give him. He didn't even remember the name of the drug. Oh, well. He did what he was told to do. Followed orders so he'll get paid. He picks up the drink he had finished a minute ago and realizes he needs another one. He stumbles off the worn couch and makes his way to the fridge.

Chapter 30

The next day a flurry of doctors and nurses look me over. I feel like I'm on some display. It feels like they are all saying, "this is rare and whatever you do be gentle, because she is about to die." I also get the impression of many people disapproving of my decision. Fortunately, Stephanie has been with me the whole time. I sent Janice home late last night. She didn't want to leave, but I made her go check on Lysa. I hope she slept more than I did. As I'm about to close my eyes, in walks another lab coat.

"Hi April. My name is Dr. Guiley. I'm a neurosurgeon. I have reviewed your chart and have seen that you have an AVM, which means you have arteries that are shaped like veins. It is very rare for people to survive after one has ruptured and from what I've read in you file, you want to carry your baby to full-term?" He lifts his left bushy eyebrow as he says the last part.

"Yes, I do. I have a peace about my decision. I know it is my right to make this decision." My hands start to move as I talk. "I was very upset to discover that Dr. Stevens tricked my husband into signing papers. My husband didn't even know I was pregnant."

"April, please calm down. Dr. Stevens is on probation and he will no longer be working on your case or anyone else's until he has been cleared to do so. We are deeply sorry for what happened to you and I hope you can please forgive him. Dr. Stevens sends his apologies as well." The new doctor pats my arm.

"Okay, it is reassuring to know that he is no longer in the building. I might be able to sleep better."

"How are you feeling today?"

"About the same. Severe headaches. I'm vomiting less though so that's good." I shut my eyes.

"I'm limited in what I can do for you, but we do have a plan. We cannot operate until your baby is born so we are going to keep you here in the hospital until you are about 23 weeks. We would like to take the baby at 25 weeks, and after that, rush you up to surgery."

"The baby won't be ready to come out then. I'm waiting until he or she is full-term."

"April, please listen to me, you cannot have this baby vaginally. You have to have a C-section. Labor will kill you." He shifts his weight and shuts his mouth. I know he was going to say that the pregnancy will kill me first but I'm glad he closed his mouth. He cannot change my mind.

"I'm hearing that a lot lately, but I'm not dead yet. I do agree that I should have a cesarean section but not at 25 weeks."

"We can't chance you going into labor either. How about 36 weeks?"

"Full term is between 38 to 42 weeks so I will wait until 38 weeks." I state.

"April, you are a stubborn woman, but I admire your strength. 38 weeks we will deliver but not a day later."

"Thank you."

"Shortly after surgery we will schedule your brain surgery."

"Oh, no. I have to have some time with the baby. He or she will need me. I'll wait a couple of months first. I need to spend time bonding with my baby!"

"April, you know you are taking many risks with your life here, right? I think you should discuss this with your husband."

"Yes, but please understand I can feel this baby inside me. I know that he or she is alive and there is no way I'm going to kill him or her. I can't do that. This baby deserves life, a fighting chance. And that is what I'm going to give him or her. I don't mean to be disrespectful. I know you are a great doctor, and I know you have said that my chance of survival is slim, but please know that I have to do this. This life inside me is much too important. This baby was meant to live." That speech takes all of my energy.

"Okay, April, please know that I will do everything I can to support you in this. I have told you and your husband that the survival rate is very small. I'm surprised you are still alive. It's your low blood pressure that has kept you alive up until now."

"I'm not surprised that I'm still alive."

"That's good. Anyway, we will keep you here in the hospital until you are 23 weeks. Then you can go home and rest. That's it, just rest. Complete bed rest. If you think labor is starting, you are to call these numbers immediately."

He hands me a paper with three different phone numbers on them.

"I'll put this up on my fridge."

"If you make it to 38 weeks, we will have the section then, but if labor starts before then, then we will have to have the surgery earlier. Any questions?"

"No. Oh wait, how far along am I exactly? I think I'm 18 weeks."

"You are 18 weeks and 5 days, anymore questions?" He looks at his watch.

"You aren't lying to me, right?"

"No, April, I will not lie to you."

"Good. I don't have any more questions."

"I'll be in to see you almost every day for the next few weeks so you can ask any new questions then."

"Okay. Thank you."

He squeezes my arm and walks out. Stephanie walks in.

"Don't you ever sleep?"

"Not when you're here." She says.

"Huh?"

"I know I'm meant to be your nurse and for as long as I can be, I will be."

"Thanks, Stephanie; that means a lot."

"You're welcome."

"You still need to sleep." She says as she turns off the lights.

"I will."

"Good, oh, and you won't be any help to me if you don't get proper rest. How about you sleep when I do?"

"I could do that."

"Great. Stephanie, you're an angel."

I think I said it aloud, either way it was the last thought I remember.

Chapter 31

They're all on a counting schedule; it's now week 20 of April's pregnancy. Janice has moved into April and Ryan's house, and she takes care of Lysa after she gets home from work. Ryan is coming home tomorrow and then she'll move in with Nancy. Nancy watches Lysa during the day when she doesn't have school. They all take turns while April is at the hospital. Her mom and Ella have been back from vacation for a couple of weeks, so they take turns at the hospital as well. Each day is stressful. April is still in a lot of pain. She has three more weeks before she comes home. Everyone is hopeful as they anxiously wait for that day.

Lysa is counting down the days and she is excited that she is going to have a baby brother or sister. She has picked out names and wants to be a part of the naming process. Janice took her shopping yesterday and they had fun picking out some adorable clothes. Lysa found some sleepwear in pink and some in blue. She insisted that Janice buy them both. She insisted that the baby would need to be properly dressed when he or she comes home from the hospital and she was going to provide the right clothes. She also said she wanted Janice to take her because she loves her style; bright and lively Lysa said. She's really like sunshine through this storm, for everyone. Her cheery attitude puts a smile on all of their faces, and they all want to be the ones to take care of her. Most afternoons, the house is filled with Nancy, Nick, Agnes, Ella, and Janice. Sometimes Ryan's parents come over too. Ryan's mom will be staying here when Ryan comes home. Janice thinks it's a way they can all feel like they're helping.

Their house has been scrubbed and the lawn has been groomed, all in anticipation for Ryan's arrival. He is doing a lot better. He is walking well and with little difficulty. He can't lift anything heavy for a few more months. He stayed at the hospital longer than expected because his doctor said he needed to. Therapy was working so well so he didn't seem to complain too much. He wants to be as strong as he can possibly be. Once he found out he was having a baby, he found a new strength. That and Janice thinks he has seen that he might be the baby's only parent, hopefully only for a little while. He knew leaving the hospital would make him have to find a new therapist and he also didn't think he would allow himself the time for the therapy he needed. They all agreed it was the best choice to stay, but they're ready for him to come home to.

Washing the kitchen counter, Janice starts to hum. A doorbell chimes in and Lysa runs to answer it. They aren't expecting anyone, well, anyone that would ring the bell, so Janice follows only a couple of steps behind.

"Doug, this isn't a good time." Janice says.

"I don't think any time is a good time, but I wanted to find out how everyone is doing."

"Lysa, can you go on up and visit with Aunt Nancy?"

"Sure." She puts on her sandals and races up to Nancy's door.

"Janice, I know you don't want to talk to me and frankly I can't blame you. I know I haven't explained myself for my actions and I can't right now either. I know I miss you and I was wondering if we could start over as friends."

She crosses her arms. "You hurt me deeply, Doug."

"I know and for that I'm sorry. Really, sorry! I never wanted to hurt you." He leans against the doorframe and looks at Janice with sad eyes.

"Yeah, well, that's too late. Will I ever get an explanation?"

"Maybe, I hope so."

"I'll admit it is really hard to talk to you right now. I'd like to just close the door on your face, but the truth is my not forgiving you is hurting me more than you and I'm tired of holding on to it." Sighing, "I forgive you, Doug."

"Thank you."

"You're welcome. I don't want to be your friend, but I need one right now so why don't you come in and we can sit and talk."

"Great." Doug follows her in. He keeps an appropriate distance. "So what would you like to talk about?"

"How is your job going, Doug?"

"It's going well. I got a promotion two months ago. It's still hard work, but I really enjoy it."

"That's good."

"How about you, Janice, how is your job going?"

"It's just a job. I don't enjoy administrative work as much as I used to. I like helping people. I'm thinking of going back to school to become a nurse." She says as she pulls out a kitchen chair and sits. Doug does the same.

"I can see you doing that. That's a great idea."

"Yeah, I don't want to go back until I know things are well with April."

"You can only help so much, Janice. And from what I saw, there's lots of help. Maybe you should start school sooner than later."

"I don't know. I'll think about it." She removes her glasses to rub her eyes and Doug sees dark circles under her eyes.

"Good, I think you have spent too much of your life trying to help April live hers."

"I've heard this too many times." She starts to get up, but Doug puts his hand on top of hers.

"I'll stop. I like your colorful top."

"Thanks."

"I also like that you matched it to your eye glasses and hair tie."

"You noticed?" Her eyebrows rise.

"Yes, I've noticed most of your tastefully chosen outfits. You have a rather unique and exquisite style."

"Thanks, I think."

"It was meant as a compliment."

"Ok, thanks then." She shrugs.

"Umm, Janice can I have a glass of water?" Water? Did he just ask for water?

"Sure, don't you usually drink Pepsi?"

"I used to. I like water now."

The whole time they were dating he always drank Pepsi. Maybe he knows that April and Ryan wouldn't have that in the house. Why is he here? She knows it's not because he likes her. She made it clear that she still wanted to date and he made it clear that he didn't. Why did she invite him in? Because she's a fool and she misses him, that's why. It's getting late. She should send him home and get Lysa ready for bed.

"Do you want ice?" She asks.

"Sure." Doug says.

She assembles a plate of fruit and vegetables that were left over from dinner and she hesitates. He doesn't like fruit and vegetables. Maybe it is better that they broke up. He was like a clam for the last month or so of their relationship and they don't eat the same foods. He thinks grease is a food group. She's sure if she thinks about it, she could find many other things they don't have in common.

"That looks great, Janice." Doug says breaking into her thoughts.

"Uh, thanks. I realized you don't like fruits and vegetables. Sorry. I eat healthy now. I've made a huge diet change and, and…" She turns with the plate toward the table then turns back to go and put it back on the counter.

"It's okay, Janice. I'll try one of everything." She turns back to the table and places the plate on the table.

"You don't have to try any of it."

"I want to."

"Okay." Wow, this is awkward. "I need to have Lysa come home so she can start getting ready for bed."

"Oh, okay, I can leave."

"Well, how about we eat and then you can leave. Excuse me a minute while I call Nancy and get your water."

He nods while looking over the plate. It's like he has never seen produce before. Did she say that aloud? She hopes not. He hasn't looked up, so she thinks she's in the clear.

She steps into the kitchen and sends a text to Nancy, who immediately responds.

"Nancy said she was really tired. She fell asleep after they had a snack." Janice looks up from her phone. She hands him his water. Now how does she get him to leave? "She has done an amazing job handling all the changes around here."

"Does she go to the hospital much?"

"Yes. We all take turns taking her. After school, she goes and visits Ryan first and then whoever is driving her goes straight to the other hospital so she can spend time with April. It fills the days. She insists on doing homework in the car because she doesn't want to miss any time with her parents. I've talked to her teacher a couple of times so far and it seems that she is keeping up in class and she has only missed an occasional assignment."

"That's great."

"Yes, she's a responsible kid." Janice smiles and helps herself to some fruit.

"How have you been keeping up with work?"

"I'm still getting my job done, but I haven't stayed extra to do the last-minute stuff that I used to do. My boss understands and I think he has realized even more how much I do that he never asked me to do but expects to be done."

"I'm not surprised that you go above and beyond what you are asked to do."

"I see a need and if I can fill it, I do. But right now, being here is where the need is and so I don't do as much as I used to do at work. And that's okay. How is your job going?"

"It's good. A couple of new guys started so that has changed the dynamics a bit."

"Do you still like the job?"

"I do, yes." He places his hands together on the table in front of him.

"Good." She lets out a yawn. She isn't sure how to convey that he should leave. She doesn't want to open up her heart to him again because she knows he doesn't want a relationship but she also wants to talk to him because maybe this will be their last conversation together. He should leave. He takes a cucumber and pops it into his mouth. She thinks that would be the best thing for both of them even though she still doesn't know why he came over to begin with. She uncrosses and re-crosses her legs as she tries to decide what should happen next.

"Well, I guess is time for me to go. It was great seeing you, Janice."

"Yeah, it was interesting Doug."

He reaches out like he's going to touch her arm then pulls his hand back quickly. She gets up and walks in front of him to the door. His shoulders slouch. He gives a little wave and closes the door behind him.

Chapter 32

The air conditioner kicked on, sending a blast of cool air into Janice's face. Normally she would have welcomed the refreshing air, but today it only made her cold. She grabs her sweater from the back of her chair and continues to stare at her monitor. Something wasn't right with the numbers. She remembers what the end balance was from when she reconciled for the month of April, but for some reason the number isn't the same. She goes over to the filing cabinet and pulls out the papers she filed for the past six months. She pulls out November and sees that everything is in order. December looks fine also. The front page for January isn't right. That is supposed to be the second page. Someone has been leafing through her files. She corrects the order and looks at the end balance. She can't remember back that far, so it could all be correct but why would someone change the order? She starts to look over February.

"Janice, here are some of the business receipts for May." Her boss hands them to her, glances at what she has on her desk, and abruptly walks away.

He has always treated her well over the years. Sometimes he barks orders at her, but most of the time they have had a good working relationship. She stacks the reconciled months together and puts them on top of the file away pile. She'll get back to that later. She needs to enter the receipts now. Maybe they will help explain last month's problem.

"Janice, I'm going to get a cup of coffee from across the street, do you want one?" Patty sweetly asks.

"Sure, I'd love one; the usual, please. I feel like my brain needs a jumpstart and this air conditioner is a nuisance today. Thanks." Janice reaches into her overstuffed purse and produces a $5 with amazing speed.

Patty answers the phones most of the day but when she steps out Janice takes over. They have worked side by side for six years now. Both single but that's about where their similarity ends. Patty wears her hair straight and the color has never changed. Janice has something new each month. Patty prefers earth tone colors and Janice wears anything that shouts. It makes her happy.

She enters the receipts and puts them away. She pulls her sweater tighter and sighs. She has been at this job for too long. It's time she finds something she enjoys doing. She used to enjoy this but the excitement is gone. She learned the job years ago and she does it well, but some of the monotony has sucked the fun out of the job.

* * *

Doug rushes into the meeting. Several sets of eyes follow him. His coffee starts to spill out of the top of his mug, so he quickly puts it to his mouth, hoping to capture most of the needed caffeine. His boss is at the white board. He points to the picture in the middle.

"This woman is who we think is behind the multi-company heist."

Doug groans as he looks at whom he points to and pulls a chair out for him to sit in.

His boss points to several company names. "These are the companies that have been robbed. We're hoping this list doesn't get longer. They have all reported large amounts of money missing from their accounts over the span of this last year. The job was hidden well but when one company figured out what was happening, they called their sister company who discovered the same entries were in their records as well. This started a chain of calls and later we became involved.

"There are several reasons why we think this woman, Janice Myers, is behind all of this. She works for the company that handles all of these companies billing. She is the woman that has access to all of their accounts and her boss believes she has been acting strange over the past few months. Asking for time off when she never took off before in previous years. She has cut back her hours considerably. We think she is getting ready to leave the country. She hasn't been home in two weeks as far as we can tell, but she is going to work. She might be suspecting that we are watching her.

Doug, can you play your recording from your last visit with Janice last night?"

Doug puts his coffee down and slowly pulls out his phone. He presses play and Janice's voice fills the room. Everyone quiets and listens to his exchange with her from last night. When she talks about switching jobs, Doug glances at his boss whose smile broadens. He thinks he has the culprit. A few colleagues chuckle when the conversation turns a bit personal. They all know about his relationship with Janice. Some think, including his boss, he set it up so that he would be in line for the promotion he received, but that wasn't the case. No one would believe him either so he has kept quiet. Janice says goodbye and he pockets his phone. There was nothing incriminating in their conversation, but it doesn't matter. He already betrayed her.

His mind drifts to how he is going to get himself out of this mess. His boss continues to strategize with the other people in the room. Doug has nothing to add. He doesn't know what to do.

"So Doug, it's your day for guard duty at the hospital today." His boss assigns tasks to three other people. One of them is to keep track of Janice. He feels sick. What a mess.

* * *

Doug plants himself in the chair in front of Ryan's hospital door. The physical therapist goes in and thirty minutes later comes out. Nick arrives after that. Doug signs them in and out. Boring! He should be focusing on how to figure out who is trying to kill Ryan but he is too distracted.

I open the door and peak my head out.

"Hey, Doug. Can you do your job in here instead of in the hall?"

"Sure." He says as he grabs his chair and follows me inside.

"Good, we are stumped and need some help." I walk back to my bed. My movements are deliberate as I think about each step but I walk much better than the last time Doug was on guard duty. Doug volunteered for it. He was becoming a friend and he wanted to help keep me safe! Doug scans the room, closes the door behind him, and locks it.

"Ryan, any thoughts on who put you here in the hospital?" Doug leans back in the rigid metal chair.

"I only have one active case. All of my other ones are closed and I have one I work on for personal reasons but that one has been ongoing for several years and presently it's at a standstill with no current leads so I've concluded that it has to be someone from my present case but we were ready to close it when I was injured. We were wondering if you could give us a fresh perspective." I know he will say yes. He has done guard duty before and since there hasn't been any action in days, Doug is looking for something to do.

"Sure, what is the case about?" Doug pulls out his laptop, ready to take notes.

Ryan and Nick go back and forth explaining the case.

"...and so the Willis's want us to still follow Tim when we can't find any reason for it."

Doug's head snaps up from looking at his laptop. "Did you say Willis? As in Edward Willis?"

"Yes." Nick says.

"Well, now this is interesting." Doug crosses his legs in front of him and rubs his chin.

"What do you know that we don't, Doug?" I lean forward.

"I know that the Willises own several restaurants and small companies throughout the East coast."

"Yes, we know that too." I sigh. That wasn't helpful.

"I also know that someone has successfully stolen hundreds of thousands of dollars over the past year from some of these companies."

"What?!" I lift my head fast and feel a twinge in my back, but I ignore it.

"Why would Mr. Willis keep this information from us?"

"I'm not sure about that. It was a dumb move for them to hold that from you. You would have handled the case differently knowing what was going on, but you must have hit a nerve since someone is trying to kill you. Who have you looked at?"

"Tim." Nick says. "But we really think he hasn't done anything. He goes to the bank a lot but his bank account has only had small ups and downs. Nothing that would indicate he was involved."

Doug closes his eyes for a second. I can tell he has more to say so I wait.

"Ryan can I see your log book?" Doug asks. Nick passes it to him. Not what I wanted to hear but there's still time. I know he already told us information we weren't supposed to hear. The Willis's are being robbed. And I didn't know this. How did I miss that piece of information? It's a good thing I'm closing shop; I botched this case. What else did I miss?

"Ryan, Nick, you couldn't have known what was going on in his company. He didn't even know. One of his accountants saw an inconsistency and followed it. From there other companies were looked at and other number inconsistencies were found. The receipts and bills all seem legit though so there is a lot more work to do."

"Who are you guys looking at?" I ask.

Doug grimaces. "I can't tell you that but I will say it would be beneficial to all of us if we started working together to find the person or persons responsible. I don't want the wrong person to take the blame."

Chapter 33

Her blinker turns off, alerting her to the evening plans. She parks in a spot far away from the church doors. The parking lot is full again for Helen's second talk. A quick glance at the clock confirms she is running late; about five minutes. Hopefully Helen hasn't started yet. She grabs her purse and cell phone, and then slams her car door. The wind has picked up, but the rain hasn't started falling. She sets her car alarm, and stuffs her keys into her pants pocket.

She was going to miss tonight because of everything happening with Ryan and April but she wants to support Helen and learn from her as well. When Janice volunteered to watch Lysa, Nancy decided to go. The door opens when she pulls on the handle. Applause greets her as she steps in. Helen must be starting. Rushing forward, she unzips her purse and rummages for her phone. She silences it and finds a seat in the back. So many women loved what Helen had to say that they voted to not wait a few months for her to come back. The feedback from the first talk said they wanted a conference series and so here they are again so soon after the first time.

* * *

"Hello, ladies! I'm so excited to be here again. Last time we talked about how God finds us beautiful and how we need to no longer believe the lies like, 'Your nose is too big or your chest is the wrong size,' or 'your thighs shouldn't rub together when you walk' or 'I shouldn't have hair there.' All right, the last one comes with age so if you are younger than I am, you haven't experienced that one yet.

"For those of you who weren't here last time, I shared about how two years ago I lost my husband of 10 years. I won't lie; these past two years have been the hardest of my life. Tonight, I have to share from my heart. Life is short. I know not all of you are married but at some point, you might be. If you aren't married, you can substitute a loved one where I say husband. You don't know when your time with your husband will be over. For me it was too short and I hope it isn't that way for anyone else in this room. In saying this, I believe I need to share something. In Philippians, it says…. 'The Lord is near. Do not be anxious about anything but in everything with prayer and petition, with thanksgiving; present your requests to God.' The part of the verse I want to focus on is 'with thanksgiving'. There is much to be thankful for but many of you, I'm sure, wouldn't be thankful for things like his facial hair in the sink or his dirty clothes on the floor." Chuckles emerge.

"I want you to think about the things that you are thankful for about your husband. You should have received a paper when you came in and if you didn't please raise your hand and someone will bring one to you. There are pens in the seat backs in front of you. Please grab it and write down five things that you are thankful for about your husband." Helen waits a couple of minutes.

"Now I want you to put it away and share it with your husband later. I have something I need to tell you. Please listen carefully. I miss so many things about my husband but there are a couple of things I really miss, like I mentioned before, his hair in the sink and his clothes on the floor. These things symbolized his presence. They were everyday reminders that he lived in the same house as me. If he left for work before I got out of bed, when I went into the bathroom I could see little signs that he was the-r-e." Her voice cracks a little.

"I miss seeing his clothes. I miss doing his laundry. Ladies, most of you here have an opportunity today that I lost two years ago. You have your husband present. Please stop trying to change him and start enjoying him. Flirt with him; don't nitpick on something he forgot to do. Be thankful for him. When you see those things that he does, that annoy you so much; thank God that your husband is there to do them. When you see the…, you fill in the blank; thank God that your husband is alive!

"Now I know there are some of you who are not in a good marriage. Some of you would say that your situation is really bad and abusive. If you are in a place where you are not safe, you need to leave and seek wise Christian counsel immediately. For those of you that are going through a rough patch, and I believe all marriages will at some point, know this: the words before the verse that say, 'Do not be anxious about anything,' reads, 'The Lord is near.' Please know that and say it when times are rough. The Lord is near! And I just want to say again that if you are going through something rough in your marriage, please don't keep it a secret. Seek wise council."

She talks for several more minutes on marriage.

"In closing, when you drive home tonight, I want you all to do something. I want you to think. Think back to when you first met your husband. Think back to how you felt when you were dating him and remember. Spend the car ride remembering. Thank you." She walks to the back of the room and sees Nancy waving to her. A line starts to form. Nancy stops by Helen and gives her arm a quick squeeze.

"You were great tonight, Helen." Nancy smiles.

"Thanks." Helen looks at her and she can see how hard tonight was for her. The line continues to grow so Nancy gives her friend a quick hug and says a silent prayer for her night. She gets in her car and sees she has just enough time to make it home before Nick shows up for dinner. I hope the crockpot worked some magic.

*　*　*

"This is nice, Nancy, and it tastes really good. Thanks for cooking tonight."

"Not a problem. I like to cook."

"I can tell; you have a gift." Nick shifts in his chair.

"Thanks." Nancy notices Nick tense.

"Nancy, we have been dating for a while but now and..."

"Aunt Nancy? Aunt Nancy where are you?"

"Oh, sorry, Nick, hold that thought." Nancy gets up and walks to the top of the stairs.

"Yes, Lysa I'm right up here." She says.

"Guess what, Aunt Nancy? My Mommy's coming home soon." Lysa yells up the steps.

"Yes, she will be home in two days. I can't wait either."

Lysa runs up and hugs Nancy.

"Daddy says we are going to pick her up in the morning so we don't have to wait all day sitting around knocking our knees together or something like that."

"Sounds like a good plan."

"Hi, Nick. I didn't know you were here."

"Yes, Aunt Nancy cooked dinner for me and it was delicious."

"Oh, why didn't you have dinner with us?" Lysa wants to know. "Daddy's home now and Aunt Janice cooked and grandma and granddad were over too."

"Oh, sorry we missed them."

"Anyway, aren't you excited?" Lysa looks at Nick, waiting for an answer.

"Very excited. Your mom is doing well."

"She is! And so is the baby. I can't wait to be a big sister."

"I think you are going to be a great big sister."

"I better be; I've been practicing with all my babies. I change their diapers and I feed them and I change their clothes too. Aunt Janice practices too. She said the last time she changed a diaper was when I was wearing them and we all know that was a very long time ago."

Nick and I give each other a look.

"So anyway, when are you two going to have a baby? I've been practicing and…"

"Lysa, first we have to get married, but right now we are only dating…" Yikes! She tries to explain, when Nick touches her arm.

"Nancy, before Lysa came up I was saying something about how we have been dating for only a little while but," he puts his hand in his pocket as he gets down on one knee. "Nancy, I love you and I have loved you for a very long time. I will be the happiest man alive if you, umm, will you marry me?"

"Really?" Her hand flies to her mouth. She doesn't say anything for a few seconds. She looks at Nick and sees the love in his eyes. "Yes! I've been wanting to be your wife for a long time too."

"Really?" He questions.

"Really!"

"So I could have asked you sooner?" He opens the box and shows her the ring. Nancy gasps.

It's beautiful and yes, you could have asked much sooner."

Nick pulls the ring out of the box and puts it on her finger. She pulls her hand to her face and examines the gorgeous ring. Nick stands up, and pulls her in for a wonderful kiss.

"Yea!"

"Lysa?" Nancy asks, but doesn't pull back from Nick's embrace.

"I'm screaming happy screams. I'm going to go tell daddy." She runs off.

Normally, they'd have liked to share the news, but now they're alone and that is more important.

"I waited because I thought you needed more time. I've tried very hard to move slowly." Nick chuckles.

"What's so funny?" Nancy pulls back so she can look at Nick.

"I thought God was teaching me patience. I didn't understand. I thought you didn't want to get married."

"Oh, no. I've wanted to marry you for a long time." Nancy says.

"Well, I guess you've practiced patience too."

"And, I've learned that I should have talked to you first. If I did, we could have been married right now and spending our time working on that baby Lysa wants us to have."

Turning away, Nancy tries to figure out how to put her fears into words. What if she still can't have a baby? Will Nick still want to marry her? Instead, she settles back into his arms and keeps those thoughts silent. After a minute, they make their way to the couch.

"The ring is beautiful!" Nancy turns it side to side to see the sparkle.

"I'm glad you like it. I asked April what you would like and she helped me pick it out. I brought her a book with lots of rings and she said you would love this one."

"Did you tell her when you were going to ask me?"

"No, I wasn't sure when but I asked April for help for two reasons. The first is that I needed help, and the second reason was to give her something else to look forward to. She was very excited." Nick wraps his arms around her shoulders and gently rubs his other hand down the side of her face.

"That was so thoughtful of you. Should we go and tell her now?"

"We should, otherwise Lysa will beat us to it."

"I don't want to spoil Lysa's fun, but I'd like to tell April and my mom and Ella."

"Okay, let's go." Nick grabs his keys and they head to the hospital.

"I have to call Helen and tell her we have a wedding to plan." Nancy lifts her hand to look at the ring again and sighs. "When do you want to get married?"

"Soon." Nick tilts his head and smiles.

"Good. I'd like a small wedding. Is that okay with you?"

"Yes. I think small is perfect." He will agree to anything, just as long as she says 'yes'.

"Good. If its small then it will be easier to plan, we can have the reception in Ryan and April's backyard."

"We can also get married there too. I'm fine with that or at our church. It's up to you."

"Um, do you mind if I think about that?" She asks.

"Not at all. I'm really not much for the details, so you can make all the decisions and just tell me when to show up."

"You don't want to help at all?"

"If you need help, I'm ready to help. I didn't mean I don't care. All I want is to marry you. And you can let me know how I can help."

The car ride passes in record time. They fill the time discussing their future plans. They walk hand in hand into April's room. She looks like she's in a little less pain. Her forehead isn't wrinkled.

"April, how are you feeling?" Nancy moves to her side.

"I'm in some pain, but I'm happy to see the two of you."

"Look, April." Nancy shoves her hand under April's eyes.

"It's beautiful." She takes a slow breath. "Congratulations. I'm so happy for the two of you."

"I love the ring, April. Thanks for helping Nick pick it out."

"You're welcome. When is the big day?"

"We haven't decided yet, but we will let you know soon. We were thinking of having it all in your backyard, then all you have to do is look out the window to watch."

She looks at Nick and he nods his affirmation.

"I can walk some, so reserve me a seat up front."

"Okay. We are planning a very small wedding; immediate family and a couple of friends. You'll help me plan it, right?" Nancy asks.

"Of course I will. I'm getting tired. I'm sorry, but I'll need to nap soon." April closes her eyes and turns onto her side.

"No need to say sorry. Oh, has the baby been moving lots?"

"Yes, a lot. I'm going to be having an ultrasound one of these days. I can't remember when, but they asked me if I want to know if it's a boy or girl. Ryan and I said no."

"Sounds good to me. I love surprises." Nancy squeezes April's hand.

"Good, I didn't want to upset anyone, but we want to wait. Lysa has picked out names for a boy and a girl. We let her know that it will be a family decision and not to get stuck on one name." Nancy runs her hand over April's scrunched forehead.

"She's very excited." Nick adds. "Yeah, she even asked Nancy and me when we were going to have a baby."

April chuckles, "I'm sure she did. She speaks whatever is on her mind."

"She gets that from you, little sis."

"Yes, she does." Nick agrees. "So, you're coming home soon."

"Yes, I can't wait. I don't know why I had to stay here this past month but all the doctors insisted that this was the best thing for me and the baby, so I agreed."

"I'm glad you stayed. They needed to monitor the baby and you." Nancy says.

"Yeah, that's true."

Nancy leans down and kisses April's cheek. April yawns and they say good-bye.

Chapter 34

"Doug, get in here!" His boss yells down the hall. Doug groans and gets up from his desk. Doug told his boss when he arrived for work that he had some new information but his boss was busy and said he would get to him later. Later has arrived and Doug's stomach turns sour. He couldn't eat lunch but that hour is now long gone. He knows he can't hold this information from him even though it is what he wants to do. He lost all hope of a relationship with Janice the moment she became a person of interest in this case. He couldn't date a potential suspect, nor did he want to but he did enjoy the dates he did have with her and that is why he is struggling with the news Ryan told him. He knows where this will lead.

"Doug, it's about time you made it into my office. Close the door." Doug closes the door, and then takes a seat.

"What is it, Doug?"

Doug shifts, opens his mouth, and closes it. His boss stares at him; waiting for him to speak.

"I was talking to Ryan about who is trying to kill him. He started talking about his work and he told me that the clients to his only open case are Mr. and Mrs. Willis. I thought that was relevant with the case we are working on with the Willises as well."

His boss leans back in his chair and stares at the ceiling. "Isn't Janice Myers a good friend of Ryan's wife?"

"Yes, her best friend. She has been at their house watching their daughter during the duration of this whole ordeal." Doug admits.

His boss snaps into an upright position and claps his hands together.

"That makes everything fit." He starts writing on a note pad as he talks. "She had access to the ladder, she had and still has free run of the house. You said she has made a lot of changes over the past few months. Weight loss, more vibrant clothes, your words, I think it has been gaudy or a bit over the top, but we'll use your words. You also mentioned that she had a dark past. You didn't say more than that but I have been curious. You can fill me in on that part later." He puts the pen down and looks intently at Doug.

Doug gulps. He should have called his boss when he first received this info but he sat on it for a while. This could get him fired. Doug didn't think Janice had anything to do with what was going on with Ryan. She's sweet. Cute. Opinionated. But he still likes her. She couldn't have hurt Ryan. She loves that family so much. April is her best friend and Lysa is like her own daughter. Janice helped raise Lysa and then April married Ryan. Doug sat back in his chair. What does that mean? Ryan invaded her world. He came in and took April from her. He took April's time away from Janice. With Ryan in the hospital, Janice moved in right away and took over. She had April and Lysa back. Could Janice really hurt Ryan?

He would have said no a few minutes ago, but now he wasn't so sure. Is Ryan in danger being back home? He hoped not, but he needed to make sure.

"Doug, you need to go pick up Janice and bring her in for questioning. No cuffs, we just want to talk to her first. After you bring her in, let her sit for a while before we question her. I want you over at Ryan Nolsen's house. We need to get Ryan's permission to search his house. I don't think that will be too hard. I'll give him a call. I want Mike and Anthony on this too. I'll take Mike; you take Anthony. Don't speak to her like she's guilty. Make it sound like you need her help in solving a case. Tell her your briefcase is at work so you need to come here to get all the information you need. Then have Anthony call you and pretend you are being called away but you will be back soon. When you leave, I want her locked in. We'll let her stew."

"I don't like all this lying, boss." Doug shifts.

"Too bad. I don't want her thinking she's in trouble, but I want her to sweat some."

"What if she doesn't want to come?" Doug asks.

"You can get creative and figure it out." He says and stands, dismissing Doug. Doug shakes his head, trying to make sense of what just happened. Could Janice have tried to kill Ryan, twice?

Did he miss something with her personality? She definitely stated her mind, but that doesn't make her abusive or a killer. She got frustrated with people but he never saw her lose it. She kept her anger in check. She seemed genuine every time they went out, but maybe he missed something. She did have an abusive childhood. Maybe she learned to hide her true self; her feelings could be deep inside and only surface when she had a plan in place. He took a deep breath. Grabbed his keys and his soda. Maybe that will soothe his stomach.

"Anthony, we have to go." Doug says as he passes Anthony's desk. Anthony gets up without saying a word. He usually doesn't say much but he hopes today he says nothing. How do you explain that your ex-girlfriend might be the mastermind behind two of their cases?

During the car ride to Janice's job, Doug briefly fills Anthony in. He got his wish, Anthony only grunts. Then chuckles. Doug parks next to Janice's car. Anthony stays behind in case Janice gets spooked and tries to leave without them. Doug's steps slow as he approaches Janice's desk. *God, please, help me with this one.*

Her fingers are flying over the keys. Whatever she is working on has her full attention. Doug's foot bumps into the garbage can and a few cans knock together. Janice's fingers pause as she looks up and gives Doug a startled look. She quickly turns back to her screen and with amazing speed finishes what she was doing and exits the program she was in before Doug makes it the last few steps to her side. She doesn't look pleased to see him.

"You keep showing up, Doug." She sighs. "It's getting old. Now you're at my work. I can't talk to you now Doug, I have to work." Her voice rises slightly and she wipes her palms on her bright pink skirt. She gives him a look and waits for him to speak.

"Umm, sorry about that, Janice. I don't mean to interrupt your workday. My boss wants me to get your opinion on a case we are working on."

"What? You're joking, right? I know nothing about solving cases." She glares at Doug. Doug visibly starts to sweat. What should he say now? He isn't supposed to let her get suspicious. He shifts his weight as he searches his brain for the right words.

"Ryan said something about you helping him a while ago with a puzzle and it stuck in my mind that you might be able to help. Please help me with this Janice." He feels dirty. Manipulative! After this he is never going to see her again. She will hate him forever and he is starting to hate himself as well, unless she really is responsible for all of this. And she might be. He needs to get her to the station!

He gives her his best smile. She opens her mouth and closes it. She's thinking about it.

"Come help me Janice, please. My briefcase is at the station so if we could go there and if you can just look over what I have on the case, I would really appreciate it."

She looks down at her computer screen and sighs. She turns off the monitor and grabs her purse.

"I have an hour and then I need to get to the hospital to visit April. Lysa is with Nancy and the three of us were going to meet there and bring him home. I prepared a killer dinner that has been simmering in the crockpot. It's one of Ryan's favorite dishes, pulled pork, but Lysa doesn't like it so I'll make her some mac and cheese." They walk to the parking lot and Janice slows down.

"You didn't tell me that you were with your partner?"

"Oh, sorry, that's just Anthony. He doesn't say much, I forgot he was here." Anthony hears Doug and shrugs. He gets into the cop car without a word.

"See, he doesn't say anything. We were on our way to the station when I asked him to stop here so I could ask you for help."

"Oh, okay, I'll follow you there." She opens her car door.

"You can ride with us, Janice." Doug insists.

"I need my car." She holds firm to her car door.

Doug starts to protest but says, "I'll ride with you, then we don't have to deal with Anthony's silence."

"Sure, whatever. I have one hour." She gets in and starts her car. Doug glances at Anthony and nods. Anthony nods back and starts his car. Doug goes to the passenger side and slides in.

They reach the station and Doug brings Janice into a room where there is a lock on the outside of the door. He asks her if she wants a drink and she says yes. When he gets back into the room his phone rings. It's Anthony. Doug answers, says a few words and hangs up.

"Janice, I'm needed down the road for a few minutes. I'll be back soon." He walks toward the door.

"Wait! I'm leaving too. I don't have time to wait for you." She grabs her purse and pushes in her chair, but Doug doesn't wait. He steps out into the hall and locks the door. Janice goes to the door, turns the knob, and nothing happens.

"Hey, Doug. The door is locked, open the door!" She bangs on it but Doug doesn't come back. She yells a couple more times but no one comes to let her out. She gives up and goes back to her seat. She puts her purse on the table and moves some papers and her wallet out of the way. Her phone sits on the bottom. She picks it up and sends Nancy a text explaining what happened. She also sends one to Doug, but she doesn't think that will do any good. She knows he locked her in here on purpose. She knows he lied to her. And she knows she's in serious trouble.

Chapter 35

I wanted this case solved before I went home but that didn't happen. Nothing has happened in about two weeks. I don't want anyone to get hurt because they are around me, but there have been no other attempts on my life. That's the good news. The bad is that I am not one step closer to solving this and April still doesn't know. There is no way I'm telling her any time soon either. That stress could cause her to die.

I spend a good portion of my day in therapy or working on achieving the new thing Jill has forced me to do. She helped me a lot and pushed me farther than I thought I could be pushed. I'm walking well now and it is because of her help. My new therapist isn't as good.

Someone knocks on the door and I go to answer it. On the other side of the doorway stands the police chief. I met him a few times over the years. A good man but also no nonsense.

"Hey, Ryan." He holds out his hand and I shake it. He motions for me to sit. Curious. I sit but I don't say anything. This is his show.

"So Ryan, we have reason to believe that someone was in your house and somehow left something that could hurt you or someone else, a lot like the sawed ladder. We would like your permission to search your house so we can make sure it is safe for you."

"Who would be doing the search?" My right side of my lip rises.

"It would be Mike, Doug, Anthony, and myself."

"Not who will search the house. Who do you think was in my house?"

He shifts his weight and takes a long moment to open his mouth. "We have someone in for questioning but nothing concrete yet. That is why we want to search your house. We know you and your daughter live there right now and we want to ensure her safety as well as yours."

"I get that but who do you have in for questioning."

"When we have something concrete we will discuss it with you, but right now it is only a lead. Can we search your house, Ryan?"

He wasn't going to budge on whom they were questioning.

"Yes, you can. I agree I want my house safe. I would like more information and I want to be here when you start looking."

"For your safety Ryan and your daughter's, we think it will be a good idea for you to be elsewhere. We can call you when we are done and let you know what we have found."

"No, I will be there when you do the search and my daughter and sister-in-law are upstairs now so the priority is getting them away from the house so they will be safe." I stand up. "I'll call them and I'll have them go to April's mom's house."

He sighs. "Okay, I already have Doug on his way over here to your house as we speak. He is probably waiting outside, in your driveway."

"Good then you can do that while I call Nancy." Nancy doesn't ask any questions but says she is fine taking Lysa to her mom's house.

* * *

Nancy's phone rings again the moment she hangs up with Ryan. "Nancy, can you come down to the station and get me? Doug locked me in a room here and no one will let me out. He got me here under the pretense that I was going to help him with a case but that was a lie." Janice leans back in the chair and looks up at the light while she holds the phone tightly in her hand.

"What? Why would Doug ask you for help on a case? And then lock you in a room?" Nancy's voice squeaks.

"He said something about my helping Ryan once before and that intrigued me enough to come. As far as I know, I've never helped Ryan with a case. And for that matter what case would Ryan need help with? He's a carpenter, right?"

"Yes, he is but Nick and Ryan have been travelling a lot. Maybe there's more to this then we thought." Nancy pauses. "Janice, give a few minutes, let me drop Lysa off at my mom's and then I'll come and try to get you out."

"Thanks."

"While you wait, keep thinking about your conversations with Ryan. Maybe there's something there. Doug didn't say you were under arrest, right?"

"No he didn't, so you should be able to get me out of this room." Janice hopes as she ends the call.

* * *

Doug and Anthony walk around the side of the house when he sees his boss motion for him to come inside.

"I did a check around the house, no forced entry and I couldn't find anything out of place." He says and holds out his hand to me. I shake it and nod.

The boss nods and all three men fan out as they walk through the entryway into the house.

"Stay back, Ryan." But I follow anyway. This is my house. I'll be able to spot something out of place quicker than they will be able to.

The living room looks neat, with nothing out of place. The same goes for the other rooms on the first floor. Doug says something about needing to test the food in the crockpot. I know that smell. It's Janice's pulled pork. Where's Janice? Originally, she was going to the hospital with Nancy and Lysa, and we were all going to visit April. Janice was the person that was here, living in my house while I was at the hospital. Since I've been home, she usually stops by when it's her turn to make dinner and she drops off her crockpot. Janice made the pork that they want to test. Janice works for the company that keeps track of all of Willis's accounts. She knows all the financials and she has access to all of the accounts. I joked with her once about how she could rob a lot of companies at once and skip town. I put this in motion. When I told Doug that the Willises were my only active case, he made a connection. They think Janice is trying to kill me!

The movement around the house brings me back to what they're doing. Janice? Really? My thoughts go into overdrive as I entertain the idea of her being responsible.

"Doug," I shout up the stairs, "where's Janice?"

He grunts. I start to walk up the stairs but only catch a mumbling exchange between Doug and his boss.

"Doug, where's Janice?" I say again when I enter the guest bedroom where Doug is. "I know you think she is responsible for this."

Doug gives me a quick look, and then goes back to looking through the dresser drawers. "Yes, some of us think she is responsible." He says.

"But what do you think Doug? You dated her." I ask.

"I'm not saying anything right now about it Ryan."

"Fair enough. Where is she, Doug? Is she with Nancy and Lysa?" I want to know.

"No, I sort of tricked her into going down to the station and I locked her in a room." Doug's back goes rigid.

"Oh, boy, she definitely won't date you after that move! Is she under arrest?" I ask.

"No, but when we are done here, we will know more and that's when we'll question her." Doug's pace doesn't slow down.

My head starts to hurt. I walk back down the stairs, to my office. I need to think.

* * *

Nancy arrives at the station and asks if someone can help her find her friend. She explains how Doug, by accident locked her in a room when she was there to only help with a case. He got called away and said he would be back but that was over an hour ago.

"What did you say your friend's name is?" The tall woman asks.

"Her name is Janice." Nancy says.

"Why don't you have a seat over there." She points to a bench that has been painted over a few too many times. "And I'll look around for your friend."

"Thanks." She says as she makes her way over to the bench. She pulls out her phone and starts checking emails. There's nothing that couldn't wait. She sends a text to Ryan to let him know that Lysa is with Nancy's mom and that she is trying to get Janice out of jail, sort of.

The lights flicker above Nancy but she hardly notices. The echo of footsteps draws Nancy's attention to the hallway on her left. She looks up and sees Janice, with a smile on her face, walking toward her. Nancy gives her a hug.

"Thank you, Nancy. I was getting really bored in there."

"Not a problem." She turns to the woman that found Janice. "Thank you for all your help."

The woman nods, and walks back to her desk. They walk out of the police station. Nancy's phone jingles, alerting her that she has received a text message. She glances at it.

"Ryan says to stay away from the jail at the moment." Nancy stops in front of her car.

"Oh, that's fine by me. I never want to go there again." Janice says. "I need to get a bag from April's house though, so I'll follow you there."

"Alright. I'll call my mom while I drive home. She can bring Lysa home." Nancy pats Janice's shoulder. "Interesting afternoon, huh, Janice."

"Bizarre." She reaches into her purse for her car keys. "I'm never going anywhere with Doug again. I don't want to see him either. Who brings their ex-girlfriend to the police station and locks her in a room? What type of joke was that?" Janice's face turns red.

"Not sure. Maybe we should just forget about it. See you at the house, Janice." She waves and gets into her car.

The drive was uneventful. Nancy arrives first and sees two cop cars in the driveway. She parks behind them but Doug and another man run out and drive the two cars away. Odd! She wonders what happened. Janice pulls in behind her after the cop cars have sped away and the two ladies walk to the front door. Before Nancy has a chance to say anything about the cop cars to Janice, Ryan opens the front door.

"Ryan, you look good!" Nancy says as they walk into the living room. She gives him a hug and steps aside. Janice leans in to give Ryan a hug next.

"We're all so glad you are home!" Janice says.

"Janice, slowly take your hands-off Ryan and put them on your head!" A voice says firmly from the corner of the room.

"What?" Her hands tighten on Ryan's back.

"I said, slowly remove your hands from Ryan and put them on your head!" Janice looks over Ryan's shoulder and sees a gun pointed at her. She screams and throws her arms in front of her, using Ryan as a shield.

A big hand grabs her shoulder and forcefully puts her on the ground. Her purse falls under her during the decent and her arm gets pinned.

Janice screams again and again. Anthony doesn't budge. He keeps one knee on her back. Janice starts to whimper and Doug walks into the room. He takes out his cuffs and gently puts them on Janice as Anthony lifts his knee off her back. Doug moves her into a sitting position and tries to make her more comfortable. He brushes some hair out of her face but Janice turns her head abruptly away. Lysa and her grandmother are standing in the doorway. I'm not sure when they arrived. No one says a word.

Lysa runs up to Anthony and kicks him in the shin. He yelps.

"Daddy, get the guy in the corner with the gun. Aunt Nancy, help Aunt Janice." Lysa gets into a fighting stance and glares at Anthony. "I have this one." She gets ready to strike when I get to her side and pull her into a hug.

"Daddy, what are you doing?" Lysa struggles.

"It will be okay now. No one is going to hurt Aunt Janice anymore." He hugs her tight and kisses the top of her head. "Nancy can you take her outside, please?"

She nods. "Lysa, let's take grandma upstairs for some tea."

I close the door behind them and make my way over to the couch. My home has been thoroughly searched. The person they think is behind the attempts on my life is my wife's best friend. The person who has been watching my daughter regularly and loving her while I was in the hospital is now in cuffs on my living room floor. April is going to be furious. What should I do? I bow my head and take a minute.

"You can't look in my purse!" Janice says.

"Yes, I can." Mike dumps it out and moves her belongings around while Anthony looks through the pockets in the purse.

"Look what we have here." Anthony pulls out a needle with clear liquid in it. Janice has a look of shock on her face. Mike gets in her face, but says nothing. He pulls her to her feet by her arm and she screams in pain. I get up and stand in front of them and look at Janice. Her elbow is at an odd angle.

"Does it hurt here, Janice?" She winces when I touch her arm.

"Anthony you either broke her arm when you pulled her down or her elbow is dislocated."

Anthony grunts.

"Anthony, you and Doug take her to the hospital. That needs to be taken care of before we bring her in for questioning. Mike and I will finish up here and we will meet you back at the station." Their boss says. Doug gently takes Janice's good arm and leads her out the door to the cop car.

"I'm not sure I agree with you guys. I've never seen Janice hurt anyone before. Please treat her well while she is in your care. Much better than what I just saw. I know you will be hearing from her lawyer soon. I'm going into my office to call him for her so he should be there in time for the questioning. I advise you to wait for him before you start. Please see yourself out." I get up and walk to my office. I need to lie down, but first I have another matter to attend to.

Chapter 36

Nancy says good-bye to her mom and puts on a movie for Lysa. Lysa was very upset over what happened with Janice, as was Nancy. She called Nick and asked him to come over as soon as he could. He's walking up the outside stairs to Nancy's apartment, Nancy races to the door and flings it open before he has a chance to ring the bell.

"Nick, have you talked to Ryan?" She asks as she grabs the sides of his shirt and looks into his eyes.

He pulls her into a hug. "Yes, he called me as soon as the last car pulled out of the driveway."

"Then what did he say about Janice? Does he think she did this?"

Nick leads her to the couch and pulls her into a side hug. He holds her for a minute before he says anything.

"Ryan is confused right now. He called a lawyer for Janice and after I talk with you I'm going to help him sort out what just happened. I can't believe Janice would try to kill Ryan but there might be evidence. They found a needle in her bag. The lab is running tests on it to see what is in it and if it was the same thing that was used on him in the hospital. If it is then the judge probably will not set bail."

Nancy sniffles. "I can't believe she would do that. She's April's best friend and over the years she has become a good friend to me as well. What do you think, Nick?"

"I'm not sure, Nancy. I like Janice. Always have, but right now we need to focus on keeping everyone safe and it's best that Janice stays away until this is all cleared up."

Nancy sits up straight. "This might send April into a coma again or worse."

"Ryan and I discussed that too. We both feel that April can't know anything right now. She might have to stay at the hospital longer. Ryan is praying about what to do. He also thinks it might be safer for Lysa to stay with you and that maybe you two should move in with your mom and Ella for now. Nothing long term, just until he is sure it's safe."

"If he is thinking we should go there then he must not think Janice is responsible." Nancy hopes. "Also, Nick, when Janice and I were talking we thought that you and Ryan might have other work you do besides the carpentry business." She doesn't ask a question but let's her statement hang.

Nick shifts, opens his mouth, but nothing comes out. He clears his throat and starts again.

"You're right, Nancy. Ryan hasn't told April and we both think now is a bad time to tell her so I'll explain it all to you but you need to keep quiet about it until April is completely in the clear."

"Okay, I will." Nancy whispers.

"Ryan started his own private investigator business a few years ago." And on he went explaining his role and how they were going to close the business once this case is over. Lysa comes in and Nick decides it's time to visit with Ryan. He says good-bye and walks down the stairs. Ryan left the door unlocked and Nick found him fast at work at his computer.

When he takes a break, he fills him in on Nancy knowing about the PI business. Ryan doesn't say anything.

"I've been thinking Nick that we should close the case. It doesn't matter anymore what the Willises say. The police are involved, there is no evidence against their daughter's boyfriend, Tim so I'm comfortable with this decision."

"I agree, Ryan. Also, if Janice has nothing to do with this and it does involve the case then closing it might deter the person that is trying to harm you."

"That's what I was thinking too."

"I told Nancy you wanted her to go to your mother-in-law's and she didn't argue." Nick grabs a soda from the mini-fridge and sits on the couch.

"Nancy wouldn't put Lysa in a potentially harmful situation. She will probably be at the door soon so that she can pack up Lysa's stuff."

"True. What do you think, Ryan? Do you think Janice is behind this?"

"Let's look at the facts. She had a needle in her bag that she says wasn't hers. That's the only thing against her. Yes, she works and has access to all of the accounts that have been stolen from but so do some other people as well. We should find out if it was only the Willis's that have been robbed. That will tell us more. Janice had access to many other accounts as well so if they weren't touched I would lean in a different direction. Also, as far as I know she doesn't know how to fly a helicopter and she might not be strong enough to lift my ladder and saw some of the rungs. But maybe she is and maybe she hired someone to fly a chopper for her. Here's the plan, Nick. You call all the places that rent helicopters and find out if anyone rented one or had someone pilot them around the day I got hurt, I'm going to call Doug and ask him about the financials."

"That's good, Ryan. Can I use your computer?"

"Sure." I say then pick up my phone and recline on the couch. Doug answers on the second ring. "Doug, it's Ryan. Any news?"

"Janice's elbow is broken." He says.

"Oh, that's bad. Any news on what was in the needle?"

"No, nothing yet."

"How about the companies that have lost money. Are they all Willis's companies or have other companies been robbed?" I ask.

"You know I can't discuss the case with you, Ryan."

"Yup, I know that and I also know that three police officers took down a woman for giving me a hug. She wasn't a threat and I didn't say she was a threat. I also know one of those three officers broke her elbow. I saw the whole thing."

"Ryan, what are you saying?" He asks but I don't say anything. "Fine, you play dirty, Ryan. The only companies that have fudged records are the Willis's, but you didn't hear that from me. I know that information changes things and right now you are probably the only person not looking at Janice so I hope you come up with something new to help the truth come out." I start to comment but he hangs up.

I look at Nick, he stopped typing when I mentioned Janice's broken elbow. "I know I shouldn't have said that to Doug, but we have nothing new so far and if I don't solve this soon, my wife's best friend is going to go to jail and my wife just might die from the news." I throw my head back onto a pillow and stare at the ceiling. Nick picks up the landline on the desk and starts talking to someone about the helicopter. He hangs up, dials again and asks the same round of questions. The fifth call starts to sound interesting so I sit up and listen.

"So you had a couple come in and pay for a full day in May. They said they wanted to just fly around. He had his pilot's license up to date so you had no concerns. Did they say where they went? And what name did they leave with you?" He listens for a minute, frowning the whole time. "What type of clothing was the woman wearing and what color was her hair?" Nick smiles. "Thank you very much."

Nick hangs up but before he could say anything, Nancy walks in. "Lysa and I are going to pack some clothes. Okay?"

"Sure, thanks, Nancy. Please send her in here before you leave, I want to give her a hug." She turns and quickly walks away.

We wait a full minute before we address the topic. "Ryan, there was a couple that took a helicopter out for a day. They said they were going to enjoy a day looking at the Catskill Mountains and the name that was left was Janice Myers."

"And you're smiling, because?" I ask.

"Because the woman who says she was Janice Myers was wearing a very neat gray dress suit. The owner remembers her because he was thinking that her outfit wasn't very comfortable for flying. Also, she was a brunette."

"That's good work, Nick."

"Yeah, I don't think I ever saw Janice as a brunette. Blond, orange, purple, pink, and I think one time green. Never a brunette."

"I have known her longer than you and I have never seen her as a brunette either. Okay, so now we know someone is framing her. Who could it be?"

"I don't think Tim is involved. Who has access to the financials?"

"That's a question for Doug but before we call him let's brainstorm a little more."

Chapter 37

Ryan hired her the best lawyer within 200 miles. A guy named Ethan Blum. Janice was relieved but she wasn't prepared for her day to turn like this. She was supposed to be celebrating the soon arrival of April coming home. And they were all going to visit April. She hopes someone called April and gave an excuse for why she wasn't there. This could kill her! And Janice doesn't want to lose her best friend. Her arm is throbbing and they gave her some pain medication, but it only reduced the pain minimally. Her lawyer has already filed a lawsuit about her broken arm. She isn't sure what to do so for now she will do as she's told. A rarity but she isn't versed in the situation she is presently in and she needs someone who is wiser than her, fighting for her.

They talked for an hour and he advised her to only answer the questions, don't add anything else. He said to let him handle the rest. Two people Janice has never seen before enter the room.

"Hello, I'm Detective Helms and this is Detective Fran. We are going to record this conversation, okay?" He doesn't wait for an answer, just presses the record button and puts the device on the table. They both sit on the other side, which is across from Janice and her lawyer.

Janice reaches for her water. Her hand shakes as she grabs it with her left hand. Her right hand is useless so she cradles the water into her left side and slowly gets the top off, but as she goes to move the water bottle from its cradled position, it falls onto the table. The lawyer quickly snaps up his papers but the recorder gets a good splash. Detective Helms glares at Janice as he wipes it on his pants. He turns it off and on again to see if it works. It seems fine. Janice turns the water bottle upright and takes the last sip. She would like to ask for more, but now didn't seem like the right time.

"Janice where were you the day Ryan was injured?"

"I was, I think I need to look at my calendar but I believe I was at work."

"So you're not sure?"

"She said she needs to look at her calendar, it was over a month ago."

"Okay, moving on, where were you the night someone tried to kill Ryan?"

"That one is easy, I was at Ryan's house watching Lysa, his daughter. Nancy was right upstairs. You can ask her. I didn't go anywhere that night."

Okay, we will ask Nancy. Now where did you get the needle that was in your bag?" He leans forward on the desk. He gets within a foot of her face and she leans back.

"I have never seen it before. I had no idea it was in there."

"Sure." Detective Fran mumbles and leans back in his chair, crossing his arms.

Janice can see the she is being viewed as guilty. Her heart starts to squeeze. She hates it when the truth isn't told and she is being accused of a crime she didn't commit, but she has no idea how to convince them that she has nothing to do with Ryan's injures.

She clears her throat and places the empty bottle on the table. Her hand continues to shake as she lets go and it topples over again.

Detective Helms shuffles a couple of pieces of paper around. "Let's switch gears. Janice, have you heard of the name, Edward Willis?"

"Yes."

"Who is he?"

"He has several accounts with the company I work for. He owns fifteen restaurants and nine office-supply stores. He's our biggest client." Janice looks at her lawyer and sees that his eyebrows are high and his jaw is clenched.

What could be going on now? She has done an exceptional job the whole time she has worked for that company. Her boss has given her adequate raises each year and has only praised her for her work. She has dedicated too many hours to her job.

"And are you in charge of all of Mr. Willis's accounts?"

"I'm not in charge as you say, my boss is in charge of all of Mr. Willis's accounts." She starts to say more but her lawyer puts his hand on her arm. She closes her mouth and doesn't say another word.

"Do you have access to his accounts?"

"Yes, but so does my boss and his boss and the two other secretaries that work for them." She folds her arms and gasps in pain. She wants to yell at these two men sitting across from her.

Detective Fran leans forward and gets in Janice's face. "Did you steal money from the Willis's accounts?"

"What? Absolutely not! I have never stolen anything in my life." She jumps to her feet. "One time I left the grocery store and when I got to my car, I lifted my purse and saw there was smoked salmon under it. I checked my receipt and saw that I didn't pay for it. And do you know what I did? I went back into the store and paid for it." She sits back down. Her face has turned the color of her shirt, pink.

"Nice story. Janice why do you hate Ryan?"

"Hate Ryan? Where did you get that? I don't hate Ryan. I think he is the best man for April. And she is truly happy being married to him. I've never hated Ryan!"

The same questions kept coming for the next hour, but they were phrased differently each time. Janice started to cry quietly during the last half hour. Does Ryan think she would hurt him? Does her boss think she would steal from accounts? She is being accused of two very serious, very different, and very bad crimes. She could be in jail for the rest of her life. Her shoulders slump and she starts to only hear pieces of what is being said around her. Her breathing starts to labor and her vision turns gray. She reaches for Ethan's shirt, but he doesn't catch her in time. She falls off the chair and hits the floor, landing on her broken elbow.

* * *

"Ethan, I need to talk to Janice!" I say.

"Ryan, she passed out and fell on her elbow. The cast helped but she might have done more damage. Right now, I'm with her in the room where they were questioning her. She came to about five minutes ago. She is on her back on the floor." Ethan says. Janice motions for the phone so Ethan gives it to her. The color is gone from her face and her lips are a pasty white.

"Ryan, how are you?" She whispers.

"I'm doing fine. Ethan will take care of you, but I have some questions that if you can answer, could help me solve this case."

"So you believe I didn't do this?" She squeaks out.

"Janice, I have only known you to love. I don't believe you tried to hurt me."

Janice sighs. Ryan is going to help her. She might not spend the rest of her life in jail.

"Besides you, who has access to the Willis's accounts?" I ask.

"You know about the Willis's?"

"Yes, Janice, stay focused, who has access to the accounts?" I raise me voice, hoping she hears the urgency.

"My head is fuzzy, Ryan, but my boss, his boss, and their secretaries. I'm one of the secretaries. I think that's it, but I'm not sure."

"Okay that's a good place for me to start. Janice, this will all work out. We serve a God who is in the miracle business. You know that, I trust that the truth will come out and I know you do too."

"Thanks, Ryan. Oh, Ryan, he's our biggest client. He owns 24 companies."

"That's good to know." I jot down the info in my notebook.

"You can't tell April what is going on with me."

"I'm not but if she asks I think I'll let her know you are taking a quick vacation."

"Ryan, that is so not funny!" Her usual attitude comes back in her voice.

"Good, I'm glad to hear you haven't lost the fight." Another call comes in. I look at the screen and see it's the hospital. Not good. "Janice I have to go, it's the hospital calling." I hear voices in the background and someone yelling that Janice shouldn't have a phone. Ethan will handle it. I end the call and click over.

"Yes?"

"Is this Ryan Nolsen?"

"Yes, it is." I keep it short, hoping they will quickly get to the reason for the call.

"Your wife, April, slipped in and out of a coma today. She is stable but we would like to keep her in the hospital longer, maybe for the duration of her pregnancy."

"Are you sure she's stable?" My heart aches.

"Yes, she is alert and wants to see you. The baby is fine too."

"Okay, I'm grabbing my keys and I'll be there as quickly as I can. Please let April know I'm on my way." I have my keys in my hands, but it takes me a moment to get my left sneaker on the right way.

I hear the nurse talk to April. "She's smiling, Ryan."

"Thank you!" I hang up and get in the car. Now that Lysa is with Nancy, I can stay with April as long as they let me but, I also have to take care of Janice now and solve this case.

I put on my Bluetooth and call Nick. He answers on the third ring.

"Nick, did you find out anything new?"

"No, I need some names."

"Janice was out of it but she told me her boss, his boss, and their secretaries, Janice included, have access to the Willis's account. She didn't give me names but I knew you could get them."

I hear clicking keys in the background. "I'm on it, Ryan. Wait, why are you calling? Aren't you in the kitchen getting us food?"

"Nope, I got a call when I was on the phone with Janice and April had a setback. I'm on my way to the hospital. You can stay at my place if you want. All our notes are in the office anyway, so it would probably be easier for you."

"Yeah, I'll stay here. What food were you going to get? I'm starved."

"There's lasagna in the fridge. Janice made it. It might be on the counter, not sure if I got that far with it." My stomach growls but food isn't a priority right now.

"I see it, yeah, you left it on the counter. How's April?"

"She's stable, so that's good. Keep my posted Nick, I need this resolved soon."

"I will. I'm planning on pulling an all-nighter and Ryan, I'm praying for April."

"Thanks, Nick! Call later with an update." I hang up before I start having difficulty talking. My baby is hurting and I'm torn with where I should be. If I don't get Janice free, April could find out, but if I'm with April, I can't work on this problem.

Did Janice say he owns 24 companies? Then why would they hire me, a no name?

Chapter 38

The doorbell rings. Nick looks through the peephole and sees Doug. He really doesn't want to let him in, but he might have information he needs or information he can get out of him.

He opens the door and Doug holds out his hand. Nick shakes it and Doug walks in.

"I made a big mess of things, didn't I?"

"You dated her for a few months. How could you think she would hurt Ryan?" Nick spits out.

"There was a lot of evidence against her, but I know she wouldn't do it. She was always putting others first." Doug plops down on the couch. Nick doesn't have time for this.

"Doug, it's nice that you stopped by but I need to work on figuring this out. Why don't you go back to work and look for some real evidence?"

"I'm off duty, my boss pulled me off the case too because he said I'm too close to it. He's right so I came over here to help Ryan but since you're here, I'll help you."

"Uh, sure, okay, let's go to the office. You can look at the board and see what we have. We know two people rented a helicopter and flew it around the day Ryan was injured. They used Janice's name but we all know that was fake. No one would use their name if they were going to do something illegal. Anyway, the woman doesn't fit Janice's description at all. I've made some calls. All the people Janice works with and works for don't have their pilot's license. That was my big lead; the people at her job that also have access to the Willis's accounts. But I struck out there. We have some age ranges and clothing styles, hair type but nothing concrete. One of the other secretaries might be a fit and she had access to Janice's bag. Janice's boss had access also and he might fit the man's description but he has never flown anything before. I'm stuck there. Any thoughts?"

"You came up with more than I did. I didn't figure out who flew the helicopter. Good work there. Janice's colorful hair and outfits might save her from jail time on this one. She was placed under arrest an hour ago. I can't believe it. I feel like this is all my fault." He runs his hand through his hair and sits down on the couch.

"Well, Doug, I'm not going there. At this point it doesn't matter but we need to work together to get her out. Her mouth will get her into trouble there." Doug groans and puts his head between his legs, making Nick go back to being solo on this.

He scans the board and a thought comes to him. He starts to type.

"Nick, is there any food?"

"Nope, Doug, I ate the last of the lasagna."

"Was it Janice's cooking?"

"Yes."

Doug grunts. "I'm going for a food run. I'll be able to work after I eat."

"Sure, whatever." Nick says, but doesn't bother to look up from the monitor.

Nick spends the next half an hour working on the computer and talking on the phone with the owner of the helicopter rental store. It turns out that he keeps all of his surveillance videos on file and he sent the footage to Ryan's computer two minutes ago. The video plays and in walks two adults. He has a tough time seeing their faces but he can tell their body shape and approximate age. Four minutes later they come out of the store and the camera gets both of their faces. A clear shot. Nick smiles and sends the video to Ryan's email. He hears Doug come back and quickly exits out of his email.

Nick starts to turn when a gunshot rings out. He feels no pain, just something wet trickle down the side of his face.

"Why, Doug?" He whispers. But his last thoughts are about Nancy before he slumps over in the chair.

*** * * ***

April is now 26 weeks along. Each day is a victory. The doctors feel the baby has a chance at surviving if he or she is born now. We are hopeful that April makes it to week 38. She has been so strong throughout all of this. Not once has she considered dying. She won't even let me bring it up. She has a complete peace from God. It's amazing to watch. I'm soaking up her faith when I sit and talk with her. She is still in pain but she hasn't vomited in a few weeks and she doesn't complain. I arrived at the hospital ten minutes ago and April was sleeping.

"Ryan?" Her voice is scratchy.

"Yes, April?" I lean forward and put my elbows on her bed.

"What do you think?"

"About what?"

"Did you hear anything I was saying?"

"No, sorry, you were asleep. You must have said it in your dreams. Can you start over?" I hope this isn't a sign of something going wrong.

"Sure. I was wondering what happened to Dr. Stevens."

"Who's Dr. Stevens?"

"He's the doctor that had you sign those papers."

"Oh, I was still on some heavy pain meds when he came in. I don't remember him saying his name was Dr. Stevens. Are you sure that's his name?"

"Yes, I'm positive. I'll never forget him."

"Huh."

"Huh, what?"

"Oh, nothing. I was just thinking. I have no idea what has happened to him. How about I try to find out?"

"You don't have to do that. I was only wondering. It shows how even though humans have a certain plan, God is still in control." She opens her eyes and touches my arm.

"I agree, April. And I'm so glad God is in control." I turn her hand over and place my hand in hers.

"Me too. Okay, I'm tired. I'm going to take a nap now."

I bend down and smooth some of April's hair behind her ears. Kissing her forehead, I turn and close the hospital door quietly behind me. How could I not have heard the name Dr. Stevens before? How did I miss that? Did he tell me his name? Man, I really don't remember. Before I make my way to the cafeteria for coffee, I put my blue tooth in my ear and call Nick.

Chapter 39

Sitting up in my hospital bed, I focus on my blessings. I'm alive today, and the baby is growing inside me. I have so many people that love me. It's amazing all the help we have here. I'm truly blessed. Even now in this time of uncertainty, I know my God will keep me safe. Occasionally someone will visit that means well, but says all the wrong things. Horror stories are not helpful. It's usually a story about someone who knows someone who is dead from the same thing or a story about a surgery gone wrong. I redirect as quickly as I can. I don't want to hear about negative stories. I'm also perplexed as to why people share them. I think they don't know what to say, so they talk about the bad things. When they leave, I spend some time praying for them. Asking God to help guide them and their words but not in a mean way, and for me to not focus on their horror stories. We all need guidance and I know I have shared my portion of those stories that only make the other person panic.

I understand more now of what a person in pain needs. They need comfort and a friend to talk to, someone who is willing to listen when they need to talk. Letting them know you care and that they can call anytime they want or for the phone to ring and ask how they are doing. There are many ways to be a blessing. I have my health today. My heart is beating on time and I know who I am. I can walk, talk, and get myself dressed. All of my blessings are from my God, and I can see them in my day today.

There are times when I cry. I know it is good to be real with myself. I try to be strong around my family, but when I am trying to nap or sleep at night, I talk to God and cry. I don't know how long I'm going to be in this state. I miss my normal way of life, when I was focused on housework and taking care of Lysa, when I was enjoying being a wife to Ryan. I cry because I miss what once was normal, and now I don't know if that will ever come back. I know God isn't upset that I cry. I know He is hugging me through this. I know He is right by my side, and I know as a parent, He wants to take this away from me. But my God uses all things for good. I choose to focus on that. Sometimes I don't understand what good will come out of me being like this, but I know that my baby is still alive and that is amazingly good. I also know that right now it's all right that I don't understand, God does and for that I'm satisfied. Today, I'm blessed because I'm alive! According to all the doctors I have seen so far, I should have died a while ago, along with the baby inside me. Now I know only God can be keeping us alive. He is performing daily miracles!

"Mommy?" A head peeks in the doorway.

"Yes, Lysa, what a great surprise!" I sit up a little straighter.

"Can I sit next to you?" She pauses in the doorway.

"Of course you can."

She pulls up a chair, and we sit holding hands.

Nancy comes in behind her. "April, I have some errands to run, can I leave her here with you for an hour?"

I smile. "That would be wonderful."

"Has the baby kicked lately?" Lysa pulls my attention back to her and Nancy slips out the door.

"Yes, a few times in the past few minutes. How about you sit up here on the bed with me and you put your hand on my stomach. Maybe you'll feel him or her kick."

"Sure!" She squeals and cautiously makes her way up. "I can't wait until the baby comes. You're 30 weeks now, right?"

"Yes, I am. How did you know?"

"Aunt Nancy and I have a chart. We cross a day off each day. We wrote how far along you are on that day, so we have a count down."

"Oh, that's great. From now on, I'll ask you how far along I am."

"Yay! I'll let you know whenever you ask mommy."

"Good. Thanks, Lysa." I wrap her in my arms and put my head on the top of hers. The smell of strawberries meets my nose.

"How are you feeling?"

"I'm okay. I'm a little tired but I just got up from a nap so now I can spend time with you."

"And me too, right?" A male voice asks.

"Hi, Ryan. Where did you go? When I woke up you were gone."

"I went to get some coffee and some snacks." He holds up a bag and Lysa reaches for it. He sits in the chair and we listen to Lysa tell us all about the fun she has been having.

"Are you tired?" Ryan leans over and touches my hand.

"Yes, but I want time as a family first."

"Okay." He looks at my eyes. "Lysa, what else did you do today?

"Daddy, I had a good day. Did you know that mommy is 30 weeks along today?"

"No I didn't. That's great news. When is, the ultrasound scheduled for?" He asks.

"It's in two days. Are we still on the same page?"

I don't want Lysa to know we're talking about not finding out if the baby is a boy or girl.

"I haven't turned any pages yet."

"Daddy, you're a very slow reader then. I've read hundreds of pages this week alone." She states.

"Wow, that's great news, so are you saying you can read faster than me?" Ryan inquires jokingly.

"Well, it does appear that way. You're either slow at reading or lazy because you haven't turned the page yet. What book are you reading?"

Ryan leans over and starts tickling Lysa. Lysa screeches and runs around the room. Ryan chases her. Watching them warms my heart. It also causes slight vertigo seeing them zigzag and circle around. Closing my eyes helps and hearing their giggles is precious. We don't need to spend money and travel to create beautiful memories. Lysa slows down.

"Mommy and Daddy I was thinking of names. I really like the name Vincent for a boy and Jasmine for a girl. What do you think?" She says as she runs back to her chair, slightly out of breath.

"I like Vincent and Jasmine definitely is unique. Can you come up with a more traditional name for a girl?" Ryan asks.

"Maybe, but I think Jasmine is a super cool name."

"I agree; it is Lysa." Ryan says.

"Good, but I'll think about other names too. This is a very important decision and I want this baby to have the perfect name."

"Lysa, I think mommy fell asleep."

I want to enjoy this but I'm really tired. "Ryan, I'm not asleep."

He helps me recline my bed back. Daily naps are a necessity, a very frustrating one. It might be a combination of pregnancy and the AVM, maybe. There isn't a point to my finding a reason; just that it's what my body needs so I'll do it.

"Thanks for reclining the bed."

"No prob. Do you mind if we take a nap too?"

"Sure."

The chair reclines too and Ryan settles into it while Lysa snuggles up to me on the bed. Ryan's breathing forms a steady rhythm. His phone vibrates, but I don't wake him. He needs his sleep. Some seasons in life last longer than others. I'm hoping mine with Ryan lasts very long.

Chapter 40

Doug opens the front door and notices a partial mud sneaker print. No sound greets him. He places his food bag on the floor and un-holsters his gun. He leaves it at his side and peeks around the corner, down the hallway. He only finds a couple more partial prints from the left foot as he makes his way to the office where he last saw Nick. He inhales a quiet, slow breath and lifts his gun. Stepping into the room, he steadily swings the gun clockwise in a full circle. The person responsible for the print is long gone. Nick is on the floor in front of the computer chair. Doug puts his gun away and races to Nick's side. He grabs his phone out of his back pocket and calls for back up and an ambulance.

"What's your emergency?" The dispatcher asks.

"A gunshot wound to the head." Doug runs to the bathroom and gets a towel.

"Is the victim alive?"

"I don't know yet." He runs back to Nick and puts the towel to his wound and presses on it. He cradles the phone in between his ear and his neck so he can check for a pulse.

"His head is still bleeding and I'm checking for a pulse now." He leans over and touches his neck. There's a lot of blood and his fingers slip. He wipes his fingers on his shirt and checks for a pulse from his wrist instead.

"I might have one. It's hard to tell." He grunts and tries again. "Is someone on their way?"

"Yes, there about a minute out."

Doug focuses on stopping the bleeding. The EMTs can determine if Nick has a pulse. Would he still be bleeding if he were dead? Doug didn't think so.

"Come on, Nick. Stay with me. You need to stay with me. Nancy will be so mad at you if you died. Do you hear me, Nick? Think of Nancy, okay." Doug can hear the sirens and knew that he would know about Nick soon. He did not want to be the one to knock on Nancy's door. He prayed that Nick would survive.

"I'm in here!" Doug screams.

Several people swarm into the room. They take the towel from Doug and move him out of the way. Doug stands by the door and watches them work. They don't say much to each other but steadily work on Nick.

"I have a pulse." One of the EMTs say and Doug's shoulders relax.

"Doug what happened?" Mike and Anthony arrive.

"I'm not sure. I came over earlier and was talking to Nick about Janice and I got hungry so I went to pick up some food, but the first place I tried was a deli and they were closed when I got there so I needed to go to another place."

"Doug slow down, what happened here?" Mike asks with a firm voice.

"I'm getting to that; I came back after getting food and I saw a mud print on the carpet when I stepped into the house and I know that wasn't there when I left. I drew my gun but I was too late. Nick was on the floor and I called it in. I haven't had time to check the house yet."

"Now that Nick is being taken care of, let's do that." Mike says.

Anthony points to the computer. "Whomever did this didn't want what was on the computer to become public knowledge." He leans down and turns the tower on its side. "The hard drive is missing. And for fun the person smashed the monitor. It looks like a really expensive one too."

"Lift." One of the EMTs says and they move Nick onto the stretcher. They start to wheel him out.

"What hospital are you taking him too?" Doug asks.

"Albany Med." Someone says as they continue to move Nick at a fast pace. Before long the siren is going at full volume.

"Guys, I have to go to the hospital and I'll call Ryan on the way and see what they were working on. Maybe that will help. Are you two okay here?" Doug asks Mike and Anthony.

"Yes, we are and that's a good idea to call Ryan. Where is he anyway?" Mike wants to know.

Doug shrugs and makes his way to his car.

Chapter 41

"Today I want to talk about forgiveness. This might seem to veer a little off course from our previous topics, but when I was thinking about what I wanted to share I realized that we have all been hurt at some point in our lives. If we haven't forgiven the one or ones whom have hurt us, then we might grow bitter, become more critical, and sometimes sever a whole or part of that relationship. Our closest relationships tend to be with our spouses and because of the time we spend with them it would most likely be that we would have some lack of forgiveness between these relationships or with our close friends and family.

"When my husband passed away, I had several people call me and question what happened? There was a lot of shock and people questioned why it happened because he was so young.

I had one woman call and practically shout at me that this wasn't right and couldn't have happened. She made me feel like I needed to defend myself. She went as far as accusing me of having something to do with his death. He died of a heart attack. She wanted to know what type of foods I was serving for dinner along with a list of other things that I did that she felt I shouldn't have done. She was blaming me for his heart attack. I was very angry with her. Here my husband just died two days before and she was telling me it was my fault. I yelled back and hung up the phone. This woman was a relative of my husband's. Weeks went by and I was starting to learn how to hold my head out of the swamp I felt I lived in. My phone rang and it was this woman again. Let's call her Franny. Franny didn't call to apologize like I thought, she called to inform me of the research she did and how she found many links to the things I was doing or letting my late husband do that surely contributed to him passing away. I let her talk and I started to feel the hurt with each word she said. It was like she was pushing my head back under that swamp I was living in. And this happened every time she called. Never an apology just her telling me what I did wrong. After a couple more calls I stopped answering the phone when she called. I had to. Those calls weren't helping me at all. But one great thing God did, was show me how to use my shield of faith. I could have wallowed in guilt about what she said when she called but I didn't. I also could have believed what she was telling me, but I didn't. It was like God was holding this shield up around me, for me, because I was too weak to hold it myself, and this shield blocked out the guilt each and every time Franny said I should be guilty. I knew that it wasn't my fault. I knew that it was just his time to go home but I missed him and still miss him terribly. Where does that leave me with Franny?

    "In the Message version of the Bible in Romans 5:20 it talks about an aggressive forgiveness called grace. I started thinking about the phrase aggressive forgiveness. I have never heard of those two words together. What does it mean? I then thought about the stomach bug. When you get the stomach bug you can't think of anything else. It is right there in the forefront of your mind bringing waves of nausea with it. It aggressively runs its course. Franny was my stomach bug. She was right there at the forefront of my mind trying to take away my peace. I wanted my peace back and God gave me a way to keep it. I had to forgive. But after I did, something else she said would pop up into my mind and take root of my thoughts and emotions. I was hurt. Then I thought about aggressive forgiveness. I made a decision. I wasn't going to passively let her words wound me; instead I was going to aggressively forgive. This meant that each time something she said came to mind I wasn't going to dwell on it. I decided I was going to forgive her and forgive her and forgive her. However long it took, with however many thoughts came to mind. I sought and pursued every area, every thought I was aware of and I chose to forgive.

"I thought of Jesus on the cross with his arms spread wide. When I pictured him there, I pictured him saying 'yes, I love you with an everlasting love, yes I know what you have done and yes, I chose to still be here for you. You are forgiven with an aggressive forgiveness because my love keeps forgiving, my grace for you, Franny,' as He breathes his last breath."

Helen lifts her water and takes a long sip.

"Who in your life do you need to forgive? Is it your husband or a family member or a friend?

"This talk is really two different ones put together. I really felt that I needed to talk about forgiveness and I also wanted to talk a little about what I originally planned to talk about tonight as well. The first time we gathered together we talked about body image and how most women are not happy with their own bodies. Instead of focusing on what we can't change, like our noses or how our feet look, we can focus on what we can change. Most of us could be healthier. Eating healthy and exercising regularly is important for all of us. When we do these things, we feel better, have more energy, and our self-confidence increases. For years, I said I didn't have the time and I truly felt I didn't. I was working full time and I was so tired when I got home. I didn't want another thing to do, so I dismissed the thought. I went through my days as I always do, helping others. I didn't have time to take time for myself. I started gaining weight, but I hid it well with my slightly baggie clothes.

"It was winter and the snow was coming down hard about an inch or two every hour. I didn't want to be late for work so I got ready quickly and started to shovel the heavy snow. It was about a foot deep at this time. I like shoveling so I wasn't upset about it. I got into a steady rhythm with shoveling, step with my left foot, scoop with my right arm. I did this for about 20 minutes; my back was sore and my arms achy. I had more to do, but I needed to get to work. Cautiously, I walked throughout my day. When I got home I saw the plow gifted me with another two feet at the end of the driveway. I, stubbornly, wanted my car in the driveway, so I got out the shovel and continued to finish the job in the same manner. My back resisted, but I continued. I'm young I thought; this shouldn't be a problem for me. I used to exercise daily when I played sports in high school. This is my exercise, I said to myself as I finished the driveway. I parked my car in the driveway and grabbed a glass of water. It was hard for me to slightly bend down to get it. Huh, why would that be? I'm young. I pulled an ice pack out of the freezer and went to bed to rest. An hour later I tried to get up to make myself dinner and I discovered that I couldn't get out of bed without having excruciating pain. I called a friend, but she didn't answer so I called another one and then another. No one was available.

"Then I thought that they couldn't help me anyway. I was stuck and I had to go to the bathroom. I knew I couldn't make it there. I didn't care that I was hungry. I weighed my options. Even if someone helped me, I couldn't make it to the car. I called 911 and waited for the ambulance to arrive. I was helpless. Why? It's because I didn't put my health first. I discovered that if I didn't help myself first, I wasn't going to be able to help others. I was in physical therapy for a while and it was months before I was able to start exercising. I didn't want to go through that again. I wanted to be healthy and I knew I couldn't rely on my past activity to keep me there. I had to do something that day and I did. I changed my thoughts and I changed my pattern of thinking. Instead of being healthy tomorrow, I decided to be healthy that day. I took time for myself. I made me a priority. I made a commitment and worked hard at keeping it. I started to believe that I was important. That I was worth fighting for and that I had self-worth. As I started to get stronger, I started to feel more confident and I started to view myself differently. I also started to like my body. I saw results.

"Now I'm not saying I was perfect. Occasionally I ate something that wasn't healthy, and once in a while I skipped a workout, but I stuck with it. I gave myself permission to move on and continue living healthy without the weighted guilt of messing up. I haven't had a problem with my back since and for that I'm thankful. I took control of what I could control. I had the ability to work out and eat a well-balanced diet and I made changes. I still can't control the way my feet look or that I have thin hair, but I've changed my thoughts on how I view them. God made me a unique individual. He made me in His image and He made you that way too. God only creates beauty so who am I to say that I'm not beautiful. We are his beautiful creation. Let's start living that way!"

After Helen briefly discusses when and what the next meeting will be about, she steps down and walks to the back. Nancy stays seated as the women leave and thinks about her day. She ran her errands and picked up Lysa from April and Ryan. They were both asleep when she arrived but Lysa was wide-awake. She rushed Lysa to her mom's house and came straight to the meeting. She didn't take time to eat much today and she was hoping to grab a bite soon.

Nancy looks up and sees Helen standing in front of a long line. Nancy's cell starts to play music. She doesn't recognize the phone number so she ignores the call.

Chapter 42

The walls are close together. She's never been in a jail before and now she is told she isn't allowed to leave. Ethan, her lawyer, said he was going to be working very hard to get her out as soon as he could. He seems nice but what he said is vague. Of course, he can work hard to get her out but he didn't work hard enough to keep her from being put in. She did nothing wrong and Doug better believe that. Maybe he only dated her because he thought she was responsible all along. Her shoulders sag as she sits on the edge of the bench. The room has several women in it. It's dirty and stale. There has been no sign of water or food and the one towel, fortunately, has been left unused.

A couple of the women whispered when Janice was brought in but that's as far as it went. No one talked to her and she was relieved. On occasion a guard would come by and take someone out. She had no idea where they went but they didn't come back. Her back was starting to hurt. She has been sitting at attention for a couple of hours. She would like to sleep but knows that isn't a good idea. The light flickers overhead but stays on.

The woman sitting next to her shifts toward Janice. She bumps her with her shoulder on purpose.

"Hey, why did you do that?" The woman says and Janice can smell the onions she must have eaten earlier.

"I didn't do anything." Janice says and moves a few inches down the bench away from the woman. The woman shoulders her again. And Janice moves again. A few snickers come from across the room. The woman glares at Janice, her arms are as big as two of Janice's put together.

"Sorry." Janice mumbles.

The woman chuckles. "A little late for that." She pounces on Janice. Her fist meets with Janice's jaw and her head snaps back, hitting the concrete wall behind her. A loud echo follows. Janice's eyes grow big and then roll back. She slumps to the floor and involuntarily exhales on impact.

Chapter 43

My stomach is nicely round. My days consist of eating, sleeping, reading, and hoping someone comes to visit. The baby kicks and Ryan walks in and hands me a small bag of Godiva chocolates.

"Thanks, Ryan. This looks tasty and fattening."

"You're welcome. I hope you enjoy them. How are you feeling?"

"That nap we took was perfect. I feel good. How has work been going?"

He visibly cringes. I can't let this go on any longer.

"Ryan, please tell me what's wrong. I know there is something you aren't telling me, and I want to know before this baby comes out."

"I haven't wanted to upset you. The doctor said to not put you under any stress."

"Your keeping it from me is stressful."

"Oh." He takes my foot in his hand and starts to massage it. "I didn't think about that."

"Good, now tell me."

"Are you sure? This might upset you."

"Yes, I'm sure." Ryan looks into my eyes as if trying to see if it's the right thing to do.

"Okay, years ago I started a side business. It became quite profitable and I have needed to hire other people to help with the work."

He turns away from me as he continues to talk, "I'm a private investigator. I help people find the truth."

"Really?" I sit up in bed.

"Yes."

He turns around and stares at me. I need to say something.

"Why didn't you tell me sooner?" I ask.

"I should have and I'm really sorry I didn't."

"Okay." I shrug.

"Okay. Are you mad?" He puts down my foot and gently picks up the other one.

"I wish you told me sooner but how can I be mad when you're massaging my feet." I laugh. "I have learned that holding secrets from your spouse is wrong. It ate me up inside every day I saw you and I didn't tell you I was pregnant. No, I'm not mad. I only hope that we both learn to trust each other with our secrets."

"Me too, April, me too. How are you feeling?"

"Better. I'm really glad you told me and didn't keep it from me any longer."

"Me too. Nick is one of my employees."

I put my head back on the pillow and close my eyes. "Ah, that makes sense. All those trips and he was going with you. I'd ask you about the danger, but I've learned that there is danger wherever one goes. For me, it is right inside my head so I'm not going to ask yet. I think it is actually a cool profession. I want to know all about it. Maybe tonight you can tell me about some of the cases you've solved. The ones where there was no danger to you, of course."

"You don't want me to close the business? I will in a heartbeat, if you want me to. I don't want a job that takes me away from you."

"Why don't we think about it for a while? The baby will be here soon. Can you take time off for a bit?"

"I can take a year off if need be or close the whole thing."

"I don't want you to do that, only take some time off for now."

"Okay, that's easy."

"Good. Has Nick told Nancy?"

"Yes."

"And?"

"And...I don't know. You'll have to ask Nancy."

Ryan leans over and hugs me as we both share a chuckle. Both of our secrets have been revealed. It's a wonderful feeling, being honest. I move over so Ryan can share some of the bed with me. He holds me for a few minutes. His phone rings and he gets up to get it from his back pocket.

"April, it's Nick, do you mind if I take this?"

"I'm in the best part of the book I'm reading now so I'm fine doing that. Go ahead."

I grab my book from the end table and open it to where I left off but the words to register in my brain. I only hear Ryan on the phone.

"Hey, Nick, what did you find out?" Ryan pauses, looks at me, and points to the hallway. I shrug.

* * *

"Doug, can you repeat that?" I say after the door is closed, and April can't hear.

"I said, I found Nick's phone on the desk and called you to tell you that someone shot him in the head. He is on the way to Albany Med and so am I. He should be there before me, probably in fifteen minutes."

"How bad is he, Doug?" I grit my teeth and feel my pulse speed up.

"He seemed bad, Ryan. He had a pulse and I'm not a doctor so I don't know how bad he really is. Your hard drive was taken and the monitor was smashed. We got a couple of partial footprints because of the rain shower we had earlier in the day so that could be a good lead. Did Nick call you with any new leads?"

"No." I lean against the wall and slowly slide to the floor.

"I don't know what he found or if you found anything but there must have been info on the drive that the person either wanted you to not have or needed for themselves. Any ideas?"

"None, Doug, none." I put my head between my legs. My best friend might die.

"I'm not sure what this means for Janice but maybe she can post bail now."

"Maybe. I'm going down to the emergency room."

"Okay, I'll find you."

I put the phone back in my pocket and open April's door just enough to put my head in. Her book is back on the nightstand and her eyes are shut. I grab a receipt from my pocket and write her a quick note saying I'm meeting Nick and I'll be back to visit later. I put the note on top of her book and quietly walk back out.

None of the elevators are on my floor so I race to the steps and run down several flights. Two EMTs wheel a stretcher in. My back twinges but I jog up to it to see an older man in the bed. I go to the window and look out. Another ambulance pulls up and before the driver gets it in park the back-door swings open. They work together well and the stretcher comes out smoothly. I see Nick. He looks very pale but his hand is moving. Maybe he's awake and talking. They start to wheel him in and I step on one of the sides. Nick's eyes are open and he looks right at me.

"Ryan, nice to see you man." Nick says.

I let out a huge breath of air. "You scared me, Nick. You okay?"

"Yeah, I might have taken a bullet meant for you though."

"You think so?"

"Maybe."

"Excuse me, but we need to bring him back to have him looked at." One of the EMTs says.

"I'll wait here to find out how you're doing, Nick." I pat his shoulder.

I step aside and watch them wheel him away. He was talking and smiling. That's a great sign. I sit down and pull out my phone. I have seven emails since this morning. One is from Nick. I click on it and open the attachment. Two people walk into a store. I pause it and look at what it's labeled. It's the helicopter rental place. And I recognize the two people. The time was three hours ago. Nick must have sent it right before he was shot. Doug sits next to me and I show him the video. He forwards it to his boss and makes a few calls.

Chapter 44

Her purse slips off her shoulder and down her arm but her body is moving too fast for her other arm to catch the strap. It falls and she quickly snatches it up, resuming her former pace. Room 2012. She knocks and waits with a constant tap of her right foot.

"Come in."

She pushes the door open too hard and it swings wide banging into the wall.

"Hi, Nancy. You look beautiful." Nick says from his hospital bed.

"My eyes are puffy and I didn't do my hair today."

"You still look beautiful."

"Nick...I'm so glad you're okay." She gingerly hugs him.

"Me too!"

She's so relieved he's going to be fine. The doctor said it only grazed his head. He will be able to leave the hospital by tomorrow if he continues to do this well. She wants to marry him desperately but she still hasn't told him about not knowing if she can have children. "I'm not sure if I can have a baby?"

"Uh, oh, Nancy, is that why you've been quiet sometimes when we were together?"

"Yes."

"Nancy if God blesses us with a baby that would be great, but that would be the cherry on top. I want to marry you; I love you and if we never have children I'm okay with that." He says.

"Are you sure?"

"I am. And I have already considered that we might not ever have children. That will be something that we can discover together and we will get through it together."

She leans to give him a hug but Nick tilts her chin up and gently kisses her lips.

"When can we get married?"

"I'd say today if it wasn't so late. How about we ask the Pastor when he's free?"

"Sounds great. Nick, I've spent the last two weeks examining your character."

"Uh, oh."

"No, it's good. You are a man of your word, you are smart, caring, and you extend yourself to help others even when you would prefer to relax at home. You love and you follow God. I want you to lead me closer to Him and I can't wait to marry you."

He kisses her again and Nancy sighs.

"How about you go visit April and I'll make that phone call."

"Great. See you soon Nick." She walks to the door but turns back and smiles. "Nick I'm so glad you're okay."

"Me too! And if I can do anything about it, the next time you see me will be when you say 'I do'."

"Oh, wait, Nick. We didn't discuss that your second job is a PI."

"Uh-oh."

"I'm still not sure…" She walks back to him; he grabs her hands with both of his.

"Nancy, I don't ever have to take another PI job in my life. I'm okay with being a carpenter."

"Okay. I'm still not sure about it. We need more time to discuss it. What I am sure about is that I want to marry you."

"Good." He pulls her down and kisses her again.

"Okay. I love you."

"I love you too."

He winks at her and she walks out the door.

* * *

Her phone buzzes at 8 am.

"Yes?" She coughs to clear her throat.

"Did I wake you, Nancy?"

"Yes."

"Oh, your voice is so cute in the morning. I can't wait!"

"Can't wait for what?" Cloudiness surrounds her thoughts.

"To get married!"

"When?" She sits up straight in bed.

"How about 9 hours from now?"

"What?" She jumps up and tries to find her slippers.

"I said the next time I see you I want to be saying 'I do'.

"You are a man of your word, aren't you?" She chuckles.

"I'll try my best to be."

"9 hours! Really?"

"Yes!"

"There is so much to do."

"Nancy, remember we said we wanted a simple wedding."

"Yes, we did but what if someone isn't free? And April is still in the hospital."

"Then we will record it. Plus, everyone that we want to come will be visiting April anyway."

"What? At the hospital? We're getting married at the hospital?"

"Is that all right?" Nick asks.

"Yes, April will be thrilled and she will be able to see everyone but what about your brothers and father?" She takes two fast breaths. "I'm trying not to hyperventilate."

"Slow breaths, Nancy. I've already talked to my dad and he said he can drive up and he will do his best trying to get my brothers here. All this wedding needs is the Pastor, you and me.

Everyone else will work out any other details. Didn't you and April and Helen work out lots of those little details?"

"We discussed a lot, but, oh, it doesn't matter. I'm getting married and I have my dress. How about you call the people you want to come and I'll do the same."

"Sounds good."

"Oh and Nick, you need to rent a tux."

"I'm on it. I already sent over my measurements. A nurse helped me out with that about thirty minutes ago." He states.

"Okay, I have lots to do so I love you and good-bye." She hears him chuckle before she hangs up. She starts to run out of the bedroom and dial Helen's number but the phone slips from her hands. She takes a deep breath, planning a wedding in less than a day is doable. Right? She takes another deep breath and calls Helen.

"Hi Nancy, I have amazing plans for tonight!" Helen sings.

"Oh, Helen, you mean you're busy tonight?"

"I'm very busy today and especially tonight!"

"Oh."

"I'm busy planning your wedding and being a bride's maid!" She states.

"How did you know?"

"Nick called me. He said he wanted to give me a heads-up. He didn't want you to be overwhelmed so he called me and I already started all of your plans into motion."

"You did?"

"Yes, I did."

"All of them? What have you done?"

"Let's see, your mom, Ella, and April are taking care of the dinner and the wedding cake. Ryan and Nick are getting the tuxes, and then Ryan and Doug have some business to take care of. April, your mom, Ella, you, and I are going to meet in April's room at the hospital for a manicure and pedicure three hours before the wedding and get our hair done there as well. I called two of my acquaintances that own their own spa and they are willing to drive over to do that. And April called another friend to arrange our hair. Ella said she knows someone who does make-up so she will be calling her soon."

"How did you do all of that? Nick just called me."

"He called me last night and asked me to start working on the plans and I called April. Then he called this morning around 7am and told me the Pastor was free, he waited one hour to call you so that you could sleep in. I've really had a lot of time to put this all into motion. Your job is to call anyone I haven't discussed and invite them. You can split your list with April, she's waiting for your call."

"Wow, this is wonderful! I'll focus on relaxing."

"Oh, and I have a massage scheduled for you before we go to the hospital for our manicures, hair, and make-up."

"What?"

"You should have one."

"I'm not going to say no; I'm just perplexed as to how you convinced so many people to leave their business and come help me today."

"Let's just say, I can be very persuasive."

"You didn't!"

"I'm good at what I do and it helped a lot that Nick is paying them double what they would normally make. Okay, maybe that's the real reason."

"Wow, thank you." Nancy does a little jump.

"Thank Nick, it was all his idea. I wonder if he slept last night. Oh, and I just pulled in, so why are you still up there?"

"Sorry, you need to come up, I'm not even dressed yet."

Chapter 45

The team assembles around the house. The shades are drawn and only a couple of lights appear to be on, but there are two cars in the driveway and after the plates were run, it was confirmed that the two people in question are the owners of the vehicles. Anthony, Mike, and two other men cover the exits while Doug and his boss take the front door. I was invited but asked to keep my distance. I'm sitting in an unmarked car on the street, which faces the corner of the house. I have a view of the right side of the house and the front.

The video put it all together. My case started to make sense after I saw the footage. I couldn't figure it out before and I probably never would have if Nick didn't come up with the needed information. Doug rings the doorbell and his boss draws his gun. Because they were trying to kill me, they're taking extra precautions. I can't hear what is said but I know they are communicating through their walkie-talkies to each other. Doug sends his boss a nod and he rings the doorbell again. I see a flutter of a curtain from one of the windows on the front side of the house. I don't think Doug can see that. My palms itch.

A window on the right side of the house opens but no one has eyes on it, but me. I slowly open my car door and duck down as I get out. I make my way over to the nearest tree without being seen. An object flies past my head and hits the car. I jump away as fast as I can, and bury my face into the ground. The car explodes and I can feel the heat on my back. I try to crawl but the blast holds me in place. Doug screams and starts to run toward the car. His boss holds him back. Another second passes and nothing hits me. I look up at the opened window and see a man climbing out. I stumble as I start to run toward the man but gain my footing right as he puts his feet on the ground. I steam roll into him before he has time to think about what was happening. I land on his back and fortunately he takes the brunt of the fall. No pain so far. The man turns and I get a good look at his face. John. Supposed employee helping me find out if Amy's boyfriend Tim was a good guy. It all started to make sense. He would call me to come down and check out something Tim supposedly did. He also didn't follow orders well. He looks at me and spits. I dodge it, and gravity takes it right back down into his face. This makes him even madder and he throws a punch at me. Doug catches his arm in mid-swing. I roll off John and let Doug cuff him.

"I thought you were a goner, Ryan. How many lives do you have?"

"I'm so glad you parked the car where you did. I had a perfect view of John opening the window. I knew you couldn't see him so I got out of the car to help out just in case he decided to run. I didn't expect him to draw attention to himself by blowing up the car." I stand to my feet and dust off my hands. "John you just did something really dumb. There's no way you are going to get away with this."

"I don't care if I get away with it. All I want is for you to be dead." The side of his upper lip curls up as he grits his teeth together.

"What I can't figure out is why you want me dead." I say.

"If you don't know then you are stupider than I thought. You let Mr. Willis see that his companies were losing money."

"How did I do that?"

"You called the company Tim was interning with and you started asking the woman in charge about the billing and receipts and too many other questions. She became curious and did some digging. She found out that the records weren't correct and let her boss know who let Mr. Willis and the police know. From there, Mr. Willis started searching for inconsistencies in his other companies and he found them. You ruined everything." He was pulling on the cuffs, trying to get to me. "I hate you, I want you dead!"

Mike helped Doug pull John to the other car. A fire truck arrives and starts to put out what is left of the fire. Mike stays with

John and Doug runs back to the front door but it opens before he gets to it. He goes to draw his gun but it's too late. The woman steps out onto the front step. Her hands are empty and she starts to tremble.

"He made me do it." She cries as she falls to the ground. Anthony runs up and cuffs Mrs. Willis's hands in front of her. He gently pulls her to her feet and eyes his boss. His boss nods and instructs him to take her to the police car. "He threatened to kill my Amy if I didn't give him access to the accounts. He said he was going to kill me too." She cries some more. Real or not real? I shrug; it's not for me to decide. I did my job, Tim is innocent and a good match for Amy, but he might choose to not want anything to do with her after he hears what has happened.

An ambulance arrives and I'm brought to the back of the truck. They lift the back of my shirt.

"You have some minor burns, some ointment and you should be fine. Do you have any pain?" The EMT asks.

"Nope, none at all." I say and smile. The job is finally over.

* * *

"Get back! What happened in here?" The guard asks the tall blond with greasy hair. Two other guards come in the room and make sure the first guard, Charlie, was safe.

She reaches down and checks for a pulse. A faint beat meets Charlie's fingers.

"Call for a medic." She yells over her shoulder. She looks at the blood on the floor and examines the situation. One of these women attacked her. She will find out whom. No one does this on her watch and gets away with it.

Someone hands Charlie a towel and she wraps it around the woman's wound. She begins to moan. That's a good sign.

The guard on Charlie's left yells, "Janice, Janice Myers? Which one of you is she?"

No one answers. "Janice, you're not in trouble, unless you hurt this woman here, you are free to go, so which one of you is Janice?" Still no one answers.

"This is probably Janice on the floor." Charlie says, then groans. Her day has just gone from bad to beyond bad. Janice was found innocent of all the charges against her. She was supposed to be walking to her car right now. Charlie makes Janice as comfortable as she can. The bleeding has stopped, she thinks, and Janice's eyes fluttered open once. She was going to be driven to the hospital.

Chapter 46

The day went as Helen described. The massage was only for Nancy. She was truly pampered. As Arlene was putting the finishing touches on her makeup in April's hospital room, she realizes that she's going to be married in less than 25 minutes. She hasn't seen Nick yet. Her dress is on, and the girls are wearing theirs. They are all set. Except for Janice. Ryan called earlier in the day to say that Janice was injured and on her way to the hospital. He asked her to keep it from April until they knew what was wrong with her. He called again two hours ago to say that Janice has a nasty concussion but that she will be fine. Her nurse volunteered to help her mask her wound and get her in her dress, but she still needed to stay in bed. They decided to wheel Janice in when she was able to be all smiles for April. That hasn't happened yet and Nancy was about to say 'I do' in twenty-five minutes. She's sure Ryan is aware of the time. He'll work it all out.

She takes a deep breath, "Helen, is Nick here?"

"He has been outside with Ryan for the past ten minutes pacing back and forth. He's constantly looking at his watch too. The flowers look amazing in here. Oh, and here's your bouquet." Helen says as she hands it to her.

Nancy pulls the flowers to her nose and takes a big sniff. "It's beautiful. I didn't think there were going to be any flowers."

"No flowers at your wedding? What type of crazy idea is that?" Ella points out. She bought a slight variation of the bride's maid dress, more modern. The lavender color looks great on all the women.

"Nancy, the flowers are gorgeous." Agnes puts her arm around Nancy. "You look so beautiful, honey. I'm so happy for you." She takes out a tissue and dabs at her eyes.

"Thanks, mom. I have no idea how you all pulled this together." Helen smiles and winks at April.

The door opens and a nurse wheels a bed in. Nancy and Helen make their way over to April so that they can answer any questions.

"April, I had to come to this unusual wedding in style. As your best friend, I didn't want you to feel left out by being the only person who gets a bed so I convinced Stephanie to find me one and she did." Janice isn't in a hospital gown but dressed in a stylish light blue suit. Stephanie wheels her to the spot that someone made moments ago. Everyone's eyes are darting back and forth between Janice and April. Janice looks completely normal. They couldn't even see her cast on her arm. The suit jacket hides it well as does the oversized hat.

"I also decided to start a blue hat society in our area." Janice chuckles as she touches the rim of her hat. It was the only hat she had that would cover her bandages around her head but she isn't planning to share that with anyone.

"I was wondering where you have been, Janice. Ryan mentioned that you went on a vacation. Where did you go and why didn't you call me?" April asks but before she could answer the door opens again.

The Pastor walks in followed by the groomsmen. This is Nancy and her mom's cue to step out and go to the room next door. Nick's family walks in with Nick, who looks a little pale. Several other people come in and stand around the two beds. How were they all free at such short notice? Music starts to play and Nancy and her mom appear in the doorway. It's a short walk. The bouquet starts shaking as Nancy consciously put one foot in front of another to where Nick is standing in his tux. All she can see is Nick. The Pastor starts talking and the few available chairs are used. He turns to Nancy and somehow she says 'I do' and she hears Nick say 'I do' as well.

"You may kiss the bride." The Pastor announces.

Nick leans in and lets everyone know who his wife is. She was more nervous than she anticipated, and she hardly heard what the Pastor said. A bunch of flashes go off and lots of people start talking all at once.

The dinner was tasty and the room next door was set up nicely for everyone to sit comfortably. Just as Nancy thought the evening was winding down, music starts playing. He even found a DJ. The men quickly fold up all the tables and most of the chairs. Nancy dances until her feet are sore. What an amazing night.

* * *

"Wasn't today a great day, Ryan?"

"Yes, it was. I'm so glad they figured it out on their own." Ryan says as he cuddles up next to April in her bed. Everyone has left, except Janice who was wheeled to the room next door when it was all cleaned up. April still doesn't know about her injuries.

"Me too, even though I wanted to meddle into Nancy and Nick's relationship, like the gift she extended to us, I held my tongue."

"It's better you didn't say anything."

"Yeah, I know. I'm so tired; I'm ready for bed. How about you?"

"Yes, since Lysa is spending the night with your mom and Ella, I think I'm going to sleep here."

"Great! It will be nice to see you in the morning." A yawn escapes. "The food was so much better than the food here. I can't believe all that happened in only several hours."

"I think it was easier to do all of the planning, and the wedding in one day. It beats months of planning for the big day." Ryan says as he pulls his duffle bag out from under my bed.

"God blessed. There's no other way all of this would have happened otherwise, too many willing people to help out last minute. It's still unbelievable."

"How are you feeling?"

"I'm really tired, but I feel good."

"Good, I was concerned that today would be too much."

"I don't think so…but I'm going to sleep now."

"Goodnight honey, I love you." He reaches over and gently runs his hand down the side of my face. Then kisses me with the same light touch.

"Love you too, and goodnight, Ryan."

The room darkens as I relax my mind.

Chapter 47

April's pregnancy is moving along nicely. The baby is growing at a perfect pace and April hasn't had any more complications. I'm still unsettled about a couple of things from this case. I've been trying to get some answers about Tim's parents. Nick and I have searched and haven't been able to track them down. I find it odd that Tim's grandparents have no idea where they are or what they do. They gave us no information. I don't think they lied to us, but I do think they are hiding something.

* * *

I pick up my phone and call Nick. "The doctor that tried to abort the baby's name is Dr. Stevens."

"Are you sure?" He asks.

"Yes."

"Do you think he's related? How did we miss that?"

"I'm not sure, but anyway, I know it could be nothing, but it's worth a shot."

"I agree. We knew Tim had an uncle but he was a doctor with a clean record. Okay, where are you?"

"I'm leaving my house now. Where are you?"

"I was on my way to your house but I can meet you wherever you're going?"

"Sure, I'm headed to the hospital."

"Okay, great."

"Which hospital?" I hear Nick pick up a drink and take a sip.

"The one where he is employed or was employed. We're hopefully going to find out if he knows where Tim's parents are."

"Tim's grandparents said they didn't feel comfortable giving us information about any relatives and we couldn't ask Tim, so hopefully this is a lead but, Ryan, odds are it isn't."

"Yeah, but if he knows something he is going to tell me because he owes me."

"He probably doesn't see it that way."

"I'll make him see it that way." I hang up and make the drive with minimal cars slowing me down.

I park and check my emails while I wait for Nick. He taps on my window and I get out. "Ryan, maybe I should do the talking."

"Why?"

"Because I think your emotions are going to get in the way of finding out what we need to find out."

As we approach the entrance, I take a minute to think through what Nick is saying.

"You're right, Nick. I don't want to admit it, but I'm really mad right now. It's best you do the talking. Thanks."

"No prob. That's why we're a team. Well at least for a little bit longer."

We approach the receptionist area.

"Excuse me, where can I find Dr. Stevens?" Nick asks the receptionist.

"Let me see."

She takes out a folder and runs her finger down a list of names. On the fifth page, she stops.

"Ah, he works on the third floor, but I don't have a schedule so I don't know if he is working today."

"Thanks. That should be all we need."

"You're welcome."

She says as she puts the folder where it belongs to the left of her desk. Nick leads us to the right elevator. Stepping off, I look around to see what floor we're on. I see a lot of elderly, but I'm not going to assume. Rage courses through my body; Nick is right about this one. I want to put this Dr. Stevens to the wall, no, through the wall.

"Kristin, where is Dr. Stevens?" Nick reads from her nametag.

"I think he's in his office," she looks up, "oh, wait, who are you?"

"I'm here to ask him some questions." Nick flashes his PI badge.

"Dr. Stevens office is the third door down that hallway, on the right."

"Thanks."

We start to walk that way, when Nick stops and tugs on my arm.

"Hey, Ryan, there's a bathroom over there. I think you need to use it."

"Nick, I think you're taking this too far." I say.

"Your anger is going to get us nowhere. You are going to blow up and blow our chance of finding out anything useful. I'm the lead on this one. You even said so yourself when we were in the parking garage. I've got this; you are going to have to trust me. You have trained me over the years and I have learned a lot. Now it's time you let me use what I've learned and I've learned that you need a cool head when questioning and you don't have that.

"Honestly, I wouldn't either if I were you, but for the first round of this, I'm doing the talking. So, please, use the bathroom and wait outside his door. I'll leave it open so you can hear, but please don't come in. I also think him seeing you, is going to cause a problem."

Opening my mouth to rebut, Nick cuts me off, "And no force and scare tactic here. Trust me."

"Okay, Nick, we'll do this your way, first. If you don't get results, I'm coming in."

"I guess that's better than nothing, oh and if we continue this business I want to talk about a partnership."

"All right, I get your point. You're the lead in this one. I'm off to the bathroom."

Nick walks ahead of me and I change my mind about the bathroom. I walk behind him and I prop myself behind the door. I don't want to miss anything. Nick knows that too.

"Hi, Dr. Stevens. My name is Nick Brennan. I'm a private investigator and I'd like to ask you a few questions."

"What is this in regards to?" His clipped voice responds.

"It's in regards to Tim Stevens."

"Oh, I thought you were here about another issue. Sit down. I have a nephew named Tim. Is he okay?"

"Yes, he's fine, but we can't seem to locate his parents. He hasn't seen them in a very long time."

Nice phrasing Nick.

"Well, that's easy, they can't be found."

"Why?"

"Because they both live in some remote country in Africa."

"Why?"

"Honestly, I'm not sure. My brother, Tim's father came here one night about three years ago. He said that his wife, Shelly, was deeply depressed. He blamed me. He said she couldn't get over her abortion. I told him that it was their choice, not mine. You see they came to me a couple of years before Tim was born. They told me that she was pregnant and that they wanted an abortion. I was just starting out as a doctor and they were in a desperate situation. It was my first abortion. I didn't want to do it, but they insisted. Shelly changed after that. They had Tim and after a little while, she lost it. She couldn't care for him. It was probably guilt. I don't know, but they basically dropped him off at her parents and moved away. They would come and visit occasionally but they weren't ever able to parent him. My brother blamed me and I blamed him for starting my career off with a horrible beginning. We grew distant and I continued to try to help women. The problem was they would come back after many years of being away, and yell at me, blaming me for their choice. I've had more hate mail than I'd like to own, more people blaming me. I don't know where I went wrong. I went back to school and studied to become a neurosurgeon. I needed a change. I was creating so much sadness and hatred that I couldn't do it anymore. After my brother left that day, I considered what he said. Was her depression my fault? I don't know, maybe.

"I've tried to be a good uncle to Tim. Are you sure he is okay?"

"He seems well. He is in a relationship and he is a Christian."

"Yeah, he told me about God. I'm glad religion is helpful for him. He has been through a lot with his parents leaving him."

"He found a relationship with God, not religion."

"Yeah, whatever." He waves his hand. "I'm glad you stopped by. I haven't seen Tim in a while so I'll give him a call and maybe he'll come up here for a visit."

"Dr. Stevens, do you know where in Africa they are living?"

"No, I don't. I've tried to locate them, but I came up with nothing. Their last letter was years ago. I was hoping to patch things up with my brother. Maybe Tim's grandparents know. You should ask them. If they do, can you tell me?"

"Sure." Nick didn't get enough information; maybe I should go in there.

"Dr. Stevens, one more thing."

"Yes?"

"What did your brother and his wife go to school for?"

"My brother followed in my footsteps. We both wanted to be doctors. He met his wife at school. That's why they wanted to have an abortion because the baby would mess up their plans. I can see now how that wasn't the right choice for them. Not having the baby hurt them beyond what they ever imagined. They both finished med school and that's when Tim was born. I was there right after he was born. They were so happy. I'm not sure what happened over the next few months, but before Tim turned two they dropped him off at her parents' and left the country. I don't know if they used their education or not but Tim told me once that they send money for him every month and that it was a lot of money. He said his grandparents saved it in a trust fund for him, and that's what he's using to put himself through college. He also mentioned that there would be money left over for him to spend his time trying finding a good job and he wanted to donate money to some religious charity. I don't remember the name of it. I wasn't really interested in that."

"Okay, thanks. Here's my card. Please call me if you hear from them. I'd really like to talk to them. And if I find out where they are, I'll let you know."

"Okay, thanks for stopping by." They shake hands and Nick walks out the door. I fall into step with him.

"He doesn't know much."

"No, he doesn't, but I think that's enough to close the case. I don't think there is anything more for us to find out."

"Yeah, I hear you Ryan; we wasted a lot of our time."

"Yes, we did. Mr. Willis believes John was threatening his wife the whole time and that she had nothing to do with it. I'm not sure I believe that but I'm also not interested in exploring that either."

"Yeah, we should just leave that one alone."

Chapter 48

I think the only hour I didn't see on my alarm clock last night was 4 am. It was the last night of my pregnancy. Many things had my attention last night. As I anxiously thought about each one, I tried to focus on the passage I read in Matthew the day before. Jesus took time for himself, sending his disciples on ahead of him in a boat. At 4 am He walked on the water to the boat. What happened last night reminded me of how I was like Peter each time a thought would come into my head. A fear, maybe, that this wasn't a good idea or what will happen to Ryan and Lysa. I would see how I was like Peter, distracting myself to the right or stepping to my left with my thoughts when what I needed to be doing was looking straight ahead at Jesus. He was holding his hand out, waiting, ready to help me through my thoughts and anxieties. He was reaching to me, lovingly, wanting to help. I started to reach my hand. A thought would come in that was distracting me from what I was going to be facing, and I would stop it and focus on Jesus' hand reaching out to me and I made my choice. I chose to take it and I spent the rest of my night praying. When I would wake after only thirty minutes of sleep, I would pray and it was like being tucked back into bed by Jesus, because I would focus back on him. I stopped my worries, my concerns, my fears, and I looked right into the trusting eyes of Jesus. I didn't sleep much last night, but I'm rested today. I'm ready for whatever is going to happen. And when those pesky 'what ifs' come crawling into my mind, I'm going to look straight into the eyes of Jesus, and take His hand as I go walking on the water with him today!

My phone rings. "Mommy, today is the day that the baby comes, right?"

"You're up really early, Lysa."

"I know, but I just woke up and I had a dream about the baby being born and I had to call you."

Chuckling, I reach over and pull the printed picture I have of Ryan, Lysa, and me off the end table and look at it.

"Lysa, do you know where daddy is?"

"Yes, he was getting me breakfast before I called."

"Okay, I'm going to send him a text. Can you ask him to look at his phone when we get off the phone?"

"Sure, he just called me for breakfast so I better go. Love you!" She hangs up.

My stomach has turned huge over the last few weeks. Today is the day. I'm not sure why a nurse hasn't been in. Wobbling, I walk to the bathroom. Brushing my teeth, I feel a contraction. Good thing I'm at the hospital. Could be nothing, but if it is labor I'm glad to know that this baby isn't coming early, but right on time!

My breathing labors as I walk around.

"There you are." Stephanie says as she sticks her head into the bathroom. She looks at my stomach. "You're having a contraction?"

"Yes."

"For how long?"

"Throughout the night." She makes a face, walks over to me, and lifts up my shirt. "Your monitor came detached. April come on and get in bed. We need to monitor you and get your section scheduled for an earlier time." She moves me back to bed. Good thing I finished brushing my teeth and sending that text to Ryan. I asked him to come right away and I'm sure he will. A flurry of activity starts happening around me. Several nurses and two doctors are now looking at me and checking to see how I'm doing. I feel fine. I answer their questions and hope that Ryan gets here soon. It seems that I should have woken up the nurse last night when the contractions started. One doctor is visibly unhappy. Neither of them are my doctor so we need to wait for him too. A brief knock on the door and Ryan and Lysa stick their heads in.

His hair is tossed to one side with a slight cowlick toward the back left.

"You didn't get much sleep, did you?"

"Nope. How can you tell?"

I reach up and try to calm his hair.

"Bad, huh?"

"You might want to look in the mirror."

"Nay, no time."

I grab some water from the pitcher and pat the top of Ryan's head.

"Hey, what was that for?"

He turns around as the water trickles down his nose.

"Oops. I guess I had more water in my hand then I thought." I say.

He pats my stomach as another contraction comes. This might only be Braxton Hicks, but it really doesn't matter now, right? Another contraction hits. It lasts less than a minute. I have nothing to be concerned about; it's too short.

"Ryan and Lysa, this isn't going to be easy for you. We don't know what is going to happen today, but we know God is in control. I want you both to think about something. Think of the road you were on as you drove her this morning, most of the time you pay attention to what is in front of you. You were focused on your destination. You went down different roads with different twists and turns but you paid attention to the road most of all. Today we are going to go down different twists and turns as well. We aren't sure where our road will take us, but what we do know is that as we focus on what is ahead of us, and we are aware of our surroundings, but not looking straight at them, most likely when we drive, we will be safe. When we drive, if we focus too much on what is on the sidelines, we can crash our car. Please try not to focus on the 'what if's' today. Don't let the sidelines; those pesky thoughts distract you from our destination. Continue to move toward Jesus' hand reaching out to you as He reached out to Peter when he started to walk on water. Today I'm going to hold Jesus' hand." Sniffling, I wipe my eyes on my sleeve, "Today I'm going to hold Jesus' hand and I ask that you both do the same."

Ryan reaches over and squeezes my hand. Lysa doesn't say a word. Blowing my nose, I pray that God keeps my family safe including this little one inside me.

"It's time for April to go into surgery." The doctor gives Ryan instructions and he brings Lysa to the waiting room where everyone else is.

Chapter 49

"I wish we were able to pray with April before the surgery." Agnes says as she squeezes her own hands together.

"I know mom, that all happened really fast. We were all supposed to be able to talk to her before the surgery, but April sent Ryan a text saying she was in labor and they were moving up her surgery time." Nancy explains even though everyone in the room already heard this.

"Ryan is going to be with her the whole time. I'm glad about that." Janice comments.

They are all a bit lost with the speed of things. Ryan called Nancy as soon as he got the text from April. He dropped Lysa off at Nancy's on his way to the hospital now that Nancy lives in an apartment with Nick. Ryan reassured Lysa that he would get her as soon as he could. Nancy called her mom, Janice, and Helen and they all met at the hospital. Nick led them to the waiting room. They've been sitting there for a few minutes trying to process what has happened and what will be happening. Nancy didn't Google any of this. She didn't want to know the percentage of survival. She couldn't see how helpful that would be. Already they've witnessed a miracle. April nor the baby were supposed to make it to this day, and here they are, both alive and well, so trying to find out previous information would only cause more worry for Nancy. And with her big mouth she probably would have shared it, nothing like lifting someone up when they are going through a hard time. She knows most people don't know what to say when times are difficult for someone. She has learned that saying stuff like, 'oh, I know someone who had that and they died or something', isn't helpful. She tries not to listen to those scary stories, but it's hard when people share them. Someone at work said to her that they know of a dad with four small children who recently passed away because they had a similar problem like April. Nancy stood there in shock. How is telling her that story helpful? She wanted to punch the woman who was talking to her but she walked away instead. She was in the middle of her next destructive sentence and Nancy kept on walking. She had no desire to be polite. Fortunately, that woman hasn't tried to talk to her since. *God, please…. I don't have words, but You know what I'm asking. Please.*

* * *

Janice rubs her arm. It has healed well and so has her head. Her memories of her time in jail still haunt her and one day she will tell April about it, but for now it hasn't been something to share. Ryan and everyone else agreed.

"Nancy, what's in the bag?" Janice asks.

"I brought baby clothes, Janice."

Janice reaches into the bag. "Oh that is so cute." She holds up a beautiful pink outfit with a shirt and skirt.

"And if she has a boy, I thought this one would look adorable." It's a Yankees shirt with a baseball cap.

"I didn't know they made caps that small." Janice folds the girl's outfit and hands it back.

She's trying to think of the positives, as they sit there in the waiting room, but she keeps circling back to the thought that her best friend might die today. She wore her loudest clothes to put a smile on April's face, but she didn't get a chance to see her. April used to mock Janice's clothing choices all throughout college. She would shrug and tell April that she liked being bold. She loves color and it makes her happy. April told her after college that all the colors put a smile on her face and that Janice brightened her day when she saw what she was wearing. Today, without any words, she did all she could to let her know how much she cared. Janice sent April a selfie this morning in case she wasn't able to see her at the hospital. April laughed. It's interesting how well they know each other. She better be okay. She has so much more life to live. *Please God let her stay with us until we are old and tired of being old.*

* * *

Being a mom is hard! It has been so difficult to watch her daughter in debilitating pain these past several weeks. Agnes wanted to take it all away. Why couldn't it have been Agnes instead? She would gladly have changed places with April in a heartbeat. She did what she could to help. She took Lysa whenever there was a need for childcare and she visited April almost every day. She stayed as long as she could. When Agnes was close to tears seeing and hearing April groan in pain, she then would have to step outside and go for a quick walk.

At night, she would put on worship songs and cry as she sang them to God. He knows. He gave His only son for them. He knows the pain in her heart. He knows how it feels to not take it away either. Agnes wishes she could but she couldn't. She would sing and cry and sing.

Her husband should be here. April needs her dad, she has needed him, but he took the easy road and left. Agnes needed him too.

God please send us a miracle today. Please keep April and this new little one in your healing hands.

* * *

Ella loves her sister but she hardly knows her, either of them really. Nancy has always treated Ella like she was her own daughter, bossing her around since Ella was born and April and Ella just didn't talk to each other much. She knows she is a lot younger then both of them, and they were close enough in age to play together. Ella was the odd one out. They even remember who their dad was. Ella doesn't remember what he even looks like.

She has started attending SUNY Albany. It's time for her to leave the shadows of her family and find out whom she really is. She loves her family, but she's felt like an outsider among her sisters. Lysa and Ella get along. She really enjoys having her around. And she can't wait to meet her new niece or nephew today. She's going to try to be around more. She knows she gave her sisters an attitude most of her growing up years. She felt they deserved it, but now she wishes she knew them better. If she were kinder she might know them better. She's sitting here next to mom and Lysa and they are the only two people she feels she can talk to and maybe Janice too. She has never seemed quite as old as her sisters. She hopes April is well. She wants her to be well.

This is her first semester and she loves it so far. She might get a job there so she can stay on campus. She's selfish, listening to her own thoughts she realizes this. Here her sister might die, and she's thinking about getting a job so she can live on campus. *God, I do love my family even though I don't show it. Please keep April well and her baby too.*

* * *

The crowd has filled the waiting room, but the low volume of chatter would say otherwise. Nick watched Ryan as he leaned down and spoke to Lysa before he went with April. He truly is an amazing dad. Nick has looked up to him since high school. He has been a true role model for him and he has learned a lot from him by watching his character throughout the years. He has waited years to marry April. Since their wedding about a year ago they have gone through challenges that normally would tear a couple apart. And now Nick is still learning from Ryan. Ryan doesn't regret marrying April either. He has loved her through her pain and sorrow and it is his pain and sorrow now too. Now that he is Nick's brother-in-law he can try to help him as well. He usually refuses help, but Nick thinks he is learning how to let others lend a hand. Nick can't help with marriage advice yet. Nancy and Nick have a lot of growing together that needs to happen first. They decided to go on an unplanned honeymoon. They both like the idea of spontaneity and adventure. When things settle around here they will go somewhere. Nick has put money aside for that already, so there isn't the stress or thought of not being able to pay for it.

They have been waiting here for about thirty minutes now. He has no idea how long it takes to have a C-section; maybe they didn't even start yet. He doesn't know nor does he want to ask either, so he's going to sit here and stroke Nancy's back as they wait. He's happy that they are no longer in a cat and mouse game of 'does she like him or not' anymore. She also explained to him how his lack of defining the relationship was hard for her to follow. They each saw their faults and he's hoping he learned enough about communicating with her to avoid further confusion and disagreements.

Ryan and Nick are taking some time off from their PI work. Nick is now working full time for the carpentry business. His head has healed. The bullet only grazed the side of his head.

He hopes things go well today. God please send Your blessings on April, Ryan, and the new baby. Keep them safe.

*　*　*

He didn't want to disturb the family so he's been waiting outside the operating room. He's close to losing his license. He finds the bottle helps him to cope with what he did. He lied and tricked a family. He's an excellent doctor and he stands by his first evaluation that this baby and/or the mother will not survive today. He doesn't want that to happen. He's not here to prove his point. He sees where he messed up and he is truly sorry for that. He was trying to save a life, but instead he almost ended one without giving him or her a chance. He doesn't understand how they are both alive today and he doesn't comprehend the strength of this woman. She completed her pregnancy. He overheard one of the nurses say that she was in early labor and she was already 2 centimeters dilated when she was checked. Amazing, the baby had all the time it was going to have anyway. He'll wait and hope for a good outcome for this family. Maybe one of them will live, maybe.

* * *

Helen's here, as a friend, and the family all know that. She's not going to counsel anyone today. She didn't think she would ever be able to find a place where she could be herself. When people find out what she does for a living, they either shy away from her or they tell her all about what's going on in their life. Lots of people approach her with their distant cousins' problems as well. She likes to help people, she wouldn't have chosen this profession otherwise, but she never imagined that it would cause such isolation. She couldn't find a true friend. She needed someone she could be real with. The reality is that she doesn't have all the answers, and she doesn't pretend to either. She enjoys helping and she has been trained to do it well. When she found a friend in Nancy, she thanked God daily. She was someone Helen could be herself around. She even jokes about what Helen does. She's honored to be here today with this amazing family. Over the past year, she has been able to become friends with them as well.

She sold her house. Greg put it on the market right away and after one month she had a buyer. Greg showed Helen a lot of apartments during that month and the timing worked out very well.

She only stayed at Nancy's for a couple of nights while she waited for her new place to be painted. The apartment is only five minutes from Nick and Nancy's place. She didn't even know where Nick lived when she put the deposit down. Actually, she didn't know they would be married by now and that Nancy would move into Nick's house. She's so happy for her. She's also trying to give them space. She doesn't want to be that needy friend. Janice and Helen have been going out for coffee occasionally too after she got out of jail. It has been fun to have some friends. Nancy wanted to set Helen up with Greg, but she's not interested. She doesn't think Greg was either.

No one is talking. They're all waiting. God, I pray for your wisdom in that operating room. I pray that today is a joyous day. Calm Ryan and give him a clear head. Please keep April and the baby strong.

* * *

Lysa is going to be a big sister! It's been hard for her to sit here and wait. She's been wiggling in her chair. She knows she's been doing it a lot because her two grandmas' and her granddad have asked her to sit by them. They put their arm around her or pat her knee to remind her to calm down. They don't know how excited she is. She wants to be in the room with her family now. She doesn't think she should be asked to wait out here. She's not doing a very good job at waiting. No one is talking. It's really odd. A baby is being born and they are all wearing sad faces. She made a card for the baby. She also wrote her name choices on the card. Mom and dad didn't decide on a name yet. She was there for all the conversations, so she knows that they're stuck. She spent the past week looking through a baby name book. When will she see the baby? She asked already a few times, and each time no one knows the answer. *God please keep my baby brother or sister safe and mommy too. I want to see them soon, very soon.*

Chapter 50

"Ryan, I'm excited. Today is the day!" I say right before the nurse announces that another contraction has started. I'm lying flat on my back.

"I'm excited too! How are you feeling, April?"

"I'm doing well."

Ryan is dressed from head to toe in the hospital scrubs. There are several nurses and doctors in the room. I was introduced to a few of them, but I don't remember any names, except for Stephanie. She has been here the whole time informing me about each step, as it was happening. She said she has prayed for me too.

"Ryan?"

"Yes?"

"If things get complicated," I'm not sure of the best way to phrase this, "If things get complicated, please hold our baby as soon as you can. Let him or her know that I love them, too."

"I will love this baby with my whole heart. And you will be there to let the baby know how much you love him or her too." He leans down and kisses my cheek.

"I know, but if I'm not..." Ryan squeezes my hand.

"Okay." He says softly.

"I didn't write any letters or anything. I didn't think to."

"Well then you will have to stay with us, now, won't you?" He half smiles, but I can see his eyes filling.

"Yes, I have to."

"Good."

Stephanie sniffles. She hasn't left my side this morning.

"Stephanie."

"Yes?"

"Thank you for all of your support. You have helped me so much and I have truly been blessed."

"You're welcome, April." She dabs at her eyes with a tissue. She looks like she has more to say, but nothing else leaves her lips.

"April, the doctor is almost ready. He'll be in very soon." Another nurse says.

"Okay."

"Hi, April, it's Donald, the anesthesiologist. How are you feeling?"

"Okay." They're all going to think I've already lost my mind if I keep saying the word okay.

"I know I've asked you that a few times already, but that's my job. I'll keep asking and you keep letting me know, okay?"

"Sure." The door to my left opens and the doctor walks in.

"What is he doing in here?" The doctor tilts his head toward Ryan as he asks someone. I don't remember his name.

"I don't know." Someone mumbles.

"Well, he can't be in here." The doctor doesn't even attempt to whisper.

"Actually, he has been given permission by the head of the hospital." I say.

I remember the day the guy in charge of the hospital came in, and talked to me when I was in the hospital. He said that if there was anything I needed to let him know. When we found out they didn't want Ryan in the room, and that he had to wait outside until the baby was born, we made a call and got permission.

The doctor grunts and succeeds in whispering this time; it doesn't matter. Ryan is here with me, which is what I want. We never thought of suing. I know it was a huge concern because I was treated like a queen during my stay here. I don't know if Stephanie is a part of that treatment or not. I'm thankful she's here. Step by step she has informed us of what is going to happen. We're not sure exactly how the events are going to play out over the next hour or so but she will let us know. I've never met the doctor that is performing this surgery. I don't think he wants his name known, but we have been told he is the best the hospital has. His bedside manner hasn't changed my confidence. I'd be lying if I said I wasn't afraid; I am, but I know God is here with me. I know this is God's will and I'm blessed for following it. In spite of my fear, I'm following my

God! He is bigger than my fear and anxiety. I have peace now knowing that I'm doing His will.

* * *

The sheet has been placed high. I can see April's head and shoulders.

"Can you feel this April?"

"Did you do it yet?"

"Yes."

"Then, no, I didn't feel it."

"How about now?"

"No."

"Good."

"What were you doing?"

"I was pinching you to make sure you were numb."

"Okay. I must be numb then because I didn't feel a thing." April's words come out slowly.

"April, he is going to start now." Stephanie whispers.

"Okay."

"April, how are you doing?"

"Umm."

"Don't start cutting!" Someone by the monitor says to the doctor.

"I already started."

"Her heart rate is slowing." A tense voice says.

"I already started."

"Her heart has stopped." The same tense voice shouts.

"Do something." I shout.

People are moving in all different directions. Two nurses bump into each other. I step back from the sheet. The doctor is moving furiously.

"I have the paddles ready."

"Not yet. I don't have the baby out yet." The doctor says.

"Hurry!" Someone shouts.

"I'm going as fast as I can."

"Go faster."

I lose track of time. Maybe a couple of minutes or so have gone by. I lean back and touch April's face. I hear the stagnant sound of the monitor. She doesn't respond. I step back again, and see the doctor pull the baby out. Close to passing out, I grab a hold of the corner of the bed. The baby is black or maybe dark blue. Not normal. That isn't normal.

"Get him out of here!"

"Clear."

I step back again. I look up, and the baby is gone. April is lying motionless. The orderly has the paddles, and someone has their arm around me trying to get me through the door.

"The machine isn't working!"

I look at the man holding the paddles. He turns to the machine and no lights come on.

"Plug the machine in!" I yell. "It isn't plugged in. Plug it in!"

The nurse pulls harder on my arm to get me to leave. The man plugs the machine in and it starts to work.

"Clear."

I see him put the paddles on my April and her body moves.

"Nothing. Do it again."

Three people pull me out of the room. I try to fight them, but can't. Practically being thrown from the room, they close the door behind me as they all run back inside.

"God, what just happened? Am I going to lose them both at once? April asked me to keep my focus on Your hand. I'm here reaching out to You now. I know you are here even though I can't see. I know there is fogged confusion filling my mind, but I know that You are an amazing God. You are the ultimate healer and I pray that You heal them. And this is painful to pray but if that healing is to mean that they go home with You then…."

Chapter 51

Listening to Ryan pray has changed Dr. Stevens. The doctor didn't know how Ryan could say such a thing. His faith is amazing.

"Hi, Ryan. I'm Dr. Stevens. I was out here waiting and hoping that things were well with your family." I look up at the doctor while my tears stream down my face.

"God...." I choke up.

"I'll sit with you."

I nod and bow my head. Dr. Stevens bows his head too. He's never prayed before. He follows Ryan.

God, I have messed up. I don't know what to say, but I pray that You keep the baby and April alive. Dr. Stevens starts his prayer.

Chapter 52

Stephanie is torn with whom she should go to, April or her baby. In the confusion, the baby was whisked away before she got a look. Stephanie didn't hear a cry, but that's normal with the drugs that are involved in a section. The technician is getting ready to use the paddles a third time.

"Clear." They all hold their breath.

"I have something." He screams. "It's faint, but I have a heartbeat."

"April, I'm here. Just relax." Stephanie whispers into her ear. She hasn't stirred, but her heart is beating. The doctor is stitching her up quickly. They need to finish this as soon as possible. Stephanie keeps talking to her. She wants to let her know about the baby, but she doesn't know how the baby is or if it's a boy or a girl. She looks around and everyone is moving fast. She wants to ask, but she's not sure if she should. She keeps talking to April.

The doctor finishes and the anesthesiologist makes his adjustments. From the other side of the room she hears a tiny cry. Instantly, Stephanie's eyes fill. The baby is alive. April knew with all her heart that this baby deserved a chance to live. She believed and even though this baby had a rough start to life he or she is alive.

"Stephanie, get the dad." A nurse from the other side demands. She rushes to the door. Ryan is standing right outside with Dr. Stevens.

"Ryan, you can come in now."

"Is..."

"Come in." Stephanie nods. He enters and looks at April.

"She's doing okay now. Her heart is stable. She will be under observation for a while."

"How is the baby?"

"Ryan, please come over here." A nurse from the far corner of the room calls.

Ryan and Stephanie walk over.

"Ryan, here is your baby girl."

The nurse hands the baby over to him. Stephanie looks around as the staff collectively stops what they are doing and watches Ryan hold his baby. They pass the box of tissues.

"She's doing well. She had a very rough start. She wasn't getting oxygen for a bit. The doctor moved very fast in getting her out so she should be fine, but we need to put her in the NICU to monitor her. You and your family can visit her there and hopefully she will be able to go home soon. She is a fighter and her color looks much better now. Her cry is a bit weak but..." The baby tries to prove him wrong by crying a little louder than the last time.

"Like I was saying, we think she will be fine, but we need to observe her to make sure."

Ryan hasn't taken his eyes off her. He walks her over to April.

"April, it's a girl. We have a baby girl."

"Ryan, April won't be able to respond for some time. We wanted you to see them both, but we have to make sure they're okay. I'm sorry, but I'll have to take your girl now. You can talk to your family. They are waiting in the waiting room for you." I reluctantly hand over my daughter.

"I love you, my baby girl. I love you."

Stephanie helps take the baby.

"Will April be okay?" I choke out.

"She's alive. A miracle. My medical opinion is invalid now. I didn't think she would make it this far. God is in control of your family, Ryan. We witnessed many miracles today. I have to get back to April now. She's in critical condition, but you have a God that is in control so..." The doctor extends his hand to shake mine. "I'm honored to know you and your family."

"Thank you, doc. Thank you!"

"You're welcome."

As I turn to the door, I spot Dr. Stevens at the doorway. His face is soaked with tears. He's sobbing. I put my arm around his shoulder.

"Alright people we have work to do. I know we will all remember today. Amazing and I wouldn't have believed it if I didn't see it."

Nods and other agreements scatter around the room. April's heart is still beating.

Dr. Stevens and I walk out.

* * *

"Hi, everyone. I have another daughter!"

Cheering fills the room.

"Daddy, where is she?"

"She is doing fine, but the doctors and nurses need to check her out to make sure she is well. We can all go see her after we go out and have lunch or brunch, whatever time it is." I don't want to leave the hospital nor can I bring myself to share all that has happened yet.

"How's mommy?"

"Umm, mommy is still being watched by the doctors too. I'm not sure when we can see her, but hopefully soon."

"You don't know when?"

Glancing around the room, I notice everyone is staring. "No, Lysa, I don't know when yet. After lunch we should know more."

"Okay, then we should hurry up and get lunch!" Lysa grabs my hand, and starts to pull me toward the door.

"If anyone would like to join us, we are going to the pizza and sub place across the street."

Dr. Stevens slips out but everyone else follows us down the hallway. I can feel the questions wanting to be asked from the people behind me. They are all respecting my wishes by not asking them and I'm thankful for that. I'm barely holding myself together. I want to be alone, but I know parenting is what I need to do right now. I could ask any of the people behind me to take Lysa, but I know she would be crushed. She needs me right now and I need her. I also need to cry and I don't want to be around anyone while I do. My head starts to throb, as I suppress my emotions, an instant result to my choice. I'm not sure how to force fake happiness. But I remember what April said. I'm trying to walk on the water, but the fog is so thick I can't see Jesus' hand anywhere. I look and turn, but I don't see him. The doctor was going to say that she wasn't going to survive. I know he was. He said she was alive at that moment. When I tried to talk to her she didn't even move. I saw three people step toward me when I went to her. I know I was going to be kicked out again. They weren't saying everything. I want to find Stephanie. Maybe she will still be there when I get back from lunch.

Why did I suggest lunch? I'm not hungry. All I want to do is go back to the hospital. My ribs work to hold my heart in. My wife died before my eyes today. I watched her go from this life and then they kicked me out. I fought but it was three against one. I couldn't get away from them. After trying to get away for a minute, I realized that all the people forcing me out needed to be in the room helping April. I stopped fighting them when they opened the door. They plopped me out there and slammed the door behind them. I could hear what was going on inside, but I wasn't able to hold her hand. They wouldn't let me comfort her. She needed me and I couldn't help. The only way I could help was to let her go. My fighting to stay was harming her by taking away the people that needed to be there to care for her so I let her go. She had a heartbeat when they let me back in. It made a beautiful sound. We need her. This new baby girl needs her and so do Lysa and I. I'm going to crack if anyone asks me any questions about what happened in there. I can't talk about it yet.

We arrive at the pizza place. Everyone orders and I pretend to eat. I can't shake what happened in there. How is she now? I need to get back to the hospital. Why does everyone eat so slowly? Can't they see we're taking too long? My leg moves from side to side as I shred my napkin into pieces. Move people move; eat faster! I stand up and walk to the door. No one moves. I pace a bit.

"Hey Nick, I'm going back to the hospital."

"How about I go back with you?" Nick asks.

"Okay," I look at my parents, "Can you bring Lysa back with you?"

"Sure. We'll get back there soon."

"Thanks."

I quickly hug Lysa and pull Nick toward the door before he tries to take a longer good-bye kiss with Nancy. Fortunately, Nick understands and he doesn't talk at all. He only walks fast. Nick keeps pace with me, but continues to remain silent. Thoughts of 'is she okay?' fill my mind. If I was in the waiting room I might know the answer to that already. No sense beating myself up. I wanted to wait with less people around so I guess I'll have that for a little bit. I love the support, but right now I want to be alone or more like I want to not talk to anyone.

This isn't going to be the last time I sit here in the waiting room waiting to hear how she is doing. She needs to have brain surgery next. How many times can I sit here and wait? I don't think I can take it anymore. *Why God? Why are we going through this? Why can't I see Your hand? I don't understand this at all.* How can one woman endure so much? She went into this with an amazing faith and focus on You God. Her faith amazes me. She was sure of what she hoped for and certain of what she didn't see. We make it to the right floor and I question the nurse at the station. She informs me that the doctor is still with her, but I can go and hold the baby.

"If there is any news about April, will you let me know?" I ask.

"Yes, Stephanie is still in there too, and she said to let you know she will find you as soon as she knows more."

"Will you let her know where I am?"

"Definitely."

"Oh, and the rest of the family will be back too." Nick adds.

"I'll point them to the NICU waiting room. Only two people are allowed in at a time, so you can all rotate, I know there are a lot of you. Holding your baby is so important right now so the more people that can help out with that, the better. Plus, it will give everyone something to do."

"Yes." I mumble.

She informs us of the best way to get there and we quickly follow.

We approach two doors. I push the button on the wall and they open. There is a waiting room to my left and a sink to my right, along with two more doors in front of me. I push another button and more of the same happens. In front of us this time is a nurses' station.

"Can we see baby Nolsen?" I ask.

"Ah, the baby without a name. And you are?"

"I'm the dad."

"Can I see your ID?"

I reach into my pocket and show her. She looks at it.

"Okay, I know that this little one had a rough entry into this world, but she is doing well. I know we didn't follow usual protocol, but now that you are here we can put the band on your arm and you can freely walk in and out. The nurse upstairs called down and told me your name and that you would be here in a minute. I was waiting for you. Please follow me and I will bring you to your baby."

"Thanks."

We walk down another hallway. There are several doors, each holding a number of little ones. She instructs us to use the hand sanitizer before we enter the room. We walk around three tiny babies hooked up to tubes. One baby could barely fit into my hand. My heart pauses. In the back is my little girl. She wasn't little compared to the others in this room. She wasn't a preemie. She has a tube connected to her nose and one in her hand. She looks so fragile.

"Can I hold her?"

"Let's ask the nurse in charge of your little one." She turns, and asks a woman monitoring several screens. She doesn't look up.

"Yes, I will be over there in two minutes." She states in a businesslike tone.

I watch my daughter. She's asleep right now. I want to touch her but there is glass preventing that so I touch the glass instead.

"Okay, you must be the dad."

"Yes, can I hold her?"

"Yes, you can. She is only here under observation. We are giving her oxygen for a couple of hours then we will remove this tube and see how she does."

She gently but quickly picks her up; adjusts the wires and places her in my arms. Sitting, I readjust her a tiny bit. I'm not sure if I'm doing this right. She seems so small in my arms. I hope I don't hurt her. She is so delicate and so beautiful. She looks just like April. She doesn't have much hair and the little she has is hard to tell the color. Her eyes pop open.

"Nick, look, she's awake."

"She's beautiful, Ryan. What's her name?"

"Ummm, I'm waiting for April before we name her."

"Okay, sounds good."

***

They were directed to the waiting room of the NICU. Lysa is bouncing off the wall. She wants desperately to meet her sister. They tried to get information out of the nurse on April's floor, but she wouldn't tell them anything. They tried several different angles of questioning but she wouldn't relent. Helen could tell she knew something, but no one could get her lips to speak it. Nancy even asked for Stephanie. She said Stephanie was still with April. That was it. Nancy asked if she could see Stephanie and she said that Stephanie wasn't leaving April's side. They didn't want to push after that. Telling them that gave the impression that April is in serious to critical condition, but she is still alive because Stephanie is still with her. The nurse mentioned that they could see the baby. They all took off for the elevator the moment the directions were out of her mouth. Maybe Nick and Ryan know more.

"Nancy, which floor did she say to go to?" Ryan's dad asks as they all pile into the elevator.

"Five."

"Thanks."

Lunch was a subdued event. Nancy watched Ryan the whole time. He wasn't very good at hiding his emotions. He, without saying a word, let her know the severity of this situation. Since they are allowed to see the baby, she must be doing well. They walk through several doors and talk to a nurse. Lysa is in front the whole way. The nurse ushers them all back into the waiting room.

"When you are called in, you need to wash your hands thoroughly here before you go through these doors here." She points to the sink. "Please follow the instructions. They are posted above the handle. And I will let the men that are visiting the baby, know that you are here. There are only two people allowed in at one time. You can keep on swapping back and forth until 5pm. Before entering the room, please stop at the nurses' station to sign in and pick up your visitor's pass. Ryan has already put you all on the list, so you can go in. Well, I think he put you all on the list;

there are a lot of you so I'm not really sure." She turns around and walks back to through the doors. They all take their seats and wait.

"Hi, Ryan." Janice says.

Nick walks out behind him.

"Hi, everyone. If you don't mind I'd like to bring Lysa in next so she can meet her sister. Does anyone have a camera?" Three hands with three cameras extend to Ryan. He grabs one and Lysa pulls him to the door.

"Oh, wait, I need to wash my hands." She quickly takes care of that and insists Ryan washes his too.

* * *

"Hi, Nancy. How are you doing?" Nick sits down next to her.

"Did Ryan say anything about April?" Several sets of eyes focus on Nick.

"He hasn't said a word. Not one word. He lit up when he saw the baby. He held her for a while. Here, I have pictures on my phone." He pulls out his phone and they all spend time looking at them.

"She's so beautiful."

"Look at those cheeks."

"She has no hair."

"She looks just like April."

"I see Ryan."

The group continues to comment as they each take their time flipping through the pictures.

* * *

"Lysa, this is your baby sister."

"Can I hold her?" She asks.

"Yes, you can."

The nurse has softened from our first encounter and was waiting right there to help us with the baby.

"Lysa, please sit down."

The nurse places her into Lysa's arms. The glowing smile on Lysa's face was priceless. I take as many pictures as I can. I forward them to Nick and April's phones. After a few minutes the baby starts to cry, and the nurse comes over to help us out.

"Lysa, you are going to be a great big sister." I say.

"I know." She states.

After thanking the nurse and informing her of the long line outside, Lysa and I go back to the waiting room.

"Can Lysa stay with you?" I ask no one in particular.

A few people say yes.

"Lysa I'm going to go check on mommy. I want you to have another turn with your sister, so it's best you stay here."

"Okay. I want to hold her again too."

"Good. I'll send a text when I know something. I'll send it to Uncle Nick because he has already been in there and then he can inform the rest of you."

"Ryan, is there anything we can do?" Janice asks.

"Actually, holding the baby is the best thing for all of you to do. I'm so glad you are all here to help with that. Soon they're going to take her off the oxygen and then they will have a better idea of how long she will have to stay. They're hopeful. She looks great. Her color is great and all of her organs are functioning well. When the doctor makes the evening rounds, we will know more. Holding her helps her so much right now. I want her to come home soon, very soon, April and the baby. I'll be back later."

Chapter 53

The nurse asked me to wait in the waiting room. She said she was going to get Stephanie. That was ten minutes ago. Nick has sent me three texts already. I can tell the family is pressuring him. I would be too. I wish I had news to tell them. I check my phone for the fifteenth time, eleven minutes.

"Ryan, I can bring you to April now." Stephanie says.

"Oh, good. How is she?"

"You can ask her yourself."

"And she will be able to tell me?" My eyebrows rise.

"Yes, Ryan, she will be able to tell you."

"Yes!" I pump my fist into the air. I start to walk in front of Stephanie, but quickly realize I don't know where I'm going. Why does Stephanie have to have such short legs?

"Ryan, April can't have any more stress so your job and those around you is to observe her. Think of poker and find her tells. Do you know what I mean? Figure out what she does when she is under stress. Things like biting her lip or pacing. Figure it out and try your best to eliminate it."

"Okay, I'll let the family know too."

"April has also been instructed but…"

"Yeah, I understand."

"Good."

Two more turns and she pushes a door open. In front of me is my April. She looks my way and gives me a weak smile.

"Oh, April, how are you?" I rush to her side.

"I'm okay."

"Good. I was so afraid but you're here now. You can talk to me."

"Yes, I can."

"What do you remember?"

"I remember the anesthesiologist asking me if I was okay, and I couldn't answer. Then I heard someone yell, 'stop cutting' and the doctor said that he already started."

"Anything beyond that?" I grab the chair from the corner and bring it to April's side.

"No. Stephanie filled me in." April looks quite pale.

"I thought I lost you. I did lose you, but God sent you back. I'm so glad. We need you so much."

"I need you too. Have you seen the baby?"

"Yes, she's beautiful."

"It's a girl?"

"Yes, it is!"

"I told Stephanie I want to hold the baby, our girl." She smiles. "She said she is doing the best she can to arrange that soon."

"I was informed that we had to wait for the evening doctor."

"Hopefully not. I can't make it over there. I don't know how long I'll be in the hospital. I want to go home when the baby does."

"I'm praying."

A quiet knock on the door and our focus changes.

"Come in." April says and Dr. Stevens walks in.

"Hi, umm, I'm sorry to interrupt. I wanted to say, umm, that I'm really sorry for everything I've done."

"I forgive you, Dr. Stevens, for all you have done." April says warmly.

Dr. Stevens looks up quickly.

"What?"

"I forgive you." April says.

"Why?"

"Because Jesus forgave me."

"I don't understand."

"Dr. Stevens."

"Please call me Grant."

"Okay, Grant, here's the thing, we all sin. We all do wrong things; that's why we need a Savior. Jesus came down to earth as a baby, He lived among us, gave us an example of how to live, and then He died for us. For all of us, Grant. There is no one here on earth that doesn't sin. We all need a savior. You can't earn your way to heaven. It's a gift, a beautiful gift that Jesus has given us and all we have to do is accept it."

"That's what I want. I've struggled with my life for so many years now. I feel so empty inside, for so many years. My wife's death threw me into a deep depression and I felt like I couldn't get out. This is the way out. I know it is. I want to become a Christian. How do I accept it?"

"You have to pray and mean what you pray. Being a Christian is a journey. This is a lifelong commitment."

"Please tell me how to pray?"

"Sure, let's bow our heads and you can repeat after me." We all bow our heads. "Jesus, I am a sinner. I need Your forgiveness. Please forgive me, I am sorry for all the wrong things I have done. I need You. Please come into my heart and be my Savior. Thank you for dying for me. Please guide me as I live my life for You. Amen."

Grant repeats the prayer. When he looks up there are tears in his eyes.

"I've been looking for this my whole life."

"You feel whole now, don't you?" April asks.

"Yes, I don't feel like a part of me is missing anymore."

"Good."

"Ryan, April, I have done so much wrong. I have killed so many babies before they even had a chance to enter this world. Are you sure God will forgive me?" Panic starts to fill him.

"God forgives you. I think you will learn a lot from the apostle Paul. He killed Christians, many Christians, but when he gave his life over to God he became a powerful man of God and led many people to Him."

"I need to read that. I need to buy a Bible."

"That's the best place to start. We should also talk about you being baptized. And if you want you can go to church with us."

"Really, you want me around you?"

April and I exchange a look. "Yes, we do."

"Thanks, you two. I'm so, so happy. Thank you." Grant shakes our hands.

"I have to go and call Tim. He has been telling me about God for a very long time but I always brushed him off and changed the subject. Ryan, here's my card. Please let me know about church."

I take the card and briefly fill him in on the when and where before he leaves the room.

"Umm, sorry you two. I didn't want to leave so I stayed in the back of the room. I also prayed that prayer."

"Really, Stephanie?" I look at her and see true joy.

"Yes, I have been drawn to you from the moment you entered this hospital April. I thought it was because I was meant to help you, but now I see it was for you to help me. I was lost, and now I have a purpose. Thank you."

"You're welcome, Stephanie. Are you able to come to church with us too?"

"Yes, I am. I'm really looking forward to it."

"Oh, and if I'm still here at the hospital when Sunday comes around, please go with the family. You know most of them now anyway."

"You are right about that."

Stephanie checks Aprils' vitals again as April and I look at pictures of our baby.

* * *

"Hey, everyone. I just got a text from Ryan. He says April is doing okay. She is talking to him."

A chorus of happiness and questions come at Nick all at once. They convince him to send back lots of questions.

"Okay, everyone, I can't send all of that at once."

Nick texts and because Nancy is the closest to him, she can lean over his shoulder to read what he's writing. She loves this man. She can't believe they're finally married now.

Nick told Nancy that Ryan said April is happy about them being Private Investigators. Nancy was very surprised to hear that. A year ago April would have run as far away from Ryan as she possibly could, if she knew that. She has really grown this year. It was a good thing Ryan didn't tell her right away. Nancy didn't think keeping things like that from one's spouse is a good idea, but they had an unusual beginning, thanks to Nancy. She's glad he did tell her. Nancy and April both knew there was something that was being kept from them. Nick puts his arm around Nancy and she leans into him. Life will be filled with challenges, but hopefully they both seek God as they go through them.

Nick's phone makes a car horn sound and he picks it up and looks at it. "Okay, everyone, Ryan said that April can have visitors, but things need to be low key. I'm thinking he means we need to be quiet."

A cheer goes up. "He also says we will be in the waiting room first."

* * *

"Come in." I say as Ryan moves to open the door.

Stephanie walks in pushing a bassinette on wheels. I start to get up, but am forced back down by abdominal pain. My baby. I have waited so long to see my baby. Without words, Stephanie lifts her out of her bed and hands her to me. I feel Ryan sit down next to me. My eyes stay fixed on her face.

"Stephanie, can Lysa come in too?"

"Yes, I'll go and get her."

"Thanks." I say still unable to take my eyes from my beautiful baby's face.

"Ryan, she's beautiful."

"Just like you."

"Did the doctors find anything wrong?"

"I don't think so, April. I really don't think she would be here if they did, but I'll ask Stephanie."

I carefully place her in front of me on the bed. My stomach hurts and I can't hold her much longer. I want to see her.

Stephanie walks in with Lysa who makes herself at home on the other side of the bed. We all stare, as I unwrap the blanket. I examine all of her toes and fingers. I can't find any birthmarks.

"Mommy, look, she doesn't have much hair."

"No, she doesn't Lysa."

"What's her name? We need to name her."

"You don't want to call her 'baby'?" Ryan jokes.

"No, when are we going to name her?"

"How about now?" Ryan says.

"Yes! Didn't we say if it was a girl we would name her Lauren?" She smiles and puts her hands together under her chin.

"That's right Lysa, and you did a good job keeping that a secret."

"I did. I didn't tell anyone even though Aunt Nancy and Aunt Janice both asked me."

I smile, knowing those two would try anything to find the name out.

"Lauren means to 'crown with Laurel', which is a fragrant plant that was used in the ancient Olympic games. The young branches and leaves were woven to make a crown for the winner. We wanted to name her that as a reminder to us about how true believers will receive the crown of glory, which will never fade away. Each day we look at Lauren, we can remember our crown of glory which will live forever."

"Maybe I'll understand that when I get older. I just like the name. What's her middle name? I don't remember us having one." Lysa wants to know.

"Faith." I say. Ryan squeezes my hand.

"That's a perfect name; Lauren Faith. Now when we look at her we can remember April's faith. Without her faith, this baby wouldn't be here." Ryan leans down and kisses her on the head.

"God is faithful."

"Yes, he is. Yes, he is!"

"I'm hungry."

"It is late, past your dinner time. Maybe we can get everyone in here so they can see that I'm well, and then you can go home and eat and go to bed. It's been an exhausting day."

"I am tired mommy, but I don't want to leave you and the baby. Can't I eat and sleep here?"

"Sorry, Lysa. You need to go home with daddy."

"He can't stay either?" Lysa scoots off the end of the bed.

"No, he can't either, but that means he will be with you."

"Okay. Can I come back tomorrow?"

"Of course you can. Your sister will be upset if you don't. She needs her big sister." I start to swaddle Lauren in her pink blanket.

"I agree mommy, she does. I've waited a long time to be a big sister. I've practiced a lot with my babies at home."

"Good."

Just then the door opens and the room fills with family and friends. Quietly they ask me how I am.

"Everyone, I don't want you walking on eggshells around me. You can talk normal. I'm doing okay. I'm very tired and Lysa is hungry so this is going to be a very short visit. At some point, we will fill you all in on the details of what happened today, but not today. God performed many miracles and I'd like to say it's really good to be alive. This little one was meant to be here. Giving her a chance at life was what I wanted and God blessed that. Her name is Lauren Faith Nolsen."

A collective ah fills the room. I try to answer the questions that come my way, but weakness overcomes. As everyone I love, surround me, I let myself relax in their chatter. I don't know what the future holds for me, but I've learned to live in the moment. I take one more peek around me. Ryan is holding baby Lauren and Lysa is cooing at her, trying to make her smile. I'll always remember this precious moment. And next time I'll try to include Ryan in on my quick decision before I make it!

"Ryan, do you have any regrets?" I whisper to Ryan as I pull on his sleeve.

"April, if I knew last year all that would happen this year, I would without a moment's hesitation say 'I do' all over again. I love being married to you. Do you have any regrets, April?"

"No, I love you too!" I ease back onto my pillow and close my eyes. What a day this has been. So many blessings! I'm not going to focus on the 'what if's' of tomorrow, I'm going to only focus on the moment I have right now. This is the moment God wants me living in.

Epilogue

April's brain surgery was four months ago. The family and I are still trying to put our lives back together. It's been hard. Before the surgery the doctor told us the odds of her survival. He said there was a 95% chance of her dying, a 4% chance of her being an invalid, and a 1% chance of her being somewhat normal. I wanted to ask what somewhat normal meant and April did ask, but I really didn't want to hear the answer. The doctor wasn't exactly sure what that would mean for April, if she survived.

We had two great months together, the first two of Lauren's life. I took time off from work and we homeschooled Lysa so she could be with us. We didn't want to waste any time and we didn't. We enjoyed all of our time together. We stayed home almost the whole time. It was an adjustment not getting much sleep at night but April handled it with joy. I was a bit grumpy, and Lysa said that she was happy her room wasn't near ours. She really enjoys being a big sister and she is good at it too. Since April's surgery, Lysa has done an amazing job caring for Lauren. I don't leave the responsibility of Lauren's care to Lysa; it's just that she has naturally gravitated toward caring for her. We have lots of family around too. I think if I were to mention that they could move in, they all would.

Maybe I should have someone move into the guesthouse since Nancy is now at Nick's. That would be helpful.

It's been four months! Four months and we still haven't fully adjusted, but we are getting there. Things will be okay one day, I know they will be, but I just wish that day were today. April made it through surgery. When she opened her eyes, we knew she was somewhere in the 5% range. The doctors couldn't answer where she was in that range at that point. They weren't sure if she would remember anything, or if she would be able to talk or see. When she opened her eyes for the first time, I was there.

'"Honey, it's Ryan. Do you know who I am?"

"Uhhh." She says, as she looks right at me. She can see me, but she can't talk. I look at the doctor.

"Ryan we will have to wait and see, but for now if you could leave the room, I'd like to examine her."

I walk out after I squeezed April's hand. She squeezed mine back and I stare into her eyes. Her eyes are big and she tries to talk some more. I reassure her that I will be back as soon as the doctor is done.

That was four months ago. She knew who I was then and she could see and hear, but she couldn't talk. Today is different. A lot has happened in the past four months.

"Ryan, can you take Lauren for me?"

"Sure." I walk over to April and gently take the baby from her arms.

"Thanks. I'm tired so if it's okay with you I'm going to go take a nap."

"That's fine. I'll take Lauren and Lysa with me to see my parents. That way the house will be quiet and my parents will be happy."

"Great. If I'm still asleep when you get back, please wake me up. Oh, and Ryan, before you leave can you please tell me if you are okay?"

"I'm fine."

"I mean with all that has happened. You have been through a lot lately."

"So have you. And we're surviving. Soon we'll be thriving but for now we are doing a great job surviving."

"I agree, we are surviving and I look forward to thriving soon!" April says and sighs.

"I love you, April!"

"I love you too!"

"There was a time that I never thought I'd hear your voice again."

"That was scary. I would try to say a word but it wouldn't come out. I could think it but I couldn't say it. When I figured out how to talk again I would say the wrong word. I still do that sometimes but it is so much better now."

"Much better! The doctor said he saw so many miracles during your time in the hospital that he couldn't help but want to follow your God."

"God is awesome."

"Yes, He is and I'm so glad you are still here with me and here to raise our girls."

"Me too. Are you going to regret not getting your boy?"

"No regrets and we also don't know what God has in store for the future."

Chuckling, April gives me a hug before she goes to take her nap.

"I'd remind you that I can't have any more kids, but you're right, with God all things are possible." April chuckles. "Oh, and Ryan, you never did tell me what was in the gym bag that the two guys took out of Tim's car."

"You're right, I didn't. When I told you everything that happened, I didn't know what was in the bag, but Doug told me later that John admitted to trying to make us think it was something of value but all it was, was a bag of workout clothes. John stole Tim's keys for the night. That's how they got in the car."

"Well, that makes for an interesting story." April mumbles as she drifts off to sleep. Lauren curls her hand around my thumb and I lean down and kiss her check.

Yes, I would marry April all over again, definitely!

Special thanks to everyone who has helped with this book! Truly, thank you Margaret, Lauren, Jen, Christine, Kathy, Sara, Kristie, Jill, Holly, and Jessi. Your input and encouragement have sincerely strengthened me. Thank you, Terry for designing an amazing cover. I'm so blessed to have you as my husband!

Thank You!

Made in the USA
Middletown, DE
29 June 2020